chaucer's bawdy

her Ulrich von Liechtenstein.

Fig. 15. *Venus as a knight's crest: bearing her dart and her brand, she is in turn borne by Herr Ulrich von Liechtenstein as he gallops over a couple of battling water nixies. University Library, Heidelberg, Cod. Pal. germ. 848 (Manessische Hand-schrift, first half of 14th c.), fol. 237*[r]*.*

thomas w. ross

chaucer's bawdy

A Dutton  _Paperback_

e. p. dutton & co., inc.

new york

for Mary

Thomas W. Ross is Professor of English at Colorado College, Colorado Springs. He has published studies of medieval and Renaissance literature, including articles on Chaucer and Shakespeare. His most recent book is an original-spelling edition of Thomas Kyd's *The Spanish Tragedy*, a precursor of *Hamlet*, published by the University of California Press.

Professor Ross took his Ph.D. at the University of Michigan, Ann Arbor. He has studied in England as a research grantee of the American Philosophical Society, and he was Assistant Director of the Salzburg Seminar in American Studies (Salzburg, Austria). In 1969, he was appointed Professor of English at the University of Regensburg, Regensburg, Germany, as one of three NATO Professors in Europe.

Published simultaneously in Canada by
Clarke, Irwin & Company Limited, Toronto and Vancouver.

SBN 0-525-47317-3

Designed by The Etheredges

contents

v

illustrations

acknowledgments

I should like to thank the following for permission to reproduce the illustrations from medieval paintings, manuscripts, and art objects: the Trustees of the British Museum for Figures 6 and 9; the Trustees of the Victoria and Albert Museum for Figures 2, 5, and 7; Foto Mas, Alinari, and the Art Reference Bureau for Figures 8, 11, 12, and 13; the Trustees of the Bodleian Library for Figures 1, 3, 10, and 14; and Dr. Wilhelm Wener, Oberbibliotheksrat, University Library, Heidelberg, for the frontispiece.

Of valued assistance to me in obtaining these illustrative materials were Professors John V. Fleming of Princeton University, Karl Heinz Göller of the University of Regensburg, and Chauncey Wood of McMasters University. The photograph of the Cranach woodcut (Figure 4) is by Michael Gamer.

I should like to thank the Houghton Mifflin Company for permission to quote from *The Works of Geoffrey Chaucer,* ed. F. N. Robinson (2nd ed., Boston: Houghton Mifflin, 1957), from which all Chaucer citations are taken.

For permission to quote from copyright material, I am grateful to: Lee Ash, ed., *American Notes and Queries,* for Norman D. Hinton, "More Puns in Chaucer," II (1964); Appleton-Century-Crofts for Albert C. Baugh, ed., *Chaucer's Major Poetry* (1963); Maurice Carlson, ed., for Haldeen Braddy, "Chaucer—Realism or Obscenity," *Arlington Quarterly,* II (1969); Barnes & Noble, Inc., and the Longman Group Limited, for Hilda M. Hulme, *Explorations in Shake-*

speare's Language (1963); Barron's Educational Series, Inc., for Vincent F. Hopper, tr., *Chaucer's Canterbury Tales* (1946); Basil Blackwell & Mott, Ltd., for Ronald Sutherland, ed., *Romaunt of the Rose and Le Roman de la Rose: A Parallel-Text Edition* (1968); the Cambridge University Press for Caroline Spurgeon, ed., *Five Hundred Years of Chaucer Criticism and Allusion* (1925); Bruce A. Rosenberg, ed., *Chaucer Review,* for W. F. Bolton, "The Topic of the *Knight's Tale,*" I (1967); Emerson Brown, Jr., "*Hortus Inconclusus:* The Significance of Priapus and Pyramus and Thisbe in the *Merchant's Tale,*" IV (1970); Stephen Knight, "Rhetoric and Poetry in the *Franklin's Tale,*" IV (1970); and for my own "*Troilus and Criseyde,* II. 582–588: a Note," V (1971), which appears here in revised form *s.v.* "hol."

The Clarendon Press (Oxford) for J. A. W. Bennett and G. V. Smithers, eds., *Early Middle English Verse and Prose* (1966); W. W. Skeat, ed., *Complete Works of Geoffrey Chaucer* (1894); G. C. Macaulay, ed., *English Works of John Gower* (1901); W. W. Skeat, ed., *Vision of William Concerning Piers Plowman* (1886); Rossell H. Robbins, ed., *Secular Lyrics of the Fourteenth and Fifteenth Centuries* (1952); W. G. Smith, ed., *Oxford Dictionary of English Proverbs,* 2nd ed., rev. Sir Paul Harvey (1948); Sir J. A. H. Murray, *et al.,* eds., *Oxford English Dictionary* (1888–1933); and for Kathleen L. Scott, "Sow and Bagpipe Imagery in the Miller's Portrait," *Review of English Studies,* XVIII (1967); Columbia University Press for Edith Rickert, ed., *Chaucer's World* (1948); Professor E. Talbot Donaldson for his "Idiom of Popular Poetry in the *Miller's Tale,*" *Explication as Criticism: English Institute Selected Papers,* ed. W. K. Wimsatt (1963); Duke University Press for George G. Williams, *A New View of Chaucer* (1965); Faber and Faber, Ltd., for W. Mackay Mackenzie, ed., *Poems of William Dunbar* (1932); Harcourt Brace Jovanovich, Inc., for Charles W. Dunn, ed., *A Chaucer Reader* (1952); Harvard University Press and Heinemann Educational Books Ltd., for Grant Showerman, tr., Ovid, *Heroides and Amores,* Loeb Classical Library (1963); and for Sir James Frazer, tr., Ovid, *Fasti,* Loeb Classical Library (1931).

Indiana University Press for Rolfe Humphries, tr., Ovid,

Art of Love (1969); Johns Hopkins Press for the following articles from *Modern Language Notes:* Norman E. Eliason, "Some Word-Play in Chaucer's *Reeve's Tale,*" LXXI (1956); J. M. Steadman, "Simkin's Camus Nose: A Latin Pun in the *Reeve's Tale,*" LXXV (1960); and J. E. Whitesell, "Chaucer's Lisping Friar," LXXI (1956); the Kennikat Press for Haldeen Braddy, "Chaucer's Bawdy Tongue," which originally appeared in the *Southern Folklore Quarterly,* XXX (1966) and has now been included in Professor Braddy's collected Chaucer papers, *Geoffrey Chaucer: Literary and Historical Papers* (1971); Macmillan Company of Canada, Ltd., for Kenneth Kee, ed., *Geoffrey Chaucer: A Selection of His Works* (1966); ABP International, London, for M. M. Mahood, *Shakespeare's Wordplay* (1965); the University of Michigan Press for Hans Kurath, *et al.,* eds., the *Middle English Dictionary* (1951–); the Modern Language Association of America for the following articles from *PMLA:* Paull F. Baum, "Chaucer's Puns," LXXI (1956) and "Chaucer's Puns: A Supplementary List," LXXIII (1958); and Helge Kökeritz, "Rhetorical Word-Play in Chaucer," LXIX (1954); the Munksgaard Forlag, Copenhagen, and Per Olsen, ed., for Per Nykrog, *Les Fabliaux* (1957).

The Oxford University Press for W. C. Curry, *Chaucer and the Mediaeval Sciences* (1926); George Ferguson, *Signs and Symbols in Christian Art* (1966); and for Alice F. Kornbluth, "Another Chaucer Pun," *Notes and Queries,* VI (1959); Nicholas Joost, ed., for Barry Sanders, "Further Puns from the *Prologue* and the *Wife of Bath's Tale,*" *Papers on Language and Literature,* IV (1968); Penguin Books, Inc., for Nevill Coghill, tr., *Chaucer: The Canterbury Tales* (1958); the Pontifical Institute of Mediaeval Studies for Paul E. Beichner, "Absolon's Hair," *Medieval Studies,* XII (1950); Princeton University Press for Ernst Curtius, *European Literature and the Latin Middle Ages,* tr. W. R. Trask, "Bollingen Series" (1953); John V. Fleming, *Roman de la Rose: A Study in Allegory and Iconography* (1969); Bernard F. Huppé and D. W. Robertson, Jr., *Fruyt and Chaf* (1963); D. W. Robertson, Jr., *A Preface to Chaucer* (1962); and for R. K. Root, ed., *The Book of Troilus and Criseyde* (1926 and 1954); Rinehart Press, San Francisco, for R. M. Lumiansky, tr., *The Canterbury*

Tales (1954); Routledge & Kegan Paul, Ltd., for John S. Farmer and W. E. Henley, *Dictionary of Slang and Its Analogues* (1966); the Scottish Text Society and the School for Scottish Studies for Sir David Lindsay, *Works,* ed. Douglas Hamer (1931); Stanford University Press for J. S. P. Tatlock, "Puns in Chaucer," *Flügel Memorial Volume* (1916); Syracuse University Press for S. B. Meech, *Design in Chaucer's Troilus* (1959); University of Toronto Press for Bertrand H. Bronson, *In Search of Chaucer* (1960); University Books, Inc., New Hyde Park, N. Y., for Gershon Legman, *The Horn Book: Studies in Erotic Folklore and Bibliography* (1964); and for Mr. Legman's introduction to Farmer and Henley (see above, under Routledge & Kegan Paul, Ltd.), "On Sexual Speech and Slang"; the Viking Press, Inc., for Theodore Morrison, tr., *The Portable Chaucer* (1949).

The Research Committee of Colorado College has awarded me grants to help with the research for this book, and the Executive Committee of the Division of Humanities, Professor Kenneth W. F. Burton, Chairman, awarded me a Ford Humanities Grant for the same purpose. Philip LeCuyer, Thomas J. Wolf, Jack Berryhill, Charles Mullen, and Donna Stavig provided me with many insights, and David Rollman also checked references. My wife helped with her unfailing intelligence, skepticism, encouragement, and patience.

introduction

1. the uses of bawdiness: character

Chaucer called a "queynt" a "queynt," but only when there was a good reason to be blunt. In all his works, there is hardly a word of bawdiness for its own sake. When he mentions sex or excretion, he almost never excites disgust or prurience.

Chaucer uses risqué words for one major purpose: to delineate comic characters and thus to make us laugh. Having said this, however, we have not really provided a meaningful assessment of the poet's methods. We need to distinguish and to judge his various devices, including the use of bawdy language for comic effect. Admittedly, in pious tracts like the "Parson's Tale," the poet uses sex for homiletic purposes, not for laughs. Much more common, however, is his use of bawdry in the portraits of the Friar and the Monk (for instance) in the "General Prologue" to the *Canterbury Tales*. They derive their humorous qualities in large measure from Chaucer's indecent innuendos.

A widely respected critic has stated—more unequivocally than I would dare—that in Chaucer's poetry "the speech always fits the speaker."[1] There are occasional surprises. For instance,

[1] Haldeen Braddy, "Chaucer's Bawdy Tongue," *Southern Folklore Quarterly*, XXX (1966), 214. See also the same scholar's "Chaucer—Realism or Obscenity?" *Arlington Quarterly*, II (1969), 121–138, referred to in the body of this study as: Braddy, "Obscenity."

Chaucer gives the smug and sober Merchant one of the most ribald tales. Usually, however, where we anticipate bawdiness, we find it. There are some Chaucerian characters for whom lewdness is singularly appropriate. We expect to hear forthright language from Alison of Bath, and we are not disappointed. Some critics speak of her as if she were the real narrator of her "Prologue" and "Tale." To counteract this sort of sentimental interpretation, we need to remind ourselves that Chaucer himself is ultimately responsible for the words his personages utter—even when he explicitly denies that responsibility. It is sometimes hard to judge the poet's tone when he forestalls possible charges of purveying scurrility. His customary trick is to claim that he is simply reporting others' words: the drunken Miller is a "cherl," as everybody knows. *He* said those words—not *I, Geoffrey* Chaucer.

Is the poet making a serious apology here, hoping to avoid the label of "foulmouthed" Chaucer, or is this another of those postures which, like self-deprecation, medieval authors assume? It is no doubt naïve to take Chaucer at his word in every passage where he makes these disclaimers. But, on occasion, he seems to be utterly serious. The "retractations" are the most familiar of these *mea culpa* apologies for smuttiness. He is ashamed, he says, of certain of the tales—"thilke [those] that sownen into [tend toward] synne." On the other hand, he is proud of his (clumsy and uncertain) translation of Boethius and of the saints' legends, which most modern readers find dull. In a very real sense, the pathological asceticism of the "Second Nun's Tale"[2] is more offensive than are the Wife of Bath's terms for her wondrous vulva.

The Wife's "queynt" was probably as taboo in mixed company in the fourteenth century as is its twentieth-century counterpart "cunt." Alison uses the term without a blush; she

---

[2] All Chaucer references are to *The Works of Geoffrey Chaucer,* ed. F. N. Robinson (2nd ed., Boston: Houghton Mifflin, 1957). Cecilie, the saint-to-be, warns her husband Valerian that she has a special guardian angel (derived from the Book of Tobit) who loves her with a great love; if Valerian touches her (his wife!) in an amatory way, the divine being "right anon wol sle [slay] yow with the dede" (G 157).

is very much aware of what she is doing. She also varies her terms nimbly enough with *"quoniam"* and *"bel chose,"* both pseudo-learned circumlocutions. It is amusing that she knows so many synonyms for her prized private part. The richness of the Wife's vocabulary tells us as much about her, indeed, as does her account of her five husbands in her "Prologue."

2. the uses of bawdiness: the poet

Chaucer often has no "persona" between himself and his readers or listeners. Most of us take at face value his remarks at the beginning of the *Book of the Duchess* that he has suffered from love for eight years. Huppé and Robertson claim that the whole thing is a Christian allegory and that Chaucer is not talking about *real* love—sexual, physical, secular love—but about Christian ἀγάπη. I doubt if these scholars have persuaded any but their most devoted acolytes.[3] The love-sickness of Chaucer is quite in tune with the amusing pose assumed in the *Parliament of Fowls*, where Scipio perceives that the poet has lost his taste for love (162) :

But natheles, although that thow be dul,
Yit that thow canst not do, *yit mayst thow* se.
For many a man that may nat stonde a pul,
It liketh hym at the wrastlyng for to be,
And demeth yit wher [whether] he do bet or he.

The encouragement of voyeurism is tempered by the wonderfully appropriate wrestling metaphor and by the notion that though Chaucer may have passed his prime, he is still experienced enough to judge lovemaking like a connoisseur.

This is not to commit the heresy of reading literature as if it were veiled autobiography. We cannot legitimately interest ourselves in the question of whether Chaucer was *actually* a voyeur; neither is it the critic's concern to try to guess

---

[3] Bernard F. Huppé and D. W. Robertson, Jr., *Fruyt and Chaf* (Princeton, 1963), pp. 32 ff.

whether in real life the poet satisfied his wife Philippa in bed, or whether his "rape" of Cecily Chaumpaigne involved forced entry or simply kidnaping.[4]

The interesting thing about Chaucer's "direct" or "personal" comments is their literary effect, not any imagined betrayal of the secrets in the poet's heart. If in a story about love a writer comments on the nature of the emotion, without using the intermediary of invented dialogue or the interior monologue of a character, his remarks will modify the significance of the erotic events in the narrative. In the "Merchant's Tale," the old lecher Januarie tells his young wife May to strip, since "hir clothes dide hym encombraunce" (E 1960), and she obeys. Chaucer interrupts to comment (E 1962):

> But lest that precious [prudish] folk be with me wrooth,
> How that he wroghte, I dar nat to yow telle.[5]

Is this simply the common rhetorical flourish called *occupatio*—feigned inability to describe something, usually because of its complexity or grandeur? Or is the pose of pudicity a subtle way of suggesting that it is best not to describe such a grotesquely mismatched coupling?

The poet continues (E 1964):

> Or wheither hire thoughte it [it seemed to her] paradys or helle.
> But heere I lete hem werken in hir wyse
> Til evensong rong, and that they moste aryse.

We know perfectly well, because Chaucer gives us plenty of hints, that May does not find it "paradys" in the arms of bristly old Januarie. And we savor the suggestion of effort

---

4 Robinson, *op. cit.*, p. xxiii.

5 Braddy, "Chaucer's Bawdy Tongue," p. 219, quotes this passage to illustrate how Chaucer fits bawdy words to situations; here, it is a "stylistic device in keeping with the morality of January's bourgeois caste. Flush at the climax, the author refuses the opportunity to become ribald and turns lamely to the insipid euphemism of 'I dar nat to yow telle.'" Braddy does not go on, however, to show that Chaucer changes his style to the direct and blunt when the situation demands—as I point out later.

that "werken" elicits. Even if this *is* merely the rhetorical trick called *occupatio,* it functions very well indeed.

Later on in the "Merchant's Tale," Chaucer chooses to be direct when describing the sexual act. It is entirely proper that he should make this shift in style here, since he wants us to understand the coarse vigor of young Damyan's lovemaking, together with the bitch-in-rut pleasure that May takes in the union. The poet begins with an apology to the ladies; but this time, claiming rudeness of education and sensibility, he proceeds (E 2350):

> *Ladyes, I prey yow that ye be nat wrooth;*
> *I kan nat glose, I am a rude man—*
> *And sodeynly anon this Damyan*
> *Gan pullen up the smok, and in he throng.*

The deliberate pleonasm "sodeynly anon" makes Damyan's haste very clear: "throng" is indeed rude—deeper and more violent than "thrust."[6]

Then Chaucer reassumes his posture of pudicity.[7] His re-

---

[6] Emerson Brown, Jr., *"Hortus Inconclusus:* The Significance of Priapus and Pyramus and Thisbe in the *Merchant's Tale," Chaucer Review,* IV (1970), 37, argues that (as the allusion to the embarrassed and disappointed Priapus shows) Damyan failed to reach a climax or to satisfy May as they "struggled" together in the pear tree. Please note the veiled pun on coitus interruptus in Brown's title—along with the echo of the Song of Solomon (*q.v.*).

[7] Bertrand H. Bronson, *In Search of Chaucer* (Toronto: Univ. of Toronto Press, 1960), p. 21, admits that despite his greatness, Chaucer baffles us in many ways: "one of these is an apparent readiness to endanger a triumphant achievement by what seems to us to be ill-timed and merely idle facetiousness—as if Laurence Sterne had suddenly seized the pen." It would appear that these shifts often involve bawdiness in unlikely places—the poet, with forced fingers rude, introduces into the narrative seemingly gratuitous references of a harsh and crude sort—at least to Bronson's ear: "we are not merely disturbed, we are sometimes disoriented and amazed by the rapid shifts of stylistic level, the apparent stoppages of narrative momentum, the commingling of the colloquial and artificial diction, the breathtaking incorporation of the whole range of language into the working texture of the verse" (p. 22). As I hope to demonstrate in this Introduction and also in the bulk of the study, these shifts are effective narrative devices in many cases.

luctance to describe what he has already portrayed, in vivid terms, is very funny. Januarie's blindness has been miraculously cured and he suddenly can see what the squire Damyan is doing to his wife May aloft in their "nest." The young stud has "dressed" May (E 2362) :

> *In swich manere it may nat been expressed,*
> *But if I wolde speke uncurteisly.*

The prim disclaimer comes too late, like an "Oh, excuse me, please!" after a particularly noisy and aromatic breaking of wind.

Chaucer thus uses various shades of comic sexual allusion and description to expose the coarseness of May and Damyan; to remind us of the senile stupidity of Januarie; and to present himself in an ironically and deliberately inconsistent light—now prudish, now forthright indeed.

3. poet or persona?

But isn't it the Merchant, not Chaucer, who is at one moment rude and demure the next? Possibly the poet wants us to imagine that when there is commentary in the tale, we are "overhearing" the voice of the putative narrator—the Merchant, a henpecked husband unhappily married to a "shrewe at al." If it is this "persona" who so slyly reveals the vixenish crudity of the young wife May, then he (the Merchant) is avenging himself, by means of the tale, on womankind in general and more particularly, though in absentia, on his own nagging wife.

This additional level of narrative subtlety is not necessary, however, for an appreciation of the bawdy humor of the "Merchant's Tale." Indeed, many readers would deny that the "persona" device functions at all in this particular story. Chaucer could have assigned the *fabliau* to several of the other Pilgrims with equal appropriateness. The bond between tale and teller is not strong, particularly when contrasted with the links between Friar, Summoner, Miller, or Reeve and their tales.

4. shakespeare's bawdy

Shakespeare's characters show a wider range of concern with sex than do Chaucer's. Hal's boisterous reference to the hot wench in flame-colored taffeta and Falstaff's boast about frequenting bawdy houses *are* like Chaucer's lubricious humor. But Lear's disgust over the simpering dame whose face between her forks presages snow; his Fool's sad little song about the codpiece; and Thersites' "greasy" talk about lust and venereal disease—these things are quite alien to Chaucer.

There are two reasons that this is true: Chaucer writes no dark comedies and no tragedies in the Shakespearean sense,[8] and therefore references like Hamlet's bitter "nunnery" (which had a second meaning—brothel) and *"count*ry matters" are not appropriate in his works. Second, and perhaps of equal importance, syphilis was unknown in fourteenth-century England. The horrors of the pox and the futile treatments of the disease made a deep impression on Shakespeare's audience, and his characters frequently refer, directly and obliquely, to these ghastly matters.[9]

5. chaucer's reputation for ribaudye

It is therefore odd, perhaps, that some of Shakespeare's contemporaries found Chaucer shocking. In his *Apologie of Poetrie* (1591), Sir John Harington condemned the "Miller's Tale" and the "Wife of Bath's Tale" (by which he doubtless meant her "Prologue") and berated Chaucer for his "flat scur-

[8] The Monk narrates "tragedies" in the narrow medieval sense: tales of the Falls of Princes.

[9] Nobody seems to know with any degree of certainty the origin of syphilis. The best guess seems to be that it, along with tobacco, came from the New World. At any rate, the disease was not known, or at least not virulent, in Chaucer's day, though it may have been confused with leprosy. By the first quarter of the sixteenth century, it was familiar in England. See **cancre**.

rilitie."[10] Harington's prudery is particularly ironic, since he is probably best known today as the author of the *Metamorphosis of Ajax*, a cloacal and coprophiliac treatise on the water closet. The title itself contains a Rabelaisian pun on "a jakes"— a privy.

Throughout the sixteenth and seventeenth centuries, indeed, "Chaucer's jest" meant something indecent and disgusting, and "Canterbury Tale" was a term of contempt, "meaning either a story with no truth in it, or a vain and scurrilous tale."[11]

Of course, Shakespeare, Spenser, and other Elizabethans revered Chaucer too—as the well of English undefiled, the first great name in English poetry. Side by side with the encomiums, however, there were expressions of prim distaste throughout the seventeenth, eighteenth, and nineteenth centuries. In her *Unfinished Sketches* (1713–14),[12] Lady Mary Wortley Montagu found fault with Chaucer's "ribaldry and rhyme," reminding us again that during the Renaissance, Englishmen had lost the key to Middle English pronunciation and prosody.[13] In his *Imitations of Horace* (1737), Pope published his often-quoted epithet for Skelton, the sixteenth-century Poet Laureate; few remember that it was coupled with an attack on Chaucer:

Chaucer's worst ribaldry is learn'd by rote
And beastly Skelton Heads of Houses quote.[14]

---

[10] Caroline Spurgeon, *Five Hundred Years of Chaucer Criticism and Allusion* (Cambridge, 1925), I. xxi, 134.

[11] Spurgeon, *op. cit.,* I. xxi.

[12] Spurgeon, *op. cit.,* I. 329.

[13] The strangest testimony to the obsolescence of Chaucer's poetry is perhaps Sir Francis Kynaston's translation (1635) of the first two books of *Troilus and Criseyde* into Latin rhyme royal stanzas— the purpose being, of course, to capture (fossilize?) the evanescent English story into unchanging Latin. One of the dedicatory verses (by William Barker) to Kynaston's translation runs: ". . . men dare know, / How Poets spake three hundred yeares agoe. / Like Travellors, we had bin out so long, / Our Natiue was become an vnknowne tongue, / And homebred *Chaucer* vnto vs was such, / As if he had bin written in High Dutch" (sig. *3ᵛ–*4ʳ).

[14] Spurgeon, *op. cit.,* I. 383.

The couplet is a satirical thrust at the evils of Pope's times, of course, not at Dan Geoffrey. Wrongheaded as it may seem today, it is at least testimony that the Augustans still read Chaucer, though "misread" might be more appropriate.

With all their reverence for native "antiquities," the Romantics persisted in expressing shock at Chaucer's bawdiness. In 1807, Byron wrote that he found the poet "obscene and contemptible." Four years later in his "Hints from Horace," he linked "Chaucer and old Ben" [Jonson], calling them "quaint and careless, anything but chaste."[15] In his notes for a lecture written in 1818, Coleridge paired Chaucer with Boccaccio, finding both guilty of "gross and disgusting licentiousness."[16] And as late as 1856, Edward Fitzgerald, the translator of the *Rubaiyat,* could still call him "licentious."[17]

6. chaucer's indecency today: the dictionaries

Victorian prudery, that familiar and often unjustly maligned whipping boy, was probably also one of the reasons that nobody has made a systematic study of Chaucer's "harlotrye," his indecorous words and innuendos. His first great modern editor was a Victorian clergyman, the Reverend W. W. Skeat, D.D., who was also a professor at Oxford. As was the custom among scholars at the end of the last century, when they were obliged to explain something indecent, they used Latin. The ladylike, of both sexes, found Skeat's Latin euphemism *pudendum* (literally "the shameful thing") less offensive than "vagina." The medical term is actually a metaphor, meaning "sheath" (for a sword). In our time, Skeat's two great followers, F. N. Robinson and A. C. Baugh—enlightened, liberal, American, Ivy-League professors and editors—still gloss "queynte" by calling on Skeat's Victorian Latin word.[18]

15 Spurgeon, *op. cit.,* II. 29, 52.

16 Spurgeon, *op. cit.,* II. 95.

17 Spurgeon, *op. cit.,* III. 29.

18 The most recent school-edition of the "Miller's Tale," ed. Constance B. Hieatt, *The Miller's Tale* (New York: Odyssey Press, 1970), *s.v.* "queynte," retains the learned euphemism *pudendum.*

Even today, Chaucer's marginal glossers and translators have trouble with the bawdy bits. For instance, the Wife of Bath tells one of her husbands that he has nothing to complain about (D 332) :

Ye shul have queynte right ynogh at eve.

In the modern "ponies," this becomes "tail"; "can have all you can take when day is done"; "have intercourse"; "you can have me all you want at night"; "evening rations"; and "i.e., lovemaking."[19] The range is amusing; from the pompous-clinical to the military, with some boys' latrine terms thrown in. These (understandably) pusillanimous paraphrases remind us again that poetry is untranslatable, and that Chaucer's comic obscenity can be appreciated only in Middle English.

In Skeat's time, scientific lexicography was just beginning: the monumental *Oxford English Dictionary* had just begun its publication, which was not completed until the 1930s. Even this great scholarly work does not include the commonest four-letter word for intercourse, "fuck." Chaucer's "swyve" is there—perhaps because the editors thought *it* could be printed with a plain (and proper) mark *obsolete.*

In the 1950s, Hans Kurath and his fellows at the University of Michigan began publication of the *Middle English Dictionary,* less than half of which has appeared. The *MED* editors were precise, comprehensive, and not squeamish. Nonetheless they, like the *OED* staff, were not always sensitive to possible double entendres.[20] Dictionary-makers *should* be sus-

19 The translations or glosses are (in chronological order) from *Chaucer's Canterbury Tales: an Interlinear Translation,* ed. and tr. Vincent F. Hopper, Ph.D. (New York, 1946), p. 325; *The Portable Chaucer,* ed. and tr. Theodore Morrison (New York, 1949) , p. 229; *A Chaucer Reader,* ed. Charles W. Dunn (New York, 1952) , p. 95; *The Canterbury Tales,* ed. R. M. Lumiansky (New York, 1954) , p. 207; *Chaucer, the Canterbury Tales,* tr. Nevill Coghill (Baltimore, 1958) , p. 283; and *Geoffrey Chaucer, a Selection of His Works,* ed. Kenneth Kee (New York, 1966) , p. 68.

20 For instance, *s.v.* "ars-metrike," one of Chaucer's most amusing and obvious puns, the *MED* cites only the literal passage in the "Knight's Tale" (A 1898) , and makes no mention of a possible double entendre. Gershon Legman, no doubt the greatest living

picious of such things, no doubt, since many of Chaucer's suspected innuendos cannot be proved with scientific lexicographic precision. Therefore many of the entries in my study cannot display an *imprimatur* like "cited in *MED*" or "supported by contemporary quotation from *OED*." I must resort to terms like "possible," "likely," and "probable—especially in this context."

7. chaucer's indecency today: scholars and critics

Between the appearance of the *OED* and the first fascicles of the *MED*, there developed three new kinds of scholarly

---

expert on pornography and certainly the most vigorous in his opinions, describes what happened to the *OED* thus in his *Horn Book* (New Hyde Park, N.Y.: University Books, Inc., 1964), p. 345: "Furnivall left the *Oxford English Dictionary*, of which he was the originator, when the boys'-school principal who was made its editor [Murray] insisted upon expurgating it; nor did Furnivall return later when the final editors made fools of themselves, and a joke of their earlier cowardice, by sneaking the omitted words ['cunt' and 'fuck'] all back in again, under the old spelling (*n.b.*), at Chaucer's and Andrew Marvell's 'quaint' and 'windfucker.' (For reasons unknown, 'cock' had not been omitted, nor any of the scatological terms.)" Legman also attacks Partridge (p. 255) for purveying the sort of analysis "done by certain modern British amateur antiquarians." He calls their method "hopelessly amateur, with *klang*-associations and wildcat etymologies blandly taking the place of any relevant research." Surely this is too strong. Even more intemperate is Legman's later attack in the Introduction to J. S. Farmer and W. E. Henley, *Slang and Its Analogues, Past and Present* (New York: Dutton Paperbacks, 1960), p. xc, where he claims that many of the entries in *Shakespeare's Bawdy* are "not sexually intended at all, except in Partridge's imagination." He gleefully goes on to point out that "this fervid compiler manages somehow to overlook both occurrences in Shakespeare of punning references to the word '*cunt*': in Hamlet's twitting of Ophelia, at the play-within-the-play, as to lying in her lap, or 'country matters' " [III. ii. 123]; and in *Twelfth Night*, II. v. 96–97, Malvolio's *C*'s, *U*'s, and *T*'s. Actually there are several more such references in Shakespeare that neither Partridge nor Legman notes—e.g., "*conc*eit," *Taming of the Shrew*, IV. iii. 162–163.

approach, all important to the study of Chaucer's "harlotrye": first, Partridge's studies of slang (however much they owe to Henley and Farmer) and his seminal *Shakespeare's Bawdy;* then the work of the critics who study Chaucer's use of rhetorical devices; and, third, the emergence of "patristic exegesis," led by D. W. Robertson, Jr.

Partridge's candid study of Shakespeare's indecent words and innuendos is an urbane, if not always critical, analysis. I have imitated its format in this book. It revealed for the first time to a popular audience the thread (warp? woof?) of "low" references that runs throughout English speech and throughout the works of England's greatest poet.

We owe Partridge an immense debt. But for him, we would miss (for instance) the obscene fun hidden, like a wickedly gleaming golden filament, in the secondary meanings of "die" in Shakespeare's day (e.g., Enobarbus on Cleopatra, I. ii. 149). Neither Partridge nor any other critic can *prove* that "die" meant to have an orgasm, but he can persuade us that in certain contexts this meaning is very likely.

Even Partridge, overzealous as he sometimes is, misses some things. He seems not to have been familiar with the popularity of rhetorical devices in the Middle Ages of Renaissance. If one knows that the puns in Chaucer (or in Shakespeare) were a "flower" of rhetoric called *paranomasia,* one need not go through the tedious business of arguing against the half-literate superstition that the pun is the lowest form of wit. Had Eric Partridge known the work of scholars like E. R. Curtius, who described the medieval and Renaissance admiration for such rhetorical devices, he would doubtless have detected many more of Shakespeare's paranomastic bawdy references.

Almost twenty years ago, Helge Kökeritz, perhaps our foremost philologist in Middle and Early Modern English, wrote a revolutionary essay in which he identified the link in Chaucer between rhetoric and puns. In it he traced the amusing story of how it slowly dawned on the experts that medieval poetry owed something to paranomasia.[21] Kökeritz began with

---

[21] "Rhetorical Word-Play in Chaucer," *PMLA,* LXIX (1954), 937–952.

Thomas R. Lounsbury, who found only two puns in Chaucer in 1892; F. N. Robinson identified nine in 1933.[22] This was "before readers became aware of Chaucer's indebtedness to the precepts of medieval rhetoric,"[23] particularly to tropes like *traductio, adnominatio,* and *significatio*—the last a variety of equivocation. Native poetry adopted these figures from Latin. Kökeritz found a large number in Chaucer, both innocent and bawdy.[24]

More recently, readers have not only identified a great many more Chaucerian puns but have begun to distinguish subtle differences among their effects. As Norman D. Hinton puts it, the puns "are not simply the result of a superabundant sense of humor, nor a 'low' mind, nor even the result of a mixed style. . . . Most of the puns tend to complicate the thing which is being said. I do not want to claim that this makes Chaucer a more 'ironic' writer, or a composer of verse with 'levels of meaning' (which is too often taken to mean that the verse in question exists in separate layers, like a Viennese torte). It does suggest, however, that Chaucerian verse is more intricate than many critics have been willing to admit—that Chaucer is saying more than one thing at a time in more places than where previously suspected."[25]

22 In his 1933 edition, Robinson stated in his note to A 297 ("philosophre" in two senses, neither bawdy) that "puns are unusual" in the poet's works; in the second edition (1957) he acknowledged the change in critical sensitivity by rewriting the note to read "puns are relatively unusual in Chaucer."

23 Kökeritz, *op. cit.,* p. 937.

24 Following Kökeritz's work, there have appeared a number of articles (but no book-length works) dealing with Chaucer's puns and their occasional bawdy meanings. Some of these treatises, which have been of greatest use in the preparation of this study, are listed in the Bibliography. Stephen Knight provides a convenient summary of the rise of rhetorical Chaucer studies in "Rhetoric and Poetry in the *Franklin's Tale," Chaucer Review,* IV (1970), 14–30.

25 "More Puns in Chaucer," *American Notes & Queries,* II (1964), 115. George Williams' remarkable study *A New View of Chaucer* (Durham, N.C.: Duke University Press, 1965) includes a revolutionary interpretation of Sir Thopas as a homosexual portrait of the King himself, Richard II (pp. 145–151). Thopas' adversary, Sir Olifaunt, is actually John of Gaunt (Williams continues). One

At about the same time as the revival of interest in medieval rhetoric—together with the recognition of the intricacy of Chaucer's poetry—there emerged the neo-exegetes. They are a group of erudite specialists whose findings run counter to, but also support, a study like this one, which depends to a considerable degree upon multiple meanings in Middle English poetry. D. W. Robertson, Jr., and Bernard Huppé are the most distinguished of these critics; they insist that Christian ethical concepts of *cupiditas* and *caritas* run through all medieval works of art. Sometimes a work that on the surface appears to encourage lovemaking ("swyvynge," as Chaucer might have called it), like the extremely popular *Le Roman de la Rose,* is discovered, by the exegetes, to have a second "truer" level: it is really a kind of anti-erotic jeremiad.

Understandably, the modern exegetical school has no central interest in Chaucer's bawdiness. The exegetes do insist, however, that what appears to be a perfectly plain meaning on the surface will turn out, upon closer inspection, to have a second, third, and even a fourth stratum of significance. Chaucer is not, they assure us, a naïve artist; on the contrary, as a learned medieval writer, and as a pre-Romantic, he was *compelled* by his own *Zeitgeist* to provide us with complex, sophisticated double meanings. He could not have written otherwise.

It is not quite fair of me to enlist the Robertsons and the Huppés in my camp, quite unbeknownst to them. They admit,

---

entire paragraph from this section of *A New View* deserves to be quoted in full to illustrate the ingenuity of Mr. Williams' argument:

> The giant is notable for three things: he has a "fel staf-slyng"; he is the protector of the "queene of Fayerye"; and he has three heads. I have already noted that the "staf-slynge" may have phallic implications—which would be consistent with Gaunt's reputation as a lover. "Fayerye" is then, very probably, the Land of Love, which the giant calls "myn haunt"; and, from Chaucer's point of view, the "queene of Fayerye" would be none other than Katharine Swynford. The three heads might then be a reference to Gaunt's three wives.

There is much more of the same, which I urge the reader to examine for himself.

of course, that there are comic passages in Chaucer.[26] But when they explain Middle English humor, the exegetes sometimes make the jests sound like Sunday School teachers' jokes.

There are those for whom the exegetical way of reading Middle English poetry is uniquely stimulating, delightful—and useful. It restores to Chaucer the high seriousness that Matthew Arnold denied him long ago. For such readers, a disquisition on the obscenities in Chaucer will seem misguided, if not outright distasteful. The exegetes should *not,* however, find my study farfetched, in view of their own methods.

8. liberated bawdiness: fun, ugliness, violence

We are ready for a new "marriage" in Chaucer studies: the old, the new, the borrowed, and (of course) the blue. With the *OED* and the *MED;* with Partridge's example to guide us; with the new awareness and information from the rhetoricians; and with something borrowed from the exegetical critics— we are ready to begin our examination of Chaucer's "harlotrye." Our contemporary literature has been "liberated" legally for about a generation, since Judge Woolsey found *Ulysses* an acceptable import. We can now read without a blush Molly Bloom's soliloquy, with its reference to Stephen Dedalus' cock. We no longer need to ship copies of Henry Miller's schoolboy fantasies home from Europe in false-bottomed trunks. John Barth and John Updike and Allen Ginsberg and LeRoi Jones can publish four-letter words as part of their natural artistic vocabulary, using the blunt terms for comic or, more often, for emetic purposes.[27]

26 D. W. Robertson, Jr., *A Preface to Chaucer* (Princeton: Princeton University Press, 1962) , p. 20: "Medieval artists did not hesitate to use what we should call 'obscenity' to illustrate a moral point. And what is true of medieval artists is . . . equally true of medieval writers."

27 Hilda R. Hulme, *Explorations in Shakespeare's Language* (New York: Barnes & Noble, Inc., 1963) , p. 90 (speaking of Shakespeare— but all the more true of Chaucer) :

. . . some present-day critics would surely claim that the defiance of linguistic inhibition by writers such as Lawrence, Joyce and

Chaucer views copulation with healthy and effervescent good
humor. The "swyvynge" that goes on in the "Miller's" or the
"Reeve's Tales" is supremely good fun for those involved directly. In the latter narrative, the daughter and the wife enjoy
immensely their (respective) fornication and adultery. We
readers, the indirect participants, enjoy the comic ribaldry too.

Where there is adultery, there must be cuckolds. In Chaucer,
they deserve their fates: they are stupid, suspicious, jealous, dishonest, and anti-intellectual. Only in Chaucer, perhaps, is the
last of these shortcomings grounds for cuckoldry.

On the morning after his delicate young wife has betrayed
him, the carpenter-cuckold in the "Miller's Tale" falls from the
ceiling and breaks his arm. Sentimental readers feel a twinge
of pity for the victim of this gratuitous violence, but the sym-
pathy does not endure. John's arm will mend, we know, just
as we are sure that the "hurt gags" in movie cartoons will not
result in permanent injuries to Sylvester the cat.

When Nicholas' scorched "toute" heals, he and the inventive
Alisoun will find another occasion to repeat their lovemaking.
They will hoodwink the stupid husband again and again, but
from us he will never elicit any lasting sense of outrage or
pity. Chaucer keeps the whole affair good-humored and comic.

Beckett constitutes a rediscovery of a source of power and truth
which was known to many great literary artists of the past. I hope
then that readers will concede that if it is useful and interesting
for the non-contemporary to try to recognise within Shakespeare's
dialogue elements of proverb-idiom alive in his day but now
gone from ordinary language, so too it may be necessary to be
alert for elements of sexual idiom, the meaning of which has been
obscured by time.

Is it worth it, Miss Hulme asks (p. 133):

Some of my readers may inwardly answer, although few, I think,
will be so unfashionable as openly to admit that they find no
great pleasure in understanding the kind of joke which is here
expounded. Others may advance the practical objection that . . .
the labour involved in understanding outweighs the aesthetic
gain. And certainly it is for the individual reader to decide what
industry and energy he can spare for such detailed exploration
into the less edifying spoken English of three and a half centuries
ago [six for Chaucer!].

8. sex and excretion: direct terms

Direct terms for sex (the act and the equipment) are actually not very common in Chaucer. He usually prefers double entendre, which will be discussed later, to the forthright "swyve" and "dight." The Middle English predecessor of "fuck" does not appear. "Swyve" is derived from a word meaning to sway and is related to "swivel." It is thus analogous to Modern English "screw" and to Italian "chiavare," to turn a key in a lock. "Dight" in the sense of "to swyve" is part of a vague verbal complex meaning generally to bring something about; it was also used in Middle English for the act of donning clothing.

"Queynte" is rare, too, compared with substitute metaphors or circumlocutions that Chaucer uses much more commonly for the vagina. He seems to have had no correspondingly direct word for the male organ. "Yerde" (yard, as in yardstick) later became the commonest term for the penis, but Chaucer used it but once or twice in this sense, and even these passages are doubtful.

Taboo words submerge and reappear, dolphin-like, as the centuries pass. Neither of Chaucer's words for intercourse is now current. But, who knows? Either "swyve" or "dight" may be resurrected.

Sometimes a perfectly innocent word may attract an indecent connotation. (Is the flies-to-honey proverb appropriate here?) Take "occupy," for example, which for a decade or so in the sixteenth century meant "swyve" (2 *Henry IV,* II. iv. 160) and then underwent amelioration, as semanticists say, and was reestablished in our neutral and unblushing vocabulary. "Quim" and "quiff" are old words for the female organ that never caught on. Nor does "spend" now compete with "come" for seminal emission, though in our grandmothers' time it was the common term.

Technical or unambiguous terms for excretion are also relatively uncommon in Chaucer's works, but when he chooses to use them, he does so without embarrassment. In the fourteenth century, "dong" and "pisse" surrounded one in the city streets and, of course, in the barnyard. You could use the "pryvee"; if the word was too euphemistic, you could call it the "gong" (i.e., "gang," the place where you *go*), a rougher word than "pryvee" in Chaucer. The fastidious Prioress calls it the "wardrobe," a hypereuphemism anticipating the modern powder room and comfort station. *Why* the Prioress uses this superpolite term should engage our critical attention. As a matter of fact, the purpose of this book is to make precisely such judgments.

Excretion was an accepted and semipublic event that Chaucer rarely uses for comedy. In the last century, these body functions have become rites performed in the shamefast privacy of a closed room, the excreta being immediately laved away by sparkling rivulets, to be seen and smelled no more. Because the act is now hidden, it is once again a source of humor. But to us, as to Chaucer, it is not so interesting or so funny as is copulation.

As there are secondary sexual characteristics, so are there secondary excretory phenomena—belching and farting. Eructation is a rare subject for jest in Chaucer. Breaking wind, on the other hand, is commoner and funnier. An entire tale among those of the Canterbury Pilgrims is built around the problem of equitable fart-division (the "Summoner's Tale"). Those who, like Absolon in the "Miller's Tale," are squeamish about this act, will not find the exercise in arithmetic very funny (see **ars-metrike** and note 20 above). I would guess, however, that the ranks of such squeamish clerks are diminishing, even among American coeds. They laugh (or titter), at least to themselves, when "Chaucer intrepidly joins sex with scatology in the 'Miller's Tale,'" linking concupiscence with the "carminative faculty."[28]

Direct allusion to excretion is uncommon in Chaucer's poetry; so too are the innuendos, metaphors, and puns related to these functions. Polite euphemisms like "passing wind" or "manure" are later inventions. In the fourteenth century,

[28] Braddy, "Chaucer's Bawdy Tongue," p. 217.

"manure" carts were filled with "dong" (what else?).
"Shit (en)" occurs rarely and seems to have been confined to
the barnyard or sheepcote. Although Chaucer does not often
exploit this vein of humor, he has amusing disquisitions on the
"reverberacioun" and "soun" of farts, and his "buf" is a
precise echoic word for a belch.

9. copulation: puns, metaphors, circumlocutions

When we enter the realm of paranomastic expressions for
sex in Chaucer, we are in the richest lode in his mine of
comedy. It is also the most hilarious and the most hazardous.
We must be cautious, or we will begin to see covert sexual allusions in almost every line.[29] I hope that I have "reformed that
indifferently with us" (as the Player says to Hamlet), if not
reformed it entirely. I am candidly uncertain about the innuendos that I suggest for "stonden in his lady grace," but
where the phrase (or its variants) occurs, it must be discussed. The suggestion of a secondary erotic meaning for such
a line is not purely whimsical or subjective; as the reader
will see, there is a basis for the notion. But I confess that I
cannot demonstrate it by citing dictionaries or contemporaneous works.[30] An analyst of connotations in poetry can express

[29] M. M. Mahood, *Shakespeare's Wordplay* (London: Methuen,
1965), p. 11, admits that the Augustans had contempt for puns.

Since then, Addison's worst fears have been realised; we have
"degenerated into a race of punsters." Where the Augustans dis-
approved of Shakespeare's wordplay and the Victorians ignored
it, we now acclaim it. A generation that relishes *Finnegans Wake*
is more in danger of reading non-existent quibbles into Shakespeare's work than of missing his subtlest play of meaning.
Shakespearean criticism today recognises wordplay as a major
poetic device, comparable in its effectiveness with the use of
recurrent or clustered images.

I think we can read "Chaucer[ian]" for Miss Mahood's references
to Shakespeare without doing any violence to her meaning.

[30] Hulme, *op. cit.*, p. 114: "To 'prove' the existence of an indecent
joke which the dramatic context seems strongly to suggest is not
always easy. Evidence which is available in the minor sources [of

opinions, guided by contexts and the scholar's critical apparatus, and he can suggest the likelihood of indecent innuendo. But, in the end, the reader, with the proper experience in analyzing this kind of literature, must decide for himself whether a naughty overtone can be heard. Like a musician who can train himself to hear high frequencies, inaudible to the layman, the reader of Middle English poetry can sensitize himself to the possibilities of sexy double meaning. However, just as the musician does not want to subject himself too often to frequencies that hurt his ears, so too the reader should not try to find scurrilities lurking behind every final -*e*.

10. copulation: clusters

The sources for copulation metaphors are as diverse as the Bible ("dette") and the arts ("daunce"). A phenomenon that surprised me is Chaucer's demonstrable habit of thinking in clusters of ambiguities.[31] This is partly due to the demands of rhyme, especially in stanzaic poetry where rhymes are at a premium:[32] "serve" will almost inevitably produce "sterve." But the prosodic requirements of rhyme royal in *Troilus and Criseyde,* for instance, will by no means explain all the clusters. "Lust-hunt-pleye" recurs often—naturally enough, since "pleye"

---

contemporary literature] may not be noted in dictionary collections; readers who come upon such evidence may not be concerned with its relevance to [the poet's] text." Miss Hulme recognizes the limitations of lexicography too (p. 131) : "How much of colloquial or vulgar vocabulary in this specialised field of sex and bodily function existed in speech only, even in less linguistically inhibited ages, we can only conjecture. Paucity of dictionary evidence is to be expected, and it may well be that such forms as get into the written language of more recent times have taken on respectability through false etymology, analogical spelling, or restricted application."

[31] Hulme, p. 105, observes that bawdiness begets bawdiness—or rather that clusters of indecent words influence one another: "A word is known by the company it keeps."

[32] Chaucer complains in the "Complaint of Venus" (80) : "rym in Englissh hath such skarsete" [scarcity].

has as its innocent meaning "divert," and "lust" could mean simple pleasure of any kind. The "pleye" of the "hunt" was for the fourteenth-century courtier one of his greatest "lusts." When, however, females like Dido are involved, the cluster takes on a blushing glow. "Pleye" is part of two other common nodules of allusion: with (1) "pryvetee" and "queynte" and (2) "jouste" and "daunce." "Pryve" seems to suggest to Chaucer "place" and "grace"; and "serve" (or "service," "servant") goes with (1) "grace," "holly"; (2) "hol," "plesaunce"; or (3) "sterve," "deye." If one is uncertain whether a word has a palimpsest of secondary sexual meaning in a particular passage, the sudden surge of clusters of associated words will often provide mutual reinforcement and heightened probability.

Derivatives must not be forgotten, though even the most perceptive analysts of Chaucer's style have generally ignored them. For instance, Kökeritz saw that the congruence of "mayden" and "hede" was suggestive. But no one has observed that "acqueyntaunce" often suggests the "queynte" referred to so shamelessly and directly by Alison of Bath.[33]

We should also be alert to changes of tempo. In the "Shipman's Tale," the movement from andante to presto is reinforced by the cluster that Chaucer assembles with ever-increasing rapidity: the wife appears pale because her husband has "laboured" her all night (B 1298); then come references to love (1330); a kiss (ostensibly symbolic of innocent agreement, 1331); love again (1343); and "deere love" (1348). By this time, the bold Daun John is practically in the wife's lap and bosom—which the Middle Ages confused linguistically, if not anatomically (see **barm**).

11. the deviates

Deviant sex does not seem to have interested Chaucer's audience much. When the poet suspects it, he expresses dis-

---

[33] Hinton, *op. cit.* p. 116, mentions one such derivative; it came to my attention after I had completed my own study.

gust—for instance in the "General Prologue" when he gives us directly his own opinion of the Pardoner's effeminacy (A 691). Thopas' unmanliness seems to amuse him, however; at any rate, it amuses *us*—especially in view of the scholarly debate that it has aroused.[34] (See **Canacee, hair, incest, nature.**)

12. amelioration and pejoration

Many of Chaucer's bawdy words exhibit marked semantic change. "Queynte" (quaint) and "luxurie" have now lost their sexual connotations: they have undergone amelioration. A word like "corage" could mean valor in the Middle Ages, but it also meant the capability to achieve and maintain an erection —the act of valor peculiar to the bedroom. The "good" sense of "courage" alone persists today. The opposite kind of semantic shift also occurs: "bawd[y]," "harlot," "lewde," "ravysshed," and "sluttish," which had relatively innocent meanings (along with secondary indecent ones) in Chaucer's day, have undergone pejoration. All are "impolite" terms in Modern English.

13. sources

In shaping his sources, Chaucer sometimes adds bawdy material, sometimes omits it, and sometimes retains it: compare Boccaccio, *s.v.* **hol,** and Vergil, *s.v.* **husbonde.** A systematic listing of what he does in each case would be tedious. However, it should be noted that in the French *fabliau*—the narrative form that he used so often for his indecent tales—the indecent diction is much like Chaucer's. That is, direct terms for sex are rare, while metaphors are plentiful. Among the former, four words make up the bulk of the references in the extant *fabliaux: foutre* (fuck, for which the seventeenth cen-

---

[34] See above, note 25, reference to Williams.

tury substituted the euphemism *ficher,* common today) ; *con* (cunt—see **hare** and **queynt** below) ; *coille* (testicle—see **coillons**) ; and *vit* (penis) .[35]

Much more common in these French tales are circumlocutions: *acoler* (embrace), *baisier* (kiss), *deduit* (amusement), *delit* (pleasure), *dosnoier* (strip, remove clothing), and *envoiseure* (frolicking sex, or organ that produces such). Lovers perform the *jeu d'amour* (game of love) or *le jolif mestier amourous* (the merry business of love) ; they do *lor bon* or *lors bons* (their "good"[s]) or *leur volonte* (their will) ; their *talant* or their *plaisir.* They *gesir* (lie) or *gesire entre les bras de* (lie in the arms of) someone. Chaucer uses many metaphors like these—sometimes translated directly from the vocabulary of the *fabliau.*[36]

If the *Romaunt of the Rose* is Chaucer's, his practices are similarly consistent. Of the passages from the *Romaunt* that I have chosen to include in this study, almost all have a direct, bawdy source in the French. See **gay,** for instance, where the Old French words corresponding to the Middle English "gaye and amorous" are *gais e amoreus.* For "aqueyntaunce," *Le Roman de la Rose* has *acointance* (e.g., in 3562 of the Middle English) , which plays on the word *cointe* in much the same way as does the Middle English upon **queynt.**[37]

14. a retractation

Chaucer ends the *Canterbury Tales* with an apology for his indecencies (see Robinson's edition, p. 265) . He asks forgiveness for those tales that are suggestive of sin and begs to be remembered for things like his "legendes of seintes." I too would like to voice a "retractation." I trust that I am not guilty of seeing bawdiness where it is not; on the other hand, I

35 Per Nykrog, *Les Fabliaux* (Copenhagen, 1957) , p. 211.

36 *Ibid.,* pp. 74, 209.

37 See Ronald Sutherland, *The Romaunt of the Rose and Le Roman de la Rose: a Parallel-Text Edition* (Oxford: Basil Blackwell, Ltd., 1968) .

cannot claim to have unearthed ("laid bare" might be a better metaphor) all of Chaucer's double meanings of a sexual or scatological sort. I have often included words and passages that are only "possibles"; but when the possibility is there, the reader should be made aware of it.

Chaucer's poetry is delightful to read. I hope that this book will make it more pleasurable. To understand that he uses bawdry as a major comic device is important; despite his own "retractations," I think the poet himself would agree.

bibliography

ABRAHAM, CLAUDE K. "Myth and Symbol: The Rabbit in Medieval France." *Studies in Philology,* LX (1963), 589–597.

BAUGH, A. C., ed. *Chaucer's Major Poetry.* New York: Appleton-Century-Crofts, 1963.

BAUM, PAULL F. "Chaucer's Puns." *PMLA,* LXXI (1956), 225–246.

———. "Chaucer's Puns: A Supplementary List." *PMLA,* LXXIII (1958), 167–170.

BEICHNER, PAUL E. "Absolon's Hair." *Medieval Studies,* XII (1950), 222–233.

BENNETT, J. A. W., and G. V. SMITHERS, eds. *Early Middle English Verse and Prose.* Oxford: Oxford University Press, 1966.

BLOCK, EDWARD A. "Chaucer's Millers and Their Bagpipes." *Speculum,* XXIX (1954), 239–243.

BOLTON, W. F. "The Topic of the *Knight's Tale.*" *Chaucer Review,* I (1967), 217–227.

BRADDY, HALDEEN. "Chaucer's Bawdy Tongue." *Southern Folklore Quarterly,* XXX (1966), 214–222.

———. "Chaucer—Realism or Obscenity?" *Arlington Quarterly,* II (1969), 121–138.

BRONSON, B. H. *In Search of Chaucer.* Toronto: University of Toronto Press, 1960.

BROWN, EMERSON, JR. *"Hortus Inconclusus:* The Significance of Priapus and Pyramus and Thisbe in the *Merchant's Tale." Chaucer Review,* IV (1970), 31–40.

CURRY, W. C. *Chaucer and the Mediaeval Sciences.* New York: Barnes & Noble, Inc., 1926.

CURTIUS, ERNST. *European Literature and the Latin Middle Ages.* Tr. W. R. Trask. New York: Harper Torchbooks, 1953.

DONALDSON, E. T. "Idiom of Popular Poetry in the *Miller's Tale." Explications as Criticism: Selected Papers from the English Institute 1941–1952.* Ed. W. K. Wimsatt, Jr. New York: Columbia University Press, 1963.

DUNBAR, WILLIAM. *Poems.* Ed. W. Mackay Mackenzie. Edinburgh: Porpoise Press, 1932.

ELIASON, NORMAN E. "Some Word-Play in Chaucer's *Reeve's Tale." MLN,* LXXI (1956) , 162–164.

FARMER, J. S., and W. E. HENLEY: See Legman.

FERGUSON, GEORGE. *Signs and Symbols in Christian Art.* New York: Oxford University Press, 1966.

FLEMING, JOHN V. *The Roman de la Rose: A Study in Allegory and Iconography.* Princeton: Princeton University Press, 1969.

GOWER, JOHN. *Complete Works.* Ed. G. C. Macaulay. Oxford: Oxford University Press, 1911.

HIEATT, CONSTANCE B., ed. *The Miller's Tale.* New York: Odyssey Press, 1970.

HINTON, NORMAN D. "More Puns in Chaucer." *American Notes & Queries,* II (1964) , 115–116.

HULME, HILDA M. *Explorations in Shakespeare's Language.* New York: Barnes & Noble, Inc., 1963.

HUPPÉ, BERNARD, and D. W. ROBERTSON, JR. *Fruyt and Chaf.* Princeton: Princeton University Press, 1963.

KNIGHT, STEPHEN. "Rhetoric and Poetry in the *Franklin's Tale." Chaucer Review,* IV (1970) , 14–30.

KÖKERITZ, HELGE. "Rhetorical Word-Play in Chaucer." *PMLA,* LXIX (1954) , 937–952.

KORNBLUTH, ALICE F. "Another Chaucer Pun." *Notes & Queries,* VI (1959) , 243.

LANGLAND, WILLIAM. *Vision of Piers Plowman.* Ed. W. W. Skeat. Oxford: Oxford University Press, 1886.

LEGMAN, GERSHON. *The Horn Book: Studies in Erotic Folklore and Bibliography.* New Hyde Park, N.Y.: University Books, Inc., 1964.

————. "On Sexual Speech and Slang." Introduction to *Dictionary of Slang and Its Analogues*. Ed. John S. Farmer and W. E. Henley. Revised edition. New Hyde Park, N.Y.: University Books, Inc., 1966. Pp. xxx–xciv.

LINDSAY, SIR DAVID. *Works*. Ed. Douglas Hamer. Edinburgh: Scottish Text Society, 1931.

LIPFFERT, KLEMENTINE, *Symbol-Fibel*. Fourth edition, revised. Kassel: Johannes Stauda Verlag, 1964.

MAHOOD, M. M. *Shakespeare's Wordplay*. London: Methuen, 1965.

MEECH, S. B. *Design in Chaucer's Troilus*. Syracuse, N.Y.: Syracuse University Press, 1959.

[*Die*] *Minnesinger, in Bildern der Manessischen Handschrift*. Intro. by Hans Naumann. Leipzig: Insel Bücherei, n.d.

NYKROG, PER. *Les Fabliaux: Étude d'histoire littéraire et de stylistique médiévale*. Copenhagen: Ejnar Munksgaard, 1957.

OVID. *Amores*. Tr. Grant Showerman. Loeb Library. Cambridge, Mass.: Harvard University Press, 1963.

————. *The Art of Love*. Tr. Rolfe Humphries. Bloomington, Indiana: Indiana University Press, 1969.

Ovid's Fasti. Tr. Sir James George Frazer. Loeb Library. London: William Heinemann, Ltd., 1931.

PARTRIDGE, ERIC. *Shakespeare's Bawdy*. New York: Dutton Paperbacks, 1960.

PERELLA, NICOLAS JAMES. *The Kiss Sacred and Profane: An Interpretative History of Kiss Symbolism and Related Religio-Erotic Themes*. Berkeley and Los Angeles: University of California Press, 1969.

RICKERT, EDITH, ed. *Chaucer's World*. New York: Columbia University Press, 1948.

ROBBINS, ROSSELL H., ed. *Secular Lyrics of the XIVth and XVth Centuries*. Oxford: Oxford University Press, 1952.

ROBERTSON, D. W., JR. *A Preface to Chaucer: Studies in Medieval Perspectives*. Princeton: Princeton University Press, 1962.

ROBINSON, F. N., ed. *The Works of Geoffrey Chaucer*. 2nd ed. Boston: Houghton Mifflin Co., 1957.

ROOT, R. K., ed. *The Book of Troilus and Criseyde, by Geoffrey Chaucer*. Princeton: Princeton University Press, 1926.

ROSS, T. W. "Five Fifteenth-Century 'Emblem' Verses from Brit. Mus. Addit. MS 37049." *Speculum,* XXXII (1957), 274–282.

———. "*Troilus and Criseyde,* II. 582–587: A Note." *Chaucer Review,* V (1971), 137–139.

SANDERS, BARRY. "Further Puns from the *Prologue* and the *Wife of Bath's Tale.*" *Papers on English Language and Literature,* IV (1968), 192–195.

SCOTT, KATHLEEN L. "Sow and Bagpipe Imagery in the Miller's Portrait." *RES,* XVIII (1967), 287–290.

SHAKESPEARE, WILLIAM. *Complete Works.* Ed. G. B. Harrison. New York: Harcourt Brace, 1952.

SKEAT, W. W., ed. *Complete Works of Geoffrey Chaucer.* Oxford: The Clarendon Press, 1894.

SPURGEON, CAROLINE. *Five Hundred Years of Chaucer Criticism and Allusion.* Cambridge: Cambridge University Press, 1925.

STEADMAN, J. M. "Simkin's Camus Nose: A Latin Pun in the *Reeve's Tale.*" *MLN,* LXXV (1960), 4–8.

SUTHERLAND, RONALD, ed. *The Romaunt of the Rose and Le Roman de la Rose: A Parallel-Text Edition.* Oxford: Basil Blackwell, Ltd., 1968.

TATLOCK, J. S. P., and A. G. KENNEDY. *A Concordance to the Complete Works of Geoffrey Chaucer.* Washington, D.C.: The Carnegie Institution, 1927.

———. "Puns in Chaucer." *Flügel Memorial Volume.* Palo Alto, Calif.: Stanford University Series No. 21, 1916. Pp. 228–232.

WHITESELL, J. E. "Chaucer's Lisping Friar." *MLN,* LXXI (1956), 160–161.

WILLIAMS, G. G. *A New View of Chaucer.* Durham, N. C.: Duke University Press, 1965.

glossary

Entries in boldface are cross-references; cross-references in quotation marks, followed by *q.v.,* indicate that the word in question is in the quotation.

I quote Chaucer by referring to a single line (usually that in which the word cited appears) rather than to inclusive line numbers. When a reference to an article has no page numbers, it may be assumed that the material therein is arranged alphabetically (e.g., Paull F. Baum's articles on Chaucer's puns), and therefore page references are unnecessary. Full information on all references may be found in the Bibliography.

Subdivisions and parts of speech have been omitted from the references to the *OED* and the *MED* unless they are necessary to distinguish one meaning or entry from another. The *MED* is now completed through the letter *L;* therefore it has been used for citations up to that point, and thereafter the *OED* has been used.

I should like to point out that *Le Roman de la Rose* is the OF poem by Guillaume de Lorris and Jean de Meun; and the *Romaunt of the Rose* is the Middle English translation of the *Roman,* parts of which are probably Chaucer's.

To avoid ambiguity, I have arbitrarily used the spellings Alison for the Wife of Bath and Alisoun for the carpenter's wife in the "Miller's Tale."

a

abedde. The bed is the "lystes" or tournament area where
Chaucer's couples engage in their (extra)marital encounters. In his various allusions to the bed, the poet
creates an erogenous "epic," complete with divine
machinery and an epic catalogue.

The gods oversee Chaucer's "lystes abedde" in the
"Complaint of Mars." Mars and Venus meet. There is no
Olympian debate: "Ther is no more, but unto bed thei
go" (73). In this obscure astrological poem, the act of
love, at least, is unequivocal.

The lubricious wife in the "Shipman's Tale" (B 1367)
provides the epic catalogue—a list of things that every wife
desires. The last, and presumably the most important, is
to have a husband "fressh abedde," a sentiment that
Alison of Bath shares. When the complicated payment of
debts (see **dette**) is completed at the end of the tale
(B 1614), the wife gives hers "abedde"—a delightful kind
of business transaction in which debtor and debtee are
inextricably involved and it is hard to distinguish one
from the other.

However, the "Shipman's Tale" adultress is at first
demure when discussing her married life with her lover-
to-be: "But sith I am a wyf, it sit nat me / To tellen no

31

wight of oure privetee, / Neither abedde, ne in noon
oother place" (B 1353). We are curious, at first, about
what sort of "private" acts have been occurring in places
other than the bedroom; but then we recall the tastes of
old Januarie in the "Merchant's Tale," and we can guess.

The climactic action of this tale of Januarie and May
occurs in an enclosed garden (analogous, perhaps, to the
walled city of epic action). Chaucer borrows this *hortus
conclusus,* with proper acknowledgment, from Guillaume
de Lorris, author of the first part of the *Romaunt of the
Rose,* who in turn got it from the Song of Solomon (*q.v.*).
In his specially built retreat, the description of which includes a pointed allusion to Priapus (see **sceptre**),
Januarie can perform sexual feats that would surpass the
heroic acts of Hector—things "that were nat doon abedde"
(E 2051). As is his usual practice, Chaucer gives us no
circumstantial details, but allows us to guess the nature of
these Pavian perversions or Lombard lasciviousnesses,
unknown (perhaps) outside those climes.

One expects epic deeds in Chaucer's Troy story, *Troilus
and Criseyde,* but actually there is much more talk than
action. Many critics would claim that this long poem is a
novel; if so, perhaps the talk is the point of it. Still, things
do happen "abedde." Part of this action is perfectly dull
and "normal"—that is, the bed is used for repose. When
Troilus returns from his night's "work" with Criseyde, for
instance, he sleeps late "abedde" (III. 1584). But we are
reminded (III. 1679) that it was Pandarus who brought
the lovers "abedde" in joy and security. When the affair
is over and Criseyde of the sliding courage has defected,
Pandarus tries to comfort Troilus by pointing out that at
least he has not seen Criseyde in bed with Diomede,
whereas many other lovers have observed their loves "in
hire spouses bed ybedded" (V. 346). Little wonder that,
even from the Eighth Sphere, Troilus can take little comfort from this philosophy.

It is neither the valiant Trojan warrior Troilus nor the
God of War who is most at home in Chaucer's "lystes" of
love. It is Alison of Bath. Although the answer to her
question in her "Tale" is concerned with women's desire

to dominate men, the Wife cannot resist interjecting a wrong guess—that some women would prefer to have, above all things, "lust abedde" (D 927). Her most potent weapon against her husbands is to deny them her favors in bed. If her mates do not accede to her wishes, she will "do hem no plesaunce" (D 408), and she reports that when they were not obedient and tractable, "namely abedde hadden they meschaunce" (D 407). [*MED*, "abedde," b with reference to amorous affairs.]

abhomynable synne. The Parson cannot bring himself to name this terrible sin—"thilke abhomynable synne, of which that no man unnethe [scarcely] oghte speke ne write." Nonetheless, it is openly referred to in the Bible (see Romans 1:26–27), he says, and we are led to guess that he refers to homosexual acts. The good Parson continues, with perhaps more knowledge (or curiosity) than is seemly: "this cursednesse doon men and wommen in diverse entente and in diverse manere" (I 909–910). [*MED* has no suggestion that the abominable sin is homosexuality.]

acorded. After their fight, the Wife of Bath and her husband "fille acorded" (D 812), which probably has a double meaning: (1) the obvious one, reached an agreement; (2) had intercourse. There is no dictionary basis for this conjecture, but there is plenty of basis in the Wife's character and in the situation, as she herself describes it.

In the *House of Fame,* the eagle says he will show Chaucer "mo love-dayes and acordes / Then on instrumentes be cordes" (695). See **conclusioun, love-dayes.** [*MED* has no sexual meanings.]

acqueyntaunce. Knowledge of a woman's private parts (derived from **queynt**). Often there is no proof that we are to see the bawdy second meaning. For example, in the *Romaunt of the Rose* (3562), the Lover has been bereft of "th'aqueyntaunce / Of Bialacoil, his moste joye." And earlier (2213) the Lover is told he should be like Gawain (the familiar type of the medieval gentleman of *courtoisie*) and not like the surly Kay; he should be wise and "aqueyntable," which simply means friendly. Now this work is of course a translation, and perhaps not even Chaucer's: still the questions of bawdy meaning arise, since after all the translator had to choose what words to use. From the same poem, we have somewhat better, and more interesting, evidence (3228): Reason speaks of Idleness, with whom the Lover went in the "daunce" (3227) and "haddest aqueyntaunce. / Hir aqueyntaunce is perilous, / First softe and aftir noious."

With the fallen Criseyde, we have a different story, and one in which her female parts play a major role. Diomede tells her that he wants "more aquayntaunce" of her (V. 129). He is very bold and is encouraged to feel yet bolder in this, his very first exchange with her. The "dynamic" of innuendo here (the increase in tempo) also forms a very clear pattern: "delit . . . god of Love . . . paramours . . . stonden . . . grace . . . servant . . . serve" (129 ff.).

Even in the relatively modest *House of Fame,* the eagle tells Chaucer that he will show him "olde forleten aqueyntaunces" (694). Actually, he has already done so, since after using "queynte" twice, he says he hasn't the ability to tell how Dido and Aeneas "aqueynteden in fere" [together] (250).

The Friar makes a vicious attack upon the Summoner, as every reader of the *Tales* knows, accusing him of employing whores and pimps as his informers—using the terms "secree" (D 1341) and "prively" (D 1343), both of which have a sexual innuendo. The spies are employees of old standing: their "acqueyntance" is not recent. There is the possibility, then, that the Summoner is using blackmail instead of paying his informers' fees.

In the "Shipman's Tale" (B 1219), the young monk is well "aqueynted" with the merchant (is this a foreshadowing of the intimate acquaintance that the monk will later have with the merchant's wife?). This hint is later made perfectly clear when Daun John says to the wife that he is not really a cousin of the merchant but that he has pretended to be one in order to gain "aqueyntaunce" (B 1342) with the wife. [*MED,* 1 (b) familiarity, intimacy between the sexes. Later citations may have bawdy implications too—e.g., the fifteenth-century *Destruction of Troy* (1865): "Syn he no knowlage ne Acoyntaunse of my cors has," where the word seems equivalent to carnal knowledge.]

amor. Even the most casual reader of the "General Prologue" knows that this is the Prioress' word. What kind of love is suggested by the brooch that she wears (in defiance of the rules of her order)? We can, I hope, never settle the ambiguities of *Amor vincit omnia.* Chaucer's satire is gentle—on that everybody seems to agree. Madame Eglentyne is not promiscuous, but maybe she *is* a little bold when she wears this piece of jewelry so prominently displayed, especially on a public occasion like a pilgrimage. [*MED,* "amour," *n.* (1) (a), love between the sexes; (b) spiritual love, charity.]

amorous. In the "Wife of Bath's Prologue," there is little question that the word is both physical and vigorous. The Wife accuses her husband of visiting their neighbor's wife too frequently: "artow so amorous" (D 240).

On the other hand, the aging Januarie in the "Merchant's Tale" (E 1680) is cautioned to "plese hire [his wife] nat to amorously," where again physical union is indicated.

In *Troilus and Criseyde* (IV. 1429), the pair are briefly reunited, "the grete furie of his penaunce / Was queynt with hope, and therwith hem bitwene / Bigan for joie th'amorouse daunce." This is intercourse. See **daunce, queynt.** [*MED* cites mostly fleshly senses, but also 4 (a) devoted (to Jesus). Chaucer's "To Rosemounde" (22) "amorous plesaunce," is glossed "love-longing." Other citations, before 1400, make it clear that "amerous *(sic)* men are lechours."]

amy. The Host calls the effeminate Pardoner "beel amy" (C 318), which of course means simply fair friend; however, in view of the Pardoner's character and of the Host's reaction to his tale, it surely suggests effeminacy—along with its established secondary meaning of rascal, knave. [*MED,* "bel ami," (a) fair friend; *iron.,* rascal, knave.]

Angelus ad virginem. The Latin phrase (normally addressed to the Blessed Virgin) is obvious irony (A 3216) in view of Nicholas' worldliness and his amorous interests in the

"Miller's Tale." An additional irony, equally obvious, is that Alisoun, the object of his interests, is no virgin. [*MED:* no entry.]

apert. See pryvee.

aqueyntaunce. See acqueyntaunce.

armes. The word "arms" has meant weapons for a long time; but even before man made these tools, he used his arms for amorous play. Chaucer exploits both these ideas in his "war" poems. In *Troilus and Criseyde* (II. 164–165), Pandarus has just mentioned Hector and his doughty brother Troilus to his niece. Criseyde says: "I holde it gret deynte [a very estimable thing], / A kynges sone in armes wel to do." Can one doubt that she refers (or Chaucer does) to his prowess both on the fields of Troy and in bed? (We are even more certain of ourselves in the "Complaint of Mars" (76): "The flour of feyrnesse lappeth in his armes," with the same pun.) One of the cleverest bits of legerdemain that the poet accomplishes is to make us believe that Troilus is the aggressor in the famous love affair. Not so. For instance, at their first encounter, she warms up to him, inviting him to "lustinesse" (perfectly innocent?); then "and hym in armes took, and gan hym kisse" (III. 182). She is still making the overt moves (III. 1128): they are in bed together, and he has recovered from his swoon (just in time). "Hire arm over hym she leyde." Then she kisses him. The tempo increases in this famous erotic Book III and pretty soon it *is* the male who is taking the initiative: "he hire in armes faste to hym hente" (1187; similarly in 1201 and 1205). Chaucer concludes his description of amorous sentiment with the most familiar of all sentimental emblems from "unnatural history," the mutual arm-entwining of the tree and vine. The "swote wodebynde . . . bytrent and writh" [encircles and twines about] the tree (1231).

Perhaps the most sensual stanza in the poem begins with Troilus stroking Criseyde, moving from her arms to her breasts (III. 1247, see also 1359, 1449, 1519, 1522). But then comes a passage of disconcerting and distasteful horseplay (if that is all it is). On the morrow, after the lovemaking between the two young people, Pandarus comes to his niece Criseyde: "With that his arm al sodeynly he thriste / Under hire nekke, and at the laste hire kyste" (1574). An avuncular thrust of the arm may be acceptable as some sort of *aubade,* but one wonders. See also **bosom, incest.**

Troilus' reaction to the night's lovemaking is different, and again there is a double entendre involving "armes": he was "the first in armes dyght" (1773). Of course this means that he got his armor on before everybody else. But also? See **dight.**

When they part, Troilus and Criseyde indulge in much intertwining of arms (IV. 1131, 1219, 1689). When she is gone, there is a kind of *ubi sunt* passage where he recalls her arms in particular: "Wher is hire white brest? wher is it, where? / Wher ben hire armes and hire eyen cleere" (V. 220). In his ominous dream, he sees his beloved lying in "his [the boar's—Diomede's] armes folde" (V. 1240).

The Legend of Good Women (2158) portrays Theseus and Ariadne dancing and singing, while he has her in his "armes": this is not ordinary song and terpsichore but intercourse.

A final example from the *Romaunt of the Rose* (2314): the Lover is enjoined, if he is a good rider, "to prike gladly, that men may se. / In armes also if thou konne. . . ." The collocation may be fortuitous in this translation, of course, but I doubt it. [*MED* recognizes the possibility of the two meanings being puns, but provides no examples.]

ars. See **ers.**

ars-metrike. When Theseus builds the lists for the great tournament ("Knight's Tale," A 1898), only those who knew geometry or "ars-metrike" (arithmetic) could have built the marvelous structures. Nobody ever suspected that there might be a double meaning in this technical term here—nor should such a suspicion be entertained.

But turn to the "Summoner's Tale" (D 2222); it is now a profoundly scientific question and the double meaning is present: how can a fart be divided into twelve equal parts? It is a matter for "ars-metrike": (1) arithmetic; (2) "ars" (ass, buttock, rectum) measurement. How the problem is solved with a wheel and its spokes should be familiar to every reader of Chaucer. If not, read the tale again. After all, the wheel was one of man's first significant inventions. Both Baum and Kökeritz mention this double meaning, by the way. [*MED* gives the meaning of arithmetic, but no hint of Chaucer's pun.]

aton. Literally, "at one," in agreement. When Alan and the miller's daughter in the "Reeve's Tale" (A 4197) reach their accord at night in bed, they are indeed "at one," quite literally joined. [*MED* has no sexual sense.]

avowtrye. Adultery—but in Chaucer's day the term was much broader. It covered a true multitude of sins (see below under *MED* reference) . So in the "Friar's Tale" (D 1306) , the attack upon the summoner is more serious than might at first appear. "Avowtrye" was, however, the act which was legally punishable by the archdeacon's court, to which the summoner had to bring the offenders. The summoner is a professional; he knows his prey, including the "avowtier."

Januarie, the talkative old lecher in the "Merchant's Tale," argues that if he should get stuck with an old wife who could not please him he would then be condemned to live in "avoutrye" (E 1435) and go straight to the devil. This is adultery as we know it today. But what of the Parson who, in his section on Luxuria (I 839) , describes the particular pains in Hell for the adulterer. One of the varieties is reserved for married couples who engaged in intercourse only for their "flesshly delit" (I 903) . The goodly Parson has much more of the same under the Remedia section against Luxuria (I 939 ff.) .

Then there is Chaucer's version of the "old army game," but with a twist. Tarquin (*Legend of Good Women,* 1809) threatens Lucrece that if she will not accede to his lust, he will kill her "knave" and lay him in bed with her, then claim that he caught them in "avouterye." [*MED* mentions that the term also covered intercourse between husband and wife for recreational purposes.]

a-werke. See **swynke.**

B

bagge. Although the dictionaries provide the basis for an obscene meaning for this word, Chaucer does not choose to use it. In the "Man of Law's Tale" (B 124), "bagge," even though mentioned along with "daunce," has the quite literal, or not wholly innocent, meaning of money-bags. See **baggepipe** and **purse**. See Figures 1 and 3. [*MED*, "genitras," "bagge of the genitras" = scrotum. Legman (p. 190) discusses a clerk's green bag and inkhorn—his genitals.]

baggepipe. A symbol of the penis and scrotum. Not only does the pilgrim Miller play one (A 565) as he leads off on the way to Canterbury, but the miller in the "Reeve's Tale" (A 3927) is also a piper. It is easy to miss this bawdy by-play between the two adversaries unless one knows the iconography of the ancient musical instrument. The Reeve is having some fun at the expense of the Miller's virility. Cf. Robertson, *Preface to Chaucer* (p. 128): "The bag-pipe . . . is, for rather obvious reasons, frequently, although not always, an instrument with which male lovers make melody." Block discusses the instrument as a symbol of both gluttony and lechery, and Legman (p. 193) refers to piper and two little drummers.

bak. An object of erotic pleasure, as in *Troilus and Criseyde* (III. 1247) where he strokes "hire streghte bak and softe."

ball. Never used for testicle in Chaucer, which is unfortunate since there are so many opportunities for comedy. In the *Legend of Good Women* (2003), Ariadne and Phaedra plot together to help Theseus by making him "balles," which he will throw into the Minotaur's mouth so that the monster will not eat him. These are not testicles, of course, but balls made of wax and tow that will glut the beast and encumber his teeth, like bubble gum. [*MED*, 8, quotes from the *Proverbes of Hendynge,* an amusing bawdy stanza that shows what Chaucer missed:

poluit prodigia super terram au
serens bella usq; ad sinem terr.
Arcum conteret et consringet
arma et scuta comburet igni.
Vacate et videte quoniam
ego sum deus exaltabo: in gent
bus et exaltabo: in terra.
Dominus virtutum nobis
cum adiutor: nr deus iacob.
Gloria pri. a Admirabit eum de
us multu suo deus in medio eius non
comouebitur. a Sicut letancium. ps.
undamenta eius in mo
tibus sanctis diligit do

Fig. 1. *Grotesque bagpiper: the details have been obliterated, perhaps by a pious hand that found them too suggestive. Bodleian
Library, Oxford, Douce MS, 62 (14th c.), fol. 40r.*

The maide that gevit [giveth] hirsilf alle
Othir [either] to fre man othir to thralle. . . .
And pleiit [playeth] with the croke [penis] and with the balle,
And mekit [maketh] gret that erst was smalle.

In the last line there is an equivocation that should be
noticed: two things are made "gret," the penis and the
maid's belly.]

bare. There is grotesque and truly perverse prudery in the
Legend of Good Women, which is not, I think, Ovid's (the
Fasti are the ultimate source), probably not Chaucer's, but
more likely that of some intermediate version. It smelleth
of the votive candle. After her rape, Lucrece (1857 ff.)
commits suicide, but in preparing for her self-destruction
she acts as if she were making a wedding-night toilet:

And of hir clothes yet she hede tok.
For in hir fallynge yet she had a care,
Lest that hir fet or suche thyng lay bare;
So wel she lovede clennesse and eke trouthe.

Even in her suicide, the genteel Roman matron observed
decorum in dress: at least Chaucer thought so. As Lucrece
dies, Ovid says, "haec etiam cura cadentis erat" (even then
in dying she took care to sink down decently—Loeb
Library, tr. Sir James George Frazer). But decorous garb
and bare feet are two different things!

barly-bred. Simple but nourishing fare. The Wife of Bath
(D 145) admits that virgins may be made of pure "whete-
seed," but she represents barley-bread, which provides the
strongest nourishment, of course. There might be some
unconscious irony in this passage, since this sort of meal
was given to criminals as punishment, as the *MED* indicates. [*MED,* "barli," 3 (a) punishment to eat "barli bred"
and drink of the brook.]

barm. Lap (Baugh); bosom (Robinson). Dalida cuts Sampson's hair while he is sleeping in her "barm" ("Monk's
Tale," B 3256). It is vaguely sexual: he is in a copulative
position, though asleep, it appears. [*MED,* 1 (a) lap; (b)
breast, bosom. The same ambiguity exists for "bosom"

itself. Perhaps the confusion goes back to the Hebrew for
Abraham's bosom.]

bawde. The term comes from an Old French word meaning—
quite innocently (for a French word) —bawdy, gay,
licentious, dissolute. This seemed to have confused the
fourteenth-century Englishman, since he could not determine what it meant with any degree of exactness. The
Parson, who should know about these things (I 885) says
bawds are those who procure, selling the flesh even of
their own wives and children. In his tale, the Friar complicates things (D 1339): he says that the Summoner has
"bawdes" aplenty, ready to hand; but whether they are
panders or spies (or both) is not clear. A little later, there
is the memorable line in which the Friar links the Summoner's trade with less savory ones: he is "a theef, and eek
a somnour, and a baude" (D 1354). [*MED,* (a) procurer
or procuress; (b) harlot. *MED* records no meaning
"spies," which the Chaucer passage seems to justify.]

bawderye. In the "Friar's Tale" (D 1305), it is explicitly
pandering. Chaucer is much subtler in *Troilus and
Criseyde* (III. 397): Troilus thinks of Pandarus' kindness
as the act of a friend or companion, not as "bauderye."
The irony need hardly be pointed out, except that
Pandarus has admitted that he *has been* practicing the
very old profession, though still "betwixen game and
ernest" (III. 254). [*MED, n.* (1) (a) pandering; (b)
brothel; (c) lechery.]

bawdy. The earlier meaning (soiled) is still present in
Chaucer. In the "Canon's Yeoman's Tale" (G 635), the
Host is surprised that the Canon, who can pave the road
to Canterbury with silver and gold, yet wears an "over-
slope" (overgarment) that is "al baudy and totore also."
But there are hosts of references in the works where the
meaning is clearly sexual. [*MED,* soiled, filthy, dirty. Skeat
points out in *Piers Plowman* (B-Text, V. 196): Avarice
wears "a tauny tabarde of twelue wynter age, / Al totorne
and baudy and ful of lys crepynge."]

bed. See **abedde.**

bedeth. See **serve.**

bedstraw. See **fyr.**

beere. The word, with a variety of spellings, meant both bier and pillowcase, among other things. Pandarus has his little joke, based on this pun, with Troilus (II. 1638): "God have thi soule, ibrought have I thi beere!" Troilus' soul is ready for its final rest—for its "bier." But it is also ready of course for that resting place on the pillowcase, with the body of the inexpressibly beautiful Criseyde. Baum comments on this pun.

The same pun is present, but not so overtly, in the lyric "Complaint of Chaucer to his Purse" (5): his "lady" (his purse, of course) has been cruel to him; "me were as leef be layd upon my bere," says he—catafalque or (preferably) pillowcase.

Something quite different and, I'm afraid, a little dull, is to be found in the Wife of Bath's "Whan that my fourthe housbonde was on beere, / I weep algate. . . ." (D 587). Unhappily, she means this quite literally, though she is keeping her eyes peeled at this very funeral, watching for husband number five. But who knows? Perhaps the word "beere," used twice, suggested bedtime to the good Wife, even in the midst of mourning. [*MED*, "bere," *n.* (3) pillowcase; *n.* (8) bier. Braddy, "Obscenity" (p. 131), remarks on "bere," pointing out that there is also the meaning that "Troilus is to have Criseyde as his *bier* to die on (sexually)." See **die**.]

bele. See *chose*.

bene. This is one of those useful Chaucerian words: things are not worth a (bean, turd, straw, etc.). The most amusing sexual use is in the "Merchant's Tale" (E 1854), where the wife May opines that her old husband Januarie's "pleyyng" (that is, his sexual prowess, of course) is not worth a "bene." See **pley** and also "flye" at **tough**.

beute. In the Garden of Love (*Parliament of Fowls*, 225), Chaucer sees "Beute withouten any atyr"; its nakedness is the only "bawdy" thing about the figure, and Kenneth Clark has explained to us the interesting differences between naked and nude. Anyway it is clear that not only Lord Clark and Euclid but also Chaucer have looked on Beauty bare. See **bare**.

bigamye. In "Anelida and Arcite" (152), we are told that since

time began men have wanted to change their mates—like
Lamech, "he was the first fader that began / To loven two,
and was in bigamye."

As is so often true of her, the Wife of Bath has a different opinion of this sort of Scriptural evidence: the text
that she likes, "wexe and multiplye," makes no mention
of bigamy (D 33) and therefore it cannot be of great
moment. [*MED,* (a) two simultaneous marriages; (b) two
successive marriages; (c) marrying a widow.]

bisy. A kind of euphemism, but not a very definite one, it
would appear, for intercourse. See the "Shipman's Tale"
(B 1508), where the doughty Daun John and the merchant's wife "in myrthe al nyght a bisy lyf they lede."
[*MED* provides no sexual meaning.]

blew. Blue is the color of steadfastness or constancy, and green
of fickleness (in love, of course). See the refrain in
"Against Women Unconstant" (7, 14, 21); "Anelida and
Arcite" (146), etc., etc.

Books like those by Lipffert and Ferguson agree that in
medieval art blue represented steadfastness, but they
recognize only liturgical or "pious" symbolic meanings for
green. [*MED,* 1 (b) symbol of constancy. Green seems not
to have had a similarly generally accepted symbolic value.
The association with jealousy is later. Cf. Robbins' Poem
No. 206: "My tombe ytt schalbe blewe / In tokyne that I
was trewe" (89).]

boce. Boss, protuberance. In his attack on scanty clothing, the
Parson singles out those fashions that permit a man's privy
members to be revealed—especially when they are in a
"horrible swollen" state, at which time they show the
"boce" of their shape ("Parson's Tale," I 422). Twentieth-
century toplessness offers an interesting contrast to this
fourteenth-century fashion. See **shap.** [*MED,* 3 (a) bulge;
cites Chaucer.]

body. It may sound strange to hear (or read) Chaucer saying
that the "delyces of body" bring anguish. Well, he did not
write it! It is from his translation of the *Boece* (III. Prosa
7) —a bleak, un-Chaucerian bit of prudery.

An interesting and much more Chaucerian occurrence
is to be found in the early *Book of the Duchess,* with its

striking parallel between *courtoisie* or *Frauendienst* on the one hand and the feudal relationship on the other. As the Baron is Lord of the Manor, so too the Fair White (the Lady—John of Gaunt's Blanche, in all probability) is Lady of the Body (1152).

There is a certain grace in the foregoing passage, but the next ("Shipman's Tale," B 1613) will strike the reader as even more typically Chaucerian in its humor. After a complicated series of financial and vaginal transactions, the faithless wife offers to pay off her merchant husband: "Ye shal my joly body have to wedde," and she will pay off her debts with intercourse. See **dette.**

There is plenty of snobbery in Chaucer, but there is one passage involving "body," which perhaps shows some egalitarianism (not unlike the Wife of Bath's arguments for natural "gentilesse"). In the "Manciple's Tale" (H 214), the Manciple himself interrupts to tell us that between a woman of high degree and a poor wench, there is no difference, "if of hir body dishonest she bee." See **honestee.**

If the reader is uncertain whether Chaucer means "body" to be equated with vagina, let him consider the "Franklin's Tale" (F 1417), where we learn that after Habradate's death, his wife commits suicide: "My body, at the leeste way, / Ther shal no wight defoulen, if I may."

But once again it is the Wife of Bath who must have the last word on the subject: the "body" as a word for sexual parts. She says she wants control over her husband's "propre body" (D 159), which is of course a general term, but in the mouth of the Wife probably refers to his penis. Later (D 314) she avers that man should not be master both of woman's body (as a sexual object) and good (her goods as well). Such a phrase sums up her beliefs, as she has derived them from her "experience (*q.v.*)." One wonders, not irrelevantly, I hope, whether she would ever consider throwing her body on her dead husband's bier, as did Habradate. Perhaps she has simply not yet found the right mate, one who could command such respect. See **beere.** [*MED*, 3 (b) refers to fornication and intercourse, but nothing so precise as vagina or penis.]

bordels. In the "Parson's Tale" (I 884), in the section on
  Luxuria, he is especially vigorous in his attack on
  bordellos, since one may unknowingly get involved in one
  of these institutions in sinning with one's own kindred.
  Extramarital sex is not his target; potential incest is. Is
  there some remote possibility that for these hundreds of
  years we have all missed a glimmer of humor in the dreary
  "Parson's Tale"? See **incest.** [*MED, n.* (1) a house of
  prostitution; earliest citation is *ca.* 1300.]

bordillers. In the *Romaunt of the Rose* (7034), Fals-Semblant
  will do business with anyone, even these bordello-keepers.
  [*MED,* "bordeller": keeper of a brothel.]

borel. Baum finds that "borel" occurs five times in Chaucer,
  always in the sense of "coarse, common"; Sanders thinks
  the word could have two meanings: coarse, woolly stuff
  and also pudendum. When the Wife of Bath (D 356)
  threatens to run out "her borel for to shewe," she means
  that she will flaunt her mons veneris and all its equipment. (I am not sure Sanders is right here, but it is worth
  thinking about.)

  Elsewhere, it is pretty clear that it is simply a word for
  a coarse kind of cloth and is used figuratively to distinguish
  levels of society: in the "Summoner's Tale" (D 1872 and
  1874) for laymen—common folk—who are contrasted with
  friars, who know Christ's secrets. [*MED* gives no support
  for the meaning "pudendum."]

bosom. When Criseyde acts cold, as Pandarus brings her
  Troilus' letter, he gets rough with his niece: "hente hire
  faste, / And in hire bosom the lettre down he thraste"
  (II. 1154). They both laugh over the matter, but it
  reminds one of Pandarus' treatment of Criseyde mentioned
  under **armes.** [*MED,* 1 (b) loving embrace; love, affection.
  But most of the citations are from pious tracts; not many
  deal with physical love.]

bouger. Fals-Semblant is making his confession in the *Romaunt
  of the Rose* (7022), admitting that he will do business
  with any "bouger." Robinson glosses it as "sodomite,"
  evidence that even in this chaste edition there are some
  "bawdy" explanations that are simply mistakes. The word
  meant a heretic. [*MED,* "bougeron," deriving ultimately

from Latin *Bulgarus.* The Latin for Bulgarian was *also* the source of "bugger," with an interesting confusion of sodomy and heresy involved.]

breche. See **breech.**

breech. The most violent passage in all the *Canterbury Tales* ("Pardoner's Tale," C 948) occurs when the Host attacks the Pardoner, who has invited him to come forward first to kiss his relics: "Thou woldest make me kisse thyn olde breech!" roars Harry Bailly. Baugh glosses this as "shorts," and although nobody really wants to kiss anybody else's underpants, it would certainly be preferable to the real thing that Chaucer has in mind, which is of course the arse *(q.v.).* To support this gloss *(pace* Professor Baugh) see the *MED* citation below. But one must grant that there *were* undergarments called by this name (cf. breech-cloth) and the other *MED* citation will make this point clear too. Braddy, "Obscenity" (p. 137), sees no humor in the Host's bold words: the passage is "that intolerable business . . . this discreditable sort of filth, Chaucer at his worst."

There is no doubt about the meaning of "breech" in that vigorous and virile blessing ("Nun's Priest's Tale," B 4638), the Host's thanks to the storyteller for his superb tale of the two barnyard fowl: "I-blessed be thy breche, and every stoon!" If there *is* any doubt, see **stoon.** [*MED,* 1 the undergarment (earliest citation before 1225); 3 the buttocks, *ca.* 1300. *Piers Plowman* (C-Text, VII. 157) makes one of these meanings clear: "baleysed (beaten with a stick) on the bar ers and no breche bytwyne."]

bren. Now that the Wife's "flour" is gone (D 478), all she can sell is bran—i.e., shopworn sex. See **flour.** [*MED,* "bran," 2 has figurative senses, but no erotic ones, even though this Chaucer passage is cited.]

brestes. See also **ye.** Probably the most innocent of the many references is that in the *Boece* (III. Metrum 12, 15), speaking of Orpheus: "Whanne the most ardaunt love of his wif brende the entrayles of his breest" it was a mighty passion!

But naturally enough most of the passion is seated in the female breasts—or at least they are the cynosure of male

attention. In the austere and almost ritualistic erotic catalogue in the *Book of the Duchess* (956), the Fair White's
"brestes" are round—perfection, like all her features.

It is good to juxtapose here the miller's daughter, with
her camus nose, alongside the Duchess Blanche: she too
has "buttokes brode, and brestes rounde and hye"
("Reeve's Tale," A 3975). In the days of girdles, corsets,
and God knows what other unmentionable deceits, we
need to be reminded that six-hundred years ago men
admired broad bottoms.

That complex psychological figure Criseyde has an odd
dream early in her poem (II. 927): an eagle tears open
her "brest" and exchanges hearts with her. This violence
reminds one of a great many medieval love lyrics, which
cannot be cited here; but the reader might glance at the
very peculiar Sonetto 1 in Dante's *Vita Nuova*.

When awake, Troilus and Criseyde are better off (III.
1250), however, when he strokes her "brestes rounde and
lite." (Recall that the second adjective means "small.")
And naturally enough one of the things that Troilus misses
when she has defected to the Greek camp is her "white
brest" (V. 219). See also **armes.**

One does not find bawdiness in Chaucer's Prioress, and
one does not expect to. But the passage in which she
praises little children who can laud the Blessed Virgin in
strange ways, even though infants, strikes me as "obscene"
in some special sense ("Prioress' Tale," B 1647 ff.):

But by the mouth of children thy bountee
Parfourned is, for on the brest soukynge
Somtyme shewen they thyn heriynge [praise]

This is explained later (1704): "Seint Nicholas stant evere
in my presence, / For he so yong to Crist dide reverence."
We are told by Baugh (from the *Legenda Aurea*) that St.
Nicholas took the breast, when an infant, only once on
Wednesdays and Fridays, out of respect for his Savior. A
juvenile act of fasting, I take it. Baugh also has a pawky
remark at this point: "here the association of ideas is all

the more natural since St. Nicholas was the patron saint of schoolboys."

There is an allied (though just how, I cannot explain) reference in the "Second Nun's Tale" (G 290) when another sort of perhaps unhealthy erotic act occurs. When St. Cecilia hears that her brother-in-law has decided to embrace the Christian faith, "she gan kisse his brest." In view of her sex life with her own husband, this is suspicious conduct indeed. (See Introduction, p. 2.) [*MED,* 3 as features to be admired; also many purely biological references (things babies suck) .]

buf. In the "Summoner's Tale" (D 1934) , the friar attacks the fat beneficed clergy: "Lo, 'buf!' they seye, *'cor meum eructavit!'* " Robinson points out that this was probably a current jest, not Chaucer's invention. It is not very sophisticated: "eructavit" means both "belched" and (in Psalm 44 [Vulgate]) "my heart is inditing a good matter," as the King James Version puts it. Robinson gives another correlative version of the joke in which the sound of the belch is spelled "puf." Belches are never very funny, but Chaucer does about as well as anyone. See also **soun.** [*MED,* Chaucer's is the only citation.]

burdoun. See **sceptre, yerde,** and Figure 6. This word and its variants present a number of delightful possibilities. In the "Reeve's Tale" (A 4165) , the miller's wife bears a "burdon, a ful strong," to her husband's *kleine Nacht-musik.* He "fnorteth" (snores) , "Ne of his tayl bihynde he took no keep." Because the "burdon" is the bass accompaniment in music, one suspects that the good wife was also guilty of a bass nocturnal tune. See **fart, tayl.**

But in the *Romaunt of the Rose* (3400) , the word has a very different sense: "I fond hym [Daunger] cruel in his rage, / And in his hond a gret burdoun," which is a spiked staff. (The combination of "rage" and "burdoun" may suggest some kind of sexual "cluster," but I cannot untangle it. Priapus' scepter may throw some light on the matter.)

The most interesting use of "burdoun," however, occurs in the familiar passage in the "General Prologue" (A 673) where Chaucer is giving us his last full-length portraits, those of the Summoner and the Pardoner:

> *Ful loude he [the Pardoner] soong "Com hider, love, to me!"*
> *This Somonour bar to hym a stif burdoun;*
> *Was nevere trompe of half so greet a soun.*

The musical meaning of the word is certainly here in this passage, but Baum thinks (and I agree) that there is yet a third (and maybe a fourth) very obscene sense. A "burdoun" was a stick, a staff: a stiff burdoun between these two possibly homosexual personages has an unmistakably libidinous sense. Finally, the word also meant a mule, a hinny (recall the Pardoner's sexual shortcomings). The only meaning of the word that Chaucer does *not* seem to exploit, as a matter of fact, is that of a nail with a big head—at least I do not *think* this sense is present. [*MED*, *n.* (1) pilgrim's staff, walking stick, club, spiked staff; (2) low-pitched undersong; (3) stud set in the boards of a book (that is, a big nail, a nail with a big head); (4) mule, hinny. Daunger in *Le Roman de la Rose* is described as bearing a *burdon* (staff), which is without sexual implications. Later in the poem, however—in the last part, which is not included in the Middle English translation—the Lover is equipped, like a pilgrim, with staff (penis) and scrip (scrotum—in which there are two hammers, his testicles). He uses these to accomplish the *factum,* the "rape of the rosebush" as Fleming calls it (see Figures 11, 12, 13).]

burel. See **borel.**

buttok. Chaucer often refers to this part of the body simply as a physical fact, as in the "Miller's Tale" (A 3803) when Nicholas is branded. But with typical Chaucerian precision, he wants to make even this minor physiological matter absolutely clear: the relative positions of "ers," "haunche-bon," and "buttock" are imprinted on the reader's mind's eye (as Nicholas is branded with the plowshare) with unforgettable clarity.

With the miller's daughter in the "Reeve's Tale" (A 3975), the significance of the buttocks has become something else—a mark of beauty, albeit rural and accompanied by a camus nose. She has "buttokes brode, and brestes rounde and hye." For the somewhat surprising idea that broad buttocks were considered marks of beauty, see **brestes.** And here we can repeat our allusion to that paragon of beauty, the Fair White, in the *Book of the Duchess* (956) who has, in addition to the perfection of her rounded breasts, "of good brede / Hyr hippes." Anthropologists tell us that most cultures have admired these signs in women, since they give promise of fecundity, but I doubt if Chaucer's readers are much interested in such matters.

The Parson has something to say about buttocks, as he does about almost everything ("Parson's Tale," I 423): to reveal these parts of the body by means of scanty clothing is Superbia (Pride): "and eek the buttokes of hem [them—i.e., their buttocks] faren as it were the hyndre part of a she-ape in the fulle of the moone." The odd thing about this passage is that he is attacking men's attire, not women's! And of course one is prompted to conjecture how the Parson knew the contours of a she-ape's buttocks during the full of the moon (when she is in heat?), or at any other time. He continues (I 427): "Of the hyndre part of hir buttokes, it is ful horrible for to see. For certes, in that partie of hir body ther as they purgen hir stynkyng ordure, that foule partie shewe they to the peple prowdly in despit of honestitee."

There is something a little nauseous about the Parson's concern with buttocks, but there is poetic justice in the "Summoner's Tale" (D 2142) when Thomas tells the greedy friar to "grope" beneath his "buttok" and he will find something hidden in "pryvetee." The resulting *carmen ani* is satisfying music! The cluster with **grope** and **pryvetee** deserves attention too: see the entries under these two headings. [*MED*, the rump; the citations are anatomical—many of them glosses of Latin terms (except for the Chaucer passages). One would think, though one would not *hope*, that Chaucer was the only Middle English poet to deal with the buttocks humorously.]

buxom. This meant simply amenable, gracious (literally

"bendable") —not "endowed in the bosom," as it does now. The psychology behind the semantic change is amusing to conjecture.

The most innocent of all the Chaucer uses is, doubtless, in that uplifting, and rather dull, "Clerk's Tale" (E 186), where Walter's people "buxomly" hear his agreement to wed. No Lily Langtrys, Mae Wests, or Raquel Welches here!

Elsewhere Chaucer is likely to use the word with various degrees of irony about wives who are, or who turn out to be, promiscuous. Januarie ("Merchant's Tale," E 1287) wants a "buxom . . . wyf." And later: "So buxom and so vertuous is she, / They moste nedes lyve in unitee" (E 1333). She of course betrays him with Damyan in the pear tree.

In the "Shipman's Tale" (B 1367), the wife turns the tables, demonstrating, of course, the older meaning of the word, too: she wants a husband "buxom unto his wyf." When her "buxom" husband leaves on a business trip to Flanders, he tells her (B 1432): "be to every wight buxom and meke." She is, indeed: to their mutual good friend Daun John, this buxom lady gives the delights of her bed: "In myrthe al nyght a bisy lyf they lede" (B 1508). [*MED,* often in the doublet phrase "buxom and bayne" (bain = willing, flexible); this dictionary gives the sense of "willing" only; *OED* shows, though not very clearly, the development of the sense of mammary endowment, but not until the end of the nineteenth century.]

byjaped. See **jape.**

C

Canacee. See **incest.**

Cancer. The sign of the zodiac that governs the genitals. It influences the "Merchant's Tale" (E 2224), the most genital of the *Tales.* But the real clincher comes when we discover that in the throbbing Book III of *Troilus and*

Criseyde (625) there is a rare conjunction of Saturn and Jupiter—in Cancer. Troilus and his beloved are forced into their lovers' bed by a rainstorm, of course; and this same portent (Saturn, Jupiter, Cancer) foretold Noah's Flood, which was sent (as everybody among Chaucer's readers knew) to punish man's lechery. Lechery and the flood should be kept in mind when one is reading the "Miller's Tale," too. [*MED*, "Canker," *n.* (2) ; but the citations do not show that the sign governed the genitals.]

cancre. This word crops up in the sermon of that ideal parish priest, the Parson, who spends so much of his time berating men for their scanty clothing (see **boce,** for instance). Men show off their privy members as if they were beset by St. Anthony's fire (erysipelas) or "cancre" ("Parson's Tale," I 426). The Parson is really concerned with an ostentatious erection (is there such a phrase as *in flagrante erectio?*), not with disease. It is not possible—or even desirable—to determine now the exact nature of the "cancre" involved, but it was probably not the chancre of syphilis. Fracostoro's poem "Syphilis" was not published until 1520, and he was alleged to have been the first victim of the disease. See **sceptre.** [*MED*, "canker," *n.* (1) ; many meanings in pathology, including cancer, but not chancre—except possibly (g) : a pathological growth on the sex organs of dogs, "a siknesse in here yerde."]

candle. Sanders contends that the sexual meanings are made clear by the context of the "Wife of Bath's Tale" (D 332 ff.) :

> *Ye shul have queynte right ynogh at eve.*
> *He is to greet a nygard that wolde werne [forbid]*
> *A man to lighte a candle at his lanterne;*
> *He shal have never the lasse light, pardee.*
> *Have thou ynogh, thee thar nat [it is not necessary to]*
> *pleyne thee.*

The only citation used by the *MED* to support the sexual meaning of the phrase is this one. And on the surface, without the arcane sex symbols which critics talk about, the lines mean quite simply that anyone who will not give

another man a light from his lantern is a "nygard" indeed, since the loan does not diminish the flame; so too
with the woman who is niggardly about her "queynte,"
at morn *or* eve. Neither flame nor "queyntenesse" is
diminished by this Christian act of sharing.

Robinson's notes on this figure, both here and in the
Book of the Duchess, are beyond comprehension; they
refer to the *Romaunt of the Rose* (7410), which has
nothing to do with lanterns or candles. Skeat gives the
right reference from *Le Roman de la Rose* (7447) —the
point (and almost the wording) of which is the same as
Chaucer's. The idea goes back to Ovid's *Ars Amatoria*
(III. 93), which Rolfe Humphries translates: "Who would
forbid us to take light from a light that is offered . . . ?"

But this is not the whole story: the Fair White, Blanche,
the Duke of Lancaster's Duchess, is involved in this complex lantern-candle imagery too. She also can "pleye"
(*q.v.*) ; and when she does, "she was lyk to torche bryght /
That every man may take of lyght / Ynogh, and hyt hath
never the less" (*Book of the Duchess,* 963). Nobody would
imagine that this idealized figure was giving away *her*
"queynte" indiscriminately. The truth would seem to be
that while the Wife of Bath uses the figure in a lewd
sense, the Man in Black employs it as a gracious metaphor.
[*MED,* "candel," 1b (b) lighten candel at (someone's)
lantern means (figuratively) to have intercourse with
(another man's) wife.]

caterwawed. The Wife of Bath is quoting herself, speaking to
one of her husbands—who in turn is addressing remarks to
the Wife herself. He says she wants to "goon a-caterwawed,"
go a-caterwauling. Sanders thinks that the Wife is developing the analogy between herself and a rutting cat.
The noise is the mournful, harsh cry of the cat in heat
("Wife of Bath's Prologue," D 354). [*MED,* "a-caterwawed," *adv.,* yowling as a cat in rut. The only citation is
from Chaucer.]

chaast. Although it is hard to agree with those who see
Thopas as a homosexual portrait of Richard II (see Introduction, p. 22, and **hair**), he is so "chaast" that it indeed
borders upon the insipid. We must remember, however,

that he *does* yearn for an elf-queen, so there is presumably hope.

What we have in the "Summoner's Tale" (D 1915) is probably a tired old pulpit joke and nothing bawdy at all, yet, knowing the Summoner, we must be on our guards:

> *Fro Paradys first, if I shal nat lye,*
> *Was man out* chaced *for his glotonye;*
> *And* chaast *was man in Paradys, certeyn.*

The words were homophones in Middle English. The pun was one of the few that Tatlock identified in 1916; in fact he found it (p. 232) "the most delightful and the most natural pun in Chaucer," which suggests that he had heard some very bad ones elsewhere. But he does go on to say that the play on words is one of the "professional glibnesses of the Sumner's friar." [*MED* does not give any indication that puns between the words were possible.]

chaffare. Literally "goods, wares," as women as sexual objects have always been. Chaucer's most amusing use of the word is in the "Shipman's Tale" (B 1475), when the rich merchant promises not only his gold to Daun John but his "chaffare" as well. As a matter of fact, the good monk gets both—money and the wife herself, a nice piece of the merchant's "chaffare."

Not unexpectedly, the Wife of Bath is a clever merchant of her wares; in her "Prologue" (D 521), she slyly points out that the cunning dealer will not display all his goods at once: "With daunger [reluctance] oute [i.e., put out] we al oure chaffare." [*MED,* 4 (a) *fig.* anything valuable or desirable, such as virtue, love, etc.; cites Chaucer, D 521. Gower, *Confessio Amantis* (V. 6114), makes clear the equation of woman's flesh and goods for sale; men when they find a

> *woman able,*
> *And therto place convenable,*
> *Withoute leve, er that thei fare,*
> *Thei take a parte of that chaffare.*]

chambre. Cecilia gives up both this world and "eek hire
     chambre" ("Second Nun's Tale," G 276); Robinson
     glosses this as "her marriage," and Skeat gives us the
     original: "ipsum mundum est cum thalamis exsecreta,"
     where "thalamis" is the wedding chamber. But the word
     would very likely recall to Chaucer's audience the "cham-
     bre of Venus" of the Wife of Bath—i.e., the vagina. See
     Venus. [*MED,* 10 (f) "chaumbre of Venus" = the vulva.
     Chaucer is the only citation, but there are figurative uses
     for other compartments in the human body.]

chose. French "thing"; Alison of Bath (D 447, 510) uses it as
     a euphemism for her vagina, but it is sad to learn that
     the term was neither her invention nor Chaucer's (see
     MED below). She always refers to it with the adjective
     "bele" preceding, and a lovely one it must have been, if
     we are to believe her "Prologue." [*MED,* only in French
     phrases "bele chose, prive chose," both referring to the
     private parts (of a woman). Chaucer's is the first citation,
     but there are three later ones in non-Chaucerian material
     —i.e., not obviously imitative of the poet. Braddy, "Ob-
     scenity" (p. 122), impishly translates the Wife's phrase as
     "play-pretty."]

clifte. The cleft between the buttocks in the "Summoner's
     Tale" (D 2145) where the greedy friar most grope.
         In the *Legend of Good Women* (740), Chaucer had a
     good chance for a bawdy double meaning, since there is a
     "clyfte" in the wall between Pyramus and Thisbe. Shake-
     speare did not miss this opportunity: see *A Midsummer
     Night's Dream,* V. i. 204.
         In Middle English, the word seems never to have been
     used for other interesting "cliftes," vaginal or mammary.
     [*MED,* 2 (a) the crotch (whether female or not is not
     clear); also cleft between buttocks. Robbins' Poem No.
     32 has the lilting line "Let me kyss yore karchos notch"
     (19), which is glossed as "carcass notch, cleft in the
     buttocks."]

clippe. In *Troilus and Criseyde* (III. 1344), the two lovers ask
     of each other "Clippe ich yow thus, or elles I it meete
     [dream]." It may mean nothing more than a fond em-

brace, but sexual intercourse certainly occurs in this book
of the great Chaucerian poem. [*MED, "clippen," v.* (1), 1
(a) to embrace; (b) as euphemism?: to have sexual intercourse with. There are no citations from Chaucer.]

coillons. It is established early in the "General Prologue" that
the Pardoner is a gelding or a mare. Hence it is particularly bitter—and indeed a very ugly passage—when the
Host says to the Pardoner, after that noble ecclesiast has
summoned him to come forth, as the foremost sinner
("Pardoner's Tale," C 952) :

> *I wolde I hadde thy coillons in myn hond*
> *In stide of relikes or of seintuarie.*
> *Lat kutte hem of, I wol thee helpe hem carie;*
> *They shul be shryned in an hogges toord!*

This is the only occurrence of the word in Chaucer. Perhaps it had better be made clear that it is the French
for "testicles." [In both *OED* and *MED*, the Chaucer
citation is the earliest.]

coitu. The Merchant (E 1811), who is telling the tale, mentions the book *De Coitu* with obvious relish, even though
he righteously condemns its author as that "cursed monk,
daun Constantyn." In the tale, old Januarie is using the
book for its aphrodisiac recipes, which he thinks he will
need for his marriage with young May. He is right.

The same book is part of the medical library mentioned
(by author only) in the "General Prologue" when Chaucer
is describing the Physician (A 433). The title means
"concerning coitus."

cok. This, one of the commonest modern cant words for the
penis, had not achieved this status in the fourteenth century—at least not in Chaucer. In the "General Prologue"
(A 823), the poet says that the Host was the "cok" for
them all, meaning simply that he woke them betimes. In
the "Miller's Tale" (A 3357), Absolon comes to Alisoun's
window "a litel after cokkes hadde ycrowe," where there
might be a hint of the obscene, though most unlikely. In
the companion piece, the "Reeve's Tale" (A 4233), the

two jolly clerks have a lively time "swyvynge" the miller's
wife and daughter "til that the thridde cok bigan to
synge." If ever there were a temptation to use a double
meaning, it would have been here, but there can only be
a "maybe." Cockcrows were medieval ways of telling time.
When pocket watches came into wider use (they were
known in Chaucer's day) perhaps things changed, and
"cock" began to rise in status. [*MED* has no sense in which
penis is intended. However, *OED*, "pillicock," 1. shows
that the meaning was developing: penis (*vulgar*), with one
citation that antedates Chaucer—"Mi pilkoc pisseth on mi
schone." Robbins' Poem No. 46, only slightly later than
Chaucer, is a bawdy verse in which "cock" is a euphemism
for the penis. It has a comb of "reed coral"; his "tayil is
of get (jet) & euery nyght he perchit hym / in my ladyis
chaumbyr."]

cokenay. An effeminate man, a milksop: the semantic evolu-
tion to cockney is a study in itself! In the "Reeve's Tale"
(A 4208), John the clerk, alone in bed, is thinking to himself that unless he acts quickly he will be considered a
"cokenay," since his colleague Aleyn has for some time
been happily "swyvynge" their host's daughter. Cambridge
men are not wont to be outdone, so he leaps from his
celibate couch and in a twinkling is in bed with the
miller's wife. She has a most unaccustomed good time:
"So myrie a fit ne hadde she nat ful yoore" (A 4230). See
fit. [MED, "cokenei," *n.* (1) probably a facetious blend of
"chiken ei" with "cok"; (2) possibly derisive use of
"cokenei" (1); or compare French *acoquiné,* degraded.
OED, 2. effeminate, milksop.]

cokewold. See **horn.** Jokes about cuckold's horns (the cuckold
is a husband whose wife is unfaithful and who is, by implication, incapable of satisfying her) were standard fare
in Europe for centuries, but during the last two seem
to have disappeared from Northern climes. I could not
guess why. They are certainly still present in Latin countries like France and Italy.

In Chaucer, the sneer begins among the Pilgrims themselves, when the drunken Miller addresses the Reeve
(A 3151):

> *Leve brother Osewold,*
> *Who hath no wyf, he is no cokewold.*
> *But I sey nat therfore that thou art oon;*
> *Ther been ful goode wyves many oon,*
> *And evere a thousand goode ayeyns oon badde.*
> *That knowestow wel thyself, but if thou madde.*
> *Why artow angry with my tale now?*
> *I have a wyf, pardee, as wel as thow.*

The wondrous thing about this passage is the tick-tock alternation between you are / you aren't a cuckold; you are / you aren't married. Careless readers, impatient for the fun of the "Miller's Tale" to begin, often hasten over this passage and miss a neat trick.

We can never know whether Osewold is a cuckold or not (though the critics have argued, futilely, about it for decades), but we are pretty sure that Mabely, the poor old woman bilked by the summoner ("Friar's Tale," D 1616) is wrongfully accused of having made her husbands cuckolds in the past. The summoner in the tale just wants to frighten her into giving him more bribes.

Chaucer uses the idea for dramatic irony and delightfully successful comic effect in the "Miller's Tale" (A 3226). John the carpenter "demed hymself been lik a cokewold" (that is, likely to become a cuckold) because his Alisoun is such a delectable little "piggesnye." Of course, he is right.

The same sort of thing happens in the *fabliau* that Chaucer uses for the "Merchant's Tale" (E 1306). Old Januarie is afraid—and his friends tell him about such matters at interminable length—"ful lightly maystow been a cokewold." We do not discover whether it is better to be made a cuckold by your wife and her lover having intercourse in a pear tree or not; but this is what happens, and Januarie's friends' forebodings are fulfilled.

That supremely gifted con man the Pardoner uses cuckoldry for his purposes (though he himself will never be one, of course). In his sermons, he encourages those among his parishioners who have not done sin to come forward and make offerings to his relics ("Pardoner's

Tale," C 382) : "any womman, be she yong or old, /
That hath ymaad hir housbonde cokewold" is forbidden,
of course. All parishioners come forward, naturally. [*MED,*
"cokewold"; cf. late OF *cucuault,* derived from OF *cocu,*
cuckoo; first citation *ca.* 1250. The name may derive from
the cuckoo's habit of laying its eggs in other birds' nests.
I have been unable to find an answer to one of my student's questions about the possible relationship between
"horny" and the cuckold's horns. There would appear to
be no logical one.]

cokkow. In the "Knight's Tale" (A 1810), the cuckoo (along
with the hare) represents a type of stupidity. In the
"Manciple's Tale" (H 243), the (then) white crow, having
observed Phebus' wife in adultery, sings out to his master,
on his return, "Cokkow! cokkow! cokkow!" The reference
here is to the **cokewold,** of course. [*MED,* "cokkou,"
1 (b) in proverbial expressions: the bird is so stupid
(or vain) that it can only sing of itself, that is, sing
its own name.].

coler. The carpenter's delectable wife Alisoun ("Miller's Tale,"
A 3265) has a large brooch upon her "lowe coler" (col-
lar), possibly (in her case *probably*) to call attention to
her decolletage.

color. See **blew.**

coltes tooth. The Reeve wants to impress the Pilgrims, especially the Miller, of course, with his youthfulness; hence
he claims ("Reeve's Tale," A 3888) : "And yet ik have
alwey a coltes tooth." Chaucer makes no use of this fact
in his tale, but in the "Merchant's Tale" (E 1847), the
proverbial expression has a function: Januarie, after an
extremely energetic wedding night, tries to act youthful:
"he was al coltissh." The context makes it clear that this
refers to his amorous behavior (see **ragerye),** but his
coltishness does not impress his young wife May. See **bene.**

Chaucer is perhaps also making narrative use of the
proverb in the "Wife of Bath's Prologue" (D 602), too,
but one cannot be sure. Alison likes her men young and
fresh abed: "But yet I hadde alwey a coltes tooth," so the
expression can serve either sex. However, if the Wife is
looking for her sixth husband on the pilgrimage (as she

says she is) who might it be? She so shamelessly reveals her desire to dominate her men, one wonders if among the Pilgrims there is one stupid enough to be attracted by her "coltes tooth" and her experience, but to ignore her terrifying determination to rule the household. As many critics have guessed, the most likely candidate (fresh, stupid—if his tale is an indication) is probably the Squire. [*MED*, "colt," 3 "haven a coltes toth," to have youthful desires, be lascivious. The only citations are the three from Chaucer. *OED*, 8. b. shows that the expression endured throughout the nineteenth century.]

come. Hinton finds that in *Troilus and Criseyde* (III. 196) the sense of "have an orgasm" is present. Pandarus speaks to the lovers, telling them to come to his house, "For I ful well shal shape youre comynge." The meaning is possible, but not at all probable, in view of the paucity of passages elsewhere in Chaucer where the orgasm is even hinted. For instance, in the "General Prologue" (A 547), Chaucer describes the brawny Miller: "that proved wel, for over al ther he cam, / At wrastlynge he wolde have alwey the ram." Or consider this passage, where the opportunity was certainly present: in her "Prologue," the Wife of Bath (D 152) says: "myn housbonde shal it have bothe eve and morwe, / Whan that hym list come forth and paye his dette." "Come forth" probably has neither the meaning of orgasm nor of extending the erotic senses.]

compaignable. Pertelote, in the "Nun's Priest's Tale" (B 4062), has many of the qualities of the ideal heroine of romance, including the fact that she is "compaignable"; of course when we see her having intercourse twenty times with her Chauntcleer, the bawdy meaning of the word is obvious.

One may object that there is no proof that this innocent word had a bawdy meaning (true!), but when we encounter it again in the "Shipman's Tale" (B 1194) where the wife of the rich merchant is both "revelous" (see **revel**) and "compaignable," we can be fairly sure. This is a good example of a passage in which a cluster of words supports one's suspicions about double entendre. [*MED* gives no sexual senses; though B 4062 is cited, B 1194 is not.]

concepcioun. In his section on Ira (Wrath), the Parson (I 575) attacks a variety of homicides, including abortion: "whan man destourbeth concepcioun of a child, and maketh a womman outher bareyne by drynkynge venenouse herbes . . . or elles putteth certeine material thynges in hire secree places to slee the child . . . ," etc. "Homycide is eek if a man approcheth to a womman by desire of lecherie, thurgh which the child is perissed," a reference to intercourse during pregnancy. See **place.** [*MED,* 1 (c) pregnancy; Chaucer is cited.]

conclusioun. In the "Miller's Tale" (A 3402), Alisoun and Nicholas agree that they will make love; they "acorded been to this conclusioun," which might simply mean that they reached an agreement (see **acorded**), but possibly also something more binding—coitus. Partridge (p. 92, *s.v.* "conjunct") glosses it "joined amorously; physically entwined." He is quoting Shakespeare, but one might conjecture that a couple of centuries did not make all that much difference in the concept. [*MED,* no bawdy meanings. *OED,* 8. provides the definition "an experiment," in the scientific sense, but the earliest citation is 1430 and the meaning did not really come into common parlance until the seventeenth century. However, it would be very fitting for the clerk Nicholas, so adept at his scientific work with the "augrym stones" and the like, to be interested in all kinds of "conclusiouns."]

concubyn. Balthasar's "concubynes" ("Monk's Tale," B 3389) are mentioned casually enough: Chaucer's was, we must remember, a pre-Reformation England in which the narrow strictures of puritanical ideas had not gained much force.

Even among the clergy, concubinage was winked at, it would seem. In the "General Prologue" (A 650), the Summoner is described as a generous type: for a quart of wine, he will let "a good felawe" have his "concubyn" a twelve-month. Robinson opines in his note that this "good felawe" was probably a parish priest. But does the line mean that the Summoner will let the priest have *a* wench in his house, or that he will "rent" him his *own* kept woman for a quart of wine a year? The former is probably right, but one could almost believe the latter of the contemptible Summoner—except that the price would probably have been higher. [*MED,* concubine or paramour, sanctioned or tolerated in custom or law . . . in Western Europe during the Middle Ages. The Chaucer passage is cited.]

copulacioun. Chaucer does not use the word. [*MED,* "copulate, -cioun," gives only senses of joining things together—abstract things mostly.]

coppe. Could it mean vagina in Chaucer? I am afraid that the evidence is disappointing. Consider the Prioress, "General Prologue" (A 134), in whose "coppe" there was to be seen no farthing's worth of grease. Surely the meaning is cleanly, well mannered, and literal.

In the "Franklin's Tale" (F 942), there occurs a perplexing line: Aurelius "withouten coppe he drank al his penaunce." Skeat explains "he drank his penance in full measure, not by small quantities at a time." This doesn't make much sense, but then neither does Baugh's "to be cheated out of one's expectation; to go without satisfaction." In this passage, since he does not gain the love of Dorigen, it might well mean the vagina. But all one can say is "might."

Troilus and Criseyde (III. 724) has an even more perplexing (and possibly bawdy) passage: Troilus asks Mars to stand him in good stead, "thow with thi blody cope." What can be suggested here? (1) Cope (= cape?) (2) Cup? Neither sense seems to help. Troilus does call upon unlikely deities to help him in his lovemaking, Mars and Diana, but what this has to do with a cup-cape I cannot guess. [*MED* provides no help.]

corage. To begin with a perfectly innocent (though archaic) meaning: in the "Manciple's Tale" (H 164), it means simply intention: "do al thyn entente and thy corage" to tame a bird.

The Legend of Good Women (1451) tells us of Jason on the way to look for the Golden Fleece: he is "lusty of corage." This is the innocent modern sense (= valor),

even though it is true that later on Jason does get involved sexually.

Old Janicula, Griselde's father in the "Clerk's Tale" (E
907) —and probably the most underdeveloped figure in
literature—gives us yet another nuance of the meanings
of "corage": when the great lord "fulfild hadde his corage"
with his daughter Griselde, he will send her back home
again. The morganatic marriage cannot possibly last. The
sense is simply "lust," and the *MED* cites this passage to
illustrate the meaning of sexual desire.

Before his marriage, Januarie worries whether May can
endure his "corage, it is so sharp and keene," "Merchant's
Tale" (E 1759) . Obviously this means his lust, but perhaps
also much more literally his penis, of which he is inordi-
nately (and undeservedly) proud, some think. His confidence seems to have faltered on the wedding night, however, since he must resort to aphrodisiacs (see *coitu*) ,
"t'encreessen his corage" (E 1808) .

With Harry Bailly, there is no question of equivocation, at least not in the "Nun's Priest's Tale" (B 4642) :
"if thou have corage as thou hast myght, / Thee were
nede of hennes, as I wene, / Ya, moo than seven tymes
seventene," referring to the seven hens that Chauntecleer
had in the "Tale." The Host admires the Priest's virility
(see **breech**) ; there can be no question here that "corage"
means sexual capability.

One of the most delightful anticlimaxes in the "Tale of
Sir Thopas" (B 1970) involves this word. And it may be
good evidence that the knight is effeminate, too. "So fiers
was his corage," says Chaucer, "that doun he leyde him
in that plas." His sexual drive is so intense that he col-
lapses and goes to sleep. In fairness, it must be recalled
that just after this, Thopas *does* mention love-illness and
goes off to seek his elf-queen. Anyway, whether "corage"
means valor or sexual prowess, the lines are very comical:
if *both* meanings are present, the humor increases geometrically. Note, too, where Thopas lies down. See
place. [*MED*, 2 (b) referring to sexual desire, lust; some
of the citations may refer to erections, but the evidence
is not clear.]

cosynage. Though not strictly bawdy, there may be a pun here between "relationship" and "cozenage" (cheating) . In the "Shipman's Tale" (B 1226), the monk claims the merchant for "cosynage," i.e., he claims that they are related, which also gives him a venue to the merchant's house and the merchant's wife's bedchamber. He also "cozens" him out of his wife's favors and out of his money, a hundred francs (1339, 1599) . The way these debts are repaid should be checked at **dette.** [*MED,* "cosin (e) ," 3, ? an intimate, a mistress; "cosinage" refers simply to a relationship; "cosin," *n.* fraud, trickery; there is no entry for the corresponding verb.]

crekes. In the "Reeve's Tale" (A 4051) the miller thinks he will outwit the "uppity" clerks, who are too educated anyway. "The moore queynte crekes that they make, / The moore wol I stele whan I take." There may be some irony here; if so, the speaker is sublimely unconscious of it. The humor emerges, however, only if "crekes" can be construed as "cracks," but it is likely that it means simply "tricks," as Robinson says. However, cracks or clefts in "queyntes" would not be un-Chaucerian. [*MED,* "crak," *n.* (2) , 2 a cleft, opening; the first citation is *ca.* 1450, and there is no evidence that during the Middle English period the word was ever spelled with an *-e-*.]

crowne. Daun John shaves his tonsure with special care before his liaison with the toothsome merchant's wife—ironic indeed, since the tonsure was of course the symbol of his vows, one of which was chastity. See the "Shipman's Tale" (B 1499) . See also **professioun.** [*MED,* "coroune," 11 tonsure of the cleric. In the widespread tale of "Dame Sirith" (in Bennett, p. 92), the wooer was a "modi clarc with croune" whom Dame Sirith's daughter spurned. "Modi" = spirited.]

Cytherea. See **Venus.**

ↄ

dalliaunce. In her husband's absence, the Wife of Bath (D
565) and her clerk have "daliance"—as Baugh says, anything from conversation to amorous play. Like so many of
these "bawdy" words in Chaucer, we have to judge the
meaning from the context.

To begin with a presumably innocent one: the Host says
about Chaucer—Chaucer the Pilgrim, who is about to tell
a tale: "unto no wight dooth he daliaunce," which must
mean, simply, that he carries on no conversations with
his fellow pilgrims ("Thopas" B 1894). This is very much
like the passage in the "Canon's Yeoman's Tale" (G 592)
where we are told that the Canon wants to ride with the
Pilgrims, "for his desport; he loveth daliaunce." In view of
the unsavory reputation that the Canon is revealed to have,
we cannot be too sure about the innocence of this passage,
however.

And what do we make of those two scoundrels, the summoner and his demonic friend the yeoman? In the "Friar's
Tale" (D 1406), "In daliance they ryden forth and pleye,"
it is probably innocent (though nothing involving the
yeoman can be completely innocent). The juxtaposition
of "pleye" (q.v.) and "daliaunce" gives one an uneasy
feeling—and perhaps this is the precise effect that Chaucer
wanted.

The Physician sounds like a latter-day fundamentalist
(C 66): in what can be described, I think, as a shocked
tone, he speaks of feasts, revels, and dances, "that been
occasions of daliaunces." Whatever "daliaunce" conveyed
explicitly to the good doctor's mind, it was not salubrious;
it might even have been illicit sexual play.

In his own lyrical exercise (I think it is no more than
that) "To Rosemounde," the refrain (8, 16, 24) is
"Thogh ye to me ne do no daliaunce." The meaning

could be pure—something like "notice" or "give companionship"—but this is a sophisticated courtly poem, much influenced by the French.

Baum deals succinctly with "dalliaunce," pointing out that in the "General Prologue" (A 211) the word applied to the Friar has a distinctly unsavory double meaning. With Alison of Bath, he is more cautious, and properly so: in D 565, the reference is to amorous play; in D 260 it is ambiguous. In the latter, it is contrasted with **daunce.** [*MED,* 3 amorous talk or to-do (*sic*), flirting, coquetry; sexual union. The only citation from Chaucer is C 66.]

dart. The Wife of Bath (D 75) says the dart is set up for "virginitee." It means a prize, as Robinson's note explains at length. It might have suggested the penis erectus, however, and I would wager that for some of Chaucer's listeners it did. See **love.** [*MED,* 2 (b) offer a dart as a prize. The Wife's is the only citation.]

daunce. Robertson, *Preface* (p. 131), is quite sure about the meaning of this very common word (and act) in medieval literature: "The Old Dance is the dance of fornication, spiritual or physical, and this is the sense in which it appears in *Le Roman de la Rose.* . . ." Braddy, "Obscenity" (p. 130), agrees: the word stands for the "sex rite." This is the sense in the "General Prologue" (A 476): "For she [the Wife] koude of that art the olde daunce." As everybody knows, this (and much of the Wife's character generally) derives from the *Roman,* where it also refers to sexual intercourse. There is, moreover, nothing equivocal about what is happening in *Troilus and Criseyde* (IV. 1431): the lovers are lamenting her imminent departure, when suddenly they find themselves in bed. The fury of Troilus' "penaunce was queynt" [quenched]. But before they know it, they have begun "for joie th'amorouse daunce." The collocation of "queynt," no matter what the lexical sense, and "daunce"ing in bed can hardly be accidental. Finally, in the "Physician's Tale" (C 79), we hear of mistresses who have in their care young ladies, yet "knowen wel ynough the olde daunce"; and in *Troilus and Criseyde* (III. 695), the lovers are in bed for the

FIG. 2. BELOW *ivory mirror-case (15th c. ?) representing a dance (note the "ryng," and cf. Fig. 14)*; ABOVE *Venus (cf. frontispiece) with her dart (and her dove?). Victoria and Albert Museum, London.*

first time: the act is about to begin, and nearby is Pandarus, who has arranged the entire affair: "Pandarus, that wel koude ech a deel / The olde daunce, and every point therinne." See also **daliaunce,** which occurs nearby.

So Professor Robertson is right. There are, however, more suggestions to Terpsichore than even he may have guessed. Arveragus of the "Franklin's Tale" (F 1098) returns after two years' absence to his wife Dorigen, and "daunceth, justeth, maketh hire good cheere." This sort of welcome-home sport could be perfectly innocent, but in view of the meaning of **juste** the amorous hint is distinctly present. A little later in the same tale, the identical sort of "confluence" occurs again. The Magician shows a vision of "his lady on a daunce, / On which hymself he daunced" (1200), which again would be purity itself if it were not for the proximity of "justyng" (1198) and "plesaunce" (1199).

Aeneas and Dido (*Legend of Good Women,* 1269) celebrate at "festes and at daunces"—discreet merriment indeed, though "justen" (1274) is nearby, and we all know what happened to Aeneas and Dido in the cave during the rainstorm.

There are other kinds of "guilt by association" for "daunce." In the (translated, but nonetheless relevant) *Romaunt of the Rose* (3227), Reason cautions Lover about Idleness: "Whanne thou yedest in the daunce / With hir, and haddest aqueyntaunce. / Her aqueyntaunce is perilous, / First softe, and aftir noious." See **acqueyntaunce.** Also in the *Romaunt* (2322), the Lover is encouraged to "daunce and play" and "if he can wel foote and daunce" it will advance him in his lady's favors. This is perhaps like the situation between Theseus and Ariadne (*Legend of Good Women,* 2157): "there feste they, there daunce they and synge; / And in his armes hath this Adryane" [*sic,* always so in Chaucer]. In an utterly different (quite low) vein, we may have an associative significance involving "daunce" in the incomplete "Cook's Tale" (A 4370, and again in 4380). The "prentys" here is called Perkyn Revelour (see **Newgate**), and "daunen he koude." The equation of dancing and coition is

Fors beissiez karole aler
Et qi amonst noblement baler
Et faire mainte belle tresche
Et mainte biau tour sur lerbe fresche
A beissiez vous fleuteurs
Et menestriers z jugleeurs
Li chantoit li vns fortiantes
I autres notes loeiantes
Pour ce quon fait en lorreine
Lus belles notes que nul regne
Ssez por tabletirresses

Fig. 3. *Dancers and a bagpiper (cf. Fig. 1): an illustration for* Le Roman de la Rose, *of which lines 743 ff. are reproduced on this MS leaf. Bodleian Library, Oxford, MS e Mus. 65 (14th c.), fol. 3ᵛ.*

not clear, but it seems highly likely that this prentice would soon (had the tale continued) have been in bed with the wife that "swyved" for her sustenance (4422) so the entire matter is more than coincidence will allow.

In his note to the "Wife of Bath's Prologue" (D 648), Robinson quotes contemporaneous sources to show that dancing and caroling (remember that it was originally dancing too) were considered evil. But there is no note for Alison's "how koude I daunce to an harpe smale" (D 457) when she was young. Maybe this is just a little sentimental nostalgia, of which Alison has more than her share, but maybe too it is a play on "daunce" and "harpe," where the latter may be equated with the *membrum virile*. It is wholly undemonstrable, but it is an idea that is not discordant with the Wife's temper.

The clerk Absolon is good at everything, including dancing, probably in both these senses. Recall the "Miller's Tale" (A 3328) where he is described thus: "In twenty manere koude he trippe and daunce / After the scole of Oxenforde tho, / And with his legges casten to and fro." If it were anyone but Absolon, one would have to be suspicious, but with him . . . ! Precisely how he cast about with his legs is interesting to speculate upon.

It is time to return to the dance as a stately and noble rite, after Absolon has been casting his legs about. Nothing could surpass *Troilus and Criseyde* (I. 517) where Troilus refers to the "daunce" of those whom Love wants to advance, however feebly—not the act of love, but the "assemblage" of lovers, which Troilus has now joined. This adds peculiar grace to Criseyde's disingenuous-naïve question to her uncle (II. 1106) : he has brought Troilus' letter; she pretends that it is Pandarus who is in love. "How ferforth be ye put in loves daunce?" she asks. [*MED, n.,* 4. a. (a) in phrases like "loves daunce, the olde daunce" there are slightly erotic hints. Naturally the equation of dancing and coition is not Chaucer's exclusive property: Robbins' Poem No. 163 has (9) : "Thys am I brought in-to louers dawnce." See Fleming on the Carol of Deduit (Dance of Mirth) and his Figs. 16, 19,

20, and 21, together with my Figures 2 and 3. Legman
(p. 421) points out that "dancing can . . . symbolize—or
even replace—sexual intercourse."]

dede. The deed of love, copulation. This idea is central in the
Wife of Bath's (D 70) personal theological system: if God
had wanted to command all men (and women!) to remain virgins, he would have "dampned weddyng with the
dede." [*MED*, 2 (c) the commission (of a sin); there is
nothing so direct as is the Wife's quotation.]

deer. In the "Friar's Tale" (D 1370), the devil compares the
summoner with a hunter's dog that "kan an hurt deer
from an hool yknowe": the demon yeoman never speaks
idly, and one suspects something grimy here, but I am
not sure what it is, except that the deer-dear pun is involved. See **hol.**

Pandarus says (II. 1535) he will bring Criseyde to
Troilus: I "shal wel the deer unto thi bowe dryve." It is
a hunting figure, but the pun is certainly possible.

As the dictionaries demonstrate, deer-dear puns were
possible in Middle English, yet Chaucer makes little use
of them. Perhaps we should be thankful: Shakespeare and
his contemporaries made up for any loss. [*MED*, *OED*,
both show that the words were homophones and homographs in Chaucer's time.]

dele. This word can, and often does, mean "to have sexual
intercourse." Dido (*Legend of Good Women*, 1158)
demonstrates how it is done: she is overcome with desire
"with Eneas, hire newe gest, to dele," and at the first
opportunity, she does. In *Troilus and Criseyde* (III.
322), Pandarus is giving Troilus some of his (often interminable) advice: "wommen dreden with us men to
dele," where the meaning is ambiguous, but taking into
account the speaker and the situation, we can be quite
certain that the off-color meaning is present. Other passages show that the primary meaning here is simply
"mix" or "argue."

The most artful use of the word is in the same work (V.
1595) where Chaucer quotes one of the false heroine's
letters. (In a sense, this is not only the first English novel,
but the first English epistolary novel as well.) Poor

Criseyde cannot avoid fulsomeness in her style. She addresses the abandoned Troilus as "Cupides sone, ensample of goodlyheede." She complains, then, of her distress: "Syn ye with me, nor I with yow, may dele." To be sure, since she is in the Greek camp—and in the arms of Diomede—she cannot "dele" with her Troilus, but she leaves a loophole, unconsciously, surely. She cannot "dele" with her beloved, but this does not mean that she cannot "dele" with others. Is this too cynical? Surely it is *not* too cynical for Fals-Semblant who says (*Romaunt of the Rose*, 6967): "I dele with no wight, but he / Have gold and tresour gret plente; / Her [their] acqueyntaunce wel love I. . . ." The juxtaposition of **acqueyntaunce** makes the interpretation unmistakable, I believe. See also **bouger**. [*MED*, "delen," 6 (b) to have sexual intercourse with, cites the Dido passage and many other contemporary examples. All three texts of *Piers Plowman* use the word in condemning beggars for promiscuity, among other evils (e.g., A-Text, VIII. 73): "They libben not in loue ne no lawe holden; / Thei weddeth no wommon that thei with deleth; / Bote as wilde beestes, with wo worcheth togedere, / And bringeth forth barnes (children) that bastardes beon holden."]

delica[a]t. See **delicacye**.

delicacye, -sye. With this word we can move neatly down the scale of creation from a god to a lowly popinjay. In the lyric "The Former Age" (57), Jupiter, because of all his amours, is called "fader of delicacye." An emperor is next: in the "Monk's Tale" (B 3669), we are told that Nero burned Rome "for his delicasie"—glossed as "pleasure," but suggestive of voluptuousness and taboo. When Chaucer describes him in the same tale (B 3661), indeed, he says there never was a "moore delicaat" emperor than he.

Januarie is not simply a lewd old man, but a knight of Pavia ("Merchant's Tale," E 1646); in contemplating his belated marriage, he thinks that he will lead a life "so delicat" that he will have his heaven on earth here. This could mean merely "delightful," but not with any plausibility, in view of the speaker. The "popynjay" in the *Parliament of Fowls* (359) is said to be "ful of delicasye,"

which Baugh glosses as "voluptuousness." He also says
that in the *Natural History*, Pliny describes the parrot as
"in vino praecipue lasciva" (particularly lecherous when
drunk). No wonder Chaucer and everybody since and
before have been attracted to Pliny: delightfully useless
knowledge even for lovebird fanciers, who now know
they should keep the spirits out of the birdseed. [*MED*,
"delicacie," 2 (a) wantonness.]

delyt. When at last Troilus and Criseyde are in bed (III. 1310),
Chaucer claims that their "delit" is simply beyond his
powers: he cannot describe it. Other passages make it clear
that we are in the presence here of what may well *be*
an indescribable physical sensation. Later in the same
poem (IV. 1678), Criseyde speaks, promising to be true
to Troilus, among other reasons because "youre resoun
bridlede youre delit" (which Baugh glosses as "sensual
desire"). In the *House of Fame* (309), Dido complains
that some men want only "delyt." Troilus, unlike Aeneas,
was, in other words, a gentleman. Criseyde appreciates
him—but not enough to remain faithful.

In the *Legend of Good Women* (1587), the false Jason
wants nothing but "to don with gentil women his delyt, /
This is his lust and his felicite." Contrast Troilus with
both Aeneas and Jason! But there is worse to come:
men always have a "likerous" appetite ("Manciple's
Tale," H 190) "on lower thyng to parfourne hire delit /
Than on hire wyves." Even *in* marriage, this sort of
bestiality cannot be avoided. The Parson tells us in his
sermon on the Seven Deadly Sins (I 903) that one of the
varieties of "avowtrie" (adultery) is that between husband
and wife, when they come together only for "flesshly
delit."

In the "Merchant's Tale" (E 1249), when Chaucer has
made one of his mistakes in ascribing tale to teller (it is
clearly supposed to be an ecclesiastic here), the speaker
sneers at the "seculeer," and most particularly at the hero
of his tale, who "folwed ay his bodily delyt / On women."
This is intercourse, of course.

And yet in the *Parliament of Fowls* (224), Delyt is one

of the allegorical figures in Chaucer's dream, in the Garden of Love. He commits no *faux pas;* but actually he does nothing at all—except stand with Gentilesse. [*MED,* "delit (e) ," *n.,* (1) , 1 (a) "fleshli delit, foul delit" = sexual gratification, but only in these phrases, apparently.]

descende. Januarie tells his young bride that he must "trespace to yow," meaning do harm to her (i.e., take her maidenhead violently) "er tyme come that I wil doun descende" ("Merchant's Tale," E 1830) . In view of his years and his need for aphrodisiacs, it would be probable that the meaning here is "to lose an erection." [*MED* provides no erotic senses.]

desport. Of course this word means pleasure in a variety of senses, but when, in the "Summoner's Tale" (D 1830) , Thomas' wife complains that when she throws her arm or leg over her husband, he grunts, but she gets no other "desport" of him—we know what kind of pleasure Chaucer had in mind.

Other occurrences are probably innocent. When the Canon's Yeoman (G 592) , reports that his master wants to ride with the Pilgrims "for his desport; he loveth daliaunce," there is probably no dark meaning. But see **daliaunce.**

It is hard to tell about the "Cook's Tale" (A 4420) , since it is not finished. The fact that the prentice "lovede dys, and revel, and disport" is probably nothing more than youthful ebullience. The *MED* quotes it, as a matter of fact, to support the general sense of fun, recreation. [*MED,* "disport," 1 (b) the game of love, flirtation.]

dette. Modern translators of the New Testament have deprived married couples of a useful metaphor. St. Jerome translated Paul's first epistle to the Corinthians, 7:3, as "Uxori uir debitum reddat: similiter autem et uxor uiro," which means that a man should pay his wife her "debt" and vice versa: intercourse.

The good Parson (whose description in the "General Prologue" is so much more attractive than his "tale"—a sermon) explains that couples should "yelden everich of hem to oother the dette of hire bodies; for neither of hem

hath power of his owene body" (I 939). The King James
Version has "due benevolence" here—no metaphors possible.

As Chaucer and his audience saw it (and so did St.
Jerome) the thing worked both ways, like any equitable
business deal. In the "Merchant's Tale" (E 1452), there
are pious mouthings about man and wife helping each
other like brother and sister, but there is a kicker: they
should "yelde hir dette whan that it is due." When the
knight is finally married, he takes his wife into the
garden "whan he wolde paye his wyf hir dette" (E 2048).

The cleverest use of this metaphor (though it is indirect) is the familiar conclusion to the "Shipman's Tale"
(B 1605, 1614). As a matter of fact, the word "dette" is
not mentioned, but it is at the center of the point of the
story. The merchant's wife will pay him her debt in bed
(she has already had the hundred francs from the monk,
of course, but she cannot admit this to her husband).
Thus she will pay back the legal debt and also the Scriptural "dette" that wives owe husbands. See **tayl** for the
rest of the joke and also "paiementz," *s.v.* **Venus.**

The shrewdest of all these marital brokers is of course
the Wife of Bath, who uses the "dette" figure with assurance and great charm (D 130 and 153). [*MED,* 4 (b)
has many citations referring to the marriage debt, mostly
from pious works; *OED,* 1. b. glosses it as a thing im-
material that someone owes another.]

Diana. Her rites, performed by Emelye, were thought by
Bronson to be obscene, and therefore the pious Knight
scanted them in his "Tale" (A 2284). See **queynt,** too,
which might be involved, though I do not think Professor Bronson was referring to this possibility.

die. As every reader of Shakespeare and Donne knows, the
Renaissance attached a secondary meaning to this awful
word: to have an orgasm. Did the fourteenth century as
well? The evidence is far from clear, but I shall present it
and let readers decide for themselves.

The *MED,* 2 (a) *fig.,* finds a suggestive meaning (but
equivocal) in the "Merchant's Tale" (E 1876) where
Damyan "so brenneth that he dyeth for desyr." If any-

body is going to have an involuntary orgasm among the characters in the *Canterbury Tales,* Damyan is my candidate. See also **sceptre.**

The trouble is that the metaphor is confused by the medieval convention about lovers "dying" (expiring) for their ladies' loves. For instance, when Troilus sees his beloved (I. 306), "sodeynly hym thoughte he felte dyen"; is this a seminal emission or just adrenalin? But back with the earthy May and Damyan in the "Merchant's Tale" (E 2332) : she must have pears to eat (she pretends to be—or is—pregnant) "or I moot dye." Immediately following this line, of course, she climbs the pear tree, does not pick or eat pears, but is boisterously "swyved" by Damyan. Later on, old Januarie, the cuckolded husband, curses the pair: he hopes they will "on shames deth to dyen" (2377) —literally, die shameful deaths, but also bitterly ironic, since we can anticipate that the two young adulterers will find many more occasions to "die" together after the conclusion of the story.

Or to revert to the romantic: Troilus, speaking to Criseyde (III. 112), threatens to take his own life: "Now recche I nevere how soone that I deye." He means that like a good Courtly Lover he will die without her love, but does he also want to imply that he would like to reach a climax with her? Why not? Criseyde swears that she is true to Troilus (III. 1049) : "if that I be giltif, do me deye."

At last (IV. 280), when Criseyde has to leave Troy, Troilus laments that he does "evere dye and nevere fulli sterve": in Middle English, of course, "sterve" was an undifferentiated word (like German *sterben*) meaning to expire from any cause. The idea that the orgasm was a little "dying" is involved in this pathetic line, perhaps, since of course the noble Troilus does indeed "sterve" before the poem ends. This last passage illustrates the fact that "serve" (to have intercourse) and "sterve" (to die, literally—also figuratively?) are linked together in Chaucer's mind. I do not think it is merely the demands of the rhymes in the rhyme royal stanza. See *Troilus and Criseyde,* IV. 319–320, 444–448, 517–525.

Braddy, "Obscenity" (p. 130), believes that Chaucer's words in *Troilus and Criseyde* (III. 1577): "What! God foryaf his deth" mean that "God forgave Pandarus's death; that is, his coition with Criseyde." (Compare **incest**.) "Die," he says unequivocally (p. 129), is used in the "Knight's Tale" (A 2243) "in the Shakespearean sense of 'to have sexual intercourse.' "

In a lighter (but not necessarily clearer) vein: the hende Nicholas ("Miller's Tale," A 3280) cries out to Alisoun: "Lemman, love me al atones, / Or I wol dyen." Perhaps another involuntary orgasm? Such an interpretation is supported by 3296, 3606, and 3612 from the same tale.

Chaucer's rather disappointing lyrics also use this metaphor—if it is one. "A Complaint to His Lady" (121) has "Wel lever is me liken yow and deye." (See **liken,** which I hope will not disturb too many readers.) Or in the "Complaynt D'Amours" [doubtful authorship] (41): "Yet alwey two thinges doon me dye, / That is to seyn, hir beautee and myn ye." Finally, how about this one, with a cluster of sexual innuendos (*ibid.*, 49): "It is hir wone plesaunce for to take, / To seen her servaunts dyen for hir sake!" See **plesaunce, serve.** [*MED* has no erotic meanings. See Partridge, pp. 101 *et passim,* and Legman, p. 189.]

dighte. This Middle English word for intercourse seems to have had a less salacious, less violent connotation than did "swyve." They are perhaps analogous to "screw" (dighte) and "fuck" (swyve). Braddy, "Obscenity" (p. 122), states: "Most editors gloss 'dighte' in its amorous meaning as 'lie with,' but obviously 'dicked,' a more homely word in which *gh* has evolved into *ck,* speaks more directly." Baum discusses the use of "dighte" by the Wife of Bath in D 398 (though he does not mention the recurrence of the word in D 767). In both passages, the Wife is speaking with distaste of a man having intercourse with a woman—that is, with the woman as an object, not a participant.

An amusing contrast is found in the "Manciple's Tale" (H 312). It is good advice, we are told, not to tell a friend "how that another man hath dight his wyf," for he will hate you forever. The connotations of "dight" make this even funnier than it might otherwise appear.

There are a couple of ambiguous occurrences: Troilus (III. 1773) was "the first in armes dyght": (1) the first dressed in armor; (2) the first in his lady's arms for the purpose of intercourse (first in quality, not necessarily chronologically—and in Criseyde's case, surely not). In the *Legend of Good Women* (1000), the case for bawdry is even slighter, but still possible: Venus tells Aeneas that to Carthage "he sholde hym dighte." Here the most common meaning of the word comes into play: to make one's way. But since he goes to Carthage to "dighte" Dido (among other things) the double meaning may be hinted at.

Harry Bailly tells us a good deal about his wife Goodelief (with her ironically gentle name). She is a fierce one! Unless he wants to stay home and fight, says he, "out at dore anon I moot me dighte" ("Monk's Tale," B 3104). This is glossed "betake me" and properly; but it could also mean that if he wants to gratify his sexual urges he must do it away from home and his shrewish wife. One must confess that this interpretation may be overingenious —especially when one recalls a similar passage that occurs only a few lines later ("Monk's Tale," B 3719) [for 3720, Robinson mistakenly prints 3270]: when the people rebel against Nero, he "out of his dores anon he hath hym dight / Allone." There is no possibility of sexual innuendo, and we even have the same conjunction of "dore" and "dighte." [*MED,* "dighten," 7 (b) to have sexual intercourse with a woman. There is only one non-Chaucerian citation. *OED,* "dight," 4. b. gives as the first citation that from D 398. It also points out that the word is from Latin *dictare,* dictate, appoint, prescribe. It also meant to put in order, arrange, clothe; make ready; direct (one's) way.]

dishonest. See **honestee.**

dong. Dung surrounds modern man as it did medieval man, but we pretend that it is not there. Chaucer accepted it, as did his audience. In fact, one of the two portraits in the "General Prologue," which critics agree is idealized—

that of the Plowman—mentions "dong" (A 530). The same sort of innocent occurrence is to be found in the "Nun's Priest's Tale," B 4208 (4226, twice; 4238, once more) where the murdered man's body is hidden in a "carte ful of dong."

Dung represents something horrid to the Pardoner (or at least he pretends it does in his marvelous sermon) when he rails against Gluttony ("Pardoner's Tale," C 535): "O wombe [belly]! O bely! O stynkyng cod [bag], / Ful-filled of dong and of corrupcioun!" It is comforting, however, to recall that the language is derived from St. Paul, Phil. 3:18, where he says that gluttons make their bellies their gods.

As might be expected, the Parson also uses "dong" to represent something morally reprehensible. Under the heading of Superbia (Pride) he condemns extravagant clothing, which trails "in the dong and in the mire" ("Parson's Tale," I 419).

The Canon's Yeoman uses it to express contempt: it is merely one of the ingredients used by the charlatan alchemist in his "conclusions" (experiments): "donge, pisse, and cley" (G 807).

Contempt is also the connotation in the *Parliament of Fowls* (597) when the tercelet ridicules the duck, who has spoken about the plenteousness of lovers ("there been mo sterres, God wot, than a payre!" [595]—which is a pretty stupid remark); the retort is "out of the donghill cam that word ful right!" [*MED, n.* (1) most of the citations are in barnyard contexts. Piers Plowman himself (C-Text, IX. 198) proudly puts all kinds of people to work in the fields, "in daubyng and in deluyng in donge a-feld berynge."]

drasty. Twice the Host calls Chaucer's romance of "Thopas" "drasty" (B 2113, 2120). Skeat notes that old glossaries use this word, or its forerunner in Old English, to translate Latin *feces, feculentus.* But it is normally glossed simply "filthy" today. If Skeat were right, "shitty" would be a better translation in Modern English, and most readers of the tale would not condemn the Host for using excessively strong critical language. However, lexical support seems lacking. [*MED*, "drast," from OE, lees, dregs; "drasti." There are no citations where the meaning "shitty" is unequivocal.]

e

embrace. Daun John "embraceth harde" the wife of the absent merchant ("Shipman's Tale," B 1393). The words and the act are not obscene except in context—a sudden and violent seduction of a willing partner. The seducer is in Holy Orders; the lady is the wife of his host and friend. When her husband returns, this generous female embraces him hard too. Simply by repeating (with variation) the line (cf. B 1567, 1568) Chaucer reminds us how easy it is for this woman to grant her favors both in and out of wedlock. [*MED*, 1 (a) embrace (someone) affectionately.]

engendrure. Copulation. The Host wishes that the Monk could "parfourne al thy lust in engendrure" ("Monk's Tale," B 3137), a passage with all kinds of double meanings and ironies. See the similar remarks made by Harry Bailly to the Nun's Priest (B 4637 ff.).

We should recall that in strict medieval ethical thought, anyone who had relations with a woman "but [unless] if it be for engendrure, / He doth trespas"—a quotation that happens to come from the *Romaunt of the Rose* (4849), but which could be paralleled in many places in Middle English writings. After the fourteenth century, the word is almost always associated with lust and lechery. [*MED*, 1 (a) the act of begetting or procreating.]

erchedeken. In the Chaucer *Concordance,* all five occurrences of this word are spelled *erc*(*h*)-. This means little, of course, since many of the Chaucer MSS may have used *ers-,* with its obvious pun (see **ers**). In the "Friar's Tale" (D 1302), the pun might be appropriate. [*MED*, "archedeken," also lists spellings *ers-* and *ars-*. Actually, *erc*(*h*)- seems to have been the most common.]

ers. In England this continues to be "arse," though in America it is, as every schoolboy knows, "ass," which provides puns with the beast of burden (Shakespeare knew about them too) .

Chaucer was not, I think we can say with assurance, an anal erotic. But he does not ignore the organ when it plays a role in his narrative. If we read the tales in Robinson's order (and all of us do, I suppose) we first encounter "ers" in its sweetest guise. It is Alisoun's "ers," naked and kissable. Absolon is outraged that he has been tricked into kissing it, but then he was suspiciously squeamish about many things. Instead of angrily wiping his mouth with dust, sand, cloth, straw, and chips, he should have enshrined those lips which kissed that "ers" (A 3755) , what though it had a "berd"!

The hende Nicholas plots to have Absolon kiss *his* bottom (A 3800) , quite a different matter. He puts it out the shot window "pryvely" (with a double meaning, perhaps the most obvious in the *Tales*) and it is "smoot" with the hot iron. Nicholas is a little *too* smugly successful up to this point, and it is satisfying to have him branded thus. In fact, only the adulterous Alisoun goes unpunished in the "Miller's Tale," but we can forgive her anything.

Unhappily, there are not many more interesting uses of "ers" in Chaucer. In the "Summoner's Tale," we are told repeatedly (and a little tediously, I think) that the nest of friars lives in Satan's rectum (see D 1690, 1694, 1698, and 1705) . The same jest is used in the *Romaunt of the Rose* (7576) , too. Here, however, Robinson's note tells us that Chaucer has mistranslated his French once again (query: why does Robinson not tell us this in his notes to the "Summoner's Tale"?) : "Fr. 'cul (var. 'puis') d'enfer,' meaning, doubtless, with either reading, 'the pit of hell.' The Fr. 'cul' may have led the English translator to introduce the idea which appears" in the "Summoner's Tale."

The abode (the manse?) of churchmen in Satan's rectum is an idea that persisted long after Chaucer and was used in Protestant propaganda like that in the Cranach woodcut. See Figure 4 and also **open-ers.** [*OED,*

Fig. 4. *The Pope and cardinals in the Devil's arse; from a sixteenth-century woodcut attributed to Lucas Cranach, the Elder (dated 1545). From the author's collection.*

1. buttocks; 2. bottom, lower end. *MED,* 1 (a) anus,
rectum, excretory organ; (b) buttocks. 2 (a) includes
"ars-holer," a sodomite? See **holour.** *Piers Plowman*
(C-Text, VII. 306) speaks of "an hore of hure ers-
wynnynge" (a whore, from her arse-winning—arse-gain) .]

eructavit. See **buf.**

ese. Hinton, following Baum, finds "eseth" bawdy in *Troilus
and Criseyde* (III. 197) : Pandarus speaks to Troilus,
telling him to come to his (Pandarus') house: "For I ful
wel shal shape youre comynge; / And eseth there youre
hertes right ynough." The meaning is, of course, "to find
sexual gratification." See also **come.**

Only the most suspicious prude would, I think, doubt
that there is the meaning of "sexual joy" when the Wife of
Bath (D 127) tells us that genitals were made for "ese of
engendrure." The meaning is not quite so clear (but still,
to me, unmistakable) when Troilus and Criseyde are in
bed (III. 1279, 1304) exchanging confidences and dropping the word "ese" to each other from time to time.

In Chaucer's chilly lyric "A Complaint to His Lady"
(72) , he claims that there is none "fayner . . . to do yow
ese." There might be some timid innuendo here.

The Lover in the *Romaunt of the Rose* (2236) is told
to do "ese" to ladies. The term seems quite neutral here
and probably is.

To that slut May, "ese" means intercourse—at least in
the "Merchant's Tale" (E 1981) where she is thinking
about the poor, sick Damyan (sick at heart for her!) :
"that from hire herte she ne dryve kan / The remembrance for to doon him ese." "Remembrance" is odd here—
as if she were remembering the delights of the "esement"
without having yet experienced them. [*MED,* "ese,"
3 includes gratification (of the flesh) ; that which . . .
affords sensual gratification; also 6 (c) relieve by evacuation.]

esement. Aleyn, the lively clerk in the "Reeve's Tale" (A 4179)
uses this word in the learned (being a clerk) legal sense,
but also in the sense of intercourse. He has just stated that
he intends to "swyve" the miller's daughter. He makes his
legal point again (A 4186) : "Agayn my los, I wil have

esement." Baum notes this double entendre and says that in this context we have both the legal sense and "the simpler enjoyment," i.e., coitus. [*MED*, "esement," 4 relieve through evacuation; excrement; no sexual senses.]

experience. Alison of Bath (D 124) tells us the *real* reasons for the creation of organs of generation: for "office and for ese / Of engendrure." "Experience woot wel it is noght so" that they exist only for utilitarian purposes, she snorts. Braddy feels that here she is equating "experience" with sexual intercourse. He does not, however, comment on what this idea does to the first lines of her "Prologue" (D 1) : "Experience, though noon auctoritee / Were in this world, is right ynogh for me." [*MED*, 3 glosses it as experience in worldly or temporal affairs, but unhappily provides no basis for Braddy's ingenious equation. He is nonetheless right.]

F

fantasye. Cenobia (Z-) in the "Monk's Tale" (B 3475) lets her husband "doon his fantasye" (have intercourse) with her but once, and that in order to engender a child. See **engendrure.** Earlier, the Monk tells us, we must understand that her husband "hadde swiche fantasies as hadde she," where it means "ideas, inclinations, tastes." But the difference is never really made clear, and later we are told that even though the husband may be "wilde or tame," she is still strict about the frequency of their intercourse and about its purpose. [*MED*, 5 amorous fancy or desire. Only Chaucer is cited in this (relatively) direct sense of "intercourse."]

fart. The most famous lover's rebuke in literature occurs in the "Miller's Tale" (A 3806). Absolon's mouth is puckered, ready for the kiss (or so Nicholas imagines), and then "this Nicholas anon leet fle a fart, / As greet as it had been a thonder-dent." Even Dorothy and William Wordsworth are alleged to have been amused by this

passage. It is delightful in itself, but Chaucer makes it all
the funnier because he has set us up for it, as a master
storyteller always does, by dropping a seemingly irrelevant
hint earlier (A 3338) that the preposterous Absolon "was
somdeel squaymous / Of fartyng."

Most readers find the farting in the "Summoner's Tale"
(D 2149) less amusing than that in the story of Alisoun,
Nicholas, and Absolon—perhaps because there is so much
of it. (See, for instance, Braddy, "Obscenity," p. 137, who
says that the "portioning of the flatus into twelve" gags
him.) The word "fart" is repeated eight times. Moreover,
there is no "sweete bryd" to speak in this story, but rather
a slimy friar, making himself all too much at home in
Thomas' house (even shooing the poor cat off its bench,
D 1775). He is so sure that his host has some precious gem
secreted in his privy parts that he puts his greedy hand
beneath the sheets without a moment's hesitation—and
Thomas gives him the gift that must be shared with his
brethren: "Amydde his hand he leet the frere a fart." See
also **ars-metrike, clifte, ferthyng, soun,** and **tayl.** [*MED,*
"fert," with several comic citations, including glosses for
Latin words like *bumbum, bumba, pidicio,* and *trulla.* Few
casual readers of the most famous of all Middle English
lyrics "Sumer is icumen in" really understand its eighth
line: "bucke uerteth" means that the buck farts to display
his ebullient joy over the coming of summer (see Bennett,
p. 110).]

feend. See **incubus, ycoupled.**

ferthyng. A quarter of a penny and also a pun on "farting" in
the "Summoner's Tale" (D 1967)—an exquisite device
that Chaucer uses to prepare us for the denouement of
the story. Baum and other commentators have noted this
pun; unhappily in Braddy's article, in which it is
mentioned, the point is spoiled by a printer's error (the
word appearing twice as "ferything"). In its original
monetary sense, "ferthyng" occurs only twice in other
passages of Chaucer's works; but see also "ferther" at
tuwel. [*MED,* "ferthing," 1 (d) cites Chaucer, D 1967, for
which the dictionary soberly tells us that the word means
"the value of a farthing." No pun is mentioned.]

fethered. Chaunticleer the cock flew down from the narrow perch (too narrow for his athletic prowess) and "fethered" Pertelote twenty times—seemingly a perfectly normal ritual, nothing beyond the ordinary. As a synonym for intercourse, it can be used only for feathered folk, alas. See the "Nun's Priest's Tale" (B 4367) and also **tredyng.** [*MED*, "fetheren," *v.* (1), 2 (c) strike or brush with the wings; cites Chaucer but does not suggest that it is a euphemism for intercourse.]

fille. See **acorded.**

fit. A "myrie fit" may be safely equated with an embrace (as Baugh calls it) or with sexual intercourse. See the "Reeve's Tale" (A 4230) where it involves the miller's wife. The young clerk who gives it to her is so successful and she is so unaccustomed to such talent, that one wonders why she did not suspect that her partner was not her husband. Rapture, perhaps.

Alison of Bath (D 42) meditates on Solomon and all his wives and the "many a myrie fit" he had with each of them on the first night (and of course succeeding nights too). See also **myrthe.** [*MED*, "fit," *n.* (2) (b) "muri fit," good time. But some of the citations suggest a sexy good time—e.g., Lydgate (not the sexiest of Middle English authors), *Troy Book,* V. 1931: "Alphenor . . . Was with the brond of Cupide brent, / And felt his part with many a mortal fyt."]

flankes. Daun John grabs the merchant's wife "by the flankes," kisses her, and makes the pact whereby he will give her the hundred francs and she will spend the night with him ("Shipman's Tale," B 1392). See **lendes.** [*MED* uses Chaucer's as the only erotic citation; all the others refer to horses or are from medical treatises.]

flour. Sanders states baldly that Alison's "flour" is her virginity, her hymen ("Wife of Bath's Prologue," D 113): "I wol bistowe the flour of al myn age." He goes on to call it "probably the most intricately developed pun in the *Tales.*" We must remember that "flour" was both a blossom and also finely ground meal. In Chaucer's pun, then, is involved the milling imagery, with grinding and grindstone having sexual significance. Sanders also quotes

Gower, and the passage is so good—so sensual and so
clearly revelatory of the meaning involved in Chaucer—
that I quote it in full (from the *Confessio Amantis*, V.
5376) :

> *Theseus in a prive stede*
> *Hath with this Maiden spoke and rouned [whispered],*
> *That sche to him was abandouned*
> *In al that evere that sche couthe,*
> *So that of thilke lusty youthe*
> *Al prively betwen hem tweie*
> *The ferste flour he tok aweie.*

Theseus' lover is of course Ariadne, whose name Gower
always spells "Adriane," as did Chaucer.

But poor Alison of Bath is old now; she admits (D 477)
that the "flour" is gone and she must sell the bran.

The meretricious May ("Merchant's Tale," E 2190)
swears to Januarie that she has been utterly faithful to
him, ever since she gave to him "of my wyfhod thilke
tendre flour"; this might be true, but she has at this point
already made her assignation with Damyan, her arboreal
lover. One doubts if May had her "flour" long after
puberty.

The two clerks in the "Reeve's Tale" (A 4174) discuss
the terrible noises made by the sleeping miller, his wife,
and his daughter. There is a hint that they not only snore
but emit sounds netherly too: they fart (see **tayl**). Aleyn
says, "Ye, they sal have the flour of il endyng," where
"flour" may have three meanings: (1) choicest sort; (2)
meal (ground wheat) ; and (3) the scent of the fart. I am
not certain of the last. [*MED,* 3 blossoming time, the prime
of life (ironically in the Wife of Bath's "Prologue") ; 2
(d) maidenhead (where Chaucer is not quoted, though
Gower is) ; 6 menstrual flow.]

foo. See **serve.**

fornicacioun. The Friar tells us, with vicious relish (D 1284) ,
that "A somonour is a rennere up and doun / With
mandementz for fornicacioun, / And is ybet at every
townes ende." "Fornicacioun" has undergone the semantic
shift known as specialization: it used to mean all sorts of

sexual misdemeanors, but now (technically) is supposed to apply only to intercourse between unmarried, heterosexual pairs. Whatever the precise meaning in the Friar's remark just quoted, "mandementz" may well be a double entendre: (1) summonses, to come to the archdeacon's court; (2) commandments, to come to the summoner's own bed. The rest of the tale makes the equivocation likely. Also "ybet" = (1) beaten; and (2) a pun on **abedde**. [*MED*, lechery, adultery, fornication, sodomy; concubinage (of priests), prostitution. *Piers Plowman* (A-Text, II. 147–155) associates summoners and "fornicatours."]

fressh. This word is so often associated with sexual prowess that it can almost be taken as a synonym. Recall, for instance, that the Wife of Bath is delighted that her fifth husband was "fressh and gay" in bed, which balances all other possible shortcomings. The merchant's wife in the "Shipman's Tale" (B 1367) also mentions this quality as the climactic final requirement that wives have in husbands. The entire catalogue should be reproduced here: "Hardy, and wise, and riche, and therto free [generous], / And buxom [*q.v.*] unto his wyf, and fressh abedde."

Observe Chaucer's clustering of the erotically suggestive words in this passage from the *Legend of Good Women* (1189), where Dido is preparing for her hunt with (and for) Aeneas, which will end in the cave-cohabitation:

> *This amorous queene chargeth hire meyne*
> *The nettes dresse, and speres brode and kene;*
> *An huntyng wol this lusty freshe queene,*
> *So priketh hire this newe joly wo.*

The oxymoron "joly wo" is not the only thing that pricks Dido. See **hunt, lust, priken.** Perhaps those spears are phallic too, but I must leave this to the reader.

When Arcite prays in the Temple of Mars, he reminds the god of:

> *. . . thilke peyne, and thilke hoote fir*
> *In which thow whilom brendest for desir,*

Whan that thow usedest the beautee
Of faire, yonge, fresshe Venus free,
And haddest hire in armes at thy wille.

The rest of the "Knight's Tale" (this passage is from A
2383) may not be erotic enough for undergraduates' tastes,
but this passage makes up for some of the catalogues that
try the reader's patience. See **gay.** [*MED,* 7 (a) gay, cheer-
ful . . . lusty; cites the tales of the Knight, the Shipman,
and the Wife—and also the "Clerk's Tale" (E 1173) . The
latter is Chaucer promising to sing a song ("Lenvoy de
Chaucer") at the end of the "Tale": "I wol with lusty
herte, fressh and grene, / Seyn yow a song to glade yow, I
wene." Under 8 (a) the definitions include: vigorous; not
weary, or tired out—but there are no Chaucer quotations!
The organization of the meanings seems confused, to say
the least.]

fruyt. The friar, Thomas' confessor, should have the first
"fruyt" of the fart, so cleverly divided on the spokes of the
wheel; but his nose will be at the hub, for the full savor.
This pristine perfume is funny only in context, of course:
"Summoner's Tale" (D 2277) . See **reverberacioun, soun.**
[*MED,* 5 (c) profit, benefit, reward, but this passage from
Chaucer is not cited.]

fundament. The greasy friar in the "Summoner's Tale" (D
2103) whines that his order needs funds for its "fundement," which simply means the foundation of a building
here; but in view of what happens at the friar's hand
from the "fundement" (in the other sense, the bottom,
the rectum) of Thomas, a dual meaning is very likely.
Chaucer is preparing us.

Baum points this one out, along with that in the
"Pardoner's Tale" (C 950) where the Host in disgust
says that the Pardoner would claim that his "breech"
were a saint's relic, "though it were with thy fundement depeint"—i.e., his undergarment (or his rectum
itself) stained with feces. Baugh thinks "breech" is a garment, others that it is the anus (see **breech**) . In either
case, it is a most unsavory passage—but the Pardoner is an
unsavory personage, perhaps the only lost soul on the

pilgrimage, in Kittredge's famous words. [*MED*, "founde-ment," *n.*, 1b (a) the basis of an institution or organ-ization; 5 the founding of an institution or an organ-ization; 7 (a) the lower extremity of the rectum, the anus; cites the "Pardoner's Tale." *Piers Plowman* (e.g., C-Text, XXII. 327) uses the word three times, always in the innocent senses.]

fynch. Chaucer's description of the Summoner in the "General Prologue" is perhaps the one that is most loaded with double meanings. For a quart of wine, he will let a priest have his concubine (see **concubyn**) and "excuse hym atte fulle." Then Chaucer adds (A 652) : "Ful prively a fynch eek koude he pulle." Robinson's gentlemanly note deserves to be quoted in its entirety: "This line, commonly misinterpreted, refers to the Summoner's own indulgences in the same sin for which he is said just before to have excused others." In other words, the Summoner has been keeping a wench and "swyvynge" her—or, as Braddy, "Obscenity" (p. 126) , puts it, in contemporary slang, the phrase "probably refers to [the Summoner's] prowess with what today one calls 'a chick' or, better, 'a bird.' "

If Robinson is right (and he quotes Kittredge!) "prively" has the familiar double meaning of "secret" and "the private parts" too. See **pryvee.** But the dictionary-makers just will not help. [Both *OED* and *MED* gloss "to pull a finch" as to pull a clever trick, and *OED* compares "to pluck a pigeon." In both dictionaries, Chaucer is the only writer cited.]

fyngres. The Parson refers to the devil's five fingers of lechery with which he catches men—probably an ancient mnemonic device: (1) "lookynge"; (2) "touchynge"; (3) "foule wordes"; (4) "kissynge"; (5) "the stynkynge dede of Leccherie" ("Parson's Tale," I 851) . Bemused by his own words, the Parson again uses a similar phrase (I 863) , when he refers to the "fyve fyngres of Glotonye," here apparently merely the fingers that thrust food and drink into the mouth. [*MED*, "finger," *n.* 3 the five means by which the devil tempts; the earliest citation is *ca.* 1290, so it must have been familiar to Chaucer's audience.]

fyr. To Chaucer, "fyr" was a symbol of sexual danger. With a

flammable substance, the peril was particularly great: "O
perilous fyr, that in the bedstraw bredeth" ("Merchant's
Tale," E 1783). The fact that it is *bed*straw should not be
overlooked, of course.

Similarly, the Wife of Bath (D 89) explains the danger
of a man touching a woman in bed or on a couch: "For
peril is bothe fyr and tow t'assemble." She is, however, an
equitable woman, and she recognizes that females burn
with lust too. She has had experience: woman's love
is like to "wilde fyr; / The moore it brenneth, the moore
it hath desir / To consume every thyng that brent wole
be" (D 373).

The Pardoner, at his most venomous in his sermon (C
481), rails against all kinds of (evidently quite innocent)
women—dancers, fruiterers, tumblers—who are the causes
of the "fyr of lecherye." The irony of such charges in the
Pardoner's mouth is very powerful.

In the *Legend of Good Women*, the same fire of lust
burns, but of course to be a "good woman" you had to
overcome this desire. In Dido (1156) there breeds "swich
a fyr" that she is overwhelmed with desire to "dele"
(*q.v.*) with Aeneas; in Tarquin's heart (1751) there burns
a "fyr" for Lucrece. And both these good women commit
suicide. Tereus (2292) lusts for his sister-in-law Philomene
[*sic*] with a "fyry herte." She is raped, of course, but does
not enjoy it and is therefore "good," presumably. See **hoot.**
[*MED,* 12 (a) heat or vehemence (of wrath, jealousy, lust,
etc.) , passion.]

G

gat-tothed. This gap between the teeth is, I suppose, the most
familiar of all the physiognomical signs in Chaucer.
Among other things, it means that the possessor of this
feature is lecherous ("General Prologue," A 468), like
the Wife of Bath. Alison herself calls attention to her

mouth (D 603): "Gat-tothed I was, and that bicam me weel." "Bicam" seems to mean both "adorned" and "fit, was appropriate." Curry's learned researches support this belief: a gap between the teeth was, he says, a sign that the person was "luxurious." [*MED* supports the meaning of lechery but has only these two Chaucer citations to buttress it.]

gay. Often associated with "fressh," this word had distinct sexual connotations too. In the *Romaunt of the Rose* (83), "gay" and "amorous" are equated.

The "Miller's Tale" (A 3339) offers an example that suggests it means sexy but a little silly too: "Absolon, that jolif was and gay." Later in the same tale, the rough smith Gervays asks what ails Absolon and guesses "som gay gerl, God it woot" (A 3769). See **girl**.

Naturally Alison of Bath has an occasion to use this sexy word (D 508) about her fifth husband, who was in bed so "fressh and gay." The Summoner uses the word (D 1727) in a much more complex and perplexing way, which I have not unraveled. He says that we are not to "holde a preest joly and gay." It is probably simple irony, but the entire passage must be examined before a decision can be ventured by the reader.

Early in her story, Criseyde hears a nightingale (II. 922), which "made hire herte fressh and gay." We should all like to think—and Chaucer gives us reason to do so— that at this point Criseyde's "gay" feeling was pure.

The modern transfer of the word to the sub-culture and -language of the homosexual probably had its beginnings in the sexual (hetero-) meanings the word had six hundred years ago. [*MED,* joyous . . . also wanton, lewd, lascivious. Cites many Chaucer quotations to support these meanings.]

gelde. There is delicate medieval beauty (gaily dressed knights riding horses in footcloths embroidered with fleurs-de-lis) and medieval horror too, which this word represents. The Monk's lugubrious tale of Nabugodonosor (B 3342) states that he "leet do gelde" the fairest children of the blood royal of Israel. This detail is not from the Bible, but from

Vincent of Beauvais, one of the encyclopedists from whom Chaucer, like most other medieval writers, got a great deal of material. [*MED,* 2 (a) to castrate (a man).]

geldyng. Normally applied to a horse (as still today) but with it Chaucer intrudes himself into the "General Prologue" (A 691) to give his opinion that the last-described Pilgrim, the Pardoner, was a "geldyng or a mare." This is the "noble ecclesiaste" (a statement both true and ironic) who preaches before us one of the best sermons we shall ever hear, including one of the best *exempla.*

The most terrible irony is, however, that if Chaucer is right (see **coillons**) the Pardoner should not even have been admitted to a church. The *MED, s.v.* "gelding," quotes the Wyclif Bible of 1382, Deut. 23:1: "A geldynge, the ballogys [ballocks, testicles] brusyd or kut off, & the yarde [penis] kut away, shal not goon yn to the chirche." This prohibition is from a terrible series of passages about deflowering virgins, incest with one's mother, and keeping bastards out of the congregation for ten generations. If these Old Covenant rules had been enforced, the Church would have been deprived not only of many of the congregation but also of supremely gifted preachers like Chaucer's Pardoner.

Braddy (p. 216) says that though the Pardoner is described as a gelding or a mare, the "noble ecclesiaste" claims to "have a joly wenche in every toun" in his own "Prologue" (C 453), thus proving that he is "hardly equivalent to a sex pervert." But perhaps Professor Braddy would also admit that there is the possibility of irony here—a compensation by the effeminate Pardoner, as shown in his boasts. Further evidence for this interpretation is to be found in his interruption of the Wife of Bath (D 166) with: "I was aboute to wedde a wyf; allas! / What sholde I bye it on my flessh so deere?" which is the same sort of protesting too much. [*MED,* 2 (a) a castrated man, a eunuch; a naturally impotent man; in Old Testament use, a royal officer (whether castrated or not).]

gerl. See **girl.**

girl. The loathsome Summoner has "girles" in his power

("General Prologue," A 664). If only young females are meant, it is bad enough. But there are two meanings even here: (1) he can summon them to the ecclesiastical court; or (2) he can summon them to his bed. The equivocation increases geometrically when we realize that "girl" meant a young person of *either* sex. Robinson reveals this in his note, but does not solve the problem of what the Summoner is doing to whom. [*MED*, "girl (e)," (a) a child of either sex; citations run from *ca.* 1300 to *a.* 1475 and include Chaucer, A 664. The specialized meaning (b) a girl, a young woman, is traced from *a.* 1375 to *a.* 1450.]

gon. The young wife May must find a privy place to read her love note from the loutish Damyan ("Merchant's Tale," E 1950). She finds an appropriate one: "She feyned hire as that she moste gon / Ther as ye woot that every wight moot neede." Chaucer calls it by its name—a privy (E 1954). The Middle English sense of "gon" has obviously persisted into modern times with our "I have to *go!*" [*MED*, "gon," 6 (b) "gon forth," to defecate.]

gong. A very blunt word for the privy (which itself is of course a euphemism). The Parson excoriates whores (I 884): they are like a "commune gong, where as men purgen hire ordure." It is a strong simile, but a little lacking in Christian charity. The word seems to have been in common use. There are recorded "gong-fermour" [cleaner], "-man," "-hole," "-hous," and "-shider" [builder]. For a scale of terms applied to the house of easement ("gong," "privy," "wardrobe") see Introduction, p. 18. [*MED*, "gang," 3 (a) privy. There are several citations in which bodies, or parts of them, are thrown into the "gong," and under 3 (b) there is "helle gang," pit of hell.]

gore. Thopas (B 1978) coos: "An elf-queene shal my lemman be / And slepe under my goore." Donaldson (p. 43) remarks: "Whatever 'gore' means here—presumably cloak—its context is unmistakable." The comedy consists in this effeminate knight plotting seduction, for Thopas (as Donaldson points out, p. 38) "though a sturdy hero, possesses some of the charms of a typical medieval heroine." [*MED*, "gore," *n.* (2) (a) wedge-shaped piece of cloth; 3 (a) woman's skirt; (b) man's coat or robe (cites "Thopas") ; (d) clothes, dress. The confusion of 3 (a) and (b) explains the humor of Chaucer's equivocation. "Gore" also meant dung—*MED, n.* (3) —but Chaucer does not seem to use this possibly bawdy double meaning.]

grace. Partridge (p. 78, *s.v.* "bottom-grass") equates it with pubic hair. It is an uncommon and rather gross pun in Shakespeare. Is there anything analogous in Chaucer?

Many times, especially in passages of a courtly import— dealing with courtiers in love, if not with Courtly Love— the knight hopes that he may "stonden in his lady grace." Most commentators stop with the observation that "lady" in this phrase is an old uninflected genitive. They do not go on to remind us that "grace" and "grass" were both homographs and near homophones in Chaucer's time; nor do they observe that "stonden" (*q.v.*) had an erotic sense.

Perhaps they are right. There *are* a number of occasions when the phrase "stonden in my lady grace" could mean "have an erection in my lady's pubic hair," but with our present evidence we cannot prove that this is what Chaucer meant.

To begin with that most sensuous of poems, *Troilus and Criseyde* (III. 472): Troilus "so ful stood in his lady grace" is suggestive indeed, but it occurs before they are actually in bed. Then Diomede (V. 171) tells Criseyde that there are many knights in the Greek camp who would strive "to stonden in youre grace": such a passage is much more likely to have an obscene meaning in view of Diomede's audacity, the situation, and Criseyde's come-hither eye.

There are dozens of other occurrences in the *Troilus,* with and without the "stonden" (if that is important). For instance, Troilus thinks (I. 370) that he might "falle in grace" (an embarrassing event indeed!). The reference is found in a "cluster" of words of a suggestive sort, including "holly" (hole-ly), "serven," and "servantes," the last two words with the familiar barnyard meanings of copulate, -ors.

More remotely possible is the passage where Criseyde

agrees to do Troilus a "grace" (III. 922). Here the word is associated with "prive" and "place."

Just as *courtoisie* has confused (and enriched) the vocabulary of love with a double meaning for "serven," so too the "religion of love" has done the same with words like "grace." Once again *Troilus* (III. 1262), when the couple is snugly in bed, illustrates the point: he calls upon "benigne Love" and mentions "grace" three times in eight lines. It is the familiar secularized "prayer" to the God of Love, but is there also the pun on "grass" (pubic hair)?

In the *Tales,* too, the phrase occurs in suggestive places: the first is in the "General Prologue" (A 88), speaking of that pattern of aspiring courteous knighthood, the Squire. He is "in hope to stonden in his lady grace." It is probably utterly innocent, but if it is even faintly suggestive of the idea of erections and the pubis, the wryly satiric portrait of the Squire takes on a new level of meaning.

In the "Miller's Tale," when Absolon says to Alisoun, "Lemman, thy grace, and sweete bryd, thyn oore" (A 3726), what reader would not be reminded that when Absolon bestows the kiss, it is her "berd" (her "bottom-grass," her "grace") that touches his lips; and again when he returns for the second kiss, he calls out in the dark, "Spek, sweete bryd, I noot nat where thou art" (3805).

Mutually suggestive juxtapositions make the possibility of a double meaning more likely in the "Merchant's Tale" (E 1997, 2018). May writes Damyan a letter in which she "graunteth hym hire verray grace"; then we are told that "fully in his lady grace he [Damyan] stood."

But just when one is about to agree that there may be a double meaning in this cluster of words, one encounters something like *Troilus and Criseyde* (II. 714): "ther I may stonde in grace," where the speaker is Criseyde. Or the lyric "A Complaint to His Lady" (125), where Chaucer asks his lady "of your grace graunteth me som drope" [drop].

All one can say with assurance is that sometimes the double meaning seems to be there and sometimes it most assuredly is not. But the reader would be unwise, I think, to discount the possibility completely. It is one of the most tantalizing ambiguities in the entire study of Chaucer's bawdy double entendre. [Neither *OED* nor *MED* offers any support, except to confirm the fact that "grace" and "grass" were spelled and pronounced identically, with only a difference of vowel length. In the dictionaries, the phrase "stonden in gras, grace" means simply to enjoy someone's goodwill or favor. The sexual double meaning is perhaps present in Robbins' Poem No. 200: "that I may be receyvyd yn-to your grace" (28), but the same questions apply here as with Chaucer. The pun, without a bawdy meaning, is in *Piers Plowman* (C-Text, XV. 23): "Ac grace is a gras ther-fore to don hem eft growe." This is one of the twelve puns recognized by Skeat in his edition (II. 482).]

gras. See **grace.**

grene. See **blew.**

grind. Sanders says that the word means to copulate, reminding one of the lost art of the striptease dancer in American burlesque. Anyway, when Alison of Bath (D 389) pronounces her homely proverb "Whoso that first to mille comth, first grynt," the sexual meaning and the suggestion of kinetic imagery are obvious. I am not so sure about the end of the "Reeve's Tale" (A 4314) where we are told that the miller "hath ylost the gryndynge of the whete." It is literally true, of course. He loses the cake made from the stolen meal. The clerks have "swyved" his wife (where the secondary sexual meaning is clear—the miller has lost the "gryndyng" of his mate) but also his daughter. And it is with her that my doubts arise. Perhaps Chaucer is simply inconsistent.

The tone is utterly different in the *House of Fame* (1798) where Fame ridicules those who are confident that "bele Isawde" could not refuse them her love, but feel that they are too good to ease the heart of the woman "that grynt at a querne"—i.e., grinds at a mill, a simple countrywoman. Grinding at the "querne" probably has the double meaning. [*MED* offers no support.]

Griselde. She seems to be a totally asexual creature. Even when she produces children, it is a mechanical and biological process without joy—pure duty. See the "Clerk's Tale" (E 442 ff) .

grope. To feel, but (as Baum says) suggestive of amorous play. He mentions the "Summoner's Tale (D 2141), of course (the most familiar of Chaucer's fumblings in erogenous [?] zones) : Thomas has told the greedy friar to put his hand down under the sheet, where he lies in bed, "doun by my bak . . . and grope wel bihynde." The friar's prize is there, a resounding old man's fart, divisible into twelve parts. Baum does not mention the humorous foreshadowing that Chaucer gives us in this same tale (D 1817) : the friar sneers at curates: "thise curatz been ful necligent and slowe / To grope tendrely a conscience / In shrift." [*MED*, "gropen," 1 (d) to touch amorously, play with, fondle; it cites the passage from the "Summoner's Tale" under the simple meaning "feel." *OED*, 3. b. gives the indecent senses and quotes some relevant material from a slightly earlier time—e.g., *Bevis* (3105) : "Thow gropedest the wif anight to lowe"; and from a work contemporaneous with Chaucer (1380) : "Heo lay stylle a luytel whil, then heo groped him atte laste," where "heo" = she. In Robbins' Poem No. 26, the erotic meaning is made very clear: "he gropith so nyslye a-bought my lape" (15) . See **lappe** and the Confession of Luxurie from *Piers Plowman* at **likyng**.]

<h1 style="text-align:center">h</h1>

hair. The length and color of hair was another of the physiognomical signs that Chaucer could use as a kind of narrative "shorthand," but which must be fully explained to us today. There are three personages in the *Tales* with similar hair and (Chaucer's audience would have perceived at once) similar characters too. The first is the inept knight, Sir Thopas (see **corage,** for instance) whose description includes (B 1920) : "His heer, his berd was lyk saffroun, / That to his girdel raughte [reached] adoun."

Then there is the Pardoner, the gelding or mare, as Chaucer calls him. He has a voice as high as a goat's, and "this Pardoner hadde heer as yelow as wex, / But smothe it heeng as dooth a strike of flex" ("General Prologue," A 675). In the later Middle Ages, the biblical Absalom had become a type of feminine beauty, as Beichner demonstrates (see especially p. 233). The prettiness of Chaucer's counterpart, the clerk Absolon, that "effeminate small-town dandy" (p. 222), was closely associated with his long blond hair ("Miller's Tale," A 3314).

Surely, someone will object, this is coincidence: these three characters have nothing in common but their hair. Curry gives us the answer, however: "Long and soft hair, immoderately fine in texture and reddish or yellow in color 'indicates an impoverished blood, lack of virility, and effeminacy of mind; and the sparser the hair, the more cunning and deceptive is the man.'" Curry is quoting Rudolphus Goclenius, *Physiognomica et Chiromantica Specialia* (p. 58).

We knew about the Pardoner's effeminacy; we have suspected that of Thopas (it is central to his humor—a reason for the Host's disgust with the "drasty" tale). We had our doubts about Absolon too. Now we have our proof. All three are rather girlish, in very different ways.

We should also remind ourselves of the hair of Sir Andrew Aguecheek in Shakespeare's *Twelfth Night* (I. iii. 100). It is fine, Sir Toby tells him, and will not curl by nature. Sir Andrew: "But it becomes me well enough, does it not?" Sir Toby: "Excellent. It hangs like flax on a distaff, and I hope to see a housewife take thee between her legs and spin it off." Sir Andrew's effeminacy is repeatedly referred to in the play, and to Shakespeare's audience his long, fine, flaxen hair (like that of Thopas, the Pardoner, and Absolon) would have been a sure sign. We can now better understand the humor in the duel between Cesario (Viola) and Sir Andrew; and Maria's invitation to let the effeminate knight advance his hand to the buttery-bar (that is, to "grope" her bosom), which he does not understand; and his own dry hand, a sign of tepid sexual desire.

In the many lyrics in the play, Sir Andrew should sing contratenor. He could be joined by the three effeminate Chaucer personages, the Pardoner, Sir Thopas, and Absolon. Perhaps we are supposed to suspect the Pardoner not only of being unmanly but also of having a homosexual relationship with the Summoner (see **burdoun**). If so, Chaucer has created a complex set of bitter ironies within ironies—very powerful though admittedly difficult to sort out. See **wench**. [*MED* provides nothing.]

hare. Robertson (*Preface,* p. 113), describing a miniature, says: "The rabbit . . . indicates what the lover, watching from the side, is actually interested in, a small furry creature of Venus and an object of her 'hunt' which owed its popularity as a symbol in part to the fact that a play on words was possible in French involving *con* [Chaucer's 'queynte'] and *conin*" [hare]. Robertson also refers to Deschamps, one of Chaucer's favorite French masters, who uses the word play just mentioned.

This tells us more about the Monk ("General Prologue," A 191) than we could have guessed, had it not been for Robertson's erudition: "Of prikyng [*q.v.*] and of huntyng [see **hunt**] for the hare / Was al his lust [*q.v.*]." We now know, if we did not suspect it before, the significance of the pin he wears, which ends in a love knot. He is indeed a "prikasour aright."

Baum sees yet another play on words (English this time) when the Friar speaks, viciously (D 1327): "For thogh this Somonour wood were as an hare, / To telle his *har*lotrye [italics mine] I wol nat spare." This, by the way, was one of the half-dozen puns identified by Tatlock in 1916, though he did not comment on its possible bawdiness.

The hare is one of the "wild" animals, along with the buck, that lurk in Thopas' forest (B 1946), and there is probably some complicated irony here, since Thopas is the reverse of the bold sexual "hunter" (see **hair**). The passage brings to mind, of course, the Host's remarks to Chaucer just before the poet begins to tell his tale of Thopas, accusing him of riding along with his eyes cast down "as thou woldest fynde an hare" (B 1886) —probably gentle self-deprecation.

Sometimes the parallel is simply not there, however, as in the "Shipman's Tale" (B 1294) where the monk compares the merchant to a hare that lies motionless in a rabbit warren, beset with hounds. There is no connection with symbolic sexual hunting here. See Figures 5, 6, 8. [*MED* offers no help.]

harlotrye. The word has undergone rich and interesting semantic changes—beginning with the noun "harlot," which was simply a man of no fixed occupation, an idle rogue (1200–1500) as the *MED* tells us. For the most part, Chaucer uses the word in this generalized sense.

We first meet the word in the "General Prologue" (A 561) where Chaucer is describing the Miller, who talks loud and long "of synne and harlotries." Here the sense is the general one of "vulgarities," but not necessary ugly ones. Later on (A 647) the Summoner is called a "harlot"—a knave, a rascal, which he certainly is.

The "harlotrye" in the "Miller's Tale" (A 3145) is ribaldry, and when Chaucer refers to the tales of both the Reeve and Miller (A 3184) as "harlotrie," he has the same connotation in mind. The "Friar's Tale" (D 1328) uses "harlotrye" for scurrility, though the context is distinctly sexual. In contrast, the "Summoner's Tale" (D 1754) uses "harlot" merely for a rogue.

As is often true, the Parson makes everything clear in his sermon (I 884) where he attacks "harlotes that haunten bordels of thise fool wommen"—i.e., these (male) rogues that go to bordellos. [*MED,* 1 base, crude, or obscene behavior; 2 low, trifling talk; foul jesting; scurrility, obscenity.]

harneys. The Wife of Bath (D 136) says that she does not claim that all those whom she has described as being equipped with "harneys" need to use it for "engendrure." The word means equipment generally—for horses, men-at-arms, and (here) mankind. The Wife refers to the genitals, of course. It is a fine word for her to employ: she has worn her own "harneys" into battle so often and with

such prowess. Admittedly, she does have trouble understanding the principle of chastity, except as it applies to
unusual personages like Christ and St. Paul. [*MED*,
"harneis," 4 sexual organs. Cites D 136. *OED*, 7. glosses it
(typically) "privy members." *MED* cites Mandeville (*a*.
1450), who describes an isle where men and women have
both "ton harneys and the othir," where "ton" = the
one.]

harpe. See **daunce.**

hende. See **hond.**

herberwynge. In his "aborted" tale, the Cook seems deliberately to misunderstand this word, which means simply
"showing hospitality to"; but in context, it involves
potential cuckold-makers, potential swyvers, the Cook
implies (see his "Tale," A 4332) . [*MED*, "herberwen," 1
(c) to shelter (an offender, fugitive, spy) .]

hert. See **hunt.**

hol- (including **hole, whole, wholly**) . "Hole" and "whole"
were not only homophones in Middle English but both
were usually written without the initial *w*. The possibilities for punning are great. But it is hard, sometimes impossible, to prove that such puns exist. The following
brief disquisition, hardly more than a suggestion of the
potential riches, begins with what has become Modern
English "hole," then moves to "whole" and "wholly."

"Hol" could be used for any external body orifice, including the female pudendum (*MED*, 2 [a]). We have no
doubts when we encounter it in the "Miller's Tale" (A
3732) : "at the wyndow out she putte hir hole"; this is
Alisoun's rectum. But what about the other Alison, the
Wife of Bath (D 573) , when she says that a good mouse
has more than one hole to "sterte to"; is there some sort
of double meaning involving her precious "queynte"?

The most interesting case occurs in *Troilus and Criseyde*
(II. 584 ff.) when Pandarus speaks to Criseyde:

And, be ye wis as ye be fair to see,
Wel in the ryng than is the ruby set.
Ther were nevere two so wel ymet,

Whan ye ben his al hool, as he is youre:
Ther myghty God yet graunte us see that houre!

Criseyde answers:

"Nay, therof spak I nought, ha, ha!" quod she;
"As helpe me God, ye shenden every deel!"
"O, mercy, dere nece," anon quod he,
"What so I spak, I mente naught but wel. . . ."

In Chaucer's source, Boccaccio's *Il Filostrato,* there is a
parallel passage, but the tone is utterly different. Criseyde
is not embarrassed by Pandarus' remarks (as she is in
Chaucer), nor does he apologize for what seems to have
been an unintended double entendre in the English. The
ring and the ruby are in Boccaccio, but, unlike English,
Italian does not convey any immodest meaning here (the
ruby is the penis, especially with its red glans, and the
ring is of course the vulva). See **ring.**

The word for "whole" in Italian is *intero.* Boccaccio's
lines are "Che deve aver di me piacere intero / Se già non
divenisse mio marito?" It is not only inoffensive, it is
sanctimonious—meaning "who could ever have complete
pleasure from me unless he were to become my husband?"
Root (p. 444) points out that this entire passage is closely
translated from the Italian, but these lines are not. And
the innocent Italian *intero* has become the equivocal
English "hol."

The cluster of "ruby," "ring," and "hole" is too much
for Criseyde, who is not so innocent as she sometimes likes
to pretend (she is a widow, after all, though we are likely
to forget it). She breaks out into uncontrollable giggles.
Then Pandarus realizes what he has said, or implied, and
tries to make amends. Perhaps Criseyde knew the lyric
which is Robbins' Poem No. 208 (31–35):

She that onys wold in a dark nyght
Renne for your loue tyl she had caught a thorn,
I wolde hyr no more harme but hangyd on the morn,
That hath ij [two] good eyen & I-chese [chose] here
    such a make [mate],
Or onys wold lyft vp here hole for your sake!

Much of this is very difficult, but the last line is the important one, and Robbins glosses "hole" (35) as "private parts."

Meech (p. 39) does not comment on the ambiguity of the *Troilus and Criseyde* passage: he remarks, however, that Pandarus' reply is "highly equivocal." What should we think, then, when Criseyde promises Troilus to "ben to yow trewe and hool with al myn herte" (III. 1001)? Or what about her "Syn I am thyn al hol" (IV. 1641)?

Much more problematical is the "Friar's Tale" (D 1370), where the summoner is compared to a hunter's dog that "kan an hurt deer from an hool yknowe." The simile involves lechers and sexual promiscuity, but the exact meaning is hard to untangle. There is the hint of the pudendum and (most likely, and much less offensively) the familiar deer-dear pun. See **deer.**

Sometimes the passages involving this word are easier to blame—or excuse. For instance, this one from the "Franklin's Tale" (F 1450) says that Portia has given her heart to Brutus "al hool"; there is no suspicion of anything irregular. It is, on the contrary, noble.

Consider next Chaucer's lyric "A Complaint to His Lady" (54): "My hertes lady, and hool my lyves quene"; his "Womanly Noblesse" (2) (repeated in line 32): "Your beaute hoole and stidefast governaunce"; or (doubtful authorship) his "A Balade of Complaint" (13): "Myn heven hool, and al my suffisaunce, / Whom for to serve is set al my plesaunce." In the latter, the cluster of "hool," "serve," and "plesaunce" (*qq. v.*) may be suggestive.

Baum recognizes the puns that are possible in Chaucer between "holy" and "wholly" and cites the "Reeve's Tale" (A 3985) where the point is that the miller in the story is intent upon marrying his daughter well, since his own wife is the bastard by-blow of the parish priest.

But what about "wholly" and "hole-y" puns? I think there are some in Chaucer—for instance, *Troilus and Criseyde* (I. 366), when the hero makes a mirror of his mind "in which he saugh al holly hire figure." What young man has not had such visions of his beloved, before

he knew her well, or in bed? There is a similar equivoque
where Pandarus says that in his niece he has put this
"fantasie" (*q.v.*) "to doon thi [Troilus'] lust and holly
to ben thyn" (III. 276) .

The friar in the "Summoner's Tale" (D 1999) is talking
to Thomas, from whom he wants alms, praising—a little
too chummily—his host's spouse: "Now sith ye han so
hooly and meke a wyf." Was this accompanied by a sly
wink? And can there be sly humor in the midst of that
most saccharine and moralistic narratives, the "Man of
Law's Tale" (B 709) ? King Alla and Custance (married,
of course!) go to bed, and the remark is made that though
wives are "ful hooly thynges," they must be patient at
night. I apologize for the rhetorical questions, but I think
that it is the fairest way to put things, and I hope most
sincerely the answer to my last one is "yes."

If the reader is about to be persuaded that these puns
are actually there (some of the time, if not all the time) ,
let me in all fairness list a couple more that will put his
mind in doubt again. The fair Blanche of the *Book of the
Duchess* (1269) is an ideal woman: "My lady yaf me al
hooly / The noble yifte of hir mercy." No pun! And
near the end of *Troilus and Criseyde* (V. 1846) , the reader
is enjoined to love Christ, and "herte al holly on hym
leye." It should be clear, then, that if this obscene pun
is present in Chaucer, we must be extremely judicious in
assessing the situation. [*MED* confirms the fact that these
words are homophones and homographs, but gives no
evidence for the puns (including the "wholly-holy" one) .
Consider the following, however: Robbins' Poem No. 189,
with the familiar cliché "Myn hertys Ioy, and all myn
hole plesaunce" (1) ; and John Bale's *King John,* written
early in the reign of Elizabeth, but for evidence that the
pun persisted: see the *Dramatic Writings of John Bale,*
ed. J. S. Farmer (New York, 1966; orig. publ. 1907) , p.
214, where there is the following dialogue: "I would thou
hadst kissed his arse, for that is holy. . . . How does thou
prove that his arse is holy now? . . . For it hath an hole,
even fit for the nose of you."]

holour. A lecher. One wonders naturally about the relationship with the word "hole," but apparently there was no etymological connection, though such puns may well have occurred to Chaucer's listeners. The Wife of Bath uses the word (D 254), quoting, as usual, one of her husbands, who says that an impoverished woman is a pitiful thing, since "every holour wol hire have."

The other occurrence in Chaucer is in the "Parson's Tale" (I 856) and it is perhaps his only joke. He describes old men who kiss with lust but cannot perform the deed—"olde dotardes holours"; they are likened to dogs that lift their legs at a bush but cannot piss. See also **arse** and (under the *MED* entry) **ars-holer**. [*MED,* from OF *holier;* a fornicator, adulterer, lecher; a paramour.]

hond. The young wife May ("Merchant's Tale," E 2005) encourages her "lemman" Damyan with an age-old gesture: she secretly takes him by the hand "and harde hym twiste" [squeezed]. Before too long, they are "struggling" together in that pear tree.

Nicholas in the "Miller's Tale" is repeatedly given the epithet "hende" [handy], and when he shows a readiness to seize Alisoun ("hire hente anon," A 3347) it is an erotic "laying on of hands" (Braddy, "Obscenity," p. 132). Donaldson (p. 36) equates "hende" with "nice," used ironically.

But there is a Chaucerian expression involving the hand that complicates these erotic mentions of the manual extremity. For instance, Alison of Bath (D 211) says: "but sith I hadde hem hoolly in myn hond," referring to her husbands. To have or hold someone in the hand meant to deceive them. Now there are three possible meanings: (1) controlled them; (2) duped them; (3) held their penis in my hand. The third is admittedly not definite, but knowing the wife it is possible. The phrase can *also* mean "prove wrong" or "accuse": variations are present throughout the "Wife of Bath's Prologue" (D 226, 232, 380, 393, 575) in all of which the indecent meaning of penis-in-hand is possible.

Perhaps the iconographical prototype for the penis-in-hand figure was Daunger in the *Romaunt of the Rose* (3401), who was portrayed in his "rage" (*q.v.*) "and in

his hond a gret burdoun." See **burdoun.** The only trouble
with Daunger as such a prototype is that he represents
what we might allegorize today as Disdain—hardly an
aggressive sexual concept! See Robinson's note at A 517,
where the matter is well explained. Compare also Priapus'
sceptre, which is relevant here.

The phrase naturally also occurs often in *Troilus and
Criseyde,* a poem filled with deceits. It probably has erotic
meanings too. For instance, Criseyde writes Troilus that
she will not "holden hym in honde" (II. 1222), but this is
a different situation from the one where she says to
Pandarus, her devoted uncle, that she will not "holden
hym in honde" (II. 477). At least I *think* that the situation is different (see **incest**).

When Pandarus is about to bring Troilus to his niece's
bed (III. 773), he says to her: "for to holde in love a man
in honde" is to do herself a shame and him a "gyle." If
there is a hint of holding the penis in hand, it would not
be beneath Pandarus to mention the fact that a female
may manually manipulate a man until emission occurs. It
would, in these circumstances, indeed be a "gyle" for her
to do so. There is little chance of such a thing occurring,
however, granted Criseyde's sensual nature.

In the same poem there are situations in which the
phrase can have no double meaning: The heroine says
she will not deceive her father, Calkas (IV. 1404): she
will not "beren hym on honde." She is merely talking
about deceit, of course. See also III. 1154, V. 1615, and
V. 1680 as well. [*MED* gives no evidence of the possible
double meaning.]

honestee. From the first time we read Hamlet's terrible shout
to Ophelia, "Are you honest?" we have known that the
older meaning of the word was "chaste." In Chaucer's
time, this was its primary meaning, but it also had another obsolete sense—neatness. The Parson (I 428) has
them both in mind when he uses the word "honestitee"
several times in the section of his sermon dealing with
Superbia (Pride).

In the "Manciple's Tale" (H 214)—as "honest" a piece
of writing as is the Parson's sermon, but somewhat more

entertaining—we are told that a woman of high degree is nothing better than a wench, if she is "of hir body dishonest," where "body" (*q.v.*) has the narrow sexual sense of vagina and "dishonest" is of course "unchaste." As a corollary, in the "Second Nun's Tale" (G 89), Cecilie's "honestee" is equated with chastity. Lucrece (*Legend of Good Women,* 1736) is the pattern of "honeste" —or at least her tears are!

Criseyde's excuse (if it is that) for not running away with Troilus (IV. 1576) is that her reputation for virtue and chastity would be sullied: "thynketh on myn honeste," she exclaims. The "Physician's Tale" (C 77) neatly divides governesses into two camps: those that have kept their "honestee" and those who have fallen into frailty and know the "old daunce"—that is, are little better than bawds. See **daunce.** [*MED, n.,* 4 (b) purity, virginity, chastity; but also 3 (a) elegance, comeliness, fairness; and 3 (b) freshness?, newness.]

hood. In Chaucer's (?) translation of the *Romaunt of the Rose* (7386), Dame Abstinence-Streyned, dressed in the habit of a Beguine, delights in being confessed by Fals-Semblant—several times a day. They are so intimate that there are "two heedes in oon hood at ones." *Le Roman de la Rose* (12063) has ".ii. testes . . . ensemble / En .i. chaperon." I cannot determine the exact meaning of this phrase, but it is likely that they are making the beast with two backs. The preceding lines certainly support such a suggestion, and the pretext of "confession" for intercourse is familiar from Boccaccio and others. [*MED,* "hod," provides no help.]

hoote. In the "General Prologue" (A 97), Chaucer tells us that the Squire gets no sleep, so "hoote he lovede." The idea of a rise in temperature during lovemaking (or thinking about it) is of course not dead today.

Troilus speaks to Pandarus (III. 1650) after his first night with Criseyde, admitting that "I hadde it nevere half so hote as now," so it is clear that Chaucer thought of it as an emotion that could both precede and follow the actual lovemaking. Later when things are desperate and it is apparent that Criseyde must leave Troy, Pandarus cannot understand why Troilus will not take her away by force. To be sure, such an act would compromise her honor—but *he* (Pandarus) would do it "hadde ich it so hoote" (IV. 583) , he exclaims.

In the *Legend of Good Women* (G-Text, 260) , the God of Love berates Chaucer: the poet, he says, thinks a man is a fool who "loveth paramours, to harde and hote." He is right: Chaucer was responsible for many tales that showed that it was unwise to love too deeply.

After Absolon has kissed Alisoun's "nether ye" his "hoote love" is "coold and all yqueynt" ("Miller's Tale," A 3754) . See also **queynt.**

The temperature of erotic emotion can be destructive indeed. Satan makes a young knight to "love hire [Custance] so hoote" that he frames her for murder ("Man of Law's Tale," B 586). And in *Troilus and Criseyde* (I. 445) , the hero's love for the Trojan widow even at this early stage is a "hote fir." See **fyr.** [*MED,* 3 (b) inflamed with sexual desire.]

hor. A whore. There are no occurrences in Chaucer's works except for the (doubtful) translation of the *Romaunt of the Rose* (7033) where we have "horis." [*MED,* "hor (e) ," *n.* (2) , la (a) whore; (b) woman who commits fornication or adultery; citations from *a.* 1225 on.]

horn. Baum suggests that in the "Manciple's Tale" (H 90) , when the Cook "pouped in this horn," the reference is to (1) drinking horn and (2) musical instrument—he belched and gulped, or regurgitated. He is drunk, we recall. Baugh glosses the passage as "has taken a gulp." But surely there is another possible meaning for "horn": the fundament, the rectum—that musical instrument, which, along with his voice, each man has. If this third meaning is present, "pouped" means farted, as it still does today. "Powped" in the "Nun's Priest's Tale" (B 4589) is innocent, by the way, though it refers to musical instruments—the "bemes" (trumpets) in which they "blewe and powped."

One might expect a great many references in Chaucer to horns as evidence of cuckoldry, since there are so many such allusions in later literature. Though the idea was current, there are very few such references. *Troilus and Criseyde* (I. 300) probably has the innuendo. The hero says he "was tho glad his hornes in to shrinke," that is, like a snail. But surely there is some foreshadowing of eventual cuckoldry too. There is irony perhaps when Troilus apostrophizes the moon (V. 650): "Ywis, whan thow art horned newe, / I shal be glad, if al the world be trewe!" Of course all the world is *not* true, including Criseyde, and Troilus only means that he will welcome the new moon because then his beloved will soon return. However, the hint of the cuckold's horns is almost certainly present. [*MED,* 1c (b) the horn of the cuckold. *OED,* "poop," $v.^1$ to make an abrupt sound as by blowing a horn . . . to gulp in drinking; b. cites an eighteenth-century quotation, which admits that it means to break wind backward softly.]

hors. Chaucer uses horses as indices to the social status of his Pilgrims in the "General Prologue," as one would use models of automobiles today. See the variety of mounts in A 74, 94, 168, 469, and 615.

Horses have no sexual significance except for the comparison of the Pardoner to a **geldyng** or a mare, and possibly the *Legend of Good Women* (1198). Dido is riding to the ill-fated hunt "uppon a thikke palfrey, paper-whit, / With sadel red, enbrouded with delyt." The details suggest a phallus, but perhaps only in the overheated context. See the two works cited from the *MED* under **juste.** [*MED* gives no help.]

hote. See **hoote.**

hunt. The Monk, whose lecherous propensities are established fully elsewhere, is discriminating, like the Wife of Bath, in the Scripture of which he approves. See "General Prologue" (A 177): "He yaf nat of that text a pulled hen, / That seith that hunters ben nat hooly men." As the entry under **hare** shows, the hunt was symbolic of sexual pursuit. It is therefore doubly ironic (though hardly any critic or reader notices it) that after the Monk has told so many dreary "tragedies," the Host interrupts to ask for "somwhat of huntyng" ("Nun's Priest's Tale," B

3995), and the Monk answers: "I have no lust to pleye."
See **lust, pleye,** and **priken** (along with **hare**) to appre-
ciate this interesting cluster. There is a whiff of the erotic
in the wind. The Monk, a lecher, has told his dull tales;
he has been reprimanded by the Host—he knows plenty
of salacious ("hunting") stories, but because he is spite-
ful, vengeful, or proud, he refuses to tell them. He plays
out the role, in other words, of his Order, with its reputation for sobriety and learning.

For Huppé and Robertson (p. 49), the hunt is of course
symbolic of a Christian myth in which the Hunter-God
chases after souls. I would maintain that there is really
very little of this sort of thing in Chaucer, at least on the
levels that we have been exploring. In the *Book of the
Duchess* (540), for example, the curious but rather insensitive poet tries to find something to say to the Man in
Black that will elicit from him more information about
his lonely mourning. " 'Sir,' quod I, 'this game is doon. /
I holde that this hert be goon.' " The remark is ironic on
two levels: (1) the Man in Black's heart is gone, lost to
his beloved; and (2) the "hert" herself, the fair Blanche,
is dead, though the poet does not know it at this point.
The familiar hart-heart pun is employed. Later in the
poem, the "hert-huntyng" ends just as the Man in Black
has finished his tale of the wooing, winning, and death
of the Fair White. The paranomasia is powerful here—
a rare use of the pun for a sober, serious purpose. It looks
forward to Shakespeare, who often uses equivoques in his
most moving poetry.

The ultimate source of the elaborate sexual hunt was
Ovid's account of Venus and Adonis in the *Meta-
morphoses;* but Vergil also gave Chaucer some material
of the same kind. In the *Legend of Good Women* (1191),
Dido arranges the chase, and she is obviously erotically
aroused: "An huntyng wol this lusty freshe queene, / So
priketh hire this newe joly wo." It is likely that the hunt-
sex metaphor is extended further (through 1213) with
"The herde of hertes founden is anon, / With 'Hay! go
bet! pryke thow! lat gon, lat gon!' " Here is the hart-heart
pun again. Consider too **fressh, hors, joly, lust, priken,**

Fig. 5. *Ivory mirror-case (15th c. ?) representing a couple on a literal and symbolic hunt; the seduction is also reflected in the dog catching the hare. Victoria and Albert Museum, London.*

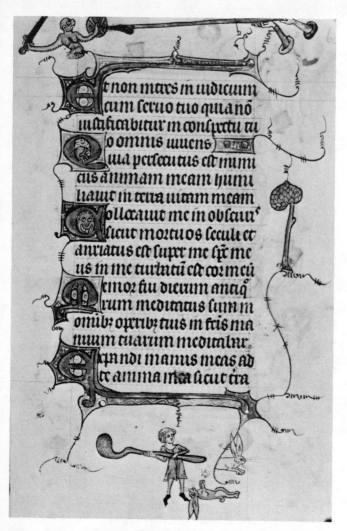

t non mors in iudicium
cum scruo tuo quia nō
iustificabitur in conspectu tu
o omnis uiuens
qua persecutus est inimi
cus animam meam humi
liauit in terra uitam meam
collocauit me in obscuris
sicut mortuos seculi et
anxiatus est super me spē me
us in me turbatum est cor meum
kmor fui dierum antiq
rum meditatus sum in
omnibz opribz tuis in fris ma
nuum tuarum meditabar
expandi manus meas ad
te anima mea sicut terra

Fig. 6. *Hunter slaying the symbolic hare with a huge phallic club. British Museum, London, Addit. MS 36684 (14th c.), fol. 69r.*

and see Figures 5 and 6. [*MED* gives no support. In his edition of *Piers Plowman,* Skeat mentions the hart-heart pun in II. 482.]

husbonde. Dido takes Aeneas (*Legend of Good Women,* 1238) in the rainstorm for her "husbonde" for life—a strange way of putting it, or so it seems to modern tastes, since this is the most famous of all unwedded liaisons. See **maydenhed.** Skeat points out, by the way, that the passage is not in the *Aeneid* but is original with Chaucer. [*MED,* "housbond (e) ," 1 (a) also used figuratively.]

hyppes. See **buttok.**

I

idleness. See **idelnesse.**

in. See **plesaunce, inne.**

incest. Braddy (pp. 214–215) finds that Chaucer is disgusted by incest, yet hints at it in the relationship between Pandarus and Criseyde, his niece (especially in III. 1574 ff.) . Criseyde hides her face under the bed sheet and blushes. Her uncle pries underneath and

> *With that his arm al sodeynly he thriste*
> *Under hire nekke, and at the laste hire kyste.*
> *I passe al that which chargeth nought to seye.*
> *What! God foryaf his deth, and she al so*
> *Foryaf, and with here uncle gan to pleye,*
> *For other cause was ther noon than so.*

Readers of the *Troilus* have always been a little alarmed at the proximity of Pandarus to the fornicating couple in Book III, during the rainstorm. Now we can perhaps understand this complex (and perhaps not wholly contemptible) character a little better. See **pley.**

The most puzzling suggestion of incest occurs just as the "Squire's Tale" is broken off—and many critics think that this unpleasant theme is the reason for the in-

terruption. The Squire is about to begin his Pars Tercia
(F 667); not much has happened in the first two parts,
and he promises to tell of "Cambalo, / That faught in
lystes with the bretheren two / For Canacee er that he
myghte hire wynne." By twisting the syntax, we can make
"faught . . . for" to mean that Cambalo is his sister's
champion. The last phrase, however, is harder to explain
away. The story was known to be incestuous, as the
reference in the "Man of Law's Tale" (B 78) reminds us:
the speaker expresses horror over Canacee's story, "that
loved hir owene brother synfully." See also **maydenhed**.

For Chaucer's audience, Nero represents a complex of
lusts ("Monk's Tale," B 3672), including the fact that he
"by his suster lay." But it is surely not blameworthy in
Chaunticleer that he had seven hens to do him "plesaunce," which (who?) were also "his sustres and his paramours" ("Nun's Priest's Tale," B 4057).

The pulpit opinion on these matters is summed up by
Parson (I 884), who says that one of the reasons to flee
adultery is that those who get involved "unwar . . .
synnen with hire owene kynrede." He deals with the matter fully—those who engaged in this sort of indiscrimi-
nate and consanguineous copulation are likened to
"houndes" (I 906). In *his* sermon (a much better one),
the Pardoner (C 485) reminds us of "dronken Looth [Lot,
who] unkyndely, / Lay by his doghtres two, unwityngly."
In Chaucer's time, and much later, the principal meaning
of "unkind" was "unnatural." [*OED*, 1.b. reminds us that
there could be a crime of spiritual incest: marriage or
sexual connection between persons related by spiritual
affinity, or with a person under a vow of chastity, etc. The
term was also used for the holding of two benefices, one
of which depends on the collation of the other.]

incubus. The Wife of Bath (D 880) says that nowadays "ther
is noon oother incubus but he"—that is, the "lymytour,"
the friar. The belief was that demons came to maidens in
the night, lay with them (or *on* them as the etymology of
the word suggests), and engendered children. It was an
ingenious explanation for unwed motherhood. There was
also a complementary creature, the "succubus," which lay

under. It is probably of the "incubus" of which the miller's wife is thinking when she cries out in the glorious confusion at the end of the "Reeve's Tale" (A 4288) : "the feend is on me falle." Actually it is the clerk John. [*MED*, (a) provides citations from 1200 on, both in the sense of a spirit that had intercourse with a female and in the general sense of a bad dream.]

inne. There is a sporting chance that in *Troilus and Criseyde* (V. 1519) "inne" means "in her vagina" in the line: "This Diomede is inne, and thow art oute." The speaker is Troilus' sister Cassandra who, as everybody knows, could not lie, although she was not believed as a prophetess. [*MED*, "in," *adv.*, 1 (b) in figurative context, including "ben stopen in," to be in an advanced stage of loving.]

instrument. Alison of Bath calls her husband's "member" his "sely instrument," that is, his blessed penis (D 132). She is ready to use her own "instrument / As frely as my Makere hath it sent" (D 149), which is a good example of the Wife's pious gratitude. [*MED*, 2 (a) cites both D 132 and 149; later citations refer to both penis and vagina; also to a bull's "stoon," testicle.]

J

jape. As both noun and verb, it usually has the meaning of joke, deceive (deceit), or ridicule. Not surprisingly, however, the Wife of Bath gives us the clearest example of the word's obscene meaning—to copulate (with). Alison addresses her husband (D 239 ff.) :

> *What dostow at my neighebores hous?*
> *Is she so fair? artow so amorous?*
> *What rowne [whisper] ye with oure mayde? Benedicite!*
> *Sire olde lecchoure, lat thy japes be!*

Here the word subsumes two neutral meanings (jokes, deceits), along with the bawdy one (copulations).

In several of Chaucer's *fabliaux,* "jape" is likely to carry this same low sense. The clever clerk John ("Reeve's Tale," A 4207) lies in bed bemoaning his loneliness, while his companion Aleyn is in bed with the miller's daughter: ". . . when this jape is tald another day, / I sal been halde a daf [fool], a cokenay!" [*q.v.*]. Again, all three meanings are present. A few lines earlier (A 4201), he has complained that his being alone, while Aleyn has a partner to sleep with, is a "wikked jape," a phrase that prepares us for the unmistakable innuendo of A 4207, if it does nothing else.

At the end of the "Miller's Tale" (A 3842), the people ridicule the carpenter. He is not only a cuckold, but he has broken his arm in the fall from the ceiling. They "turned al his harm unto a jape." The sense is "a joke," of course, but there is a suggestion of "intercourse," too. The honest sense is the only one earlier in the same tale (A 3390): where Alisoun says she will turn Absolon's "ernest . . . til a jape"; and where Chaucer says that Nicholas "thoughte he wolde amenden al the jape" (A 3799) and make his absurd rival kiss *his* "ers" (*q.v.*) too.

Two of the Pilgrims use the word with multileveled significances in their on-the-spot literary evaluations. The Host comments on the "Shipman's Tale" (B 1629) with: "A ha! felawes! beth ware of swich a jape!" In the story, the monk Daun John has "japed" the merchant in three ways: he has played a good joke on him; he has cheated him out of a hundred francs; and he has cuckolded him with his promiscuous wife. Similarly, the Cook gives us his critical analysis of the "Reeve's Tale" (A 4338) by using "jape" in the same three senses. The miller is duped—"he hadde a jape of malice in the derk," when both his wife and his daughter are "swyved," under his very nose.

Chaucer uses the word more subtly in the "Friar's Tale," (D 1440): the summoner admits he must live by extortion; his victims are prostitutes and panders, among others. He callously exclaims: "Ne of swiche japes wol I nat be shryven." The obvious sense is "deceits," but the summoner's sexual involvement makes the obscene sense come close to the surface too.

The occurrence of the word in the "Pardoner's Tale" (C 319) is powerfully effective. The Host encourages the Pardoner to tell his tale: " 'Thou beel amy [*q.v.*], thou Pardoner,' he sayde, / 'Telle us som myrthe or japes right anon.' " It is doubly ironic: (1) the "Tale" is hardly a "myrthe" or joke; rather, it is a superb but grim *exemplum* warning us against excesses; (2) the gelding Pardoner can have only ironic relationships with "japes" in the sense of "copulations," and of course the Host is well aware of this. The irony is reinforced, perhaps, by the lines about the Pardoner in the "General Prologue" (A 705): "with feyned flaterye and japes, / He made the person [parson] and the peple his apes."

The apes-japes rhyme is often the only excuse for appearance of the latter word, however (e.g., "Nun's Priest's Tale," B 4281; *House of Fame,* 1805; *Romaunt of the Rose,* 6835). One suspects, too, that sometimes Chaucer uses the formula "jape . . . pleye" without any thought of the bawdy meanings attached to either word (for instance, "Merchant's Tale," D 1389; "Manciple's Tale," H 4; *Troilus and Criseyde,* V. 509). He also uses the word in a formula to describe Pandarus, but here it has a clear narrative function, revealing something about the character that is important. When the cynical go-between cannot think of a dignified response, he will begin to "jape," to joke, with Troilus or with his niece (II. 943, 1096, 1164; III. 555).

This long erotic poem does have some "japes" with suggestive overtones, however. Early in the story (I. 531), Troilus worries that his hidden sorrow will be bruited abroad; if it is, "I shal byjaped ben"—(1) ridiculed; (2) "screwed," just as in the vulgar modern English expression. This same rude sense can also be found in the cynical remark in the last book (V. 1134), "Fortune hem bothe [the two lovers] thenketh for to jape!" The word has more complex meanings, perhaps: Pandarus teases Criseyde, and she accuses him of practicing "some jape" on her (II. 130). As is frequently true, the reader suspects that the heroine is

deliberately using "jape" in a double sense. Pandarus re-
torts (II. 140) : "I jape nought, as evere have I joye." He
is a self-confessed unsuccessful lover; consequently the
word has a wry, ironic significance. When Pandarus arranges for Troilus to "jape" Criseyde in his house, the
hero is overwhelmed with gratitude. He promises his
friend his sisters (see **suster**), "whether this servise a
shame be or a jape" (III. 408). See **serve,** too.

In the *Legend of Good Women* (1699), Chaucer says
that Tarquin "gan for to jape, for he was lyght of tonge"
—harmless enough, but perhaps a foreshadowing of the
cruel "jape" (rape) he will play on Lucrece.

The Parson is at his sourest when he cites the authority
of St. Paul, who frowned on joking (I 650) : "japeres" who
make people laugh at their "japerie" are committing a sin;
the Apostle forbids such "japes." Earlier in his exhaustive
treatise on the Seven Deadly Sins, the Parson advises his
listeners to come to Confession earnestly, not as "japere[s]"
(I 88).

A final innocent derivative of "jape" should be mentioned; even though it is not bawdy (and usually in
Chaucer the word is not), it is vigorous and amusing.
Dame Philosophy describes the prophecies of Tiresias,
which he claims will either come true or not. Such
prophesying is "japeworthi," she says (*Boece,* V, Prosa
3. 132), as indeed it is. [*MED,* "jape," *n.,* 2 (c) bawdiness
(cites "Parson's Tale," I 651) ; "japen," *v.,* 3 to have sexual
intercourse with (citations from 1400, but nothing from
Chaucer).]

jolif. See **joly.**

joly. In Modern English this word has lost all suggestion of
sex, but in Chaucer it almost always is associated with the
play between the sexes. As the *MED* points out, in the
generation just before Chaucer the religious writer Richard Rolle equated "iolife" and "lechurs" (i.e., lecherous).
Rarely, indeed, can one say with assurance that Middle
English "joly" and its derivatives do *not* have obscene
significance. One such occurrence is, however, to be found
in the "Reeve's Tale" (A 3931) where Chaucer tells us
that the miller carries a "joly poppere" (dagger).

As a word with sexual innuendo, "joly" is often linked in Chaucer's verse with other bawdy terms—e.g., **daunce, gay, light,** and **lust**—as doublets. For instance, in the "Miller's Tale" (A 3339), Chaucer describes Absolon "that jolif was and gay." The word "joly" is, indeed, used seven times in this tale in lines that refer to the absurd amorous clerk.

Birds, those charming "smale foules" who change their mates on Valentine's Day, are often described as "joly" too. Oddly, Chaucer does not seem to apply the term to the **sparwe,** but he frequently uses it for the jay and the "pye" (e.g., in the "Wife of Bath's Prologue" [D 456], she recalls herself in her youth, with her fourth husband: "I was yong and ful of ragerye [see **rage**], / Stibourn and strong, and joly as a pye").

One of the (wrong) answers given to the question in the Wife's "Tale" (What do women most desire?) is "jolynesse" (D 926), which occurs along with "lust abedde" (*q.v.*). The youthful mating season, spring or May, is also called "joly" many times. It is "joly Veer" in *Troilus and Criseyde* (I. 157, variant); the "joly time of May" in the *Legend of Good Women* (G 36, also F 176). In the *Romaunt of the Rose,* the word occurs frequently: the God of Love Himself is "jolyf and lyght" (1003).

Three or four times Chaucer uses erotic oxymorons involving "joly." In *Troilus and Criseyde* (II. 1099), Pandarus delivers Troilus' letter to Criseyde, saying that he himself is suffering from lovesickness: "I have a joly wo, a lusty sorwe." Criseyde sees through this smoke screen, with its rhetorical excesses (her uncle is not really suffering) and responds (1105): "Tel us youre joly wo and youre penaunce. / How ferforth be ye put in loves daunce?" See **daunce.** That other tragic lover, Dido, also suffers from "joly wo" (*Legend of Good Women,* 1192, where it is associated with **priken**).

These samples show that "joly" does not mean simply "happy" when we read about the two lusty Cambridge scholars in the "Reeve's Tale" (A 4232) who spend the night with their host's wife and daughter: "This joly lyf han thise two clerkes lad / Til that the thridde cok bigan

to synge." [*MED*, "joli," 2 (c) amorous, lecherous; of animals: ready to mate; (d) "joli wo" . . . a pleasing
pain? amorous woe?]

jurdones. Jordans, chamber pots. They, along with the Physician's "urynals," are blessed by the Host ("Pardoner's
Tale," C 305). Harry Bailly is a great one for blessing
inappropriate objects (e.g., see **stoon**). Both these vessels
were used by doctors for urine and fecal specimens, the
analysis of which made up a large measure of their diag-
nostic practices. See Figure 9. [*MED* traces the word to
Latin *Jordanes;* the *OED* is uncertain. Partridge says
confidently that the name comes from the River Jordan.]

juste. Joust—a familiar euphemism or substitute term for
coition. (In Modern English, by the way, the word should
be pronounced as if it were spelled "just," but you will
find only a handful of professors of medieval literature
who do the right thing.)

In the "General Prologue" (A 96), Chaucer says that
the Squire can "juste and eek daunce," the first example
of the common "cluster" of these two words. On the literal
level, of course they are associated: dancing and jousting
were the sports of gentlemen. But the same is true of their
bawdy connotations, both of which naturally mean intercourse.

At the beginning of Part Four of that most genial of
romances, told by the Squire's father, the "Knight's Tale"
(A 2483), occurs a passage that should be quoted in its
entirety, to give the reader the proper flavor of festal
sublimity (to borrow a term from C. S. Lewis):

> *Greet was the feeste in Atthenes that day,*
> *And eek the lusty seson of that May*
> *Made every wight to been in swich plesaunce*
> *That al that Monday justen they and daunce,*
> *And spenden it in Venus heigh servyse.*

The cluster of "juste," "daunce," and "servyse" is gracious
but distinctly sexual. Just in the next line there is a reference to the necessity that they should "ryse": let the

reader decide for himself if we have an allusion to an erection here. I do not think so.

After a two-year absence, Arveragus returns to his wife Dorigen and "daunceth, justeth, maketh hire good cheere" ("Franklin's Tale," F 1098), as it is meet he should. The conjunction of the two words "juste" and "daunce" once again makes it more likely that there is a double meaning. Then a strange thing happens, for the magician shows Arveragus a vision in which there is a reflection of this same "rite" of dance and tourney. There are "knyghtes justyng in a playn; / And after this he dide hym swich plesaunce / That he hym shewed his lady on a daunce, / On which hymself he daunced, as hym thoughte" (F 1198). Here are two levels of erotic experience, one real, the other magical; each supports and intensifies the other.

In *Troilus and Criseyde* (III. 1718), Chaucer summarizes the lovers' frequent lovemakings, describing a Troilus who "spendeth, jousteth, maketh festeynges; / He yeveth frely ofte. . . ." The acts are literal, but unmistakably sexual too. See **spendeth,** however, where the evidence for erotic meaning is weakest.

Finally we return to the type of clandestine lovers, Dido and Aeneas, *Legend of Good Women* (1274): Aeneas would "justen" for her—literally, of course, but figuratively too—especially because of the proximity of "daunces" (1269). See also **hors.** [*MED*, "justen," 3 (b) to be married, enter into a union; 2 (d) *fig.* to copulate. Cites (*ca.* 1460) *My fayr lady,* p. 204: "Hire cote armure is duskyd reed, / With a boordure as blak as sabyl, / A pavys (convex shield—i.e., mons veneris) or a terget for a sperys heed. . . . For who shalle justyn in that stabyl, / But he shodde he is not sene," which is a very complicated "icon" for the female organ and for sexual congress. Also cited is (*a.* 1425) *At the northe,* 11: "I leyde my ware, a bogeler (buckler—again the mons veneris) brode, & euer he . . . smote by syde . . . shalle ther neuer man justy ther-at but yf he can hyt smyte," another extended sexual double entendre, where "iusty . . . smyte" means

to copulate and have an orgasm. This is Robbins' Poem
No. 30, which he entitles "Silver White." With Middle
English "smyte," cf. Shakespeare's "hit it," as recorded by
Partridge. Though very late (1554), Lindsay's *Ane Satire
of the Thrie Estaitis* (545) shows the persistence of the
indecent metaphor when Wantones suggests to Hameli-
ness that they "go iunne our justing Lumis" (go join our
jousting tools, have intercourse). The figure of jousting
was not always erotic in Middle English poetry; cf. *Piers
Plowman* (C-Text, XXI. 184) where Peace tells Righteous-
ness how they will respond at the Harrowing of Hell: "ich
shal daunce ther-to—do al-so thow, suster! / For Iesus
Iousted wel. Ioye by-gynneth to dawen." Here Christ's
"jousting" is associated with the dancing of the two allegorical figures.]

k

kiss. The custom of pressing lips together plays many narrative roles in Chaucer. First is the familiar greeting, prac-
ticed particularly among the English in former times—a
casual gesture of recognition (like hat-tipping) or of concluding an agreement (like shaking hands). When the
friar greets the wife of his good friend Thomas in the
"Summoner's Tale" (D 1804) with a kiss, we are to take
no erotic notice of it. It is, however, a little too familiar
when the friar also "chirketh as a sparwe." See **sparwe.**

Such kissings and chirkings could have more obvious
seductive and illicit meanings—as in the "Shipman's Tale"
(B 1331) when the monk and the merchant's wife agree
not to betray each other's confidences and seal the com-
pact: "and heerupon they kiste." When the seduction becomes overt (1393), this phrase is changed to
"kiste hire ofte," after a hard embrace.

The kiss of greeting took place even between males, as
it still does in some Latin countries today: see *Troilus and
Criseyde* (V. 77), Troilus and Antenor. But in Chaucer

this sort of greeting never develops into anything homosexual.

The kiss between lovers can show dramatic differences —i.e., can be used cleverly as a dramatic device. In the bridal bed, the repulsive Januarie, with a bristly face like a dogfish, "kisseth hire [May] ful ofte" ("Merchant's Tale," E 1823). Chaucer forces us to recognize how repulsive this is to the young bride. After the deception and the intercourse in the pear tree, Januarie's suspicions are easily allayed. He is a stupid old man; or perhaps he *wants* to believe the young lovers' outrageous lies. The language is almost the same as we had earlier in the description of the wedding night (E 2413): "He kisseth hire, and clippeth hire ful ofte, / And on hire wombe he stroketh hire ful softe." Chaucer does the same thing in changing pace and repeating language in the "Shipman's Tale"; see Introduction, p. 21. See also **myrthe.**

By arranging the order of events (including a kiss) in an amusing way in the "Miller's Tale" (A 3305), Chaucer tells us something important about the progress of the seduction. Nicholas first seizes the delectable Alisoun by the "queynte"; then he "thakked hire aboute the lendes" (*q.v.*); and *then* "he kiste hire sweete." The pattern is not what is advocated for the Courtly Lover.

But those two Courtly Lovers Troilus and Criseyde break the rules too (III. 182). As she warms to him, she invites him to "lustinesse"; then: "and hym in armes took, and gan hym kisse"—i.e., *she* takes the initiative. As the tempo increases in Book III, one can follow it by watching, and listening to, the kisses (972, 1129, 1252, 1275, 1350, 1353, 1403, and 1519). They kiss "a thousand tyme" (1252); the osculation continues, but more slowly, dying out like a lover's sigh of satisfaction. When they part, there is of course plenty of kissing again (IV. 1131, 1161, 1219); and after Criseyde leaves, there is the silly business of Troilus wanting to kiss the "colde doores" of her house (V. 551). Silly but psychologically perfect.

Equally, or rather utterly, silly are those star-crossed lovers Pyramus and Thisbe (*Legend of Good Women*, 768) who "kysse" the wall that separates them (Shakespeare does more with this motif in *A Midsummer Night's Dream* than does Chaucer) .

A strange passage occurs in the translation of the *Romaunt of the Rose* (1999) : the Lover is invited to do the God of Love homage, "and sithe [then] kisse thou shalt my mouth." If nothing else, the sensuality is a little disconcerting.

Finally we have the kiss of peace, the *pax*. After the terrible violence between the Host and Pardoner, the Knight persuades them to kiss; and, sure enough: "anon they kiste, and ryden forth hir weye" (C 968) . No reader is ever satisfied, however, that the peace symbolized by this kiss was genuine or lasting. [*OED* shows that the gesture was used for nonerotic purposes. See also the Confession of Luxurie from *Piers Plowman* under **likyng**. The misdirected kiss of the "Miller's Tale" (A 3734) is not unique to Chaucer. In Robbins' Poem No. 36, an equally disdainful maiden shows her contempt for her lover in exactly the same way: "Whan she hym at the wyndow wyst, / She torned out her ars & that he kyst" (26) . It might, of course, be simply an imitation of the famous incident from the *Tales*. Tatlock (p. 229) finds Middle English puns on "cyssan" (kiss) and "cyst" (virtue) , but I have been unable to trace the latter. Legman (p. 189) discusses "kiss" as a metaphor for intercourse.]

knyf. In the "General Prologue" (A 233) , Chaucer tells us that the Friar carries "knyves and pynnes" as presents for the "faire wyves" of his district. They are literal gifts, and probably of considerable value in those days before mass production of metal objects.

Does the knife in Chaucer suggest a phallus, here or elsewhere? I cannot say for sure, but consider the "Merchant's Tale" (E 1840) where Januarie tells his young wife on their wedding night that a man may do no sin with his own wife "ne hurte hymselven with his owene knyf." Januarie perhaps means his own penis. He is obsessed with it and with the sex act generally, though his performance is pitiful.

The Parson (I 858) shows how the connection between intercourse and knife was made. The good padre uses homely language to drive his point home: "And for that many man weneth that he may nat synne, for no likerous-nesse that he dooth with his wyf, certes, that opinion is fals. God woot, a man may sleen hymself with his owene knyf, and make hymselve dronken of his owene tonne" (knife = penis, tun = scrotum?) .

When the Host's wife Goodelief cries out to him ("Monk's Tale," B 3096) : "By corpus bones, I wol have thy knyf, / And thou shalt have my distaf and go spynne," it becomes clearer that the knife (which stood "astrout"—sticking out before the bodies of the young gallants who carried them) probably has phallic significance. [*OED* and *MED* offer no help. Because of Skeat's squeamishness, one cannot be sure what he made of the "pissares longe knyues" of *Piers Plowman* (C-Text, XXIII. 219). His note says: "The knife itself had what was probably a cant name" and refers to (B-Text, XV. 121) "ballokknyf," i.e., "balls-knife." See piss.]

kynrede. See incest.

L

labour. Sometimes copulation is hard work, and Chaucer does not hesitate to tell us when it is. In the "Merchant's Tale" (E 1842) , we naturally find it. Old Januarie "laboureth" all night at his lovemaking—to no avail. On the morn, his wife May finds his prowess "nat worth a bene." The old man tries too hard, perhaps—tries to be too coltish (see coltes tooth) . After the wedding night, May stays in her chamber until the fourth day: "For every labour somtyme moot han reste" (E 1862) —suggesting that she too is weary? Or, more likely, bored? Perhaps Chaucer suggests that Januarie returns each day, or night, for four days, though this seems hardly plausible. (One

MS reads "laborer" for "labour," which makes better sense; but as Baugh points out, "labour" has overwhelming MS authority.)

In the "Shipman's Tale" (B 1298), Daun John very boldly suggests that his host's wife is pale because she has been kept up by her husband: he "hath yow laboured sith the nyght bigan." It may have been true, but if so it was not enough to incapacitate the merchant's wife, who is soon enough in bed with the friar himself. See also **swynke.** [Neither *MED* nor *OED* includes any obscene senses.]

lanterne. Troilus apostrophizes Criseyde's empty house (V. 543): "O thow lanterne of which queynt [quenched] is the light." It can be no coincidence that we have here, first, one of Chaucer's familiar double entendres involving **queynt;** and, second, that we also have the reassuring folk wisdom of the candle and the lantern. See **candle.** What seemed at first to be a bit of sentimental silliness on the hero's part is still silly, but it is a very erotic memory, as Chaucer's cluster of suggestive words shows. [*MED,* 4 (d) house empty of someone loved; the *Troilus* passage is the only citation.]

lappe. Canacee holds her "lappe abroad" to catch the falcon when it falls from its tree, weak from wounds and exhaustion, in the "Squire's Tale" (F 441). At first one wonders if there might be some dim and confused sexual innuendo in this dim and confused tale. But no: it simply means a fold of her garment. However, in some of Chaucer's audience, the line would have aroused a smirk, I think, since the word also meant the female pudendum.

We get some funny possibilities, then, in *Troilus and Criseyde* (III. 59) when Pandarus leads Criseyde by the "lappe" to Troilus. The innuendos (by their absence!) are even funnier when, as Pandarus is about to leave, Criseyde catches *him* by the "lappe" (II. 448); and when the good uncle of the heroine leads Troilus to *her,* once again by the "lappe" (III. 742). Pretty clearly, one must consider the setting of these bawdy references. [*OED,* "lap," *sb.*[1] 1. flap, lappet; 2. b. a fold of flesh or skin; occasionally the female pudendum. The earliest citation for this last meaning is 1398, which means that it was just coming in while Chaucer was composing the *Tales*. In 1615, the sense was still current, since we are told that the clitoris is "placed in the height of the lap." *MED*, 6a (b) the female pudendum; *pl.* "lappes," the lips of the pudendum?]

large. This word means, generally, "generous," and in the "Shipman's Tale" (B 1621) it means this too. The merchant tells his wife not to be so large in his absence. However, the circumstances give the word a second meaning, since the wife has had a liaison (for 100 francs) with the good friar Daun John. So the meanings are (1) generous with my money (and the merchant loses 100 francs in the complicated deal); and (2) generous with your body to others, though of course here the merchant speaks with unconscious irony of which only the reader is aware. [*MED*, 1b overgenerous; cites B 1621.]

launcegay. This was a particular kind of lance, the exact nature of which we do not know. It has been suggested that it is an appropriate weapon for Sir Thopas to carry on his forays against three-headed giants, but I do not believe that its appropriateness has been demonstrated. Edith Rickert (p. 146, *n.*) quotes Manly and tells us that it was a light, slender lance—apparently of Arabian or Moorish origin.

In any event, Williams (p. 148) finds possible homosexual implications in Thopas' threat to pierce the giant's "mawe" (B 2013) with his launcegay. Such an implication is very difficult to demonstrate. See **gay.** [*OED's* and *MED's* first citation (1383) is from an Act of Parliament during the reign of Richard II: "Le Roi defende que desoremes null homme chivache deinz la Roialme armez . . . ovesque lancegay" (the King forbids that from henceforth no man shall ride in the Realm armed . . . with a lancegay). This makes the weapon sound formidable enough. Chaucer is the second citation in both dictionaries.]

Launcelot. After all the magical devices, the Squire asks, who could give a proper account of all the strange dances and "subtil lookyng and dissymulynges / For drede of jalouse

mennes aperceyvynges." The answer is "No man but
Launcelot, and he is deed" ("Squire's Tale," F 287).
Launcelot was of course the epitome of the jealous, fur-
tive, and destructive lover. Note that he is "deed," whereas
Gawain (F 96) still lives in "Fairye" (fairyland), the
Avalon of Arthur.

In the "Nun's Priest's Tale" (B 4402), there is another
allusion to Launcelot: "This storie is also trewe, I un-
dertake, / As is the book of Launcelot de Lake, / That
wommen holde in ful grete reverence." Baugh says that
the reference has no relevance but as a comic aside. The
comedy is certainly there, though Baugh does not explain. Chaucer is referring ironically to the fact that (1)
everybody knew that the tales of Arthur were fables (not
a bawdy reference, of course) : (2) women have reverence
for the book because, like Pertelote, they dream of their
perfect lover, their Launcelot (her Chaunticleer). It is
therefore a hint at Pertelote's sexual nature—not, I think,
at Chaunticleer as a Launcelot-like adulterer, even though
he had seven wives. [*OED* has no entry.]

laxatyf. Defecatory comedy is not the subtlest, in Chaucer's
time or now. In the "Nun's Priest's Tale" (B 4133), Pertelote counsels her mate to take some "laxatyf" in order
to purge himself; he has a superfluity that has caused his
bad dream. He should complete the purge both "bynethe and eek above," i.e., shit and vomit. Pertelote is
wrong about the nature of the dream, by the way. [*OED*
uses Chaucer as the earliest citation.]

lay. To have intercourse with, as is familiar today. Baum thinks
that this sense is present in the "Manciple's Tale" (H 222)
where women of high and low birth are compared—those
that are free with their bodies: "Men leyn that oon as
lowe as lith that oother"; in the "Miller's Tale" (A 3269),
Alisoun is a "piggesnye" that any yeoman might wed, or
"any lord . . . leggen in his bedde"; and in the *Romaunt
of the Rose* (1421), which describes grassy banks "on
which men [*sic*] might his lemman leye." The association
of the word is, in all three quotations, with illicit love.

Baum neglects other possibilities. For instance, surely
the sexual sense is present in the lively scene where John

the clerk is having intercourse with his host's wife ("Reeve's Tale," A 4229) : "and on this goode wyf he leith on soore." And in the "Friar's Tale" (D 1358), the wenches report to the summoner who "lay by hem," where the word has the familiar biblical euphemistic sense. Thomas' wife in the "Summoner's Tale" (D 1828) uses the word in a different (more literal, but still clearly erotic) sense: she complains that in bed she will "over hym leye my leg outher myn arm," but she gets no "desport" out of him. Januarie ("Merchant's Tale," E 2394) says that he saw Damyan "leyn" by his wife—a very peculiar way of describing intercourse in a pear tree, but perhaps the only way the old man can explain what he means. In any event, Januarie is troubled with difficulties of vision. There are similar passages in the "Pardoner's Tale" (C 486) and the "Monk's Tale" (B 3470).

In the *Book of the Duchess* (1023), there is a peculiar passage that can only be an unfortunate ambiguity, which a more mature Chaucer would certainly have avoided. The Fair White—John of Gaunt's Blanche—would not give false encouragement to any man: "But if men wolde upon hir lye." "Men" is the impersonal pronoun that has disappeared in Modern English (analogous to French *on* or German *man*) ; we have to remind ourselves of this phenomenon in reading Chaucer, especially if we are beginners with Middle English. "Upon . . . lye" means to lie about her, to tell untruths about her. An erotic meaning, which seems (out of context) so obvious in this passage, is simply unthinkable at this point in the graceful *Book of the Duchess*. [*OED* has no erotic senses, though the general idea of violent attack is there.]

lecchour. Alison of Bath is, as usual, direct and clear when she addresses her husband as "Sire olde lecchour" (D 242) and accuses him of being interested in neighbors' wives. She also has plenty of other kinds of worldly wisdom and insight: drunken women have no defense, "this knowen lecchours by experience" (D 468), that is, they have tried out the drunken wenches, of course. See **experience**. It is another example of Alison's contrast between "experience" and "auctoritee." From "auctoritee," however, comes

another example in the "Wife of Bath's Prologue" (D
767), where her husband reads her horror stories about a
wife who slays her husband and then has intercourse
with her "lecchour" all night long in the same room where
the corpse of the husband lies on the floor "upright" (face
up).

The "Friar's Tale" (D 1310) tells us that the archdeacon punishes many kinds of wrongdoers, including
those guilty of usury and simony; but he does "grettest
wo" to "lecchours"—the general sexual offender. The
Friar tells us (D 1325) that the summoner in the story
uses "lecchours" (whom he pardons) as his informers
to lead him to others. He knows his "lecchour" along
with his "avowtier" and his "paramour" (qq.v.).

Chaucer (or the Merchant, perhaps) intrudes into the
narrative in the "Merchant's Tale" (E 2257) to point
out Damyan, waiting for May: "Lo, where he sit, the
lechour, in the tree!"

Finally there is Thopas, who, we are told, is no
"lechour," but is terribly "chaast" (B 1935). And insipid.
There may be something more to this unlecherous knight,
for which see **hair.** [*OED* has citations from *ca.* 1175 to
the present. Ultimately the word is associated with roots
meaning to lick.]

lecherous, -ly. The "General Prologue" tells us directly that the
Summoner is lecherous (A 626), despite (or because of)
his unappetizing appearance. Baum points out that in the
"Wife of Bath's Prologue" (D 466), we have a combination, punning powerfully, of lecherous and "likerous,"
which is not only a variant spelling but also carries the
implication of fondness for drink. The same spelling may
be found in the "Miller's Tale" (A 3244), but without
the secondary meaning. The same is true of the passage
from the "Manciple's Tale" (H 189) where were are
told that men "han evere a likerous appetit / On lowere
thyng to parfourne hire delit / Than on hire wyves"—an
unpleasant, naturalistic truth. Chaucer does not do much
with puns on "liker-" in the "Pardoner's Tale" (C 549):
"a lecherous thyng is wyn," but perhaps the association
was so common that the audience would "hear" it anyway.

The Parson, preaching against Superbia (Pride), once again finds fault with current fashions of dress: though faces may be chaste, garments may "notifie" others of "likerousnesse and pride" (I 429).

In Griselde's heart, there runs no likerous lust ("Clerk's Tale," E 214); some readers have wondered if there is any blood in that organ either.

Lecherousness is associated even with divine beings (in pagan literature, of course) and Chaucer takes occasion in the "Monk's Tale" (B 3747) to describe the wicked Holofernes, whom Fortune kissed "so likerously," only to betray him later, as was Fortune's habit. (Holofernes is from the Apocrypha; his lover Fortune is pagan.) In his short poem "The Former Age" (56), Chaucer refers to "Jupiter the likerous," naturally because of all his illicit loves about which Chaucer and his audience knew so much (from Ovid).

We know what happens to all these lecherous people. In the *Parliament of Fowls* (79), Chaucer paraphrases the *Somnium Scipionis,* part of which reveals that after their deaths "likerous folk" shall whirl about the earth forevermore in pain. [*OED* provides spellings that support the "lik-" "lech-" pun.]

lecherye. In one of her perhaps uncharacteristic learned allusions, the Wife of Bath (D 737) refers to Clytemnestra's "lecherye," not unlike her own with her fifth husband, with whom she was having an affair before the death of her fourth. Alison says that Venus has given her all her "likerousnesse" (D 611), and she is grateful. It is equated with "lust" (*q.v.*).

The "Merchant's Tale" (E 1451) has plenty of "marriage manual" advice. Husband and wife are told that to avoid "leccherye" they should yield to each other their debt (see **dette**)—simple and easily acceptable counsel.

Sometimes, but not very often, the word can have a neutral, nonsexual meaning, as in the "Physician's Tale" (C 84) where the homely advice is that a thief of venison who has left "his likerousnesse and al his olde craft" is your best forest keeper: the old idea of "to catch a thief. . . ." Baugh says the word here is simply equal to "appetite." But in the same tale when the plot to get Virginia begins, it is called "lecherie" (C 150) and there is no mistaking the erotic significance of the word this time. It is repeated (C 206), where the plan is "in lecherie to lyven."

There is nothing subtle in the story told by the physician: its lechery is simple. On the other hand, Chaucer can use the word and the idea for powerful ironic purposes. How bitter it is that the Pardoner, that lost soul, claims that all sorts of innocent people are likely to incite others to sin—"wafereres" (sellers of wafers), for instance, who will "kyndle and blow the fyr of lecherye" (C 481).

Zenobia, who sleeps with her husband only to get a child ("Monk's Tale," B 3483), considers all intercourse that is done for pleasure as "lecherie and shame." It would do her good to read something like the "Manciple's Tale" (H 259), where the telltale crow describes for Phebus how his wife and her "leman" have "doon hire [their] lecherye. . . . For on thy bed thy wyf I saugh hym swyve," which is clear enough. [OED, habitual indulgence of lust. MED, 1a (a) includes sexual intercourse in marriage for purposes other than that of begetting children.]

leith. See **lay.**

lemman. See also **wench.** There is always an aura of the illicit and the delicious around this word, which means something more delectable than does "mistress." Good fortune has smiled upon the miller's daughter in the "Reeve's Tale" (A 4240), with her round, high breasts and her broad hips, when she is in bed with a vigorous and attractive young university student. "Deere lemman," she calls him, and again "goode lemman" (A 4247).

In the "Man of Law's Tale" (B 917) the "lemman" is again a male lover and again the act is extramarital, as is true in the "Manciple's Tale" (H 204), and where Phebus' wife sends for her "lemman" (H 238). The Manciple (or Chaucer) appears shocked (H 205): "Hir lemman? Certes, this is a knavyssh speche! / Foryeveth it me, and that I yow beseche."

These are men, but most of the "lemmans" in Chaucer

are females—as for instance Dalida (Sampson's) alluded to by the Wife of Bath (D 722), and also in the "Monk's Tale" (B 3253). The smug friar in the "Summoner's Tale" (D 1998) cautions Thomas against striving (arguing—and thus producing wrath, the Deadly Sin of which the friar himself is later so patently guilty) either with wives or "lemmans." To this confessor, the "striving" was more culpable than the existence of any "lemman."

In the *Legend of Good Women* (1772), Tarquin swears that willy-nilly Lucrece will his "leman" be, even if force is necessary; and, as everyone knows, it was needed to bring her to bed.

Finally, there is Thopas: the gentle knight has dreamed all night that an elf-queen will be his "lemman" (B 1978), a fantasy (*q.v.*) that is never fulfilled, of course. See **hair**. [*OED* refers to illicit lovers of both sexes and to one's marital partner (a sense that Chaucer does not seem to use).]

lendes. Loins or (possibly) buttocks; at any rate, on a svelte creature like Alisoun in the "Miller's Tale" (A 3237), something very attractive. In this line, Chaucer tells us that Alisoun wears a white "barmclooth" (apron) upon her "lendes." The detail seems pleasant but inconsequential. However, the superlative narrative artist is preparing us, ever so subtly, for something later on in his tale. The "barm" is the lap (*q.v.*) and white of course suggests purity. It is not long, however, before we learn that Nicholas "thakked hire aboute the lendes weel" (A 3304), and we recall the first passage. This is what is meant by "good structure" in storytelling. See also **flankes, syde**. [*OED*, "lend," *sb*.1, the loins; also the buttocks.]

lepe. As in the later term "leaping-houses," this word sometimes has an ugly sexual connotation in Middle English. It is true at least once in Chaucer. Alison of Bath (D 267) says that foul (ugly) women will "lepe" on every man, like a spaniel: (1) to get attention; (2) to solicit love-making.

In *Troilus and Criseyde* (II. 955), Chaucer gives the word a different connotation. Pandarus has told Criseyde of Troilus' love; he reports his action to the latter, adding the gleeful: "and ches [choose] if thow wolt synge or daunce or lepe!" Because it is Pandarus speaking, sexual innuendo may be present (see **daunce**), but the line is certainly not ugly. [*OED,* 9. only of certain beasts; to spring upon (the female) in copulation; the earliest citation, however, is 1530].

lere. Thopas' "leere" (B 2047) means the flesh, particularly the muscles of the thigh (Skeat). It is mildly erotic, perhaps, in Chaucer (and is more than mildly so in Shakespeare: cf. Hulme, p. 122). See **hair.** [*OED,* "leer," *sb.*4, the flank or loin; the hollow under the ribs. Chaucer's is the earliest citation.]

lest. See **lust.**

lewed. As the *OED* citations show, the word has undergone interesting semantic changes: lay (as opposed to clerical); unlearned; vulgar, obscene. The first two of these (and especially the second) are those to be found most often in Chaucer, although the third is developing. For instance, in the "Friar's Tale" (D 1346), the narrator tells us that, without a summons, the summoner could summon to the archdeacon's court any "lewed" man, where we see both the old senses of lay and ignorant, together with the emerging (new) sense of the lascivious.

In the "Merchant's Tale" (E 2149), there is a wonderfully complicated passage in which this word figures. Januarie has paraphrased the Song of Songs to seduce his young wife May. In his mouth, even lovely phrases like "How fairer been thy brestes than is wyn" (E 2142) sound slimy. At this point, Chaucer (or the Merchant?) interjects "swiche olde lewed wordes used he." The Bible cannot be "ignorant" (though the interjector, if it is the Merchant, could be). Therefore the words are "lewed" in the erotic sense, at least as used by Januarie. [*OED,* 1. lay; not in holy orders; 2. unlearned.]

light. As Baum and Kökeritz have observed, this word carried the punning meaning of "morally irresponsible" along with its references to luminance and weight. In the "Reeve's Tale" (A 4154), this is clear: the miller's wife "as any jay she light was and jolyf." It appears innocent here, but it is, again, Chaucer's preparation for what is to follow. The wife enjoys her adulterous intercourse far more than she ought to have done. See **joly.**

The poet uses the same meaning in "Complaint of Chaucer to His Purse," the little lyric that makes us wish that he had written much more such light (intended pun) verse. The point of the poem is to equate his purse with a lady: "I am so sory, now that ye been lyght" (3), the clever equivocation of which need hardly be pointed out.

Absolon shows his "lightnesse" (gaiety) by playing Herod, by being an actor ("Miller's Tale," A 3383). Such a performance is not morally reprehensible—quite the reverse. But the word prepares us, perhaps, for his visit to Alisoun later on (A 3671), "ful joly . . . and light," where the sexual meaning is not in doubt.

A very complex occurrence is to be found in *Troilus and Criseyde* (IV. 313): "Syn she is queynt [quenched—i.e., must leave Troy], that wont was yow to lighte." Criseyde was "light" to Troilus—undependable, faithless. And she was his "light," which gave, however briefly, a luminous quality to his life. She is, moreover, **queynt.**

In the same poem there occurs a pun that is probably not really erotic, but which I think has not been noticed before. The lovers are in bed (III. 1136) and Pandarus (always nearby—*too* nearby) remarks that "this light, nor I, ne serven here of nought. / Light is nought good for sike folkes yen!" [eyes]. Three lines later he says: "lat now no hevey thought / Ben hangyng in the hertes of yow tweye." There is play here on weight, luminance, and "hevey" (sad).

If the voiceless velar fricative [x] was being lost during Chaucer's time (and there is evidence that it was, despite the time lag in spelling change—i.e., spellings like *gh* were retained, even though the sound was lost), then there are possibilities that "lite" (little) could be a close homophone. In the "Reeve's Tale" (A 4283), occurs the line: "For she was falle aslepe a lite wight," where there may be a suggestion of moral laxity *if* the sound change had occurred. [*OED, a.*[1], 14. b. of persons (chiefly of women) and their behaviour: wanton, unchaste; citations from *ca.* 1375 to the present.]

likerous, -nesse. See **lecherous, -ye.**

likyng. At the end of the tale of the Wife of Bath (D 1256), the hag-turned-beauty is the model wife: "And she obeyed hym in every thyng / That myghte doon hym plesance or likyng." There is a temptation to see a pun between "like" and "lick," even though the difference in the Middle English vowels militates against it. Cf. "Thopas" (B 2040): "love-likynge"; and *Troilus and Criseyde* (III. 613): "And wel was hym that koude best devyse / To liken hire," which of course means simply "please her." Or does it? For Thopas' reputation, see **hair;** also see **plesaunce.** [*OED* shows that the vowels were not identical in Middle English; however, they were close enough that puns might have been suggested. "Lick" as a sexual act is present in Robbins' Poem No. 32; the woman speaks: "Well, ffor a kyss I wylle not stycke, / so that ye wyll do nothyng but lykke; / but, and ye begyn on me ffor to prycke, / I-wyss, ye shall not kyss me" (37). See also *Piers Plowman* (C-Text, VII. 179): "somme gan ich taste / A-boute the mouthe, and by-nythe (beneath) by-gan ich to grope (*q.v.*), / Til our bothers wil (lust of both of us) was on; to werke we yeden / As wel fastyng-daies as Frydaies . . . puterie and of paramours . . . handlynge and halsynge (necking) . . . and al-so thorw cussynge" (kissing). This is part of the Confession of Luxurie (Lechery). Cf. C-Text, XI. 286: "lecherye is a lykynge thyng."]

lite. See **light.**

love. Even though this is a study of Chaucer's bawdy language, there must be an entry for love. It is the theme of many of the poet's works, in all its guises—sublime, casual, corrupt. I can mention only a representative selection of passages containing the theme.

Most engaging—saddest and at the same time gayest—is the Wife's "Allas! allas! that evere love was synne!" (D 614). This is the same love that exists between lower creatures too—e.g., the falcon and her tercelet in the

"Squire's Tale" (F 529), where, in the ninth line of a long periodic sentence, she "graunted hym love." The relationship is as carnal as is that between Alison of Bath and her five husbands (along with all the "others"), but in this gentle bird story, we do not think of physical love-making ("feathering," *q.v.*, in this case), nor are we supposed to. In any event, Chaucer (or the Squire) makes nothing of the story anyway. See **incest,** which may be the reason for the breaking-off of the tale.

In the *Book of the Duchess* (766 ff.), the relationship of the Lover and the God of Love is portrayed: it is of course analogous to that of the feudal relationship in politics— the baron to his king, for instance. And in *Boece* (Chaucer's translation; II. Metrum 8. 21 ff., end of Book II), we have a famous paean of praise: "This love halt togidres peples joyned with an holy boond, and knytteth sacrement of mariages of chaste loves; and love enditeth lawes to trewe felawes. O weleful were mankynde, yif thilke love that governeth hevene governede yowr corages."

This reminds one, not unnaturally, of the graceful Religion of Love referred to so often in a poem like *Troilus and Criseyde,* and coming to a climax, perhaps, in this stanza (I. 43 ff.) :

And biddeth ek for hem that ben at ese,
That God hem graunte ay good perseveraunce,
And sende hem myght hire ladies so to plese
That it to Love be worship and plesaunce.
For so hope I my sowle best avaunce,
To prey for hem that Loves servauntz be
And write hire wo, and lyve in charite.

Note well the last word, and see the entries for **ese, plesaunce,** and **serve.**

A few more references to the God of Love: in the last Book of *Troilus and Criseyde* (V. 143), Diomede, grow-ing very bold (his audacity approaches the disgusting), says that both he and Criseyde serve the "god of Love"— which, sensing that he has gone too far and fast, he im-mediately changes to "love of God." It is a nice hysteron-

proteron kind of rhetorical figure; it also tells us something important about Diomede's slippery mind. In the
Legend of Good Women (F 327), the God of Love accuses Chaucer of thinking it folly "to serve Love," and
of course he must make amends. In a lyric like "A Complaint to His Lady" (36), he claims that "Thus am I
slayn with Loves fyry dart"—rather cold and stillborn.
We would rather hear Chaucer speak through his characters like the Wife of Bath. Out of fairness, see **synne**
and also frontispiece.

love-dayes. This is one of the most familiar of all the erotic
double meanings in the *Canterbury Tales*. In the "General
Prologue" (A 258), the Friar "in love-dayes ther koude he
muchel help," which means: (1) preside at the formal
occasions set aside in medieval society for the settlement
of disputes; and (2) add to his own erotic triumphs
among the women in his area.

It is sometimes forgotten that in the *House of Fame*
(695), the eagle says he will show Chaucer "mo love-dayes
and acordes / Then on instrumentes be cordes." The
musical figure is terrible—existing only for the rhyme; but
not all eagles are good poets. He does not keep his promise
about the love days either; however, the poem is not
finished. See **acorded**. [*OED*, day set for amicable settlement of disputes.]

love-knotte. The fact that the Monk wears one ("General
Prologue," A 197) not only reinforces our idea that he
cares nothing for regulations, but also that he is an erotic
man. Remember what the Host says to him before he
tells his dreary tragedies ("Monk's Tale," B 3135) and
consider all the other evidence, like **hare**, for instance.
[*OED*, supposed to be a love token.]

lussheburghes. The Host pays the Monk a nice compliment
(though "nice" is hardly the word, I know) when he says
that when religious persons like him pay "Venus
paiementz," they pay in no "lussheburghes" ("Monk's
Tale," B 3152). These were coins from Luxembourg of
inferior metal, and Chaucer uses them for a complicated
jest: (1) to copulate was to pay one's marriage debt (see
dette); (2) to pay in good coin was of course to give

satisfaction sexually. The fact that the "debt" was reserved for those bound by the Sacrament of Marriage seems not to disturb Harry Bailly. See **Venus** too. [*OED*, "lushburg," a base coin; Chaucer is cited but no puns are pointed out.]

lust. Like a great many other words in this study, "lust" has undergone the semantic change known as pejoration; that is, its earlier meanings were less tainted than are the modern ones. As was true for the entry on **love,** we can provide only a selection of representative passages.

Let us begin with those that have a pejorative connotation in Middle English—immoderate sexual desire. In the "Man of Law's Tale" (B 925), it is the "foule lust of luxurie," where the last word translates the Latin *luxuria* (lechery), one of the Seven Deadly Sins. To the Wife of Bath, who has heard plenty of sermons on the matter—and has heard her fifth, clerkly husband read from his misogynistic books, too—"lust" means something else. She knows how to "wyn," which means to make a financial profit: "For wynnyng wolde I al his lust endure," she says (D 416), meaning sexual desires. When her husband is absent, she finds occasion to "pleye" with "lusty folk" (D 553). It means simply "merry," but since Alison speaks the words, and since it is spoken along with "pleye," one wonders.

The Wife is actually proud and ostentatious about her sexuality: "Venus me yaf my lust," she boasts (D 611). In her "Tale," this is its point: some women claim that what women most desire is "lust abedde," and the Wife does not sneer at *that,* but the magical old hag, who will turn into a lovely princess, knows better. Though she frankly accepts lust in herself and others, Alison of Bath does draw the line somewhere, however. She finds the bestiality of Pasiphaë's "lust" and her "likyng" (*q.v.*) insupportable (D 736).

Before we turn to the next most important expert on lust in Chaucer, Criseyde, let us consider some less significant figures. In the *Parliament of Fowls* (219), Lust is one of the allegorical personages met in the Garden of Love, but nothing happens. There are some humorous

"lusty" figures, like old Januarie, who is advised to use
"the lustes of youre wyf attemprely" ("Merchant's Tale,"
E 1679). In view of his age and his confessed need for
aphrodisiacs, the idea is amusing indeed. It is something
like the Host's appellation for the drunken Cook, this
"lusty man" ("Manciple's Tale," H 41), wild irony, since
the poor Cook cannot even sit upright on his horse.

Then there are the innocents—a great many of these,
but they are not interesting, and a few will therefore
suffice: take Walter, for instance ("Clerk's Tale," E 80),
whose "lust" is innocent pleasure—the older meaning of
the word—and he likes only hunting, not women. Or consider the three young people in the *Legend of Good
Women* (716, 1038, and 1451): they are Pyramus, one of
the "lustyeste" youths in the land; Dido, "so yong, so lusty,
with hire eyen glade" (be careful about *her,* however!);
and Jason, "yong, and lusty of corage." All three are
innocent, lively young people in the passages just cited,
but all three become entwined in the toils of "lust" in its
more modern sense.

In concord with this innocence is Chaucer's own tone
in his "Complaint of Mars" (175), a kind of lyric, where
Venus is called the source of "beaute, lust, fredom, gentil-
nesse"—a catalogue that suggests decorum and grace.

There are strange and sometimes rather sad mixtures,
like that in the "Shipman's Tale" (B 1307), where the
lovelorn merchant's wife says there is no wife in all of
France who has "lasse lust . . . to that sory play" (less
pleasure in sexual intercourse with her husband). Here
"lust" is (1) pleasure and (2) sexual gratification—a
most satisfactory blend.

The Host does not help matters; that is, he complicates
the ideas of "lust" in Chaucer because he deliberately involves the clergy in them, and he means "earthy, sensual,
sexual, physical copulation" when he uses the term in
conjunction with clerics. In the "Monk's Tale" (B 3137),
Harry Bailly says that if the Monk had permission, as he
has the might (power) "to parfourne al thy lust in
engendrure," then he would have begotten many a
creature. This should be paralleled with the "Nun's

Priest's Tale" (B 3996), when the Host, weary to death of the Monk's tragedies, asks for something about hunting (*q.v.*). But the good cleric answers: "Nay . . . I have no lust to pleye." The cluster of "pleye" and "lust" suggests that the Host is dealing with a very complex figure here.

Now for *Troilus and Criseyde*: to begin at the end, which has puzzled and annoyed so many modern readers, we find Troilus safe in heaven now (V. 1824); he looks down and laughs at those who follow the "blynde lust, the which that may nat laste." After sym- and empathizing with the personages for five long books, it is a little hard for the modern reader to take this sort of offhand dismissal. The theme of the wonderful "novel" is shrugged off as if it were totally insignificant after all. I shall not try to settle this matter, nor to determine the exact position of Troilus' eighth sphere here, but I shall simply ask the reader to note that Chaucer chooses to use the key word "lust" at this key point.

At the beginning, we have Criseyde's candid interior monologue (II. 752) where she assesses herself as fair, young, and "unteyd [untied] in lusty leese" [pasture]. She is ready for sex, for lust, and we should not forget it as we watch her artful posturings and deceptions. It is about this time in the development of the narrative (II. 787), too, that Criseyde thinks to herself (aloud) about fickle men: "right anon as cessed is hire lest [their lust], / So cesseth love, and forth to love a newe." The irony is profound—for some readers, too much so. Chaucer is excessively heavy-handed in this passage, according to some tastes. When they part (III. 1550), Criseyde remembers his "lust" (pleasure from her? her own pleasure? both?). At the actual separation (IV. 1573) they argue: if they should run off together, Criseyde thinks that people would say it was either "lust voluptuous" (which *was* the basis for their relationship) or "coward drede." The latter is an important characteristic of Chaucer's heroine, though not, of course, of Troilus. She is "slydynge of corage" (V. 825) and we are (usually) as ready as is the poet to forgive her.

Perhaps the most urbane of all the lovers in Chaucer is Dido (*House of Fame*, 287), who recognizes that her feeling for Aeneas is "nyce lest" (foolish desire) but cannot help it. [*OED*, 1. pleasure, delight (through the sixteenth century) ; 4. sexual appetite, from the beginning of English to the present. Now the chief sense.]

lustiheed, -nesse. Something strange occurs with this word—perhaps miraculously true, psychologically; perhaps confused textually or philologically. In the "Manciple's Tale" (H 274), after he has slain his adulterous wife, Phebus calls her "gemme of lustiheed." It is hard to determine the tone here. He regrets having to kill his wife, but she has engaged in lust with her "lemman," and there is no alternative for a man of honor. He goes on recalling her as a wife "that were to me so sad and eek so trewe," which of course she was not. And he accuses himself of being rash. She might have been guiltless: after all, he has relied upon the testimony of a talking bird!

In the warm, middle Book III (line 177), after Criseyde has rather coldly warned Troilus, her words rise in temperature, and she tells him "draweth yow to lustinesse," which is unequivocal. A few lines later they are in bed.

luxurie. Directly from the Latin *luxuria,* one of the Seven Deadly Sins—lechery; and, as it is called in the "Man of Law's Tale" (B 925), the "foule lust of luxurie."

One wonders about that great preacher, the Pardoner: is he interested in the heterosexuality of *luxuria*? He opines that "luxurie is in wyn and dronkenesse" (C 484). See **hair.**

But we are on surer ground when listening to that much more orthodox, and duller, preacher, the Parson (I 836 ff.), in his section on Luxuria. Here one can learn of the penalties for women taken in lechery; of the relationship of Gula (Gluttony) and Luxuria; and of lechery as the cause of the Flood.

Even from the reserved and puritanical Boethius (in Chaucer's translation) we encounter fierce condemnations: if man "be plongid in fowle and unclene luxuris, he is withholden in the foule delices of the fowle sowe" (IV. Prosa 3. 121). In medieval iconography, the sow is usually associated with gluttony, though not here. See **delicacye,** too, for "delices." [*OED*, lasciviousness, lust; citations from 1340 to the present.]

lye. See lay.

lymes. See membres. Januarie is talking about his penis when he says ("Merchant's Tale," E 1458): "I feele my lymes stark and suffisaunt / To do al that a man bilongeth to." The comic (pathetic?) irony is that he is of course wrong (see bene). Later (E 1465) he claims that his heart and all his "lymes been as grene / As laurer thurgh the yeer is for to seene." For "grene," see tayl. [*OED*, *sb*.1, any organ or part of the body, including a citation from 1484 "lymes of generacion"; a similar, but less succinct, citation occurs in the fourteenth century too.]

m

malkyn. See maydenhed.

manly. See serve.

mare. See hors.

mariage. In the "General Prologue" (A 212), two meanings for this word are relevant to the Friar: he can perform the sacrament, but he is also involved in temporary "marriages" with local girls.

Totally different is the amusing anticlimax that occurs in the "Man of Law's Tale" (B 217), where it finally dawns on the Sowdan (Sultan—a Paynim, not a Christian) that the only way to have Custance is by way of marriage. [*OED* provides no help for the double meaning in A 212.]

mawe. See launcegay. [*OED*, *sb*.1, 1. the stomach; 3. the throat, gullet—earliest citation 1530.]

maydenhed. Kökeritz points out the complex sort of punning buildup in the "Wife of Bath's Tale" (D 886–888), with its "mayde," "mayde," "heed," "maydenheed." Something similar happens in the "Knight's Tale" (A 2328) where Emelye prays to Diana: "Mayde and kepere of us alle, / My maydenhede thou kepe and wel conserve, / And whil

I lyve, a mayde I wol thee serve." Here the iteration has a point, which it really does not in the Wife's "Tale": the irony is of course that though the virginal Emelye is under the protection of Diana, her "fate" is to marry one of the knights in the story and to lose her maidenhead. In the same prayer, Emelye mentions **queynt** (quenched) and actually asks to lose her hymen, since she prays Diana to "sende me hym that moost desireth me."

These two passages might suggest that Chaucer takes maidenhead lightly. Not so. St. Cecilie swears to keep her "maydenhede" ("Second Nun's Tale," G 126) even though married, and her husband Valerian agrees. If he touches his wife Cecilie "in vileynye" (that is, with amorous intent) her guardian angel will kill him. See Introduction, p. 2, on this repellent asceticism.

The Parson explains the concept to us in his sermon (I 867): "Another synne of Leccherie is to bireve a mayden of hir maydenhede," and whoever does so casts her out of the "hyeste degree that is in this present lif."

It is precisely with this concept that the Wife of Bath disagrees (D 96), though she does admit that "maydenhede" is better than bigamy. There are many other tales and passages that testify to the value placed on maidenhood—some unintentionally amusing, I think. There is the Amazonish Cenobia (Z-) in the "Monk's Tale" (B 3459), fond of hunting, wrestling, and keeping her "maydenhod from every wight." She does not succeed completely, but almost. When she at last marries, she persuades her husband to come to her but once, and then in order to engender children. Reminiscent in some ways of Zenobia is the patient, patient Griselde, that combination of treacle and tears. In the "Clerk's Tale" (E 837), she gladly relinquishes her maidenhead to Walter, her high-born husband: it is the symbol of her purity and the only dowry that she brings to her marriage (866, 883).

A maiden who has been "oppressed" (raped—"Franklin's Tale," F 1436) also tells us of the fantastic value placed upon maidenhead: she kills herself after losing hers, and "with hire deeth hir maydenhede redressed." Chaucer tells Ovid's famous story of Tereus and his rape of his sister-in-law, Philomene [*sic*]: she too is bereft of her "maydenhede," which makes the crime all the more reprehensible. Chaucer chooses not to give us the details of the rape (*Legend of Good Women,* 2325) ; this is one of the reasons, perhaps, that the poem in which the story occurs is such a sodden failure. At the beginning, the God of Love has told Chaucer to write of those good women who have kept their "maydenhede, / Or elles wedlok, or here widewehede" (G-Text, 294) . He does so, but the result is a series of "Second Nun's Tales." The only exception is the Dido story: she has of course already lost her maidenship; she befouls her "widewehede" through the affair with Aeneas, but after this "adultery" she commits suicide and therefore qualifies as "good."

There is the familiar horror of incest involved with maidenship too: in the "Man of Law's Tale" (B 83) , there is mention of the father who "birafte his doghter of hir maydenhede," a story that comes from one of the versions of the Apollonius of Tyre tradition, though Robinson cannot trace it. The father is King Antiochus.

After all this sober talk about a filament of tissue and the state that it represents, it is refreshing to hear the Host refer to it in a homely, proverbial remark. He says that lost time will never return again, no more than will "Malkynes maydenhede"—Malkyn being a traditional name for a country slut ("Man of Law's Tale," B 30) . The contrast with the Antiochus story (see just above) is surely deliberate, and is very amusing.

It is worth noting, though not surprising, that the "maydenhede" is not mentioned in Chaucer's most famous love story, *Troilus and Criseyde.* From the very beginning, the heroine is no maiden, but a widow. Chaucer lets us forget this fact—properly and deliberately, since even a shadowy predecessor to Troilus would intrude upon the lovers' relationship.

It was believed (the source of the notion cannot be found) that to be able to look directly at the sun was proof that one was still in her [his?] state of maidenhead. And everybody knows the wry old legend that tells us that in order to catch a unicorn you need a virgin in whose

lap he will lay his head. The reason for the rarity of the
beast is obvious. [OED, virginity. The equation with the
intact hymen is not made clear. However, see Robbins'
Poem No. 25: "he gafe my mayden-hed a spurne (stroke) /
and rofe my kell" (broke my membrane) (7). Piers Plowman (A-Text, I. 158) mentions the worthlessness of
Malkyn's "maydenhod, that no mon desyreth." In a note
(p. 373) to the Interludium de Clerico et Puella, Bennett
writes: "Malkyn: although OED does not recognize the
sense 'slut, drab; lewd woman' till nearly 1600, several of
the ME contexts quoted s.v. have contemptuous implications that seem near to it."]

meede. From the beginnings of English to the present this
word meant "wages," but in Chaucer's time it carried an
aura of evil—a reward dishonestly offered or received;
corrupt gain; bribery (as the OED puts it). It is odd,
therefore, that Chaucer tells us in the "Miller's Tale"
(A 3380) that Absolon sends Alisoun presents (sweet
wine, for instance) in order to gain her favors, but he
also "profred meede." What was her reaction to this in-
sult—or what would it have been? Chaucer gives us no clue
in so many words. That is, in an otherwise perfectly con-
structed story, here is a loose end of some significance. For
some readers, the extremely subtle reaction to his wooing
is, however, enough, and there *is* no loose end. The tale
gains power in *not* being direct and clear. See **ers.**

There can be no question of the word's pejorative
connotation. In the Parliament of Fowls (228), Meede is
an allegorical figure described along with other unpleasant
concepts and acts. And the Parson tells us, as he does so
frequently, what moral stance we should take toward
meed in his warning against corruption (I 167): "ne for
preyere ne for meede he [any man] shal nat been corrupt."
[OED, 1. wages; 2. reward dishonestly offered or accepted;
corrupt gain; bribery: the first citation is from Piers Plowman, 1362.]

melodye. See **revel.**

membres. The Parson cites Genesis when telling us (I 330)
that after the Fall, Adam and Eve "sowed of fige leves a
maner of breches to hiden hire membres." These are of

course the members of generation, the genitals (see **breech, lymes**). The Wife of Bath (D 116) admires their perfection and the perfection of their Creator—a sentiment of which the Parson would probably not approve though he does not interrupt her on the Pilgrimage to say so.

However, when he turns his righteous wrath on current fashions (men's), which he does so frequently under the heading of Superbia (Pride) in his sermon, we discover that the Parson thinks the "membres" are shameful objects indeed. Men now wear scanty garments that show their "shameful membres," "horrible swollen membres," "wrecched swollen membres," "shameful privee membres," and, last, "privee membres" (I 421 ff.) . His point of view is clear. [*OED,* 1. b. privy member (s) .]

meschaunce. Braddy (p. 218) says that "meschaunce" in the "Wife of Bath's Prologue" (D 407) is a synonym for coition. I am afraid that this is simply wrong. She says that to gain what she wants from her husbands, she torments them: "Namely abedde hadden they meschaunce"—i.e., they were *denied* coition. We should have known, of course, that Alison of Bath would not use a pejorative synonym for the act of love. [*OED* provides no meaning like Braddy's.]

mete. In modern parlance, "meat" can be either a female used for coital purposes or the male member. In Chaucer it is neither. Just consider the Prioress in the "General Prologue" (A 127) . [*OED* offers no evidence of an erotic meaning at any time.]

mevynge. In *Troilus and Criseyde* (I. 289), Hinton (p. 116) points out that there is a double meaning, the second one mildly erotic: "Troilus is startled both at Criseyde's beauty as she walks and at the stirrings she causes in his breast . . . ; he was pleased with both." The passage says that the hero "gan for to like hire mevynge." [*OED,* 1. c. bodily movement; 2. *fig.* a disturbance or commotion (the first citation for which is 1450) .]

mixne. Dunghill. Even though Holy Writ speaks of vile things, it does not touch Holy Writ, any more than it befouls the sun to shine upon a "mixne": "Parson's Tale" (I 910) . [*OED,* "mixen," dunghill, with citations from all periods

up to the present, but it is not, I think, familiar in
America today.]

mouth. For many of Chaucer's characters, the mouth is an
object of erotic attraction—as it is for everybody, I would
guess. Alison of Bath, who knows all about such things
(D 466), tells us—about herself and about women generally—"a likerous mouth moste han a likerous tayl."

What exactly is a "likerous" mouth (with both meanings of "lecherous" and "liquorish"—see **lecherous**)? First
some negative evidence: when Criseyde faints (IV. 1161),
Troilus kisses her "colde mowth," which is clearly not
"likerous." However, she regains her senses quickly and in
a trice the couple is in bed having intercourse.

I can offer two more pieces of evidence from Chaucer,
and then the reader will have to investigate for himself.
In the "Miller's Tale," Chaucer's description of Alisoun
takes up some fifty lines, with each detail more toothsome
than the last (including A 3261): "Hir mouth was sweete
as bragot or the meeth" (both sweet drinks). Finally we
must not overlook the Prioress. Even though she is in
Holy Orders, she is a beautiful woman, and ("General
Prologue," A 153) "Hir mouth [was] ful smal, and therto
softe and reed." [*OED* offers no help. See the Confession
of Luxurie from *Piers Plowman* at **likyng.**]

multiplye. See **wexe.**

myddel. Old Januarie has fantasies in bed, thinking of his beloved's body, especially of her "myddel smal," which for
him is especially erotic ("Merchant's Tale," E 1602). The
small waist was a conventional attribute of the medieval
beauty (*Romaunt of the Rose,* 1032): "Yong she was . . .
Gente, and in hir myddill small." (For more of Januarie's
fantasies, see **streyne.**) [*OED,* B., *sb.* 3. the waist. In fourteenth-century lyric poetry it recurs repeatedly as an ideal
quality, modified by "smale" or "gent"—e.g., Robbins'
Poem No. 127: "myddyl small" (46); No. 129: "medyll . . .
gaunte & small" (20), etc.]

myrthe. In some passages, "myrthe" is a kind of euphemism (a
lively one) for intercourse—e.g., the "Shipman's Tale"
(B 1508) where the monk and the wife "in myrthe al
nyght a bisy lyf they lede," in bed, of course. The amusing

thing about this passage is that once again Chaucer has used a parallel to remind us of how libidinous is this unfaithful spouse. When her husband returns from his journey, she does the same thing with him (B 1565) : "And al that nyght in myrthe they bisette." See **fit, kiss.**

The relationship of "myrthe" with venereal activity is made clear in *Troilus and Criseyde* (III. 715) , when the hero, about to go to bed with his beloved, calls thrice upon Venus—the third time as "O Venus ful of myrthe." [*OED* gives no support to any erotic meanings.]

n

naked. See **bare, strepen,** and Figure 10.

nature. In his passage on Ira (Wrath), the subdivision on homicide, the Parson says that it is murder if a woman abort, and also "or elles dooth unkyndely [unnaturally] synne, by which man or womman shedeth hire nature in manere or in place ther as a child may nat be conceived" ("Parson's Tale," I 575) . The references are to coitus interruptus and to "unnatural" sexual positions or entries. Skeat glosses "nature" as "seed." See also **concepcioun.** [*OED,* 7. a. semen; 8. the female pudendum, especially that of a mare (which seems not to be relevant here, but perhaps elsewhere) .]

nekke. In the "General Prologue," Chaucer tells us that the Friar has a "nekke whit" (A 238) . Baum refers to this fact, and Robinson's note tells us that the physiognomists interpreted a white neck as evidence of licentiousness (cf. the Friar's lisping, too) .

In the *Book of the Duchess* (939) , the Fair White's "nekke" is also white: it "semed a round tour of yvoyre," and perfection without a blemish. The Man in Black seems to know the significance of this feature. See **throte.**

For Pandarus' nonavuncular toying with Criseyde's "nekke," see **incest.** [*OED* offers no substantiation for the erotic significance.]

Newgate. Baum thinks that the prentice had perhaps been
guilty of adultery ("Cook's Tale," A 4402), since it was
the practice to play adulterers into Newgate Prison with
musical accompaniment: Chaucer's "revel."

Baum does not mention the much more indirect reference in the same (unfinished) tale (A 4370): "Dauncen
he koude so wel and jolily, / That he was cleped Perkyn
Revelour," which at the very least is a foreshadowing of
the "Newgate . . . revel" reference that comes up a little
later. [*OED's* first reference to Newgate Prison dates from
1596, Shakespeare.]

Nicholas, St. See **brestes.**

nycetee. If her husbands please her, the Wife of Bath lets them
do their "nycetee," which is manifestly copulation (D
412). [*OED,* "nicety," 2. b. lust (also quotes Hoccleve,
ca. 1412).]

O

odious. In the "Summoner's Tale" (D 2190), the friar complains bitterly to the lord to whom he is reporting Thomas'
"gift" that "an odious meschief / This day bityd is to
myn ordre and me": (1) offensive; (2) odorous (recall
that the gift was a fart). [*OED* does not recognize the
possibility of a pun between "odious" and "odorous"; it
is of course the familiar malapropism uttered by Bottom
in *A Midsummer Night's Dream,* III. i. 83.]

open-ers. A descriptive (open-arse) if unappetizing name for
the medlar, the fruit which was eaten only when half-
rotten and which we keep encountering in Chaucer and
Shakespeare. In the "Reeve's Tale" (A 3871), the Reeve
says that old men are like the open-ers: "Til we be roten,
kan we nat be rype." We recall Mercutio's use of the fruit
to represent the female organs (*Romeo and Juliet,* II. i.
34), an equation that had not occurred to Chaucer (at
least in this passage) it would seem. It is a vulgar name for
the medlar, in any event, and this tells us something about

the Reeve. [*OED,* "openarse," in reference to the large open disk between the persistent calyx lobes; still common among the working class in the late nineteenth century. And this dictionary entry is much funnier than Chaucer's use of the word!]

oppressed. This seems to be a rather pompous euphemism for "raped." In the "Franklin's Tale" (F 1435), the narrator, who is perhaps addicted to pompous euphemisms, tells us of the Theban maiden "oppressed" by a Macedonian. She commits suicide, and thus "hir maydenhede redressed." See **maydenhed.** [*OED,* 7. to force, violate, ravish; obsolete in the seventeenth century.]

p

paramour. Since the word was both an adverbial phrase (with or without "for" or "as") and a noun meaning a lover, there is sometimes some uncertainty of exact meanings in Chaucer. However, we can always be sure that illicit love is involved somehow.

To illustrate the ambiguity, consider the *Legend of Good Women* (G-Text, 260) where the God of Love accuses Chaucer of thinking that anyone who "loveth paramours" is a fool: (1) loves illicit lovers; (2) loves illicitly or clandestinely. Similarly, there is a doubt about the syntactic function in the "Miller's Tale" (A 3354) where the absurd Absolon "for paramours he thoghte for to wake."

The distinction between "paramour" and licit love-making is made clear in the "Merchant's Tale" (E 1450), which praises the lawful procreation of children, to honor God above, and condemns sensual pleasure, which is only "paramour or love."

Maidens long for Thopas "paramour" (B 1933) —either *as* a paramour or "with licentious lust," neither of which is likely (nor does Chaucer expect us to take it seriously). See **hair.**

As *Troilus and Criseyde* draws toward its end (V. 158),
Diomede swears to Criseyde that never before has he loved
a woman "as paramours," which is, like the Thopas reference, a statement that we are not intended to believe. Here
the result is disgusting, while in "Thopas" it is amusing.
Its meaning is simple, but it also occurs in a very complicated passage in the *Troilus*. Pandarus speaks to Criseyde,
his niece (II. 234 ff.) :

And by the blisful Venus that I serve,
Ye ben the womman in this world lyvynge,
Withouten paramours, to my wyttynge,
That I best love. . . .

Part of the rich ambiguity depends on the double meaning of "withouten" (see **Wife of Bath**) : (1) without; (2)
not counting, as inconsequential. There is the possibility
too that the adverbial and the substantive senses of
"paramours" are both operative; the result is that we have
(1) not counting lovers; (2) except I do not mean in the
way of passionate, physical love, of course, since I am your
uncle; (3) "ye . . . withouten paramours" = you, who
are a widow without lovers. There are more permutations
possible—a complicated piece of multiple significance
worthy of Shakespeare's poetry at its most mature and
complex.

There are many lines in which the word is simply a
synonym for "illicit lover (s) "—a funny one, for example,
in the "Miller's Tale" (A 3756, repeated at A 3758), which
should be compared with A 3354, treated above, to see
what Chaucer does with a single word to show a change in
character.

We may merely mention the "Cook's Tale" (A 4372)
and the "Friar's Tale" (D 1372), but we may pause over
Chaunticleer in the "Nun's Priest's Tale" (B 4057) who
has seven hens to do him his "plesaunce," which were his
"sustres and his paramours." The contrast of this Oriental
luxury with the simpleness of the widow's barnyard and
house (in which the tale takes place) is one of Chaucer's

master touches of providing background that functions in the narrative.

Last there is the bitter irony of *Troilus and Criseyde* (V. 332) where Pandarus betrays the fact that he has misunderstood all along the depth of the love in which he has been so deeply, though perhaps peripherally, involved. He comforts Troilus, whose beloved has betrayed him, with the information that other knights have "loved paramours as wel as thow." One can hardly endure the poignance of the complex innuendos. Troilus did *not* love Criseyde merely "paramours"; and the double meaning of "as wel" makes the line doubly powerful. [*OED, adv. phr.* and *sb.;* both "fantasy" and real physical love are suggested; there was also an early "weakened" sense (which Chaucer seems not to use) meaning "of your kindness, as a favour." See also the Confession of Luxurie from *Piers Plowman* at **likyng**.]

Pardoner. See **hair.**

Parson and **Plowman.** Along with the Knight (probably) the only completely idealized Pilgrims in the *Canterbury Tales,* despite the latter's **dong** (*q.v.*) . The Plowman tells no tale, so we cannot judge him on this score. But the Parson does. It is the last one in Robinson's edition—a very long (though beautifully balanced) sermon. One feels that it is far too intellectual for the simple country preacher, and it reveals (to some readers, including this one) a morbid concern with, and a misunderstanding of, sex. See, for instance, **membres.**

partritch. "Ful many a fat partritch hadde [the Franklin] in muwe" ("General Prologue," A 349) . The birds are associated with fish—a common term for a prostitute—and with "stuwe," both a fishpond and a brothel. However, there is no evidence that "partritch" was a word for a whore or concubine. The Franklin's birds are real, and he, a son of Epicurus, keeps them for his table. [*OED* offers no evidence that "partridge" was a cant word of any sort.]

Philomene (or **Philomel**) . See **rape.**

pipen. See **baggepipe.**

piss. In Chaucer's time the word was not "dirty" or taboo.

Pissing was an everyday occurrence, as it still is, though it was perhaps done more publicly in the fourteenth century. Not until the seventeenth century did the word pass out of polite use.

More than once Chaucer mentions the necessity for urinating: in the "Miller's Tale" (A 3798) : "This Nicholas was risen for to pisse," which is the occasion for the thunderous fart and the toute-branding. Similarly, in the "Reeve's Tale" (A 4215) , the miller's wife "gan awake, and wente hire out to pisse." Everybody in this story is a little (or more) drunk; hence the verisimilitude of the act. When she returns, there is the confusion of the bed with the cradle at the foot. Everybody wakes up, and there is the riotous melee as a finish—almost as good as that at the end of the "Nun's Priest's Tale."

Alison of Bath (D 729) is rather tired of listening to her fifth husband's tales of wicked wives, including: "How Xantippa caste pisse upon [Socrates'] heed." Even this seemingly irrelevant detail is made useful in the narrative: Alison loses her patience, like Xantippe, tears pages from the book in which these stories are written, is smitten on the ear, deafened, etc., etc. A little earlier she is talking about wives who cannot keep their mouths shut, and she says: "for hadde myn housbonde pissed on a wal" (an illegal act, apparently, not a disgusting one) and had she told on him, there would have been trouble (534) .

Under **kiss,** I have already mentioned what is the only gleam of humor in the "Parson's Tale," but since it is so rare, it should be treated here again. It is a fairly amusing little piece of excretory humor. Old men like to kiss, says the Parson, but they are incapable of the deed of love: "Certes, they been lyk to houndes; for an hound, whan he comth by the roser or by othere [bushes], though he may nat pisse, yet wole he heve up his leg and make a countenaunce to pisse" (I 857) .

For the Canon's Yeoman's contempt for alchemy and its ingredients, including piss, see **dong.** [*OED* offers evidence that "piss" was no longer in polite use in the seventeenth century. In a very roundabout note, Skeat admits that "pissares" in *Piers Plowman* (C Text, XXIII. 219) means exactly what it appears to and is a term of contempt for soldiers.]

pissemyre. Thomas' wife says to the overfamiliar friar in the "Summoner's Tale" (D 1825) that her husband is as angry as a "pissemyre" (ant). There is no evidence that this was a common or proverbial comparison, but it is apt: first, Thomas is indeed angry, since his wife has admitted the unctuous friar in the first place; and, second, the furious racing about of the little insect does indeed suggest uncontrollable ire. [*OED,* "pissmire," states that the word comes from the urinous smell of the anthill. The earliest citation is this one from Chaucer.]

place. I think that it is just barely possible that, given the proper circumstances, of course, this was a euphemism for the pudendum. In the "Parson's Tale" (I 575), the good pastor, sermonizing on Ira (Wrath), tells us that abortion is murder—by potions or else by putting "certeine material thynges in hire secree places to slee the child." See also **concepcioun.**

Even without the qualifying adjective, the word may suggest the vagina, perhaps even in the "Knight's Tale" (A 2399) where Arcite says that he hopes to win Emelye "in the place." Literally, of course, this refers to the arena for the tourney, but if the other erotic meaning is present, we have an amusing tremor in the otherwise serious fabric of the romance. Thopas (B 1910—cf. also B 1971) is said to have been born in the "place," which Baugh glosses as "manor" or "marketplace." The second of these meanings is comical: if the sexual sense is also here, we have a triple complex of satirical innuendo. He was—*mirabile dictu!*—born from his mother's pudendum! See also **poperyng.**

In *Troilus and Criseyde* (III. 1271), we learn that the hero was about to die, but that through the bounty of Love is now bestowed "in so heigh a place / That thilke boundes may no blisse pace." We can never be sure whether this is the widow's vagina or not, but in view of the rampant double entendre elsewhere in the poem, it is possible—certainly more so than in the "Knight's Tale" line just discussed. But even this narrative has some latent

erotic possibilities. See **maydenhed** and **queynt**, for instance. [*OED* gives no support for any erotic meanings.]

plesaunce. The word means simply "pleasure," but very often
it has unmistakable overtones of sexual joys. When Januarie says that if he had an old wife, "that I in hire ne
koude han no plesaunce, / Thanne sholde I lede my lyf in
avoutrye," "Merchant's Tale" (E 1434), he is talking
about orgasms. (Hinton, p. 115, points out that in this
passage the first "in" is also bawdy. See **inne**.) The same
dirty old man asks his young wife May to strip naked, since
he will have "som plesaunce" of her, and her clothes are
an encumbrance to him (E 1959).

There is an interesting gradation in sexual pleasure
revealed in the *Legend of Good Women* (1770) where
(though the passage is syntactically confused) Tarquin
wants "not pleasaunce but delit" from Lucrece. It reminds
one of the blunt joke of some years ago about "intercourse,
hell! I said 'fucking!' "

In the *Parliament of Fowls* (389), Dame Nature makes
the birds choose their mates "as I prike yow with
plesaunce," which Baugh glosses as "desire." That nobler
fowl, Chaunticleer, has "seven hennes for to doon al his
plesaunce," and there is no question that this is coitus.
See **tredynge**.

Naturally throughout *Troilus and Criseyde* there is
much mention of "plesaunce," usually with its erotic
overtones. For instance, on the morning after his first
meeting with Criseyde (III. 426), Troilus goes about his
business with remarkable self-control, though he is burn-
ing "for sharp desir of hope and of plesaunce." When she
agrees to admit him to her bed (III. 944), she asks: "That
I honour may have, and he plesaunce." She has her sexual
pleasure too, of course, though (because she is a lady) she
is reluctant to admit it; later (III. 1422), she calls him
her "plesaunce."

After the separation of the lovers, the callous Pandarus
tries to comfort Troilus by asserting that love is but
"casuel plesaunce" (i.e., caused by chance, IV. 419).
Troilus himself recalls that he lived with Criseyde (IV.
493) in "lust and in plesaunce." She too (V. 731) recalls

the "plesaunce" of being with Troilus, but in her letter to him (V. 1608) she accuses him of thinking only of his own "plesaunce," which (if it *is* equivalent to sexual pleasure here) is a very perceptive piece of psychological truth about women.

Let me mention only a couple of occurrences when the word seems not to have an erotic meaning: in the "Shipman's Tale," Daun John is "ful of diligence / To doon plesaunce" (B 1235) in the merchant's house. This seems, and probably is, innocent enough. It is only later that we remember his willingness to "doon plesaunce," when the wife promises to pay the friar back the loan of 100 francs: she will "doon to yow what plesance and service / That I may doon" (B 1381). The word has assumed its erotic mantle, as the conjunction with "service" helps to show. And if we are still uncertain, the following action, which occurs without interlude, makes the erotic tone clear, for he seizes her, kisses her, and they make their pact to meet in bed.

Chaucer the lyricist uses the word often, but his verses are to most readers such obvious exercises, rather than expressions of personal emotion, that it is hard to tell when his "plesaunce" is sexual. There is no doubt that in "Complaint of Mars" (46) Venus is "causer of plesaunce," but in "To Rosemounde" (22), what are we to make of "I brenne ay in an amorous plesaunce," since this is a "petition" lyric, begging for the lady's favors. Perhaps it suggests that "plesaunce" can be experienced and enjoyed in anticipation. In "Womanly Noblesse" (4), Chaucer writes: "you to serve is set al my plesaunce" (note **serve**) and calls her "lady of plesaunce" (27). All that one can say here is "maybe."

In poems of doubtful authorship but included by Robinson in his edition, there occur equally problematical passages in which we have apparent erotic "clusters" but in which the meaning of "plesaunce" is left unclear. No doubt the very ambiguity was the charm and the utility of the word for writers of love poetry. Consider "Complaynt D'Amours" (48): "It is hir wone [custom] plesaunce for to take, / To seen hir servaunts dyen for

hir sake." See **die, serve.** And "A Balade of Complaint"
(14): "Myn heven hool, and al my suffisaunce, / Whom
for to serve is set al my plesaunce." In addition to **serve**
(again), see **hol.** [*OED* has many suggestive citations,
none of which demonstrates conclusively an erotic significance.]

pley. Sanders (p. 194) suggests that there were puns between
"pley" (to have intercourse) and "pleyn" (to complain),
since the infinitive of the former could appear with a final
-*n* inflection. The pun is certainly possible, but I have
not found many occurrences. There is an interesting one
(Sanders') in the "Wife of Bath's Prologue" (D 390):
"I pleyned first, so was oure werre ystynt" [quarrel between husband and wife stopped]. The passage should
be read in context, of course, and compared with the entry
under **grind.**

There is possibly a similar equivoque in *Troilus and
Criseyde* (III. 1020); the heroine appears to be addressing
Jove in a complaint, but it is equally possible that the
"the" is Troilus: "O were it leful for to pleyn on the, /
That undeserved suffrest jalousie, / Of that I wolde upon
the pleyne and crie!" There is also a double meaning in
"suffrest": (1) permittest; (2) sufferest from.

There are probably hundreds, certainly dozens, of passages in which "pleye" is used in a neutral sense, erotically
speaking—as are such words as **desport,** with similar
pairs of meanings. Symkyn the miller in the "Reeve's
Tale" (A 3958) is angered if anyone dares to "rage or
pleye" with his wife (see **rage**). If there were *real* sexual
play going on here, Symkyn would be more than angered:
he is a dangerous man, and well armed, as Chaucer is
careful to point out at the beginning of the tale. It is
probably merely a matter of heavy-handed coquetry. In
the same story (A 4004), the two young scholars are described as "testif . . . and lusty for to pleye," which is
harmless enough in the opening part of the narrative; we
are reminded of it, however, when the serious sexual
"pleye" begins later on, and one clerk "swyves" the miller's daughter while the other sports with his wife.

The Wife of Bath is fond of using the word in possibly

ambiguous senses. When her husband expresses the jealous suspicion that she visits a friend's house for immoral purposes, she says she is there only to "pleye": (1) amuse myself; (2) have amorous dalliance; and she does the same thing in D 551. Her cleverest use of the equivoque, however, is when the Pardoner interrupts her "Prologue" (D 192) and she politely says: "myn entente is nat but for to pleye." The fun lies in the Pardoner's reason for the interruption (he talks, with profound irony, about getting married) and his character (see **hair**). The Wife can remain completely demure, using the word to mean both (1) amuse and (2) have intercourse, which, with the Pardoner, is ironic indeed.

In the "Merchant's Tale" (E 2043), Januarie likes to walk and "pleye" in his garden, where both senses are very likely, since he has built the *hortus conclusus* especially for amorous "pleye" with his wife May. There is doubt, but also narrative foreshadowing, in the "Shipman's Tale" (B 1249), when the merchant sends word to Daun John (who is destined to cuckold and cheat him soon) that the young monk should come to his house "to pleye / With hym and with his wyf a day or tweye." The word occurs again later (B 1263), though the wife is not mentioned.

The Man in Black (*Book of the Duchess,* 875) says that though his beloved "pleyde," she was always careful with her eyes, with her "lokynge"; and thus she remained demure. The passage makes it clear that here the word is innocence itself. But later (961) the innuendo is stronger: "Therto she koude so wel pleye." After all, the Duke and Duchess were married. (The passage is also associated with the idea of the undiminished candle flame: see **candle**.)

In the *Legend of Good Women* (1495), Jason tells a messenger that he has come from the sea to rest—to "pleye," which is literal and nonerotic, though again it does foreshadow his sexual play, which occurs afterward. (See also 1497.) In the same poem (2300), there is a strange double meaning where the word may simply be clumsily used. Pandyon, Philomene's father, says that

Tereus should give Philomene leave to come visit him
(Tereus) —leave to "pleye." In view of the rape that
Tereus soon enacts upon Philomene, the hint of sexual
play is odd indeed.

Before turning to *Troilus and Criseyde,* which I shall
treat by itself as an example of a single work in which
the word "pleye" can be used in a number of interesting
poetic ways, let me move to some passages in which the
sense is unmistakably "intercourse." Nicholas and Alisoun
("Miller's Tale," A 3273) "pleye," and the Reeve interrupts his own tale to address one of the characters, "Now
pley, Aleyn, for I wol speke of John" (A 4198), when
Aleyn is in bed with the miller's daughter. The poor old
fool Januarie tells May, his young wife, that it makes no
difference how long they "pleye" ("Merchant's Tale,"
E 1835) on their wedding night, since no workman can
work both well and hastily—a transparent excuse for his
own slow, senile performance in bed. All the aphrodisiacs
from the book *De Coitu* (q.v.) were valueless! He uses
the word again (E 1841): "We han leve to pleye us by
the lawe." But we get the real information from May herself (E 1854): "She preyseth nat his pleyyng worth a
bene."

Similarly, the wife in the "Shipman's Tale" (B 1307)
tells the monk that intercourse with her husband is "sory
pley." In this tale, Chaucer uses some subtle variations on
the word, since he also tells us that when this husband,
the merchant, is away, he neither "pleyeth" (at dice) nor
"daunceth," which makes him sound very upright indeed,
for a traveling man. But consider his wife's complaint,
and see **daunce.** On the other hand, we are reassured (and
frankly very much surprised) when the merchant returns and his wife accepts him as her partner at "pleye"
even though she has barely left her lover's bed. On the
night of the husband's return, they have a merry time in
bed; then in the morning he asks for more! She says
"no" but appears not really to mean it, since in a moment
"wantownly agayn with hym she pleyde." We are led by
Chaucer to anticipate some weariness in her, or at least
some disdain for her less capable husband (compared

with Daun John), but evidently she is ready for any and all, at any time of day or night. We must admire her durability, if not her taste.

The repulsive Zenobia ("Monk's Tale," B 3478) permits her husband to have intercourse with her but once; if she conceives, "namoore sholde he pleyen thilke game"; we are told in the same tale (B 3484) that it is lechery if women have intercourse for other reasons—if men "pleyde" with them for other purposes.

In the *Romaunt of the Rose* (2322), the Lover is encouraged to "daunce and play" to gain favor with the ladies; both words have double meanings. It is not surprising, therefore, that in his "Complaint of Mars" (178) Chaucer himself calls Venus the source of "love and pley."

Venus presides over *Troilus and Criseyde,* though there are also malign influences (Fortuna, for instance) that make it the fascinating narrative that it is. Even in the variations he plays upon "pley," Chaucer shows us his mastery. There are some neutral meanings: Pandarus says (II. 121) that he could tell Criseyde something that would make her "pleye"; she has just refused to "daunce" (*q.v.*) since she is a widow. Then, they "pleide" of this and that (150)—talked idly, that's all. These are some of Chaucer's finger exercises for his variations on the word.

Criseyde thinks to herself that it "were honour" to "pley" with such a lord as Troilus (II. 705). After long inner debate, she goes to "pleye" (nice foreshadowing!) in the garden with her nieces (II. 812). Pandarus tells Troilus (III. 250) that he has begun "a gamen pleye," which he will never do for anyone else: it is "pandering," not real participation in the sport of intercourse, which perhaps makes the reference more obscene. Criseyde is about to have Troilus in her bed (III. 821), but she talks with her uncle Pandarus of the transience of man's joy ("O brotel wele") ; "with what wight so thow be, or how thow pleye." Can this be a sly Criseyde, pretending to be philosophical, but actually telling the foxy uncle that she is ready to "pley" with "some wight"? Yes.

Chaucer refuses to describe in detail their lovemaking, the rhetorical device of *occupatio* (III. 1313), but lets

them judge who have been at the feast of such gladness,
"if that hem liste pleye": (1) playfully try their hands at
such description; (2) like to have intercourse. In the
actual "pleyinge" (III. 1368) they interchange their rings.
I do not know what it means for Criseyde to receive
Troilus' ring, except in the literal sense, of course. Her
gift to him represents the vulva: see **ryng.** It is here, too,
that the oddly ugly note is struck about Pandarus putting
his hand under his niece's neck and she "with here uncle
gan to pleye . . . and Pandarus hath fully his entente"
(III. 1578) . See **incest.**

When Criseyde laments the necessity of leaving Troy,
her lady friends think that it is because she can no
longer "pleye" with them—in all innocence, of course.
The word is used for the diversion that Troilus and Pandarus have *chez* Sarpedoun, to help the hero forget his
lover (V. 402, 429, 431, 509) . When Troilus is recalling
the past (V. 569), his "pleye," along with "lustyly,"
"plesaunce," and "daunce," is probably suggestive. [*OED,*
10. c. to sport amorously; *euphem.,* to have sexual intercourse. The last citation in this sense is from *Paradise
Lost* (IX. 1027) where the reader will find, not surprisingly, that the old associations of "play," "toy," and
"disport" are still present, even though Milton was probably consciously using archaic connotations here. The passage concerns what C. S. Lewis calls the "fallen sexuality"
of Adam and Eve. Non-Chaucerian lyric verse is full of
plays on the word—e.g., see Robbins' Introduction (p.
xxxvi) where he quotes a carol: "y-loren is my playnge";
and his Poems Nos. 24, where the maiden will not let "with
me a clerk for to pleyn" (16) and 26, in which the word
"pley" (2) has the erotic sense.]

plit. The young wife May has to find a ladder or stool that
she can use to start her climb up the pear tree to Damyan,
who is waiting aloft to have carnal knowledge of her sweet
young body. To her blind old husband Januarie, she says
that "a womman in my plit / May han to fruyt so greet
an appetit / That she may dyen, but she of it have." She
is hinting that she is pregnant and that she must have

pears. Januarie obediently bends down. She steps on his back and in a trice Damyan has lifted her smock ("Merchant's Tale," E 2335). In his note, by the way, Skeat alludes to the "vulgar error" that pregnant women have these lusts.

In addition to her need for a stool, May has another motive for claiming to be pregnant. The old man is flattered that he can sire a child at his age. If Damyan is really successful at his game, the child can be explained to the dim-witted old man as arriving a little late. The flattery works, in any event, and after the improbable explanation of the "swyvyng," the cured blindness, and the struggling, Januarie is reconciled to his worthless little wife and strokes her on the "wombe" (E 2414). This is perhaps merely a gentle erotic act, but more likely it is evidence that he is persuaded that she is really *enceinte*. [*OED*, "plight," *sb*.², 4. b. evil condition—nothing more explicit.]

polucioun. Involuntary emission or orgasm, viewed in Chaucer's time (and by later puritanical moralists as well, of course) as an abominable sin. In dealing with Luxuria (Lechery) the Parson says that it comes during sleep: "ofte to hem that been maydenes, and eek to hem that been corrupt" (I 911). He also has a formula for this embarrassing event: it can occur in four ways, including having villainous thoughts before you go to sleep. [*OED*, 3. seminal emission apart from coition; self-pollution; citations from 1340 to the present.]

Poperyng. It is a town in Flanders, Thopas' birthplace (B 1910); but in view of its conjunction with "in the place" (*q.v.*), a bawdy meaning seems likely. By the sixteenth century "poppering" had come to mean a particular variety of pear; paranomastically, it was also a term for the male organ (pop-'er-in): see *Romeo and Juliet* (II. i. 38). The indecent sense seems to have arisen even in Chaucer's time, and the poet uses it as part of his "remarkable-commonplace" description of Thopas: the knight was born, he says, in an extraordinary way—by a union of the male and female organs. [*OED*, "poppering," cites the Shakespeare passage as the earliest reference to the fruit; it does not recognize any bawdy sense, though most modern editors of Shakespeare point out that the word was commonly used for the male parts.]

post. Baum hesitantly gives it a possible second meaning (penis) in the "General Prologue" (A 214), where the Friar is called a "noble post." In *Troilus and Criseyde* (I. 1000), Pandarus says to Troilus that since he has been converted from a scoffer to a supporter of love: "thow shalt ben the beste post, I leve, / Of al his lay" [law]. The idea is again "support," but perhaps there is the second meaning here too, since Pandarus speaks it. [*OED, sb.*1, 6. support, prop, stay. Cites Chaucer and (*ca.* 1430) Lydgate, *Minor Poems* (Percy Society, 29): "Ful ofte a wife is a broken poste," which is obviously not very good evidence for the secondary meaning, "penis." But Lydgate was not particularly sensitive to double entendre of an erotic sort, being a monk himself.]

pou-, powped. See **horn.**

press. In *Troilus and Criseyde,* Criseyde thinks that Pandarus will "Troilus upon hire for to presse" (II. 693), which means simply and innocently: (1) bring to meet her; but also (2) literally press her with his body. She is right on both counts, and it would seem likely that she deliberately uses the double meaning of the word, since (as we see often elsewhere) she is often given erotic equivocation. [*OED* has no support for an erotic meaning.]

prest. Priests are not really the continual butts of Chaucer's anticlerical and bawdy humor, as some critics think. Other members of the ecclesiastical hierarchy and organization, perhaps. . . . The Pardoner uses a particularly vicious kind of attack, and gratuitous too. He has a special medicine, he says, which when brewed with his pottage will make a man lose jealousy of his wife, "al had she taken prestes two or thre" ("Pardoner's Tale," C 371).

The "prest" in the "Canon's Yeoman's Tale" (G 1014) seems to be innocent enough; he was "so servysable / Unto the wyf, where as he was at table"; that is, he was useful to the woman with whom he took his meals. The alchemical canon gulls him later on, but nothing is made of his

(possible) sexual malfeasance. See **quene** and Figure 9.
Priapus. See **sceptre.**
priken. As a synonym for "to have intercourse," the word does
not really occur very often in Chaucer. It means to spur
a horse, to hurt oneself (as with a thorn), or to feel a
twinge (as of conscience) much more often.

Baum agrees, however, that in the "Reeve's Tale" (A
4231) the reference is to coitus: John is in bed with the
miller's wife and "he priketh harde and depe as he were
mad." The metaphor derives from riding, of course, and
one can see how easily erotic senses could develop.

But the noun "prick" for penis was not yet in use, and
consequently development was slow. If the Wife of Bath
misses a chance for an erotic equivocation, there must
have been little possibility—and she does so (D 656), with
her quotation of the rather foolish four-line, one-rhyme
proverb that contains the word but suggests nothing lascivious to the Wife: "Whoso that buyldeth his hous al of
salwes [willow-twigs], / And priketh his blynde horse over
the falwes [plowed lands], / And suffreth his wyf to go seken
halwes [saints' shrines], / Is worthy to been hanged on
the galwes."

Much more frequent are the innocent uses like the
familiar one in the "General Prologue" (A 11): "so priketh
hem nature in hir corages," which means that nature re-
vives the spirits of the birds in the spring. The juxtaposition of **corage,** however, may to some suggest that something more is happening here, perhaps the general sexual
awakening that many critics sense is part of it. We have
the same thing in the "Knight's Tale" (A 1043): "For
May wole have no slogardie a-nyght. / The sesoun
priketh every gentil herte." If this be bawdry, it is the
most gracious sort. The auditors are the true subjects and
audiences of romance, Gottfried von Strassburg's *edle
Herzen,* Dante's *cor gentil,* Chaucer's "every gentil herte."
The erotic overtones are faint and quite lovely.

With the famous passage from the "General Prologue"
describing the Monk, we are on a different plane. "Of
prikyng and of huntyng for the hare / Was al his lust"

(A 191) : see **hare** and **lust.** We should go back a couple of
lines, where Chaucer tells us (A 189) that "he was a
prikasour aright." It is the only occurrence of the word
in Chaucer's works; its literal meaning is one who follows
the "pricks" (hare's tracks). But this is the *Monk!* I
think we cannot deny that there is subtle bawdiness
throughout his description and every time he appears in
the *Tales,* except (oddly and significantly enough) when
he tells his own lugubrious stories. That he chooses to
relate tragedies, serious and irreproachably moral tales,
is his gesture toward his position in the Church and
society.

Even more frequent in Chaucer are innocent remarks
like that of the Parson, who finds occasion to allude to
bees (I 467) : "And therefore thise flyes that men clepen
bees, whan they maken hir kyng, they chesen oon that
hath no prikke wherwith he may stynge." He uses this
as an example of gentle monarchs and humility in good
subjects. More familiar is a phrase like: "o thyng priketh
in my conscience" from the "Merchant's Tale" (E 1635).
This is the *Agenbite of Inwit,* the Middle English treatise
whose title Stephen Dedalus cannot get out of his head
on June 16, 1904.

There are a couple of suggestive passages in the *Romaunt
of the Rose,* and even though they are, of course, Chaucer's
translations of the French, they may be cited. The Lover
is told to "prike gladly" (2314), which seems to refer to
riding. However, Chaucer (or whoever actually did the
translating) did not *have* to choose "prike" here, since
something like "spur" would have done just as well,
metrically and otherwise. See, too, 2438 ff., with its cluster
of "eased," "desyr," and "prikketh," where a subtle erotic
aura may be suggested. It is very much like Chaucer's
own *Parliament of Fowls* (389), where Nature tells the
birds that they are to choose their mates "as I prike yow
with plesaunce," where the presence of the last word
throws "prike" into a slightly different light.

The wild hunting scene (see **hunt**) in the *Legend of
Good Women* also shows that an erotic encrustation was
forming on "priken." See 1192 where Dido is planning

the hunt: "this lusty freshe queene, / So priketh hire this newe joly wo"; and—when the "hertes" appear, they cry "pryke thow!" (1213). See the discussion at **fressh**.

Last we have "Thopas," in which the word occurs eight times in eighty-three lines, as George Williams reminds us (pp. 146–147). He concludes that all this pricking is comically ironic in view of the effeminacy of the gentle knight. "The ribald meanings of the word are well known. According to the [*OED*], the noun *prick* was used to refer to the penis in the late sixteenth century." He is right: the first citation is found in literature written two hundred years after Chaucer. This is just the point. The erotic meanings for "prick" are not easy to demonstrate; neither is it easy to assume that certain meanings are present because we should like them to be there. This study, and more particularly the foregoing remarks on "prick," have, I hope, made this clear. [*OED,* 17. where the first citation for the meaning "penis" is 1592; it is marked "now low." The citations for the verb illustrate no erotic meanings whatsoever! See Robbins' Poem No. 28: "he prikede & he pransede" (28); and No. 32: "and ye begyn on me ffor to prycke" (39), which the editor glosses as "to have intercourse with."]

professioun. The monk's "professioun" was his vows, including that of chastity. Chaucer makes delightfully ironic use of this fact when Daun John in the "Shipman's Tale" (B 1345) protests to the wife that he loves her above all women, swearing on his "professioun." [*OED*, 1. vow made by one entering a religious order.]

pryvee, -ly, -etee. Chaucer has a marvelous time with these richly suggestive words, and so can his readers. I shall deal with four meanings: (1) private parts, genitals; (2) the suggestion of privates, with other suggestive words in the neighborhood; (3) privy, outhouse, house of easement, "a necessary" (as the *OED* calls it); and (4) nonerotic senses like "secret."

Baum cites the passage from the "Monk's Tale" (B 3905) to show that the word could indeed mean private parts. When Julius Caesar is dying, he throws his mantle over his hips so that none might see his "privetee"—a remarkable example of "honestee" (*q.v.*). One should also compare Lucrece, the shamefast suicide: see **bare**. A horrid corroboration of Baum's point is found in the *Boece* (II. Prosa 6. 40) where we are told of the frailty of man, who may be slain "with the entrynge of crepynge wormes into the pryvetees" of his body.

More interesting are the double meanings. I shall begin with one that I do not think is really there, but that should be pointed out. In the "General Prologue" (A 609), Chaucer says about the Reeve: "ful riche he was astored pryvely: / His lord wel koude he plesen subtilly," which suggests a relationship between the Reeve and his lord that is something other than business. Much surer and funnier is the "Miller's Tale" (A 3164): "An housbonde shal nat been inquisityf / Of Goddes pryvetee, nor of his wyf," which provides such exquisite preparation for what will happen in the tale proper: Nicholas, the overeducated clerk (his landlord thinks), presumes to look into "Goddes pryvetee," or rather to pretend to, when he predicts another Deluge. Actually, he is looking into the carpenter's wife's "pryvetee" (her private parts) and he succeeds in getting her to bed with very little difficulty. Chaucer makes these links and innuendos clear when Nicholas says he will not "tellen Goddes pryvetee" (A 3558).

Innuendos involving "privy" are not common in *Troilus and Criseyde*, though Baum thinks there is one suggested in "pryve wente" (III. 787), which means literally a private way. The exact double entendre is not explained, neither is it very clear, but Baum is probably right that something is going on: there may be an oblique reference to Criseyde's vagina. Criseyde, considering Troilus' "prive comyng" (III. 921), will grant him "grace" (the passage is also associated with "place"). It is a complex cluster in which sex is hinted at but in subtle ways. See **come, grace,** and **place.** After the lovers' night together, Troilus sends for Pandarus "pryvely" (III. 1585), which I think is an innocent meaning of the word (and thus could have been treated later on) —simply "privately."

In the "Summoner's Tale," Thomas tells the grasping friar to grope (*q.v.*) behind, "Bynethe my buttok there shaltow fynde / A thyng that I have hyd in pryvetee" (D 2143). The "thyng" is the infamous fart, and the double meaning of "pryvetee" (secret; private parts) cannot be doubted. Neither can it in the "Miller's Tale" (A 3276) when Nicholas "prively" seizes Alisoun. We might be in doubt about the word (it could—and does—mean simply "secretly, in private") were it not for the words that immediately follow: "by the queynte" (*q.v.*). The same joke recurs, though not quite so overtly, a few lines later when Alisoun asks Nicholas to "wayte [watch] wel and been privee" (A 3295).

The Wife of Bath bears the mark of Mars on her face "and also in another privee place" (D 620), which is "private" in both senses. We never discover the exact location or shape of the mark, but perhaps Alison's sixth husband, for whom she is searching on the Pilgrimage, will do so. In her "Tale," the Wife presents a long disquisition on "gentilesse" (or rather the hag in her story does), in which she says that if this quality were planted naturally, "pryvee and apert," then the gentle-born would never cease to act genteely (D 1136). There may be something sexual here, but I am not sure—genitals opened wide to those who wish to enter, like the Wife's? One must confess that here one is on less sure ground.

The summoner in the "Friar's Tale" (D 1343) has his spies, including whores; they act as his "approwours [agents] prively," surely a suggestion of sexual intimacy. See also **acqueyntaunce**.

When the Reeve has finished his tale, the Cook comments on the dangers of bringing strangers into one's "pryvetee," which he decides, wrongly, is the moral of the story. This lovely double entendre (A 4334) is made even more attractive because the ignorant and drunken Cook cannot be aware of his own subtlety: (1) private chambers; (2) private parts of the wife and daughter.

In his own tale (A 4388), unhappily unfinished, the Cook tells us that Perkyn the prentice is a dicer; no one is as free of his "dispense, in place of pryvetee." As things

stand in this tale, all we can be sure of is the surface meaning—"spending money in a private place." But I am certain that if the tale were to be finished, it would be a
fabliau, complete with the traditional themes of the
bilking of a middle-class character and the "swyvynge"
of a woman. Therefore, it is probable that Chaucer was
planning to use this reference with two more meanings:
(1) that the prentice takes his master's money from its
secret hiding place; and (2) that he expends his "goods"
(semen) in a woman's "secret place." Admittedly this is
speculation, but there are very good grounds for it, since
we know what happens in *fabliaux.*

The devil tells the summoner in the "Friar's Tale" (D
1637) that he will soon know of "oure privetee," which
seems merely to mean "secrets." But since in the "Summoner's Tale" (D 1690) we are told that friars live in Hell
in the devil's "privetee," his arse, there is probably an
indecent second meaning too. See Figure 4.

There are plenty of occasions in which the words mean
only "private" or "secret (s)." Let me suggest *Troilus
and Criseyde* (III. 1585), treated earlier; or the "Miller's
Tale" (A 3603) where the carpenter tells Alisoun all his
"pryvetee." [*OED,* "privy," *adj.,* 1. c. sexually intimate;
8. d. privy members, privy parts, privy *chose* (of a female) —see *chose; sb.,* 3. a private place of ease, a latrine, a
necessary; 4. short for privy member.]

purge. The Parson rails against indecent clothing, sometimes
in amusing (or at least surprising) contexts. In his attack
on Superbia (Pride), he expresses his horror at garments
that show off the buttocks, the "hyndre part," and "that
partie of hir body ther as they purgen hir stynkynge
ordure" (I 427). See **laxatyf.** [*OED, v.*1, 4. to empty
(the . . . bowels).]

purse. Because of similar shape and valuable contents, this
word also had a secondary erotic meaning, "scrotum." This
is what the Wife of Bath is talking about when she boasts
that she has picked out the best partners for herself (in
lines declared uncanonical by Robinson and relegated to
the bottom of the page). She chooses those who excel

"bothe of here nether purs and of here cheste" (D 44b).
"Purse" = (1) moneybags and (2) manly scrotum; and
"cheste" (not erotic, but a pun) = (1) money chest and
(2) manly thorax.

Chaucer seems not to have used this amusing double
sense elsewhere. In his delightful "Complaint of Chaucer
to His Purse," he equates the purse with a woman in a
witty way. See **light** and Figure 13. [*MED*, "ballok": "bal-
lok-purs," the scrotum (*ca.* 1410 and other contemporary
citations); *s.v.* "instrument." *MED* mentions the bull's
"stoon" (testicle) and the "porce" in which it is (they
are?) kept. *OED*, "purse," 8. b. the scrotum. Cf. Robbins'
Poem No. 7: "I haue a poket for the nonys, / therine ben
tweyne precyous stonys," where the allusions to scrotum
and ballocks are clear.]

putery, -ours. These are learned or "pulpit" words for whore-
dom and procurers. See the "Parson's Tale" (I 885 ff.)
where he condemns the procurer who may sell the "bodily
puterie" of his own wife or child. [*OED*, "putery," har-
lotry, prostitution; "putour," whoremonger, pimp, fornicator; citations from Wyclif and Langland.]

pyrie. Pear tree, but also a commonplace symbol for the penis.
It is not completely clear how this works in the "Merchant's Tale" (E 2217) where Damyan sits "upon the
pyrie," but like the tree his penis is erect and ready. May
expresses an uncontrollable desire for "peres" (E 2333) —
testicles?—climbs the tree, and soon is in Damyan's arms.
[*OED* provides no erotic meanings. However, see Robbins'
Poem No. 21, where the "peryr" and the "pery tre" (6,
12) represent the penis. It bears no pears, but the "per
Ienet" (that is, it bears the weight of a girl). A maiden
comes into the garden and asks for a grafting, which she
gets. The man "gryffid her / ryght vp in her home"
(17–18). The verb "gryffyn" is glossed "to insert (a shoot
of one tree) into a different stock." Robertson, *Preface*
(p. 328 *n.*), describes an obscene marginalium in a MS
of *Le Roman de la Rose* in which a woman plucks fruit
in the shape of male organs.]

q

quene. Quean, harlot. In the "Manciple's Tale" (H 18), the
Host is extremely (and justifiably) rude to the drunken
Cook; no doubt as a professional innkeeper he had had
experience with such types. He asks the Cook if he has
"yswonke" (labored; had intercourse) all night with a
"quene." In the circumstances the word, spoken by Harry
Bailly, has grimy connotations. It is also humorous, since
the sodden Cook does not have the strength to **swynke**
with anyone. There is the same sense in the *Romaunt of
the Rose* (7032), in reference to a "prest that halt his
quene hym by" (cf. **prest**).

But in a couple of Chaucer's lyrics, I am not sure of the
meaning. "A Complaint to His Lady" (54) has "My hertes
lady, and hool my lyves quene," which I would not give a
second glance (accepting the meaning as "queen") were
it not for the potentially corruptive presence of **hol.**
"Fortune" (43) is easier to judge and actually shows us
the bawdy Chaucer at work with his materials. Fortune
answers the Pleintif that she has been his "quene"—a
double meaning (queen and whore), first because it is the
conventional strumpet Fortuna who is speaking, and,
second, because of the proximity of **plesaunce** in the preceding line. The source is *Boece* (II. Prosa 1. 99–100),
where Boethius chooses Fortuna as his *lady.* When he
transfers this material to his lyric, Chaucer deliberately
gives the word a second, libidinous sense. [*OED,* "quean,"
at first simply a woman, a female, but soon degraded into
strumpet, hussy, harlot. In Middle English, the word was
distinguished from "queen" by its open *e,* which in the
fourteenth to fifteenth centuries was sometimes denoted
by the spelling with *ei* or *ey,* and later (as in other words
of the class) by *ea.* As the Chaucer material shows, the
qualification *"sometimes* distinguished" should be made
here. As an example of what the *OED* is talking about,

see *Piers Plowman* (C-Text, IX. 46) : you cannot tell a knight from a knave or a "queyne fro a queene," where the former is the harlot.]

queynt. The word had a number of significances in Chaucer's day, which makes it perhaps the most interesting of all the sexual double-meaning locutions in the poet's work. First it was the forerunner of "cunt" and the normal, if vulgar, name for the vagina. It also meant strange; curious, curiously contrived; elaborate, ornamented; neat, artful, sly; graceful; "make it queynt (e) ," be offish or disdainful, make it strange or difficult; also, show pleasure or satisfaction (from Robinson's glossary) . Further, it was the past participle of "quenchen," i.e., "quenched"; and it formed part of words like **acqueyntaunce.**

Baum sees unequivocal references to the pudendum in the "Miller's Tale" (A 3276), a line that must be quoted with its predecessor for the *rime riche* (identical rhyme, which Chaucer and the French of his time admired extravagantly—to use it here makes the couplet very funny indeed!) :

> *As clerkes ben ful subtile and ful queynte;*
> *And prively he caughte hire by the queynte. . . .*

See Figures 7, 8, and 9 where this act is graphically shown.
    The same perceptive scholar has also found an unequivocal vagina in the "Wife of Bath's Tale" (D 444) : her husband does not want her to go out; "Is it for ye wolde have my queynte allone?" she shrieks at him. In the tale (D 332), Baum says that the meaning is "semi-abstract," a judgment with which I simply cannot agree, since it seems as forthright as the other two. In speaking of her old dotard husband, she tells him that he will have "queynte right ynogh at eve" (see Introduction, p. 10) . Baum agrees with me, however, that we have an unmistakable double meaning, when she confesses that she, like all woman, has a "queynte fantasye" (D 516) : (1) curious habit of mind; (2) concern with her own pudendum. Kökeritz says, about this passage (p. 951) , that it "cannot have failed to produce delighted chuckles from

Fig. 7. *Ivory mirror-case (15th c. ?): the gentleman has the lady by the "queynt," just like Nicholas in the "Miller's Tale." Victoria and Albert Museum, London.*

Chaucer's listeners or readers, who were familiar with the word used in l. 444."

Baum also sees sophisticated double meaning in the "Merchant's Tale" (E 2061; he prints 2057 by mistake), in the passage on the evanescence of worldly joy, with its explosive oxymorons: "O brotil joye! o sweete venym queynte!" The particular example of worldly joy under consideration is the female, the wife to be enjoyed in bed, either by her husband or by another. The "venym queynte" is therefore clearly (1) strange poison, and (2) poisonous pudendum.

No one has commented, I think, on the obvious parallel to this passage that occurs in *Troilus and Criseyde* (I. 411), in the "Canticus Troili," the hero's love song: "O quike deth, O swete harm so queynte." The oxymorons remind one of the "Merchant's Tale" lines and also of influential passages like the "swete helle" and "soroufull paradys" of the *Romaunt of the Rose* (4743) —where, however, there are no bawdy second meanings.

Baum and Kökeritz do not mention the "Knight's Tale" (A 1531), where Chaucer writes about manic-depressive lovers, now up, now down, "as boket in a welle"—these lovers "in hir queynte geres." The figure of the bucket and well helps to suggest, however timidly, that we also have an equivoque here. Arcite is thinking of Emelye and even though she is a devotee of Diana and one of the purest (dullest?) heroines of romance, she too has a "queynte." And when she is praying in the Temple of Diana (Kökeritz does mention the play on words here, without commenting on the eroticism), the Knight says (A 2333 ff.) :

> *But sodeynly she saugh a sighte queynte,*
> *For right anon oon of the fyres queynte,*
> *And quyked agayn, and after that anon*
> *That oother fyr was queynt and al agon;*
> *And as it queynte it made a whistelynge. . . .*

The fires are omens of future events. One of her suitors will be vanquished in battle, but the other will die in a

nonmilitary accident. There is also, I believe, some suggestion of Emelye's leaving the followers of Diana and
turning to those of Venus. To Chaucer's audience, all
those "queyntes" in a row could suggest only one thing.
Braddy, "Obscenity" (p. 129), agrees, quoting Bolton:
"With four 'queynts' and a whistle in five lines, Chaucer
leaves no doubt where the fire is."

Perhaps Chaucer was uncertain about maintaining the
tone of the high romantical in the "Knight's Tale." It
seems to be an example of what Bronson calls "rapid
shifts of stylistic level" (Introduction, p. 5n). In a
fabliau like the "Miller's Tale," the tone is more consistent, and when (A 3605) we are told that Alisoun knows
"what al this queynte cast was for to seye," both meanings
are there—"cunning contrivance" and "cunt." When
Absolon has kissed Alisoun's "nether ye" (see ye) by mis-
direction, his once hot love is "coold and al yqueynt"—
i.e., quenched, but surely a whiff of the pudendum too
(A 3754). Miss Hieatt does not hesitate to point out the
puns in this tale that involve "queynt" and "yqueynt,"
and as she astutely observes: "While these puns are
patently obscene, they also have an ironic function characteristic of the poet's treatment of this material" (p. 10).

The miller in the "Reeve's Tale" (A 4051) suspects that
the clerks will make "queynte crekes," glossed as "clever
tricks," and indeed they do. They also become closely
acquainted with the "queyntes" of their host's wife and
daughter. See **crekes.**

In the "Squire's Tale" (F 234), authorities have written
on the "queynte mirours" and (F 239) on Achilles "with
his queynte spere," and it is probable that neither is
obscene. But later in the tale Canacee awakens from her
sleep (F 369) "for swich a joye she in hir herte took /
Bothe of hir queynte ryng and hire mirour, / That twenty
tyme she changed hir colour. . . ." Does this Oriental
heroine change color for shame (embarrassment over the
vision she has had in the mirror) or is it an allusion to her
repeated orgasms, as she takes joy in her "queynte ryng"?
The latter seems preposterous, yet in view of the passages
where "queynte" occurs elsewhere, one can hardly doubt

Fig. 8. *Detail from a mural by Francesco del Cossa (1436–78) at the Palazzo Schifanoia, Ferrara; note the gentleman's hand and the symbolic hares. Alinari-Art Reference Bureau.*

that Chaucer's audience would have raised an eyebrow. Her "queynte ryng" is mentioned again (F 433), but she is bearing it on her finger, and with its magical help, readers will recall, she can understand the language of birds. See **ryng**.

The merchant in the "Shipman's Tale" bores his wife almost to distraction (he *does* bore her into adultery) by explaining his business deals at intolerable length. The ironic double meanings in the following passage make it all the more amusing, because we know that the listener will cuckold the tedious speaker (B 1420 ff.) :

> *We may wel make chiere and good visage,*
> *And dryve forth the world as it may be,*
> *And kepen oure estaat in pryvetee,*
> *Til we be deed, or elles that we pleye*
> *A pilgrymage, or goon out of the weye.*
> *And therfore have I greet necessitee*
> *Upon this queynte world t'avyse me. . . .*

See **pleye** and **pryvee**.

In his loftier pieces, as we have already seen in the "Knight's Tale," Chaucer sometimes puzzles us with his tone. In the *Book of the Duchess* (784), for example, the "impressions" of love in the Man in Black's heart are figures on a wall or tablet, "be the werkes never so queynte." And at the end (1330), the poet says that it was "so queynt a sweven" [dream] that he will put it into rhyme. The *Book of the Duchess* is a love poem, but I do not think we are to understand these "queyntes" in two senses here. One cannot, however, ignore the faint suggestion of the carnal.

So too in the *House of Fame* (126), in the Temple of Glass Chaucer sees more "queynte maner of figures," which seems innocent (the word used in the sense of "curious") . The poet knows, however, that this is Venus' Temple (133) because he sees her figure "naked fletynge [floating] in a see." So there is a possibility, and maybe more than that, of something erotic in the "queynte."

Hinton (p. 116) writes about "queynte": "This is one of Chaucer's favorite obscene puns, noted by Baum in several places. Two others should be added, both at the *House of Fame*, 245–250. After saying that Dido granted Aeneas 'al that weddynge longeth too' (244), Chaucer first says 'What shulde I speke more queynte' (245), then notes 'the manere / How they aqueynteden in fere' (249–250)." These are valuable additions, but Hinton has missed one from the same passage that also deserves to be recorded: Aeneas meets Venus "goynge in a queynt array" (228), which may be innocent, but is certainly preparation for the adulterous affair that is to follow. It also reminds us of the organ with which Venus is naturally associated. Her "array" is curiously wrought, too, of course.

In *Troilus and Criseyde,* the abandoned hero can no longer behold his lover. She must leave Troy, and the metaphor for her absence is an extinguished light: "syn she is queynt, that wont was yow to lighte" (IV. 313). This occurs in the neighborhood of **stonden** and **light.** Of course "queynte" = (1) quenched and (2) vagina; and "light" = (1) give you illumination and (2) morally loose. We are reminded of this later on when Troilus apostrophizes Criseyde's empty house (V. 543): "O thow lanterne of which queynt is the light." See **light** for more illustrations.

The great fury of Troilus' penance (i.e., the fury of his despair) "was queynt with hope" (IV. 1430), and he and Criseyde begin "th'amorouse daunce." The primary meaning is "quenched," but the erotic significance is also hovering nearby. See **daunce** too.

In the *Legend of Good Women* (F-Text, 353), there are in court many a "queynte totelere accusour"—glossed as "cunning, tattling accuser," though Baugh says that "totelere" is properly a noun. Since this is a slander against women, dealing with their fragility in love, it might be suggestive.

Let us examine a final (perhaps) obscene example before we turn to the innocent occurrences. In the "Wife of Bath's Prologue" (D 361), Robinson does not print, but points out that one MS has "though queynte he be" for "so moot I thee" (a tag meaning "so may I thrive"). The primary significance is probably "sly." The change was doubtless scribal: it demonstrates that the scribe was aware of the effect of the incremental repetition of this double-meaning word, though perhaps he overdid it.

Chaucer *could* use "queynte" in its commonplace and nonerotic senses. In the "Man of Law's Tale" (B 1189), the Shipman says he knows no "termes queinte of lawe," where it simply means "curious, involved, complicated." So too the Franklin protests ("Franklin's Tale," F 726) that he knows no "colours"—"colours of rethoryk been to me queynte." He means, with engaging honesty, that rhetoricians' devices are not familiar to him. The Canon's Yeoman (G 752) tells of the alchemists' "elvysshe" craft, the terms of which are so "clergial and so queynte" (learned, strange). Note that all three of these passages are spoken by relatively unlearned men who disclaim acquaintance with technical language.

The labyrinth in the *Legend of Good Women* (2013) has "queynte weyes"—curious turnings. And in *Troilus and Criseyde* (IV. 1629), Criseyde asks, who can keep a thing that has the desire to escape, and answers herself: "my fader naught, for al his queynte pley." One cannot possibly harbor any suspicions here of "queinte" *or* of "pley." See also **acqueyntaunce**. [*MED*, "cunte," *n.*; also "conte," "counte," "queynte" (corresponding to Old Irish "kunta," OFris, MD and MLG "kunt"). A woman's private parts. "Cunt-beten" = impotent (man). Earliest citation *a.* 1325. The only example from Chaucer is D 444. *OED* is uncertain of origin: from the adjective "quaint"? Cites Florio, *Becchina* (1598): "A woman's quaint or priuities." Partridge (p. 95), *s.v.* "coun," claims an etymology "from the Aryan radical" present in "quean," "cow," and Greek *gyné*. Farmer and Henley report that "quaint" for the pudendum was still in use in the seventeenth century; and Halliwell states that in 1847 it, along with "quim," was still used "in the North of England by the colliers and the common people." (They were speaking Chaucer all their lives without knowing it.)

Fig. 9. *An ecclesiastic—probably a monk or friar—with his hand between a prostitute's legs outside her place of business; the "bush" protruding from above the doorway suggests that it is a tavern. Note the chamber pot (see "jurdones"). British Museum (London), Yates Thompson MS, 13 (14th c.), fol. 177ʳ.*

"Quiff," by the way, was not a noun, but a verb (to copulate) in the eighteenth century. For some more amusing synonyms, see Robbins' Poem No. 26: it is the "box" wherein the clerk puts "hys offryng" (11); a "mouse-trappe" (13). See also **lappe.** Robbins' Poem No. 211 has "wemen, for all theyre cheres queynt" (8) and "Hit ys full queynt theyre fantasy to aspy" (20). (The first of these is glossed with an error—210.8. for 211.8. The editor recognizes no sexual meanings for the last two quotations.) *Piers Plowman* has several passages that suggest the double meaning (B-Text, XVIII. 344), "queynte was thorw synne," where the parallel passage in C-Text, XXI. 394, has "aqueynt thorw synne"). Even clearer are the lines describing Lady Meed (Bribery)—e.g. (A-Text, II. 14), where she is dressed in scarlet, with rings on each of her five fingers (see **fyngres**)—"ther nis no qweene qweyntore." Neither of the other two versions has parallel passages. See **quene.** Langland wrote (C-Text, V. 161): "the comune called hure queynte comune hore," where "hure" refers to Mead (B omits "queynte"; A has neither). The meaning is "the common people called her 'quaint common whore,'" but there are also double meanings for "comune" (= also everybody's property) and "hure" (her, whore). Under the pudibund rubric "monosyllable," Farmer and Henley record "coynte," "quaint," and "queynte," along with "cunt." Their list of synonyms is fairly exhaustive (though they rarely cite Chaucer). It includes "coney" (see **hare**); "nature" (*q.v.*); "ring" (*q.v.*); "Temple of Venus" (see **Venus**); and, among the French words for the monosyllable, *la lanterne* and *lampe amoureuse* (see **candle**).]

quoniam. All the husbands of the Wife of Bath told her "I hadde the beste *quoniam* myghte be" (D 608). The Latin word literally means "because"—as we might say today, "what-do-you-call-it." It is one of Alison's synonyms for her vagina, suggested no doubt by the identical initial letters of **queynte.** See Figure 10. [*OED* does not have the word in this sense, but cites it as a term used in the seventeenth century for a particular kind of drinking glass.]

Fig. 10. *A grotesque with a second face for genitals, apparently applauding a nude woman; the word* quoniam *begins two of the prayers on this page and just above the drawing there is a reference to beauty* (pulcritudo), *which the drawing may illustrate. Bodleian Library, Oxford, Douce MS 62 (14th c.), fol. 43ʳ.*

R

rage. Baum refers to this word as a synonym for sexual activity. See the "General Prologue" (257) where we are told about the Friar: "rage he koude, as it were right a whelp. / In love-dayes ther koude he muchel help." See **love-dayes.**

The same word is used to describe the love play of the adulterous Nicholas and Alisoun in the "Miller's Tale" (A 3273) : when the old husband is away at Oseneye, the young clerk "fil with this yonge wyf to rage and pleye." In three lines, he has seized her by the **queynte,** and they agree to get into bed together as soon as possible. Clearly "rage" does not mean "copulate" here, but some kind of precoital caressing. See **pleye.**

The relative innocence of the word is clearer in the "Reeve's Tale" (A 3958) where the miller becomes angry if anyone dares to "rage or pleye" with his wife. But in the "Wife of Bath's Prologue" (D 455) , her description of herself "I was yong and ful of ragerye" is blatantly and actively sexual.

After their wedding night, Januarie tries to act coltish and "ful of ragerye" ("Merchant's Tale," E 1847), but it does not deceive May, his young wife. See **bene.**

In the *Romaunt of the Rose* (3400) , we have Daunger in his "rage, / And in his hond a gret burdoun"—a cluster that suggests some sort of Priapic scene that I cannot quite envision. It seems inappropriate for this allegorical figure, which symbolizes aloofness, to be represented in a coital posture with penis in hand, but this is what the erotic double entendres indicate. It is odd for Daunger to rage and to carry a big stick anyway. See **burdoun** and **sceptre.** [*OED,* 3. to behave wantonly or riotously; to take one's pleasure; to play. Robbins' Poem No. 24 has: "Now wyll I not lete for no rage / With me a clerk for to pleyn" (15) .]

ragerye. See **rage.**

ram. Williams (p. 148) finds something sexually suggestive in this word in "Thopas" (B 1931). The lines are "Of wrastlyng was ther noon his peer, / Ther any ram shal stonde," and we have Robinson's note on the ram as a wrestler's prize (cf. "General Prologue," A 548), all of which seem innocent. Williams insists, however, that there is the suggestion of "a plunging action," which "must have long phallic associations," where "long" is, I think, used in the temporal sense. There are other passages in "Thopas" of an erotically suggestive nature. I believe, however, that "ram" is here without indecent overtones, despite the second reference in the *OED* citation, which would have helped Williams' case, if he had chosen to use it. [*OED* has no relevant meanings under *v.*1, but *v.*2, *obs. rare,* to leap (the ewe), with two seventeenth-century citations, is perhaps of some help. See **lepe.**]

rape. In the phrase "rape and renne," from the "Canon's Yeoman's Tale" (G 1422), we must not jump to conclusions. As Skeat explains, it has a complex history of mistaken substitutions, but it means merely "snatch and catch."

In the *Legend of Good Women* (2228 ff.), where we have a real rape (perhaps the most famous in all myth) in the tale of Philomene (as Chaucer always calls her), the poet is strangely silent about the details. Perhaps he was reticent, or perhaps the whole thing was too familiar. [*OED, v.*2, 1. b. to take a thing by force, cites the Chaucerian alliterative tag.]

ravysshed. In the "Summoner's Tale" (D 1676), the word is innocent of sexual meaning. It means "carried off." Indeed, this is true wherever it occurs in Chaucer: "Nun's Priest's Tale" (B 4514), where Chaunticleer is carried away by the fox's blandishments; and *Troilus and Criseyde* (IV. 530, together with several later passages in the poem), where it is suggested that the hero "ravish" his beloved in order to prevent her going to the Greek camp, but he refuses. [*OED,* 1. to seize and carry off a person; 2. b. to commit rape upon a woman—first citation, 1436.]

rebaudrye. See **ribaudye.**

rebekke. See **ribibe.**

refresshed. The Wife of Bath (D 38) marvels at Solomon, with all his wives: "As wolde God it were leveful unto me / To be refresshed half so ofte as he!" This gives special piquancy to Alison's equating of wives (ready for intercourse) with barley bread (D 146) : "And yet with barlybreed, Mark telle kan, / Oure Lord Jhesu refresshed many a man." Easygoing wives are God's (Christ's) gift to mankind.

It has the same double meaning in the heroic poetry of the *Legend of Good Women* (1081). Dido takes pity on Aeneas: "refreshed moste he been of his distresse," which, in light of what the pair was famous for, and in light of the bawdy tone of the entire "Legend," doubtless has a libidinous second meaning—the peculiarly refreshing act of intercourse. [*OED* has only general senses. Cites the *Legend of Good Women* passage under 2. c. to relieve *of*, to set free or clear *of*.]

religioun. In the "Monk's Tale" (B 3134), the Host expresses his dismay that the Monk is in Holy Orders and cannot propagate: "I pray to God, yeve hym confusioun / That first thee broghte unto religioun! / Thou woldest han been a tredefowel aright." Harry Bailly makes very similar remarks to the Nun's Priest; in fact, the similarities are so great that it is possible that Chaucer meant to cancel one or the other when he edited his MS of the *Tales* in the final version (which never appeared, of course). See **tredefowel.**

A few lines later, the Host tells the Monk (B 3150) that "religious folk" are better at "engendrure" and therefore lay peoples' wives should go to them for "Venus paiementz." He hastily adds that he is joking, but "Ful ofte in game a sooth I have herd seye," one of Harry Bailly's favorite explanations of his own and others' levity.

In the "Parson's Tale" (I 890), one of the species of "avowtrie" is that devoted to the religious—when one or both partners in the sin are also in Holy Orders. [*OED*, the state of life bound by monastic vows.]

revel. A playful euphemism for copulation. Alisoun and Nicholas in the "Miller's Tale" (A 3652) are cosily in bed while the cuckold husband is suspended from the ceiling in his kneading-tub, awaiting the Deluge. "Ther was the revel and the melodye; / And thus lith Alison and Nicholas, / In bisynesse of myrthe and of solas." See **myrthe**.

The lamentably unfinished "Cook's Tale" contains a couple of references to "revel," the bawdy sense of which would doubtless have emerged had Chaucer finished the story. The "prentys" is named Perkyn Revelour (A 4371). He *is* a "revelour" (4391); and, though he is able to play on the "gyterne" and the "ribible" (see **ribibe**), "revel and trouthe" are ever at odds. The likelihood—nay, the inevitability!—is that if the tale were complete, this apprentice would be in bed at least once with somebody, and "revel" would take place. The passage in which Chaucer (or the Cook) speculates that he was "somtyme lad with revel to Newegate" (A 4402) takes on new auras of erotic suggestion in context. See **Newgate**.

The rich merchant's wife in the "Shipman's Tale" was "compaignable" (*q.v.*) and "revelous." Both are innocent, perhaps, at the beginning of the tale (B 1194), but Chaucer is preparing us for the lewd double meanings that will be made manifest later on in the story.

The Wife of Bath defines the word for us, in case we need it: "My fourthe housbonde was a revelour; / This is to seyn, he hadde a paramour" (D 453). [*OED*, "revel," *v.*¹, to make merry (no particularly erotic senses); nor is there any citation from Chaucer, though "reveler" is illustrated by the Wife's definition. The dictionary refuses to recognize an erotic significance, despite the reference to "paramour."]

revelour, -ous. See **revel**.

reverberacioun. This polysyllable for "echo" is humorous and bawdy only in context, where it is used as the scientific explanation for a fart. See the "Summoner's Tale" (D 2234). See also **soun**. [*OED*, 1. a. the fact, on the part *of* a thing, of being driven or forced back, especially after impact—a ponderous definition funnier than Chaucer's use of the word, which is the earliest citation. The last comes from 1601.]

ribaudye. Like many Middle English words, this one has

undergone pejoration over the centuries; it originally had a meaning not quite so low and wicked as it has now—it was a little vulgar, perhaps. The Reeve (A 3866) says that if he wanted to repay the Miller for his tale, he could speak of "ribaudye," but he is old, and he is indeed too old to "pleye." There is nice dramatic irony here, for (although we are never assured of the Reeve's own virility) his "Tale" is certainly ribald enough—probably the second or third on the scale of bawdiness.

Later the "gentils" in the entourage cry out against the Pardoner, asking that he be forbidden to tell them "ribaudye," where the modern meaning of "obscenity" has clearly developed fully. They want "som moral thyng" ("Pardoner's Tale," C 324). They get it: his sermon is unexceptionable.

The modern sense is probably not present yet, however, in the *Romaunt of the Rose* (2224): the Lover is told not to speak words of "rebaudrye," which could be nothing stronger than "slang." [*OED,* "ribald," *sb.,* 1. one of an irregular class of retainers who performed the lowest offices in royal or baronial households . . . hence a menial or dependent of low birth. "Ribaldry," 1. debauchery, lasciviousness, vice.]

ribibe. The summoner calls the poor old woman a "ribibe" in the "Friar's Tale" (D 1377). There is some lost joke here (Skeat) that we can only partially recapture. It is obviously an insulting term and probably also lewd.

The "ribibe" is a synonym for the "rebekke" (D 1573), both stringed musical instruments. There may have been some allusion to the harsh sounds made upon these instruments, which were likened to the voices of aged scolds. Skeat felt that there was an allusion to Rebecca, in the marriage ceremony (a pun that scholars perennially rediscover). Whatever the explicit meaning, there is a hint that the old woman is a worthless object, no longer good for sexual purposes, perhaps like an old fiddle without strings.

The apprentice in the "Cook's Tale" (A 4396) can play upon the "ribible," but since the tale is not finished we cannot guess what the relevance of this information might be. It was to be a *fabliau* about a wife who "swyved for hir sustenaunce," so perhaps the "ribibe, -ible" pun would have been explained. See **swyve**. [*OED*, "ribibe," 1. = "rebeck"; 2. an opprobrious or abusive term for an old woman. The note is made (Skeat does the same) that both Skelton and Jonson doubtless took the word from Chaucer.]

rise. See *Troilus and Criseyde* (III. 69) : "allas, I may nought rise, / To knele and do you honour in som wyse." Hinton (p. 116) says: "In view of the situation, there is almost certainly a coarse pun when Troilus greets Criseyde from his bed" and speaks this speech. "Pandarus (of whom we might expect such talk) repeats it at lines 202–203: 'Whan thow mayst ryse, / This thing shal be ryght as you devyse.' " Hinton's remarks are marred by a host of typographical errors, but his point is not affected by them: the reference to an erect penis is quite obviously in the air at this point in this most erotic book of this erotic poem. [*OED, v.,* 1. g. of hair, etc., to become erect or stiff. The earliest citation is from Dunbar (one of Chaucer's followers as a "Scottish Chaucerian") , *Poems* (1500–1520, lxxv. 34) : "Your heylis . . . Gars ryis on loft my quhillelillie." A more modern edition, that of Mackenzie (p. 54) , prints "Garris" (24) but otherwise the quotation is the same. It is worthy of note. "Heylis" is a Northern English word (that is, a Scottish word) for the neck—Chaucer's "hals." For the erotic significance of the white neck (and Dunbar does describe her neck as white in this poem) , see **nekke**. The marvelous "quhillelillie," a Scottish word for penis, should be made known to a wider audience.]

romances. The principal kind of erotic literature in the Middle Ages. Thopas finds himself confronted by a three-headed giant while he is on his questing; inexplicably (and unhappily) he has forgotten his armor on this quest, and therefore must return home ("drow abak ful faste") for it, before engaging in battle. As he is being armed, he arranges for "geestours" to tell him tales, probably to rouse his courage: "romances that been roialcs, / Of popes and of cardinales, / And eek of love-

Figs. 11, 12, 13. *The climactic events of* Le Roman de la Rose: *the God of Love wounds the image; with pilgrim's staff (penis) and scrip (scrotum) the Lover approaches her; the defenses are down and the act is consummated (note the two hammers [testicles] in the scrip). University Library, Valencia, MS 387 (ca. 1420), fols. 144ʳ, 144ᵛ, and 146ᵛ.*

likynge" (B 2038). This is part of Chaucer's parody—
an amazing confusion of quite impossible elements in the
narratives to which Thopas listens. See also **hair** and
likyng.

When Troilus and Criseyde have snuggled up in bed
during the rainstorm, Pandarus retires to the fireplace
and pretends to "looke upon an old romaunce" (III. 980),
the old voyeur!

Among the *Tales*, by the way, the "Knight's Tale," the
"Wife of Bath's Tale," and the "Squire Tale" are romances.
"Thopas" parodies their conventions and those of similar
narratives. [*OED*, II. 2. a tale in verse, embodying the
adventures of some hero of chivalry. . . .]

ronyon. Baum refers to the "Nun's Priest's Tale" (B 4638),
which must be a mistake, since this is an erotic passage,
all right, but not one involving this word (see **stoon**).
However, he points out that "runnion" meant the male
organ and also was an abusive term applied to a woman.

See these references in context: it is the exchange between the Host and the Pardoner before the "Pardoner's
Tale" (C 309–310, 320):

> HOST: "So moot I theen [so may I thrive], thou art a propre
> man,
>   And lyk a prelat, by Seint Ronyan!"

> PARDONER: "It shal be doon," quod he, "by Seint Ronyon!"

The echo is very odd, unless Chaucer wants to call our
attention to this obscure saint and to the double meanings and puns associated with his name. The Host also
calls the Pardoner "beel amy" (*q.v.*), which may be suspicious, and their vicious exchange of insults and double
entendres at the end of the "Tale" is in the most violent
language that Chaucer wrote.

When we add here the earlier gloss of "ronyon" as the
bottom, the fundament, we have invective that may be
translated "arse," "prick," which is enough to arouse
anyone's wrath. The Pardoner waits until he has finished
his sermon to get his revenge (C 941 ff.). [*OED*, "runnion," 1. an abusive term applied to a woman; 2. the

male organ. Neither has fourteenth-century citations—
only later ones.]

rouncivale. Tatlock (p. 232, *n.*) says that "rouncival" in the
sixteenth century meant a mannish woman. " 'Rouncy'
means a riding horse, and the Pardoner is called 'a gelding
or a mare.' The passages are not close together, so I feel
no confidence in this suggestion. But there may be some
such forgotten point." Robinson found the equation with
"rouncy" unlikely; but Baum finds that it is, after all, a
probability—an equation with a mannish woman. Robinson explained "Rouncivale" in the "General Prologue"
(A 670) as a reference to Rouncivalle, a hospital near
Charing Cross, but this has not completely satisfied anybody. For more peculiar suspicions about the Pardoner, see
hair. [*OED*, "rouncival," 3. a woman of large build and
boisterous or loose manners; the illustrative citations
range from 1596 to 1654.]

ryde. At night on a narrow perch, the noble Chaunticleer
knows that he cannot "ryde" Pertelote; that is, to "treden,"
to have intercourse. The terms are usually used only for
fowl ("Nun's Priest's Tale," A 4358) , but these are very
human birds, of course, since it is a beast fable.

In the lyric of doubtful authorship, "Complaynt
D'Amours" (19), the poet calls himself the unworthiest
that "may ryde or go," which is probably just a rhyme-tag
(ride or walk—as "go" always meant) . But perhaps it is
also suggestive of copulation, since "go" might denote
ability to have an orgasm.

In the *Romaunt of the Rose* (2313), the Lover is told:
"For if that thou good ridere be, / Prike gladly, that
men may se. / In armes also if thou konne. . . ." See
armes and **priken.** [*OED*, 3. to mount the female, copulate; now only in low and indecent language. Citations
from the thirteenth through the eighteenth centuries that
refer to human copulation.]

ryng. Criseyde, playing coy, says to Pandarus (III. 885) : "have
heere, and bereth hym [Troilus] this blewe ryng, / For
ther is nothyng myghte hym bettre plese, / Save I myself."
The ring, the "O," the "null," the "nought"—all these
have been recognized for a long time as suggestive of the

female pudendum. The sensuous metaphor goes back at least as far as Ovid's *Amores* (II. xv), on the gift of a ring to his mistress:

> *Anule, formosae digitum vincture puellae . . .*
> *tam bene convenias, quam mecum convenit illi.*
> (O ring, that art to circle the finger of my fair
> lady . . . mayst thou fit her as well as she fits
> me—Loeb Library tr. by Grant Showerman.)

He imagines himself to be the gift ring, touching her breasts:

> *sed, puto, te nuda mea membra libidine surgent.*
> (But I think that, seeing you naked, my member
> would rise lewdly—my translation.)

The symbolic ring, the metal one, that Criseyde sends is equipped with a blue stone, which stands for steadfastness and constancy, ironic indeed for a gift from Criseyde, though appropriate for Troilus. See **blew** and Figure 14.

In the *Book of the Duchess,* which otherwise impresses us as a work of almost ceremonial purity, the Man in Black says that his lady was his "al hooly" (1269) and "therwith she yaf me a ryng" (1273). Like Criseyde's, this ring was both a metal symbol and the real thing. See also **hol.**

Similar is the passage from *Troilus and Criseyde* involving the ring, the ruby, and the whole, which we have dealt with fully at **hol.** See also: "A ryng? . . . Ye, nece myn, that ryng moste han a stoon / That myhte dede men alyve maken; / And swich a ryng trowe I that ye have non" (III. 890). The **stoon** is the testicle; the magical ring that will bring the dead back to life is perhaps some reference to Criseyde's never-to-be-regained hymen (she is a widow). Or perhaps it is simply a reference to the refreshing (see **refresshed**) powers of the vulva.

The two lovers are safely in bed, and "pleyinge [they] entrechaungeden hire rynges" (III. 1368). These rings are literal pieces of jewelry again, but in Criseyde's case the gift represents something else. See **pleye** too.

In the last book, Criseyde has left her lover. He speaks:

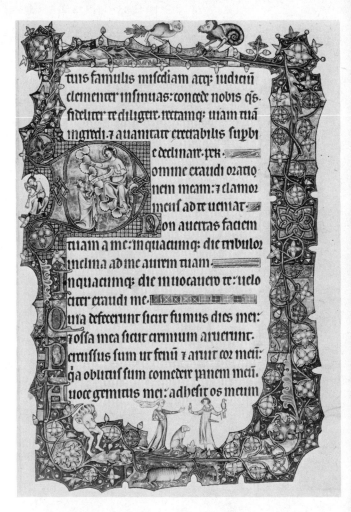

tuis famulis miscdiam atq̃ iudiciū
clementer infinuas: conceδe nobis q̃s.
fidelitcr te diligere.rectamq̃ uiam tuā
ingredi.⁊ auanitate crecrabilis fupbi
e declinare.prx.
omine craudi ozatio
nem meam:⁊ clamoz
meuf ad te ueniat.
on auertas faciem
tuam a me:inquacumq̃ die tribuloz
inclina ad me aurem tuam.
inquacumq̃ die inuocauero te: uelo
cirer craudi me.
uia δcfecerunt sicut fumus dies mei:
⁊ ossa mea sicut crimuum aruerunt.
ercuffus sum ut fenū ⁊ aruit coz meū:
q̃a obitus sum comeδere panem meū.
uoce gemitus mei: adhesit os meum

Fig. 14. *In the lower margin, a man with sword and falcon offers
a ring to a lady; the grotesque figure, with animal head for genitals,
watches lasciviously. Bodleian Library, Oxford, Douce MS 366 (14th
c.), fol. 131r.*

"O ryng, fro which the ruby is out falle" (V. 549). He
is apostrophizing his absent lover's *house,* to be sure,
but the suggestion of pudendum and penis is unmistakable.

In "Anelida and Arcite" (131), the heroine says her
heart is wedded to Arcite with a ring, which is, I think,
quite literal. The poem is pretty dull, which may have
been one of the reasons Chaucer did not finish it.

Under **queynt,** I have already discussed the suspicious
and difficult passages from the "Squire's Tale" (F 369,
433). The problems here may be attributed to the in-
herent nature of magic rings, perhaps. Canacee's is a
literal piece of metal jewelry, but there is also something
planned for her figurative "ring," her pudendum, later
in the tale. If she is destined to be wooed and won by her
own brother, no doubt it *is* better that the Squire breaks
off. We can say only that it is indeed odd that he has
begun the story at all. His choice betrays his naïveté.

In the "Man of Law's Tale" (B 712), there may be a
hint of something involving the female parts. When
women are wedded with "rynges," they must lay aside
their "hoolynesse." See **hol.** Perhaps there is a half-remem-
bered ritual of natural-magical exchange: the imperfect
ring (vagina with hymen) for the perfect ring of precious
metal. [*OED* provides no help. Partridge (p. 179) equates
the ring with the pudendum and compares the circle and
the *O.* Root, in his note to II. 585 ff. (p. 444), reminds us
that the proverb that lies behind these lines: "Wisdom
added to beauty is like a ruby set in a ring" is from
Scripture. Nonetheless, the "iconology" of penis and vagina must occur even to the most learned scripturalist.]

S

savour. See **soun.**

sceptre. This represents a phallus, and a god's at that. Chaucer
   sees Priapus in an embarrassing situation, when "the

asse hym shente" (*Parliament of Fowls,* 256). He was
about to have intercourse with the nymph Lotis when an
ass brayed, awakening her and others, who laughed at his
discomforture as he stood there with "hys sceptre in
honde."

As the god of gardens, Priapus is also present in the
hortus conclusus in the "Merchant's Tale" (E 2034). As
a tutelary deity, he is particularly appropriate for *this*
garden, since he was always portrayed with an immense
phallus, no doubt as an encouragement to the fertility of
the flora. We know that there is at least a flourishing pear
tree in the garden, strong enough to bear the "struggling"
bodies of two adults, but the presence of the god encourages not horticulture but copulation. May claims, of
course, that she is pregnant (E 2335). It may be that in
this tale the Lotis adventure is also glanced at, and we
are to imagine that the pear-tree intercourse between
Damyan and May was not consummated. See Introduction, p. 5n. [*OED* provides no erotic senses.]

seed. Semen. If none were sown, asks the ever-practical Wife
of Bath, how would virginity—which others prize so highly
—be created? See her "Prologue" (D 71). [*OED* provides
the meaning.]

serpent. Baum thinks that in the "Summoner's Tale" (D 1994)
it means the penis. He finds "complex irony" here, since
there is probably also a pun on hire-ire (D 1993). The
friar is attacking Thomas' wife and cautioning him about
the attractiveness of intercourse. [*OED* has no erotic
meanings.]

serve. Two medieval cults (whether real or merely literary is
a matter of some dispute), the Religion of Love and
Courtly Love, with their parallels between lady-service
and the feudal relationship, have complicated this word
when it appears in erotic passages. In the barnyard, there
is no question about it: "serve" is to copulate. But an
acolyte serves at the altar of Love, and a feudal underling
serves his lady (as he does his lord) and receives in return her favors. See **Venus** and frontispiece.

The medieval feudal ideal is illustrated in the "Franklin's Tale" (F 792): "hir servant and hir lord,— / Servant

in love, and lord in mariage." The Religion of Love, with
its deity Venus, is most succinctly shown in the "Nun's
Priest's Tale" (B 4534), in a passage that is far enough
along in the story that we have forgotten that Chaucer's
"tale is of a cok" (B 4442), and we accept the anthro-
pomorphism. Thus Chaunticleer's "servyce" to Venus does
not seem ridiculous. The equivoque immediately becomes
clear: (1) service of a divinity and (2) the act of copulation. In the "Complaint of Mars" (34), we get the same
thing, though it is Mars himself, not Chaunticleer the
chicken, who is in Venus' "servise." The sexual relationship in the poem is underscored by the repetitions of
"servaunt" (187) and "servise" (189).

Sometimes the word is ironic, as in the "Merchant's
Tale" (E 1911): Januarie, soon to be cuckolded, praises
Damyan as "manly, and eek servysable." The irony is
heavy-handed, since this same "servant" will mount Januarie's bride in the pear tree. In the same tale (E 1784),
the suggestion is simply *there:* the old man is cautioned
"O famulier foo, that his servyce bedeth," where the "foo"
(foe) is almost certainly the penis. It is accompanied by
the warning against the "perilous fyr that in the bedstraw
bredeth" (1783): see **fyr.** In the first passage, "bedeth"
(asketh) probably also contains a pun on "bed."

There is less doubt of equivocation in the "Shipman's
Tale" (B 1381). The wife will do the monk "service,"
which occurs along with "plesance." The erotic suggestion
is unmistakable, since he grabs her, they kiss, and the pact
(to copulate) is made.

Naturally Chaucer rings the changes on "service" in his
great poem of Courtly Love, *Troilus and Criseyde.* Troilus
imagines Criseyde and in turn imagines himself in love
(I. 370): "to serven hir . . . Or ellis for oon of hire
servantes pace," which occurs along with "holly" and
"grace" (*qq.v.*). Pandarus says (I. 817) that a lover
should be ready to "serve" his dear heart's queen. Troilus
is a fighting man by day (III. 440); by night he lies
awake "and thoughte how that he myghte serve / His
lady best, hire thonk for to deserve." In bed (III. 1290),
he asks Criseyde if he can amend his "servyse . . . syn

God hath wrought me for I shal yow serve." When Criseyde must leave Troy, he sees himself as a "combreworld" [encumbrance to the world] "that may of nothyng serve" (IV. 279). He says that his spirit will leave his body, "that shal ay yow serve" (IV. 321). The last cited passages (along with IV. 444–448, 517–525) are in palpitating erotic clusters that include "d[e]ye" or "sterve," which may carry the connotation of orgasm. See **die.**

As the poem comes to its pathetic end, the word crops up again (see V. 173–174), with both "servant" and "serve"—probably suggestive since Diomede has been boldly insinuating and familiar with Criseyde. In Troilus' letter to her, he assures her that none of his "servyse" has been elsewhere (V. 1318), which is true—making all the more poignant the "slydynge of corage" (V. 825) of the heroine.

In the shorter pieces, the concept occurs frequently too. Chaucer expostulates that someone should help Theseus (*Legend of Good Women*, 1957) "hire servaunt for to be, / And ben hire trewe lovere yer by yere!" In his lyric "A Complaint to His Lady" (39), the poet says that Love has taught him to "serve alwey," which is the first of a series of occurrences of the word and its derivatives (83, 91, 93, 105, and 111). In this same poem occurs the pathetic: "Of alle servantes, bothe of goode and badde; / And leest worthy of alle hem, I am he" (66).

In the poems of doubtful authorship, "serve" naturally occurs very often too, perhaps with stultifying frequency: "Against Women Unconstant" (2): "Many a servaunt have ye put out of grace" (see **grace**); "Complaynt D'Amours" (49): "It is hir wone [custom] plesaunce for to take, / To seen hir servaunts dyen for hir sake!" (if taken figuratively and erotically, this one is decadent indeed, since it suggests that the lady gets pleasure from watching her lovers in the throes of their orgasms—see **plesaunce** and **die**); and "A Balade of Complaint" (14): "Myn heven hool, and al my suffisaunce, / Whom for to serve is set al my plesaunce." A glance at **hol** will bring out some possible new reverberations in this simple little lyric. [*OED*, "serve," *v.*1, 8. d. to be the "servant" or lover of a lady. Chaucer is the earliest citation. 52. of a male animal, to cover the female; especially of stallions, bulls; the first citation here is 1577, which cannot be right. Two contemporary lyrics from Robbins' anthology help bring out the erotic meanings: Poem No. 200, "wold to god I were able your seruaunt to be, / Euery nyght yn your armes that I myght slepe" (38); No. 179, where a woman, it is said, will "ofte change hir seruyse" (60), glossed as "professed love."]

shap. Tarquin thinks about Lucrece's "shap"; he seems given to erotic fantasies, since the word means not only "shape, beauty of form" but also "the sexual organ—especially the female pudendum." Tarquin is up to thinking of both at the same time, in the same word: see *Legend of Good Women* (1747).

As we have seen frequently, the Parson is outraged by men's fashions. There are those, he says, that show the "boce of hir shap" (I 422), which encourages lust, since it means "protrusion of their penis." See **boce.** [*MED*, "chose," as in *"bel chose,"* cites, from *ca.* 1425, an attempt to describe the shape of the vagina, comparing it with a bishop's mitre: "It hath also the prive schap or chose as a hellyng (*OED*, covering) or mytre." Note the "prive schap." *OED*, 4. b. excellence of form, beauty (1382–1535); 16. the sexual organs; the distinctive organ of either sex; now *dial.* in narrower senses, "the private parts of a female"; quotes I 422.]

shepe. The Wife of Bath, trying to seduce her husband—that is, to restore his good humor and to obtain some favor from him—will say to him: "Goode lief, taak keep / How mekely looketh Wilkyn, oure sheep" (D 432). Nobody has been able to explain this, though editors like Skeat and Baugh conjecture that Wilkyn is the name for a pet sheep (like Malle in the "Nun's Priest's Tale," B 4021), which does not help at all.

A century or two after Chaucer, as every reader of Shakespeare and Partridge will remember, "mutton" was a common, low word for a woman, especially for a whore. I think that Chaucer's line demonstrates that the later obscene meaning was developing here, and what the Wife means is: "Look, darling, at 'Wilkyn,' my willing 'queynte.' " She is using hypocoristic language to entice him to bed or at least to arouse his lust. [*OED,* "mutton," 4. food for lust; loose women, prostitutes; nothing under "sheep." A contemporary lyric, cited by Robbins in his Introduction (p. xxxviii) is perhaps parallel: "Ie haue so longe kepe schepe on the grene, / Wilkyne, that alle yowere hert ys so for-hew (forsaken)" etc. "Willkin" is a conventional shepherd's name, and maybe that is all we have in the Wife's allusion.]

shit. The simple noun and verb do not occur in Chaucer, though they were commonplaces, especially in rural areas. However, we do have the remark, with its participial adjective "a shiten shepherde and a clene sheep" ("General Prologue," A 504), no doubt proverbial. It occurs in the description of the Parson, but it does not describe him, since this clean old man is the opposite of "shiten."

Because the word was so common—and not a taboo word—it was not useful, as it is today, to express disgust or to use in invective. We must not be misled by passages like that in the *Romaunt of the Rose* (2767) where we are told that "Love hath shit in his prisoun": here "shit" is simply one of the forms of the past participle of "shut." [*OED,* "shit (e)," to void excrement; citations from the fourteenth century to the present, with the note "not now in decent use." One of the quotations used by the *OED* not only deserves to be recorded in its own right, but also shows the difference between Chaucer and his much more homely contemporary, William Langland, traditionally the author of *Piers Plowman,* in which occurs the proverbial expression "the wolf shiteth woolle" (C-Text, X. 264), which is a much better example of circumstantial evidence than Thoreau's famous "to find a trout in the milk." The Langland phrase translates a Latin proverb, *lupus lanam cacat.* Chaucer knew this expression, since he uses it himself in the "Physician's Tale" (C 101), though choosing to translate different portions. The complete proverb, not quoted in the *OED,* but given in Skeat's edition of *Piers,* is *Sub molli pastore, lupus. . . .* The gentle Chaucer (*or* the Physician) emphasizes the first part of the proverb and omits the crudity, along with the humor, with: "Under a shepherde softe and necligent / The wolf hath many a sheep and lamb torent" (torn to pieces).]

shoppe. The Host tells the Cook that "in thy shoppe is many a flye loose" (A 4352). Hulme (p. 94) states that in Shakespeare the word means organ of generation. However the evidence is shaky (see *OED* reference). In Chaucer, too, it is another example of a word that might be thought obscene, but in fact is not. [*OED*, 3. c. a place where something is produced or elaborated, or where some operation is performed. Often said of the heart, liver, or other internal body organs. The citations, ranging from 1545–1737, do not refer to the penis.]

shryfte. In Shakespeare's time, "shrift" meant copulation, according to Hulme (pp. 122 ff.). If the same were true earlier, the line where it occurs in Chaucer's version of the Pyramus and Thisbe story (*Legend of Good Women*, 745) is very amusing rather than insipidly "poetical." The lovers have found the hole in the wall through which they may converse: "Ye founden first this litel narwe clifte; / And with a soun as softe as any shryfte, / They lete here wordes thorugh the clifte pace." See also **clifte.**

The summoner in the "Friar's Tale" (D 1442) naturally condemns the "shrifte-fadres everychoon" since they are his professional competitors. Knowing the summoner, however, one might suspect something much more indelicate.

Pandarus swears that if he meant any harm "here I me shryve" (II. 440), which has an indecent meaning only if the reader suspects a more than avuncular relationship between Pandarus and Criseyde. See **incest.**

Usually not even an ingenious reader can find wicked innuendos connected with the word—for instance, consider the "Summoner's Tale" (D 2095), which in other passages is extremely forthright; here "shryve" is literal but not obscene: the sick man, Thomas, tries to get rid of the unctuous friar by telling him "I have be shryven this day at my curat." [*OED* has no support for any obscene meaning at any time.]

skyn. It was proverbial that when a singed cat's hair grows back, out she goes to "shewe hir skyn" ("Wife of Bath's Prologue," D 354). Perhaps "skyn" is the equivalent of pudendum, but the only justification for such a conjecture is that Alison of Bath is the speaker. See also **caterwawed.** [*OED* provides no help.]

slepynge. The Parson, who seems suspicious of almost everything natural, says that "slepynge longe in greet quiete is eek a greet norice to [a great nurse to—i.e., encourages] Leccherie" (I 951). He is probably thinking of masturbation.

In *Troilus and Criseyde* (IV. 93), Calkas thinks with pity of his daughter, abandoned in Troy, "slepyng at hom"—nice irony, though natural enough. She *has* been sleeping regularly with Troilus. [*OED,* "sleep," *v.,* 1. b. implying sexual intimacy or cohabitation; citations from all periods.]

sluttissh. The Host calls the Canon this, and it obviously means merely "slovenly" ("Canon's Yeoman's Tale," G 636). The present meanings did not develop until the next century. [*OED,* dirty and untidy in dress or habits; G 636 is the earliest citation. "Slut" as a (female) slattern did not develop until the fifteenth century.]

smok. Among the catalogue of details that Chaucer gives us concerning the delectable Alisoun ("Miller's Tale," A 3238) is: "Whit was hir smok, and broyden al bifoore / And eek bihynde." If the reader is captious and concerned with verisimilitude, he wonders how Chaucer—or, odder still, the Miller—knew about this intimate garment, which is the equivalent of the modern slip.

Just how intimate it was we discover in the "Merchant's Tale" (E 2353), when we watch the lusty and impatient Damyan in action in his pear tree: "And sodeynly anon this Damyan / Gan pullen up the smok, and in he throng." Elsewhere I have commented on the deliberate pleonasm (see Introduction, p. 5), which shows us how eager is this Damyan; see also **throng.** Later in the story, Januarie, his vision restored, complains about the position of the smock on Damyan's body: "thy smok hadde leyn upon his brest" (E 2395) —of course, if you are going to have intercourse in a treetop! [*OED,* a woman's undergarment; a shift or chemise; now *arch.* or *dial.* (common down to the eighteenth century). In a lyric from Harley MS 2253 (Bennett, p. 119), the lover wishes he could hide between the "curtel ant . . . smok" of his beloved.]

Solomon. The lovely Song of Solomon is paraphrased in the "Merchant's Tale" (E 2138). Januarie uses it (one is surprised that he knows it well enough to employ in this situation or any other) to arouse his young wife May, and Chaucer (or the Merchant) gives his opinion of these erotic words: "Swiche olde lewed wordes used he" (E 2149). The opinion does not really fit either the poet or the narrator. However, the words are certainly appropriate to May, who has no taste in language or in lovers; perhaps if Chaucer had revised this tale, he would have put the opinion in her mouth. See **lewed.**

The Wife's envy of Solomon (D 35) is discussed under **refresshed.**

soun. The musical tone of the fart in the "Summoner's Tale" (D 2226), where it occurs in the phrase "soun or savour of a fart" (music or perfume . . .). It is amusing to recall here the explanation of sound that Chaucer gives, seriously, I think, in the *House of Fame* (765): "Soun ys noght but eyr ybroken." We are naturally reminded of the broken wind in the comic tale.

The Pardoner fills his belly gladly enough before his tale, but in the sermon, he professes to be horrified by the "bely." He addresses it, accusing it of being full of "dong" (*q.v.*) and "at either ende of thee foul is the soun"—belching and farting. This is a good example of Chaucer *not* being amusing with bawdy language. See "Pardoner's Tale" (C 536). [*OED, sb.*[3], 1. b. music, melody; earliest citation *ca.* 1320.]

sparwe. In the "General Prologue" the Summoner is said to be "lecherous as a sparwe" (A 626), and in the *Parliament of Fowls* (351), Chaucer calls the sparrow "Venus sone." The Chaucer scholars do not seem to know why this association arose (see Robinson's dead-end note, p. 795); however, Legman (p. 189) points out that for centuries

birds have been metaphors for the male genitals (cf.
Catullus' lyric about Lesbia's sparrow). Thus when the
friar "chirps" with his lips (kiss-kiss-kiss), Chaucer does
not compare the action with the song of the robin or the
wren, and for good reason. The friar is *too* familiar with
Thomas' wife, to whom he directs this sound and gesture
("Summoner's Tale," D 1804): he "kiste hire sweete,
and chirketh as a sparwe / With his lyppes." [*OED* does
not mention the bird's association with lechery. In a contemporary poem, which cites a number of incredible
things, the poet illustrates when to trust women thus
(Robbins' Poem No. 114): "Whan sparowys bild chirches
& stepulles hie" (15). Not only is this impossible for the
tiny bird, but its association with lechery makes the building of churches all the more incredible.]

speed. Appius ("Physician's Tale," C 134) is afraid he cannot
"speede" with the virginal Virginia. It means "succeed,"
but if Hulme is right (pp. 97–98) it might also mean,
much more specifically, have one's will with, have an orgasm with. Pandarus explains to Troilus (I. 1041): "God
spede us bothe two!" which, since they are both lovers,
might have the secondary sexual meaning. He also assures Troilus later (II. 954): "Thy nedes spedde be!"
[*OED* has no erotic meaning.]

spendeth. There is a remote chance, but at least a chance, that
the word means "has an orgasm" in *Troilus and Criseyde*
(III. 1718): in summarizing the lovers' affair, Chaucer
says that Troilus "spendeth, jousteth, maketh festeynges; /
He yeveth frely ofte. . . ." See **juste.** [*OED* does not
record an erotic meaning for the word, though readers of
nineteenth-century pornography can testify that it was the
common term for which we now use "come." *S.v.*
"give," *OED* also fails to provide erotic meanings.]

sperme. Not a bawdy but a rather unhealthy reference occurs
in the "Monk's Tale" (B 3199) where Adam is described
as being made with God's own finger, not of "mannes
sperme unclene." [*OED,* seed of male animals; Chaucer's
is the earliest citation.]

spille. The common Middle English meaning was "to die" (or,
as a transitive verb, "to kill"). This is probably the mean-

ing in the "Miller's Tale" (A 3278) : "For deerne [secret] love of thee, lemman, I spille," but it is also possible that it meant "to have an involuntary emission." In the hot love affair between Nicholas and Alisoun, such an event is perfectly possible. [*OED* has no erotic meanings.]

staf-slynge. The three-headed giant Olifaunt has one in "Thopas" (B 2019) , which may be a phallic symbol. Such a meaning is possible only if we concur with Mr. Williams (p. 148) that "Thopas" is full of homosexual innuendos, of which this is another. The shape of the weapon—a staff at the end of which was a pouch in which the stone to be slung was placed—would indeed lend itself to a symbolic function. See **baggepipes.** [*OED*, "staff," no erotic meanings; "staff-sling," citations from the fourteenth-century, but again nothing erotic.]

stand, -t. See **stonden.**

steede. Williams (p. 148) thinks that the recurrence of this word in "Thopas" (six times) "may have phallic connotations by being related to the word *stud,* meaning both a stallion and an upright prop or projecting knob." Unless one accepts the "secret" of Thopas (see **hair**) , the suggestion is preposterous. [*OED* indicates that in OE it meant a studhorse or stallion, but that in Middle English it had come to mean simply a high-mettled horse; "stud," *sb*.^{1}, 1. a post; 5. ornamental round knob.]

-stere. See **tappestere** (it is a general feminine ending) .

stew. See **styves.**

stif. The Summoner bears a "stif burdoun" to the Pardoner, "General Prologue" (A 673) . If "burdoun" (*q.v.*) means both (1) bass accompaniment and (2) penis, then "stif" of course refers to erectness. The whole thing fits this pair of degenerates (and homosexuals?) . See also **honde.** [*OED*, 1. rigid; 15. of voice or sound: powerful, loud (citations from the fourteenth century, including Chaucer) .]

stonden. To make the penis stand; to have (get) an erection. In some of Chaucer's poetry it does have this naughty innuendo, and often, of course, it does not. I shall try to give the reader some guidance.

The word occurs in passages along with "grace" (*q.v.*) , with which we shall begin. Whether or not the latter word means "(bottom-) grass" (pubic hair) is unimportant here, since "to have an erection" and thereby to achieve a lady's favors is quite enough. "Stonden" occurs first in the portrait of the Squire in the "General Prologue" (A 88), who is "in hope to stonden in his lady grace." He lives for love and lovemaking; his desire to achieve his lady's favor by this special means is understandable. The satire of the Squire is genial; I think it not at all improbable that there is a suggestion of an erect penis in it.

We encounter the same passage, but in different circumstances, in *Troilus and Criseyde* (III. 472). It is a little puzzling since it occurs *before* they actually get in bed together: "he so ful stood in his lady grace" that she thanks God they have met. Then there is the very much by-the-way passage in the "Canon's Yeoman's Tale" (G 1348) where the Yeoman compares the happy (though gulled) priest to a knight: "to stonden in grace of his lady deere." Lastly, and with much more assurance, one may mention the pathetic last book of *Troilus and Criseyde* (V. 171), in which Diomede tells Criseyde that in the Greek camp there are many knights who will strive "to stonden in youre grace." In view of Diomede's outrageous boldness in this scene, his intention is very likely bawdy.

We come next to possible erections without "grace." Williams (p. 148) thinks that the "stonde" in "Thopas" (B 1931) is suggestive. Again this depends upon whether one can accept Williams' ingenious arguments about Thopas the homosexual: see **hair.** But there is no question in the reader's mind when the Wife of Bath (D 394) reveals the ways in which she tricks her husbands, accusing them of having affairs: "whan that for syk unnethes [scarcely] myghte they stonde": (1) stay on their feet; (2) get an erection.

In the "Shipman's Tale" (B 1298), the young monk has suggested to the wife that she is pale because her husband has "laboured" (*q.v.*) her all night in intercourse. She answers: "It stant nat so with me" (i.e., he can get no erection with her, B 1304), which she repeats: "dar I nat

telle how that it stant with me" (B 1310). This sounds
like the cliché of the lusty young wife whose merchant-
husband does not understand her, to use a current and
appropriate euphemism. However, as the end of the tale
shows, she is lying. Her husband is actually as lusty as (if
not lustier than) the monk. The wife is simply insatiable.

When Criseyde promises to speak to Troilus "to-morwe"
about the false rumor of her infidelity, Pandarus answers: "Nay, nay, it may nat stonden in this wise" (III.
851); he has just said, "thus fallen is this cas . . ." (841),
so it is likely that some subtle Pandar-ean obscenity is
being hinted at here. For an even subtler Pandarus, see
hol.

Kornbluth (p. 243) comments on IV. 312 of the same
poem, finding that the references to "eyes" = naughts,
zeros, O's. Troilus, lamenting the fact that Criseyde must
leave Troy, says that his eyes "stonden for naught." The
syntax is a little involute here, and perhaps the idea of a
useless erection is being hinted at. "Syn she is queynt
[quenched—but see **queynt**] that wont was yow to lighte"
(313) follows fairly closely, reaffirming our suspicion that
"stonden" may have something to do with an erection.

We should conclude with a couple of passages where
there is really very little basis for a suspicion of obscenity,
though some readers might think so. For instance, Criseyde
(II. 714) asks why she should call down upon herself a
powerful prince's disfavor (she means Troilus) when
she might gain his favor: "ther I may stonde in grace."
The passage sounds exactly like that with which we began
this entry, except the sex is wrong, and there can be no
possibility of a double meaning. It is the right sex when
Harry Bailly quotes his wife Goodelief to the Pilgrims
("Monk's Tale," B 3102): "Thou darst nat stonden by
thy wyves right!" In the context, it probably means just
what it says: you are a coward and will not stand up for
(i.e., defend) your wife's rights. Because of the juxtaposition of "knyf," there is just a vague possibility that she
is saying that he cannot have an erection. (Very vague—
see **knyf.**) There cannot be even this sort of suspicion

about the passage near the end of the "General Prologue" (A 778) when the Host asks if it will be agreeable to all the Pilgrims "to stonden at my juggement." He means "abide by," that's all. [*OED,* "stand," *v.,* 17. to be in an upright position. Lyrics contemporary with Chaucer illustrate the bawdy meaning. In Robbins' Poem No. 7 the speaker boasts: "I haue a Ielyf (jelly, i.e., penis) of godes sonde (God's gift), / Withoutyn fyt (feet) it can stonde" (9). The entire poem is an obscene double entendre. A similarly bawdy poem is Robbins' No. 31, in which the speaker boasts that he has a tent (probe) "of xv ynche" (3), which will drive away dogs, rats, or flies —and presumably also perform other services. See also Robbins' poem quoted at **stoon.** Though much later (1554), Lindsay's *Ane Satire of the Thrie Estaitis* (200–204) shows how the idea persisted in ribald poetry: "I wald renunce all this warld quyte / For till stand in hir grace: / She is wantoun and schoe is wyse / And cled scho is on the new gyse / It wald gar all your flesche vp ryse. . . ."]

stoon. Most of the occurrences of this word in Chaucer are simply references to rocks. But there are some marvelous exceptions: when used for testicle, it is a very bold, very male, word. The Host is mightily pleased with the "Nun's Priest's Tale" (B 4638) of Chaunticleer and Pertelote, as are all who read or hear it, and he compliments the narrator by giving him a blessing—for his "breche" (*q.v.*) and every "stoon." For a man in Holy Orders, who has sworn vows of chastity, such a compliment is particularly gratifying (or inappropriate, I suppose, if you are prudish). The Host has just given the Monk the same sort of praise (see **hunt**) *before* the Priest begins his beast fable (B 3995); and also just before the Monk himself has told his tragedies (B 3133 ff.).

Criseyde sends Troilus a "ryng" (*q.v.*) by Pandarus; he exclaims (III. 891): "that ryng moste han a stoon / That myghte dede men alyve maken": (1) a gem with magical properties and (2) a testicle (probably). Since it is Pandarus who speaks, the likelihood of obscenity is greater. Most of the other occurrences of "stoon" in

Troilus and Criseyde are, however, doubtful. For instance, consider: he who has a head of glass "fro cast of stones war hym [let him beware] in the werre" (II. 868) —funny, perhaps, but not sexual. Or where Pandarus swears "by stokkes and by stones" (III. 589), which is the familiar old alliterative doublet (by which Pandarus—since it is he —*might* mean penises and ballocks, but I do not think so).

The "Parson's Tale," that endless sermon with its beautifully logical organization, has a couple of occurrences—not allusions to testicles, however, except for the lewd-minded in his congregation—(I 835–840), the section on Luxuria (Lechery), where he tells what should be done to a woman taken in this sin: "if she were a gentil womman, she sholde be slayn with stones." This is alluded to again (I 885–890) and is rather like the practice of hanging for murderers from the lower classes but beheading for peers.

An utterly different but peripherally sexual, and amusing, use of the word may conclude our selection. On her wedding night, May is brought to bed with the disgusting old Januarie, "stille as stoon" ("Merchant's Tale," E 1818). This means that she is quiet, of course, and makes us wonder why—from fear? (unlikely in view of her later escapade in the pear tree); apathy? (unlikely for the same reason); disgust? [*OED*, 11. testicle, with citations from the twelfth century on. There is doubtless bawdy innuendo in Robbins' lyric, contemporary with Chaucer, which he quotes in his Introduction (p. xxxix): "Atte ston castinges my lemman i ches . . . allas, that he so sone fel; / wy nadde he stonde better, vile gorel?" The allusion to testicle is here accompanied by references to a falling and standing penis. See **stonden**.]

straw. When a chamber is on fire (its floor strewn, as was the custom, with rushes or straw), it is not worthwhile to ask "how this candele in the strawe is falle," says Pandarus (III. 859), where "strawe" might mean pubic hair. Hulme (p. 117) suggests the meaning for the word in Elizabethan English—as she does for "thatch," but Chaucer seems not to have used the latter in any sort of vulgar sense. See **grace**.

On the other hand, from the same poem (IV. 184), the lines have perhaps a political overtone (one of the very few in Chaucer—referring to the Peasants' Rebellion and Jack Straw), but not a sexual one: "The noyse of peple up stirte thanne at ones, / As breme [fierce] as blase of straw iset on-fire." Furthermore, the material that Absolon uses to wipe his mouth, after it has kissed Alisoun's bare bottom in the "Miller's Tale" (A 3748) is literal enough: "Who rubbeth now, who froteth [rubs] now his lippes / With dust, with sond, with straw, with clooth, with chippes."

An equally common form of the word in Middle English was "stree," and when the narrator in the "Reeve's Tale" (A 3873) compares himself and other old men to the medlar, the fruit that is not ready to eat until it is rotten, "in mullok [refuse] or in stree," the literal meaning is *kept* in refuse or straw. But a subsurface obscenity is possible; see **open-ers**. [*OED* has nothing applicable.]

strepen. Januarie asks May ("Merchant's Tale," E 1958) to "strepen hire al naked" before they have intercourse, which would be most natural were it not for the speaker. This particular copulation takes place at some time other than bedtime. We must recall, however, that it was customary for ladies and gentlemen to sleep in the nude in the Middle Ages: when Chaucer himself finally gets to sleep at the beginning of the *Book of the Duchess* (293), he is "al naked."

The stripping in the "Clerk's Tale" is totally without erotic significance, but that is because the heroine is Griselde, that sexless puppet. When her husband casts her aside (apparently) without reason or cause, she recalls with humble gratitude how "ye dide me streepe out of my povre weede" (E 863). Naturally she promptly returns her rich clothing to her highborn husband at this time of "divorcement." The pathos in one of her lines here is almost beyond endurance (of heart or stomach) when she pleads "lat me nat lyk a worm go by the weye" (E 880). [*OED,* to unclothe.]

streyne. A violent embrace, but not necessarily one that would put undue stress upon the strainer's heart (the aged Januarie's, for instance). As a matter of fact, the whole matter in the "Merchant's Tale" (E 1753) is a sex-fantasy in the old man's mind. In his heart he "gan hire to manace [threaten] / That he that nyght in armes wolde hire streyne." See also **myddel** for more of his fantasies.

What Januarie only makes up fantasies about is what really happens in *Troilus and Criseyde* (III. 1205):

This Troilus in armes gan hire streyne,
And seyde, "O swete, as evere mot I gon,
Now be ye kaught, now is ther but we tweyne!
Now yeldeth yow, for other bote [remedy] is non!"
To that Criseyde answerde thus anon,
"Ne hadde I er now, my swete herte deere,
Ben yold [yielded], ywis, I were now nought heere!"

Criseyde's frank confession of sensuality in this passage is only one of the multitude of facets that Chaucer gives this character. [*OED*, *v.*1, 2. to clasp tightly in one's arms; cites the *Troilus* quotation.]

strugle. Though May may be a slut, she is quick of wit; when her husband (previously blind, but sight suddenly restored by divine intervention) sees her in intercourse with Damyan in the pear tree, she tells him that the only way to cure his eyes was to struggle with a man in a tree. She hopes to persuade her credulous old husband that she was indeed "struggling" ("Merchant's Tale," E 2374), and she apparently does, even though Januarie grumbles for a moment: "Strugle! . . . ye algate in it wente" (E 2376). The word becomes (for the nonce) a synonym for intercourse. See also **kiss**. [*OED*, continual effort to resist force; no erotic meanings. Partridge (p. 92), *s.v.* "conflict," glosses it as "amorous struggle" and gives cross-references to "wrestle" and "contend." But in the fourteenth century "struggle" had not yet come this far, it would appear. Chaucer helped it on its way.]

styves. The Friar says the summoners have no jurisdiction over friars and never will have. The Summoner interrupts indignantly: "Peter! so been the wommen of the styves . . .

yput out of oure cure!" ("Friar's Tale," D 1332). The "stews" were brothels; the development of the term shows why the euphemisms like "massage parlor" or "Turkish bath" have continued into our time.

The Summoner's great and good friend the Pardoner mentions wicked people in his sermon ("Pardoner's Tale," C 465), those who "haunteden folye," including "stywes." Such a condemnation from this gelding is deeply ironic.

There is a problematical reference in the *House of Fame* (26) where, in discussing dreams, Chaucer says: "prison, stewe, or gret distresse," in which it is uncertain whether these are causes of dreams or whether we dream that we are in such places.

On the night of his assignation with Criseyde, Troilus is hidden in a "stewe" (III. 601, 698), glossed by Robinson as a small heated room; by Baugh, as a room generally used for bathing; by Skeat, as a small chamber, closet (and compares the German *Stube,* with mistaken philology, as the *OED* shows). This is heavy-handed equivocation, surely, since Chaucer did not *have* to hide his hero in a nook the name for which will recall the brothel!

Finally there is the apparently similar word in the "General Prologue" (A 350), describing the rich Franklin, that son of Epicurus, who has fat partridges and many fish "in stuwe." This is a fishpond where the fish were kept until needed for the table. But "stuwe" would certainly *suggest* the brothel. "Fish" was later a cant word for a whore (see Partridge). Also see **partrich**. [*OED*, "stew," *sb*.1, 2. a pond or tank for fish (from OF *estui*), first citation 1387; *sb*.2, 4. a brothel (citation from 1362), from 3. a heated room used for hot air or vapor baths (1390).]

suster. See **incest** and then consider *Troilus and Criseyde* (III. 409). In return for Pandarus' procurement of Criseyde, Troilus offers his friend his sisters, Polixene, Cassandra, and Eleyne (really his sister-in-law, Paris' paramour). He does so with arrogant confidence: they will be Pandarus' "to han for thyn, and lat me thanne allone" [leave it to me].

swynke. Alison of Bath confesses (with glee!): "How pitously a-nyght I made hem [husbands] swynke!" Literally the word means "work" ("Wife of Bath's Prologue," D 202), but here it is a synonym for **swyve**, of course. Just a few lines later she says (D 215) she set her husbands "a-werke," which again is literal, and also figurative and erotic. See also the "Cook's Tale" (A 4337), where "yset a-werk" means something utterly different—"has duped." One must, of course, always consider the context.

Before the "Manciple's Tale" (H 18), the Host asks the Cook if he has been with a "quene" (*q.v.*) all night—if he has her "yswonke" (had intercourse with her). It is funny because the Cook is so drunk he cannot keep his seat on his horse. See **labour** and **swyve**. [*OED*, "swink," to toil, labor; no sexual meanings, though in the sixteenth century the *OED* recognizes that it developed (briefly) a secondary sense "to drink deeply, tipple." For a good example of "werke" in the sexual sense, see the Confession of Luxurie from *Piers Plowman* under **likyng**. "Swink" is used in a sexual sense in the "Land of Cokaygne" (Bennett, p. 143): after the monks have satisfied themselves with women ("aftir her [their] swinke") "Wendith meklich hom to drink, / And goth to har (their) collacione / A wel fair processione."]

swyve. To have intercourse with. It has brutal or coarse connotations, much like Modern English "fuck," I would guess. As the conclusion for the marvelously lively "Miller's Tale" (A 3850), Chaucer gives us "Thus swyved was this carpenteris wyf," which is amusing but undeniably crude. Similarly, as the "Reeve's Tale" progresses, the two clerks see their chance for revenge on the dishonest miller. Alan eyes their host's daughter and whispers to his mate: "yon wenche wil I swyve" (A 4178). He does. And he boasts later: "As I have thries in this shorte nyght / Swyved the milleres doghter bolt upright" [i.e., she was on her back] (A 4266). His bed-companion to whom he makes this confession is not, however, his friend John, but the "swyved" girl's father. The confusion, as Chaucer describes it, is lovely! When the tale is over, Chaucer concludes (or the Reeve does, A 4317) with a neat summary of the action and a statement of the moral (be an honest miller!) : "His wyf is swyved, and his doghter als. / Lo, swich it is a millere to be fals."

The last line of the (regrettably) unfinished "Cook's Tale," which promised to be a vigorous *fabliau* like its predecessors, tells us of a wife who keeps a shop as a "front," but who "swyved for hir sustenance." Some critics have felt that the reason for Chaucer breaking off here was that the material in the story was simply too gamy.

The climax of the telltale crow story ("Manciple's Tale," H 256) makes one wonder, however, if rawness of material would ever make him break off. He certainly does not here. He tells us as bluntly as possible: "For on thy bed thy wyf I saugh hym [her paramour] swyve." The only ambiguity here is a grammatical one: (1) I saw thy wife swyve him; or (2) I saw him swyve thy wife. The equivocation cannot be accidental.

Nor does Chaucer mince words at the end of the "Merchant's Tale" (E 2378) : old Januarie cries out to May in outrage: "He swyved thee, I saugh it with myne yen" [eyes]. He is right, but he is so dull-witted that May can persuade him that it did not really happen. See also **plit**. [*OED*, "swive," 1. to have sexual connection with, copulate with (a female) ; it is from OE *swifan,* to move in a course, sweep; *swivel* is also derived from the same root. The earliest citation is that from the "Miller's Tale."]

syde. When Chaunticleer feels Pertelote's "softe syde" at night, he is sexually excited, even though he knows he cannot "ryde" (*q.v.*) her on the narrow perch ("Nun's Priest's Tale," B 4357) . In the most sensual stanza of all, Troilus strokes Criseyde on her "sydes longe, flesshly, smothe, and white" (III. 1248) . See **lendes**. [*OED* provides no specifically erotic meanings.]

synne. The pulpit opinion on this matter comes not from the Parson, for once, but apparently from Chaucer himself, in the notorious "Melibee" (B 2454) : "The proverbe seith that 'for to do synne is mannyssh, but certes for to persevere longe in synne is werk of the devel.' " Skeat traces the proverb to St. John Chrysostom and Vincent of Beauvais; Robinson adopts his note. We should listen to Chaucer when he is speaking in his own person and telling us his opinion about the nature of innate human evil, about Original Sin. But it is hard to pay attention to "Melibee." See also **love.**

t

taille. See **tayl.**

talent. Illicit appetite. Apparently, though the syntax is not too lucid, Tarquin feels "unrightful talent" for Lucrece, *Legend of Good Women* (1771). [*OED*, 3. evil inclination or passion, usually anger. Citations from the fourteenth century.]

tappestere. A female barkeep: the ending *-ster (e)* indicates the feminine gender in Middle English. The casual reader is likely to miss this grammatical fact, since the ending has become a neutral "agent" suffix in Modern English.

Absolon, the foolish clerk in the "Miller's Tale" (A 3336), frequents taverns where "any gaylard [lively] tappestere was," and the Friar ("General Prologue," A 241) is very familiar with "tappesteres."

In the "Merchant's Tale" (E 1535), the "chidestere" is a bad wife, a scold; and in the "Pardoner's Tale," the narrator, who probably has no real (i.e., sexual) interest in women, rails against "tombesteres" (female tumblers) who are "fetys and smale, and yonge frutesteres" (C 477). [*OED*, "-ster," as a feminine suffix in the late fourteenth and early fifteenth centuries. *Piers Plowman* (A-Text, II. 79) associates barmaids with other low-lifers: "taberes and tomblers and tapesters fele."]

tayl. The spelling "taille" permits some interesting puns, some of which have been recognized for many years. Baum finds the double meaning of "tail" (intercourse) and "tally" (keep accounts; derived from *tailler,* to cut; and in the past notched sticks were used) in the "Shipman's Tale" (B 1605, his error for 1606). The quick-thinking and sexually insatiable wife says that her husband can regain the loan of a hundred francs in a special way: "I am youre wyf; score it upon my taille." The joke depends upon the double meaning, and also upon the idea of the marriage **dette.** Chaucer (or the Shipman?) drives the point home with the last line, where the teller asks that God send us "taillynge ynough unto oure lyves ende" (B 1624). There is yet a third meaning woven into this wondrous complex—"tale": the Shipman has just said (B 1623) "Thus endeth now my tale. . . ."

Baum also sees the double meaning in a couple of other passages that puzzle me. The first is in the "Reeve's Tale" (A 3878) : the speaker is defending his age—"to have a hoor heed and a grene tayl, / As hath a leek." The idea of a lecherous "tail" is there, but the double meaning with "tally" is certainly not intended. The same is true in the "Wife of Bath's Prologue" (D 466), in which she talks about the relationship between drink and copulation: "A likerous mouth moste han a likerous tayl," with an added pun involving **likerous.**

Whether there is double meaning in the "General Prologue" (A 570) depends on how "gentil" you think the Manciple is. Chaucer tells us that he did business in two ways: "he payde or took by taille," where the latter is usually construed as meaning "on credit." But we have always had petty officials who accepted women's favors for payment, when they could.

There is no doubt about the "Reeve's Tale" (A 4164), which tells us of the sleeping habits of the drunken miller. He snores mightily, and also "ne of his tayl bihynde he took no keep." The ambiguities are particularly rich: (1) farting; (2) "tail" of his wife, of which he makes no use, but which will be used shortly as an instrument of copulation by the clerk John.

In the "Man of Law's Tale" (B 111), there is *Schadenfreude* of the most reprehensible but simplest sort. The envy one feels for one's neighbor is gratified, we are told, by imagining the day "whan that his tayl shal brennen in the glede" [coals]. "Tayl" is simply arse here. [*OED*, *sb.*[1] spelled "tayl, taille," etc., in the fourteenth century;

5. lower and hinder part of the human body (citations from the fourteenth century); c. sexual member; penis or (oftener) pudendum (also fourteenth century). "Tally," *v.*[1], to notch a stick . . . to mark, score, set down a number; the earliest citation for this word is *ca.* 1440, an obvious error. To illustrate "tayl" more fully, the entire concluding stanza of Robbins' Poem No. 41 deserves to be quoted; the poet is warning against marriage:

> *Of madenys I wil seyn but lytil,*
> *For they be bothe fals & fekyl,*
> *& vnder the tayl they ben ful tekyl* [*ticklish, touchy*];
>   *A twenty deuel name, let hem goo!*

The tail-tally pun occurs in *Piers Plowman* (B-Text, V. 395): Sloth is reluctant to rise from bed, "but if my taille-ende it made": (1) my tail's demand to relieve itself; (2) my profit.]

tete. References to the teat or tit seem to have been confined almost exclusively to the barnyard. That is why the use made of the word by Absolon in his marvelously inept simile is so funny. He wants to express his love for Alisoun, and he tells her, "I moorne as dooth a lamb after the tete," "Miller's Tale" (A 3704). It is the only occurrence of the word in Chaucer. [*OED*, the nipple; the whole breast; used very early for human females, and in the earlier citations there is no hint of embarrassment. Sexual and sensual meanings were developing, however, as a lyric from Harley MS 2253 (Bennett, p. 115) shows. Here the beloved's "tyttes" are compared with "apples tuo of Parays" (*sic*).]

thakked. Patted amorously. The *order* of events in the "Miller's Tale" deserves attention: first Nicholas seizes his landlord's wife by the "queynte"; then he declares his love; next he "thakked hire aboute the lendes [*q.v.*] weel" (A 3304), and finally he kisses her on the mouth. This is followed by some music and eventually, of course, by some hard-and-fast copulation. [*OED*, "thack," *v.*[2] to clap with open hand; to pat, slap lightly; Chaucer's is the earliest citation. In the "Land of Cokaygne" (Bennett, p. 143), the monks gather around the wench whose bottom has been turned up and "thakketh al hir white toute" (*q.v.*) ; then they have intercourse with her.]

Thopas. Braddy (p. 216) called my attention to George Williams, who "speculates (p. 147, *n.* 151) that Chaucer wrote the 'Tale of Sir Thopas' to ridicule King Richard's alleged homosexuality." But, as Braddy shows, the only basis for this idea is Shakespeare's fictional account of Richard, which in turn was influenced by "Marlowe's portrayal of the homosexual King in *Edward II*." Despite Braddy's wise words, one wonders: see **hair.**

thought. Daun John, the young monk in the "Shipman's Tale," tells the wife of his host, the merchant, that she is pale from being "laboured" all night by her husband. Then "of his owene thought he wax al reed" (B 1301). The "thought" that makes him blush has two meanings, as the remainder of the tale shows: (1) of the connubial "labor" between wife and husband and (2) of his own fantasy, wherein he takes the merchant's place. [*OED* has no obscene meanings, but then the erotic sense here depends totally upon context.]

throng. The past tense of "thring," a rough, vulgar word, which has unfortunately become obsolete. It is the only possible term, however, to describe the movement of the crude stud Damyan's penis into the willing pudendum of May in the "Merchant's Tale" (E 2353). See Introduction, p. 5.

Without any sexual meaning, but with the connotation of violence and rudeness, is the action of old Calkas in *Troilus and Criseyde* (IV. 66) : "He gan in thringe forth with lordes olde." Even better evidence for the connotation is the action of Mars, who stirs up both the Thebans and the Greeks to violent battle in "Anelida and Arcite" (55) : he "throng now her, now ther, among hem bothe, / That everych other slough, so were they wrothe." [*OED*, "thring," 2. *intr.*, to press or push forward.]

throte. To Troilus it is an erotic object and, presumably, to Criseyde it is erogenous, as he strokes her in bed on "hire snowisshe throte" (III. 1250). See **nekke.** [*OED* has no erotic citations from the fourteenth century.]

thynges. The Wife of Bath (D 121) calls them, tenderly, "thynges smale": the genitals. She insists, nay, she demonstrates, that they were made for purposes other than urination and differentiating the sexes. [*OED,* "thing," 11. c. privy member, private parts. Chaucer is the earliest citation.]

tool. A little after Chaucer's time this word, along with "yard," became a familiar name for the penis. But in the late fourteenth century, it still had no obscene meaning.

Pertelote says to her husband, whom she is accusing of being fainthearted ("Nun's Priest's Tale," B 4106) : "Ne hym that is agast of every tool," which is glossed as "weapon." If "tool" had had a secondary sexual meaning, Chaucer would surely have taken advantage of it here.

Pandarus speaks to Troilus with a different air. He says that he himself may be unsuccessful in love, but this does not mean that he cannot give advice (I. 632) : "A wheston [*sic*—whetstone] is no kervyng instrument, / But yet it maketh sharpe kervyng tolis." Again this has the four-teenth-century meaning of "weapon, sword." Knowing Pandarus, however, it might have the erotic overtone of "penis," if it had developed that early. He does indeed act as a "wheston" to sharpen Troilus' tool for operation on Criseyde. [*OED,* 1. b. a weapon of war, especially a sword; 2. b. a bodily organ; especially the male genera-tive organ; the first citation here is 1553: "Al his toles that appertayne vnto the court of Venus," which clearly illustrates how the shift in meaning occurred. Cf. also *Piers Plowman* (C-Text, XI. 287), where we are advised to marry when young and "yep" (active) and "thy wepne kene."]

toord. See **turd.**

torche. See **candle.**

totrede. See **tredyng.**

touchyng. It is one of the devil's "fyngres" (*q.v.*) of lechery. In *Troilus and Criseyde* (III. 517), Pandarus is con-triving to get the lovers together at his house where they can find time to discuss the entire matter "touchyng here [their] love." It means (1) in regard to; and, with Pan-darus as speaker, probably also (2) literally fondling each other, doubtless in the genital area. [*OED,* "touch," *v.,* 2. a. to have sexual contact with; citations from the fourteenth century. See also the Confession of Luxurie from *Piers Plowman* at **likyng.**]

tough. The phrase "to make it tough" had three meanings: (1) to make it difficult; (2) to be persistent; (3) to achieve an erection (though the *OED* does not provide substantiation for the third).

The worthless, but clever and tireless, wife in the "Shipman's Tale" greets her husband warmly after his absence —during which time she has had some merry games with the young monk Daun John. She spends a night of "myrthe" (*q.v.*) with her husband, and when he is ready again in the morning, so is she: "And up he gooth and maketh it ful tough" (B 1569), which Baugh glosses as "shows great vigor." The particular kind of vigor wanted at this moment is to achieve penis erectus, which the merchant does. It is all especially amusing since she has told Daun John (in order to seduce him, to make him pity her?) that her husband's prowess in bed leaves something to be desired (B 1360): "he is noght worth at al / In no degree the value of a flye" (note the emphatic nature of the double negative). There is another act, however, in this little bedroom drama: when in the morning he asks his wife for a second round of intercourse, she responds with "Namoore, by God, ye have ynough!" which is followed immediately by "And wantownly agayn with hym she pleyde" (B 1570–1571). Her protestation lasts exactly as long as the pause between two decasyllabic lines. Even Robinson recognizes that this passage in the "Shipman's Tale" is expressed in *sensu obscoeno,* as he puts it (see p. 820, a note on *Troilus and Criseyde,* II. 1025).

It is this same passage that next comes to our attention. Pandarus tells Troilus in his letter to "make it with thise argumentes tough" (II. 1025). Baugh glosses the passage as "make it difficult"; Robinson has a long note citing several senses not in the *OED* (from special and privileged communications with Professor Kittredge). Here he thinks that the phrase means "don't make a display by using

arguments." Robinson is, indeed, probably right, and
even though the foulmouthed Pandarus is involved here,
there is no obscene sense that one can detect.

In the same work, Criseyde says she likes Troilus because he does not make it "tough" (III. 87) —is not boast-
ful or overweening. Since they are about to be very intimate, however, and since he *will* then "make it tough"
in the third sense, perhaps this is a bit of humorously
ironic foreshadowing.

Diomede thinks (V. 101) that it would be futile if he
were to "make it tough" with Criseyde because she is already in love with a Trojan—meaning (1) to be too
forward and (2) have an erection. Diomede is, most
pathetically, mistaken.

The *Book of the Duchess,* which usually seems so
austere and pure, has a very curious passage in which this
phrase occurs. Chaucer, the somewhat insensitive and
dull-witted speaker at the beginning of the Man in Black's
story, finds that the Man is more willing to speak than
he had thought he might be (529 ff.) :

> *Loo! how goodly spak thys knyght,*
> *As hit had be another wyght;*
> *He mad hyt nouther towgh ne queynte.*
> *And I saw that, and gan me aqueynte*
> *With hym. . . .*

It is simply impossible that there are obscene meanings
at this point for either "towgh" or "queynte" (*q.v.*) ; the
juxtaposition is either incredibly clumsy and inappropriate,
or it foreshadows the union of the Man in Black and his
Blanche in a way that is difficult to accept. [*OED, adj.,* 3.
stiff, severe, violent; 8. "to make it tough": (1) to make
it difficult; (2) to be persistent.]

toute. The arse, buttocks. Absolon is a preposterous character,
   with his hair like a fan and his playing-at-love, but he
   deserves *some* vengeance for his ill-treatment at the
   "hands" of Alisoun and Nicholas. (It is the girl's "nether
   ye" and the "hende" clerk's musical anus that actually
   punish Absolon, of course.) Absolon's revenge is to brand

Nicholas on the "toute" ("Miller's Tale," A 3812). As every careful reader of the tale has observed, the lissome Alisoun is the only personage (besides the "walk-on" Gervase, the smith) who does not get poetic justice. If this is immorality, we accept it and excuse Chaucer, the Miller, and, of course, Alisoun.

Chaucer reminds us of the funny word (the connotations of which are like Modern English "keister") and of the hot plowshare applied to the buttock as he concludes his tale. It is probably one of the best examples of how to use a couplet to call attention to the important (rhymed) words, tying everything up neatly. To show how brilliant the passage is, here are the last five lines (A 3850–3854):

Thus swyved was this carpenteris wyf,
For al his kepyng and his jalousye;
And Absolon hath kist hir nether ye;
And Nicholas is scalded in the towte.
This tale is doon, and God save al the rowte!

[*OED,* "toute," the buttocks, fundament; last citation 1460. In the "Land of Cokaygne" (Bennett, p. 143), the abbot "taketh maidin of the route (crowd) / And turnith vp hir white toute, / And betith the taburs (drums, i.e., buttocks) with is (his) hond" to summon his monks from their wandering. (They are evidently not cloistered.) They return and join in the fun: they "thakketh (*q.v.*) al hir white toute."]

trad. See **tredyng.**

tredefowel. The Host laments ("Monk's Tale," B 3135) that if only the Monk had not been in Holy Orders (vowing chastity and the rest of it) "thou woldest han been a tredefowel aright." It was, perhaps, a common (coarse) name for a sexual athlete, since in the "Nun's Priest's Tale" (B 4641) the Host repeats it to the Priest: "Thou woldest ben a trede-foul aright." To call a man a chicken-fucker today is not a compliment; however, Harry Bailly means it as one, even though it is applied to two clerics. We must remember, too, that the chicken-hero Chaunti-

cleer was capable of remarkable sexual feats. See **tredyng**.
[*OED* cites the phrase as "the male bird," *s.v.* "tread,"
sb., 12. without any indication that praise or blame was
attached; under 9. a. the action of the male bird in coition,
Chaucer is cited.]

tredyng. Copulation. The Host bewails more than once the
fact that "religioun" (*q.v.*) seems to have attracted all
the good, virile men ("Monk's Tale," B 3145); that is,
"religioun hath take up al the corn / Of tredyng." It is
a good metaphor, in addition to being an obscene innuendo, quite appropriate for Harry Bailly: (1) threshing;
(2) copulating.

The word was, however, usually applied to fowl. Chaunticleer flies down from his narrow perch, feathers (*q.v.*)
Pertelote twenty times, and "trad hire eke as ofte" ("Nun's
Priest's Tale," B 4368). The question here is, does
"feather" = copulate, or is it simply to cover with feathers?
I opt for the former, and this means that he has intercourse with his gentle mate not a mere twenty, but *forty*
times. Baugh equates the two terms (i.e., he agrees with
the number 40); Skeat ignores the matter.

In his frightening sermon, the Parson (I 863) tells us
that among the punishments in hell for lechers (including
Chaunticleer? surely not!) is to be "totrede . . . withouten respit and withouten ende." The obvious meaning
is "trampled," but the secondary one is not impossible,
and it would neatly fit the crime: to fornicate and be
fornicated forever and ever. In Middle English, the
prefix "to-" can be an intensive. [*OED*, "tread," *v.*, 8. of
the male bird, to copulate with; citations from the thirteenth century.]

trespace. Old Januarie warns his young wife ("Merchant's
Tale," E 1828): "Allas! I moot trespace / To yow, my
spouse, and yow greetly offende." Evidently he is telling
her that the breach of the hymen will be painful. It is
not too uncharitable to suppose that the warning is gratuitous. [*OED* has no precise meaning like this.]

tribulacion. Like many half-educated people, the Wife of
Bath likes big words. When she tells us that her husband
will "have his tribulacion withal / Upon his flessh" (D

156), she means that he wants intercourse. [*OED* has no such sense.]

turd. The Host expresses his literary opinions with confidence and vigor. Chaucer's "Tale of Sir Thopas" is, says Harry Bailly, "drasty rymyng . . . nat worth a toord!" (B 2120). He is right, of course, which is part of the fun.

On the other occasion when the Host uses this word, he is not being a literary critic; he is defending his good name against the insinuations of the contemptible Pardoner, who has suggested that the Host is perhaps the greatest sinner among all the Pilgrims. The passage, which contains the most violent invective in the *Tales,* should be reproduced fully (C 952 ff.) :

> *I wolde I hadde thy coillons in myn hond*
> *In stide of relikes or of seintuarie.*
> *Lat kutte hem of, I wol thee helpe hem carie;*
> *They shul be shryned in an hogges toord!*

The terrible irony is, of course, that Chaucer himself has told us in the "General Prologue" that the Pardoner is a gelding or a mare (A 691). See also **coillons** and **hair.** [*OED,* a lump or piece of excrement; it seems to have passed out of polite use in the eighteenth century.]

tuwel. Old Thomas promises the greasy friar a present if he will grope (*q.v.*) about his "tuwel." Only when we, and the friar, discover that the gift is a fart do we recognize that the word is a metaphor. The "tuwel" is, one might say, the old man's nether chimney, his anus ("Summoner's Tale," D 2148).

The other occurrence of the word in Chaucer makes the metaphor clear. In the *House of Fame* (1649), Aleolus blows "his blake trumpe of bras, / That fouler than the devel was . . . / Loo, al on high fro the tuel," where the meaning is simply "chimney." The smoke that comes out grows larger, Chaucer notices, "the ferther that hit ran" (1651). It would not surprise me at all if "ferther" has the same punning meaning as that involved in **ferthyng:** the "fart-er" that it ran. But if there is obscenity in this passage it is not clearly developed. [*OED,* "tewel," 1. a chimney; 2. the anus (Chaucer is the first citation).]

twiste. As a signal that she will give him her "queynte," May "taketh hym [Damyan] by the hand, and harde hym twiste / So secrely that no wight of it wiste" ("Merchant's Tale," E 2005), an age-old gesture welcoming seduction. [*OED*, III. to wring, wrench.]

U

unkyndely. See **nature.**

upright. Not sitting up, but on one's back (supine): Alan has "swyved the milleres doghter bolt upright" ("Reeve's Tale," A 4266). It is perhaps an unimaginative, but a perfectly satisfactory, position. At any rate, Malyne, the grateful daughter, takes eight lines of pentameter couplets to thank her "ravisher." Chaucer prepares us carefully for this scene a few lines earlier, when he tells us that the wench lies upright (A 4194).

In the "Shipman's Tale" (B 1506), the monk lends the merchant's wife 100 francs. She agrees that he will have her in his arms all night "bolt upright"—and we now know what to expect, as does the monk, Daun John.

Utterly different, of course, is the "Prioress' Tale" (B 1801), which modern readers find so distasteful and, in a way, "obscene" because of its intolerance and its concern with the details of the grotesque murder of the "litel clergeon." To be offended is to read the miraculous tale "anachronistically," but some readers cannot help making this mistake. At any rate, Chaucer (or the Prioress) describes the little lad still singing the *Alma redemptoris mater,* though "with throte ykorven [he] lay upright." "Ykorven" may remind us of a joint of veal, though it should not do so; we must keep our attention focused on the little martyr, "this gemme of chastite, this emeraude." [*OED,* 2. lying on the back; citations from all periods up to the seventeenth century.]

urynals. After the "Physician's Tale," the Host asks that God
save the tale-teller's body, "and eek thyne urynals and thy
jurdones" [chamber pots, *q.v.*], "Pardoner's Tale" (C 305).
He speaks wholly without embarrassment, though in his
usual boisterous fashion. It is like his blessing for the
Nun's Priest: see **stoon.** The Physician does not reply
to Harry Bailly's well-meant remarks, so we cannot know
how they were received.

"Urynales" are used in the alchemist's experiments in
the "Canon's Yeoman's Tale" (G 792). Baugh explains
them as glass vessels (to hold any liquid) for making
solutions. See **dong** and **pisse,** however. [*OED,* glass vessel
to receive urine for medical examination or inspection;
citations from the thirteenth century. The modern sense
for the device in men's lavatories arises in the middle of
the nineteenth century, when it was invented, I suppose.]

uryne. The Wife of Bath (D 121) says that genitals were
made "for purgacioun / Of uryne," but of course for
other and more important purposes too (see **thynges**).
She is deliberately using the "learned" polysyllable here
for comic purposes. She would normally and naturally
have said, "to voyden pisse," or some such. [*OED,* first
citation *ca.* 1325.]

V

venerie. Baum recognizes that in the "General Prologue" (A
166) the Monk who "loved venerie" presents a genuine
equivoque: (1) hunting and (2) copulation. This possibility is made a certainty in view of the many other hints
in the description of this fair ecclesiastic (see, for instance,
hare and **priken**).

The same word occurs in the "Knight's Tale" (A 2308)
where Emelye says (to Diana): "I am, thow woost, yet
of thy compaignye, / A mayde, and love huntynge and
venerye." A true devotee of the maidenly life, we might

exclaim. Yet just a few lines later she prays (more from
the heart, perhaps) : "As sende me hym that moost desireth me" (A 2325), i.e., either of the two knights, Palamon or Arcite. Perhaps her earlier use of "venerye" was
a foreshadowing of what will eventually occur in the romance, when one of the two knights weds her. See also
hunt. [*OED* labels them "venery[1]" and "venery[2]." The
first = hunting (citations from the fourteenth century) ;
derived from Latin *venari* (no Chaucer citations) ; the
second = the practice or pursuit of sexual pleasure; indulgence of sexual desire (from *Venus*) ; the earliest citation is from 1497, a palpable error.]

Venus. Naturally Chaucer alludes to, devises prayers to, and
makes other narrative uses of the Goddess of Love in his
poetry. She is often pictured in the Middle Ages with a
dart and a blazing torch (see Figure 2 and frontispiece),
for obvious iconographical reasons. In the "Merchant's
Tale" (E 1727), she laughs and dances about with her
"fyrbrond"; and (E 1777) her "brond" has hurt Damyan,
the lustful squire.

Even though Chaucer himself no longer cares for love
(so says Scipio in the *Parliament of Fowls,* 162 ff.), he is
still exposed to it and to its goddess in the poem. There
is an invocation (113) : "Cytherea! thow blysful lady
swete, / That with thy fyrbrond dauntest whom the lest."
And in "A Complaint to His Lady" (36), Chaucer says
that he himself is "slayn with Loves fyry dart," though
one suspects that this is conventional, not romantic,
lyricism.

Often Cytherea is associated with other things. The
Wife of Bath says, for instance (D 604) : "I hadde the
prente of seinte Venus seel." Does she mean: (1) a literal
seal, a semiprecious stone engraved with the planet's sign
(cf. Robinson's note to A 414, p. 661) ; or (2) some kind
of birthmark? Recall that she also has "Martes mark"
both on her face and "in another privee place" (D 619).
See **place.** The former seems more likely to me. It makes
little difference, since the point is only to underscore her
devotion to the goddess and all she represents.

Alison of Bath confesses (or is it a seductive ploy to at-

tract a man among the Pilgrims?) that she will not with-
draw her "chambre of Venus" from any "good felawe." It
is a poetic euphemism for her "queynte," her *"quoniam,"*
her *"bel chose,"* but perhaps the venereal circumlocution
is the best (D 618). She also refers to "Venus werkes" (D
708) and says that when a clerk is old, he cannot perform
these "werkes" satisfactorily any longer—they are not
worth an "olde sho" [shoe]. See **bene.**

Chaucer uses "werkes" for a complex narrative purpose
in the "Merchant's Tale" (E 1971). The narrator (the
Merchant?) says that he does not know if the constella-
tions or the time were propitious "for to putte a bille of
Venus werkes," but at any rate it was efficacious. The
meanings are: (1) Damyan's "complaint," actually his
protestation of love, which he has written down; or (2) a
plea for venereal favors (Baugh). "Bille" meant a piece
of writing; also to "putte a bille" meant to make a plea.

Aurelius, the "lusty squier" in the "Franklin's Tale"
(F 937), is a "servant to Venus," and he makes passionate
love to Dorigen in the absence of her husband. The
same phrase occurs in the "Nun's Priest's Tale" (B 4532),
in the apostrophe to Venus herself. Why, asks the narrator, would you let him die that was your servant? He ex-
erted himself in your service, "moore for delit than world
to multiplye." When one remembers that the subject of
this fustian prayer is a chicken, it is all the more amusing.
See **delyt, lecherye, serve,** and **tredyng.**

The *House of Fame* has an invocation to "Cipris" (518)
and Chaucer is already aware that the Temple of Glass
was Venus' Temple, where he sees many "queynte [q.v.]
maner of figures" (30). The conjunction of "queynte"
and Venus' Temple might remind the reader of Venus'
"chambre" (see above), and perhaps there is indeed a
connection. The Temple of Venus in the "Knight's Tale"
(A 1918) is filled with sighs (not sensual ones) and tears.
A little later there is a reference to the Mount of
Citheroun (A 1936 and 2223), which is possibly the mons
veneris, but when Chaucer describes Venus' statue (A
1955) it is covered from the navel down. Such a passage
may be meant to convey the Knight's embarrassment when

he confronts pagan deities: cf. **Diana.** We are disappointed
again in the *Parliament of Fowls* (269), when we see
her in the Garden of Love, which is part of Chaucer's
dream. Once more she is naked but "from the brest unto
the hed."

In the "Monk's Tale" (B 3151), the Host (joking?)
says that wives go to the religious for their sex because
churchmen pay better "of Venus paiementz" than do secular folk. It is, in any event, an appropriate commercial
metaphor for a man with a merry business—the innkeep-
ing business, with its bar.

Often references to Venus occur without other "properties" such as torches, temples, and the like. She is of
course not only a goddess, but also an important part of
medieval astrological computation, and therefore she
figures in many of Chaucer's pieces. On the day that
Criseyde sees her Troilus returning from battle and falls
in love with him (II. 680) "blisful Venus" was in the
seventh house. There may be astrology at work in the
"Complaint of Mars," too, where the "chambre" (79 and
85) "may refer to some subdivision of the sign regarded
as a house" (Robinson). However, the Wife of Bath's
reference to Venus' "chambre" (see above) makes one
suspicious of these "astrological" references, since Mars
and Venus have just been brought to bed (see **abedde**),
and Chaucer continues: "Sojourned hath this Mars, of
which I rede, / In chambre amyd the paleys prively" (78–
79—see also **pryvee**). Chaucer writes "Venus chambre"
again (84), though the equivocation is blurred by "the
chambre, ther as ley this fresshe quene" (85). See **fressh**
and **quene.**

Imagine what fun the "patristic exegetes" (see Introduction, pp. 12, 14) have with *Troilus and Criseyde* (III.
1254): the hero is embracing his Trojan widow in bed
and hardly knows what to do next. He cries out: "O
Love, O Charite / Thi moder ek, Citherea the swete. . . ."
Earlier in this exclamatory and lustful Book III, Troilus
has exclaimed just before climbing into bed: "Now, blisful Venus, thow me grace sende" (705, 712, 715). See **grace.**

After wine, confesses the Wife of Bath (D 464): "on

Venus moste I thynke," and she knows well the relationship
between Bacchus and Cytherea. "For certes," she admits
(boasts?) : "I am al Venerien / In felynge" (D 609). The
"Physician's Tale" (C 59) has a similar reference to Venus
and Bacchus, but here it is a warning: "wyn and youthe
dooth Venus encresse," we are told. It is ultimately derived from Ovid's *Ars Amatoria,* a book that the demure
Virginia in the tale had never read, I same sure. Neither
had Alison of Bath, though her fifth husband might have.
[*OED,* "Venus," 2. the desire for sexual concourse; indulgence of sexual desire; lust, venery. The earliest citation is 1513 (!). There are many attributive citations
under 11. with "werkes," "play," etc., of which the earliest
are *ca.* 1400.]

vessel. Literally, a cup—that made of wood being more service-
able than that of gold, according to the Wife of Bath (D
100). The context suggests, however, as does the character
of the speaker, that this "vessel" might be the "chambre"
of Venus (*q.v.*). See also **coppe.** [*OED,* 5. in the fourteenth century, numerous references to membranous
canals, ducts, tubes, but no precise reference to the
pudendum.]

virginitee. Naturally Virginia has perfect "virginitee," but
she, like Constance and Griselde, is too saccharine to be
very interesting; see the "Physician's Tale" (C 44). As a
good corrective, compare the "Wife of Bath's Prologue"
(D 62, *et passim*). [*OED* offers citations from 1300 to
the present.]

virytrate. In the "Friar's Tale" (D 1582), the vicious summoner calls the widow this name (along with "rebekke"
and "ribibe," *qq.v.*). It is glossed as "trot," and Skeat
suggested a connection with *tratte,* "anus." What Skeat
means, of course, is the Latin *anus,* which meant "old
woman." But the more familiar, and identical, word meant
"rectum" as well. In his introduction to Henley and
Farmer (p. xxxvii), Legman prints a comic Latin rhyme
(apparently medieval) in which the joke depends upon
the two meanings of *anus.* Hence one is perhaps justified
in scenting a learned pun of this sort in Chaucer, too:
anus = (1) old trot, but also (2) rectum.

The combination of *tratte* (anus, rectum) and vir- tempts one to make yet another conjecture about "viry- trate." Vir- is close to the Romance root for "glass." The word means "glass-arse." (Unhappily the dictionaries give this brilliant gloss no support. I am afraid that we must admit that although we suspect that the summoner is saying something obscene, we do not know what it is.) [*OED* gives up with "obscure origin."]

ω

wanton. In Chaucer's day, it could mean both "jovial" and "lascivious," though the former was still more common. Baum says that in the "General Prologue" (A 208) both meanings are present in the description of the Friar. He also finds double meanings in "daliaunce," "rage," "nekke whit," and also perhaps in "noble post" (*qq.v.*).

The Host uses the homely proverb (see **maydenhed** for its significance) in the "Man of Law's Tale" (B 31) that Malkyn has lost her maidenhood through her "wan- townesse," where the connotation of promiscuity is patent.

After his laborious wedding-night efforts, Januarie ("Merchant's Tale," E 1846) tries to appear spirited in- stead of exhausted. He makes "wantown cheere": (1) merry looks; (2) lascivious leers. But he cannot deceive his wife May, who sneers at his efforts at lovemaking. See **bene.**

The wife in the "Shipman's Tale" is unquenchable. She has just dallied with Daun John; on her husband's return, she has spent a vigorous night of sexual play with *him;* on the morn, he asks for more, and she tells him she has had enough—lying, since immediately (in the next line!) "wantownly agayn with hym she pleyde" (B 1571). [*OED,* "wanton," *adj.,* 1. undisciplined, unruly; 2. lascivi- ous, unchaste, lewd; also, in a milder sense, given to amorous dalliance (both 1. and 2. have fourteenth-century citations) ; 3. jovial, waggish; cites Chaucer, A 208, first.]

wardrobe. The Prioress' euphemism for "privy" (B 1762). Naturally, she is the only personage in Chaucer's works to use the word. It somehow makes the murder of the "litel clergeon" all the more distasteful since the tale-teller uses this prim circumlocution for his burial pit. [*OED*, 5. a privy; refers to Wyclif's translation of the Bible of 1382, where the word translates *latrinas* (and where the Prioress—if there had really been one!—could have read it) . In later translations, it becomes "privy."]

wench. The word was undergoing pejoration (taking on bad connotations) even in Chaucer's time, as the quotations will show.

The clearest distinction is made in the "Merchant's Tale" (E 2202) where May swears her fidelity to old Januarie: "I am a gentil womman and no wenche." The irony of this self-congratulatory claim is marvelous, since it is made by the most famous adulteress and pear-tree-climber in all literature.

The summoner in the "Friar's Tale" (D 1355) has at his command "wenches." They report to him the names of those who "lay by hem." The term clearly means "prostitutes" or at least "doxies" here. The same meaning is present in the "Pardoner's Tale" (C 453) : he claims he will "have a joly wenche in every toun." Chaucer makes a different narrative use of the word, however, since it tells us something pathetic about the speaker. In view of his presumably missing **coillons,** one wonders if this is a fallacious boast rather than a confession.

Balthasar's "wenches" in the "Monk's Tale" (B 3417) are contrasted with his wife. Earlier, his wife and his concubines are mentioned, thus glossing "wenches" for us. See **concubyn** for evidence of their acceptability.

The same distinction between marrying somebody and having somebody for bed only is made, in a by-the-way passage, in the "Miller's Tale" (A 3269) . Alisoun is described as perfection—worthy "for any lord to leggen in his bedde, / Or yet for any good yeman to wedde." An

identical specimen of such class feeling is found in the
"Manciple's Tale" (H 215): a woman of high degree
is no better than a "wench" if she be "of hir body dishonest"; however, the "gentile" (gentle-born) will be
called "his lady, as in love; / And for that oother is a
povre womman, / She shal be cleped his wenche or his
lemman" (H 220). Of the last two words, I would judge
that "wench" was clearly the more insulting. See **lemman**.
[*OED*, 1. a. a girl, maid, young woman (from thirteenth
century to the present); 2. a wanton woman, a mistress
(fourteenth century on); cites the "Merchant's Tale"; 3.
female servant (1380 to the present).]

werke. See **swynke**.

wexe. In the Scriptural phrase "to wexe and multiplye" (D
28) is a gentle text that the Wife of Bath can readily understand, though of course she interprets the causal act
as more important than the effect. As a matter of fact, despite her fondness for this phrase and for copulation,
there is no mention of a child in all her long "Prologue"
—one of the pathetic things about this charming, candid
character.

Chaunticleer has been in Venus' service ("Nun's Priest's
Tale," B 4535) "moore for delit than world to multiplye."
Contrast Zenobia's idea of **lecherye**. [*OED*, "wax" (with
-*e*- a very common spelling), *v.*, 1. grow, increase; citations from the time of King Alfred to the present.]

whore. See **hore**.

Wife of Bath. This most famous of all Chaucer's "lewd" pilgrims is given a remarkably chaste description in the
"General Prologue," until the very end of it (see **daunce**).
Her tale is also irreproachable in its morality. See **wexe**
for the fact that she never alludes to children from any
of her five marriages.

Baum points out that "withouten" (A 461) has a double
meaning: (1) not having any; (2) not to mention—a
wonderfully contradictory innuendo. Tatlock recognized
the ambiguity long ago (p. 229) and noted that Chaucer
"leaves us guessing whether or not the Wife of Bath had
lovers before she married." However, Braddy ("Ob-

scenity," p. 125), who is highly sensitive to Chaucer's
bawdiness, disagrees: " 'Withouten' more likely means
'without' than 'not excepting' in this passage."

Baum also mentions that "wandrynge by the weye" (A
467) refers both to her literal pilgrimages and to her wandering eye. However, see the *OED* entry that follows.
[*OED,* "without," *adv., prep., conj.,* 5. in addition; 6. not
including; 7. with absence of. "Wandering," 1. b. wanton
(earliest citation 1450–1530) ; c. of the eyes, roving, rest-
less, turning this way and that (earliest citation 1578) .]

wilde. Amorous. Whether her husband is "wilde or tame"
("Monk's Tale," B 3481), Zenobia will let him have intercourse with her but once, and then only to engender a
child. He was, one can imagine, "wilde" often enough.
Chaucer pretends that we are supposed to admire the vir-
tuous Zenobia, but I do not think we are reading anachronistically to suspect that there is some irony here too.
[*OED,* 7. b. giving way to sexual passion; also, more
widely, licentious, dissolute, loose.]

will. Sexual passion. The Reeve is talking about old men
(A 3880), but he admits that "oure wyl desireth folie evere
in oon." In Chaucer's dream, he sees Cupid and his
daughter "Wille" (*Parliament of Fowls,* 214), who is
tempering arrows to slay or wound lovers. Robinson's note
points out that (1) this may be a misreading of *voluntade*
for *voluptade;* but (2) also there is evidence that "wille"
was used in the sense of *voluptas.* We are sure that later
it had this meaning. See Partridge, who glosses it as "a
passionate, or a powerful, sexual desire," and consider the
"Will" sonnets, Nos. 135, 136. See also **shepe.** [*OED,* 2.
carnal desire or appetite (the last citation is 1603) . See
also the Confession of Luxurie from *Piers Plowman* at
likyng.]

withouten. See **paramour** and **Wife of Bath.**

wombe. See **plit.** Chaucer's audience was evidently fond of the
obscenely horrible story of Nero, who his mother's "wombe
slitte to biholde / Where he conceyved was" ("Monk's
Tale," B 3674) . The source is *Boece* (II. Metrum 6. 5 ff.),
which Chaucer translates "he was maked moyst with the

blood of his modir (*that is to seyn, he leet sleen and slitten
the body of his modir to seen wher he was conceyved*)."
This horrid story is, by the way, in Hamlet's thoughts (III.
ii. 412) just before he visits his mother in her "closet," but
most editors seem unaware of it. [*OED*, 1. belly (including
c. the bowels) ; 2. the uterus. Both senses have been present
in English from its beginning, though the first became
archaic in the seventeenth or eighteenth centuries.]

wommen. Bawdiness cannot exist without them. In the Middle
Ages (and as some feel, still today) there was widespread
misogyny, alongside the opposite, the *Frauendienst* of
Amour Courtoise and the developing cult of the Virgin.
Even in the midst of the unreadable moral tale of
"Melibee" (B 2246), one finds the narrator (Chaucer)
saying: "I seye that alle wommen been wikke, and noon
good of hem alle," which he supports by alluding to
Scripture. This occurs in a tale in which the point is that
Melibee wants to avenge his daughter (who was, or is,
presumably a female) who has been mortally (?) wounded
in five places by marauders. Dame Prudence, his model
wife, argues with him and counsels patience. The anti-
feminism is wildly misplaced.

Another example of a gratuitous misogynistic passage
is in the "Monk's Tale" (B 3252), referring to Sampson:
"For wommen shal hym bryngen to meschaunce!"
Chaucer usually uses the tradition more functionally. In
the "Nun's Priest's Tale" (B 4456), the teller disclaims
any responsibility for saying wicked things about women:
they are the cock's words, not his. He explains: "I kan
noon harm of no womman divyne." This Priest is in the
entourage of the highborn Madame Eglentyne, the
Prioress—in her service. She is (presumably) one of the
listeners to his tale of the cock and the hen. "Kan" may
mean (1) am able or (2) know (more often). Consider
now the intriguing ambiguity of "divyne": (1) guess; and
(2) adjective, modifying "womman." It reveals an
admirably complex, humorous, and gracious mind in the
Priest.

The Manciple sums up the dilemma neatly (H 148):

A good wyf, that is clene of werk and thoght,
Sholde nat been kept in noon awayt [under watch], certayn;
And trewely, the labour is in vayn
To kepe a shrewe, for it wol nat bee.

ℊ

ybedded. See **abedde.**

ybet. See **fornicacioun.**

ycoupled. The word meant both simply mated (married) and coupled, joined, in the act of intercourse. Both are present when the Merchant complains about his wife just before telling his tale (E 1219): "thogh the feend to hire ycoupled were, / She wolde hym overmacche, I dar wel swere." [*MED,* "couplen," *v.,* 1 (a) to unite in marriage; 1 (c) to have sexual intercourse.]

ydelnesse. The Second Nun says that "ydelnesse" is the "porter of the gate of delices," nurse and minister unto our vices. "Idleness" is the name of the Porter in the *Romaunt of the Rose*—itself an idle, secular book, which was conducive to sin (*pace* Professor Robertson—see Introduction, pp. 12, 14). The narrator uses the word four times in the Prologue to the "Second Nun's Tale" (G 2, etc.). One wonders how the Second Nun knew about this identification of Porter and "Ydelnesse."

In the *Book of the Duchess* (798), the Man in Black says that his mistress, Youth, governed him in "ydelnesse" when he was first initiated into the ways of love. The word meant both the Preacher's *vanitas* and also, literally, the condition of having nothing to do. Both (certainly the latter!) are necessary to lovemaking in the slow medieval way. [*OED,* "idleness," 1. vanity (the last citation is from the *Romaunt of the Rose*); 4. being idle (citations from the beginning to the present).]

ye. Eye. The "nether ye" that Absolon kisses ("Miller's Tale," A 3852) is equipped with a beard, too. It is of course Alisoun's rectum.

Troilus' "herte, which that is his brestes ye" is a strange
figure (I. 453). Skeat, Root, Robinson, and Baugh ignore
it. I would venture to bet that it has its roots in an
"emblem" concept. See my article on the emblem verse in
the fifteenth century. [*OED* ignores obscene meanings.]

yerde. In Middle English, "yerde" could mean: (1) penis; (2)
enclosure; (3) rod (especially as a symbol of authority).
Chaucer uses the second two, but it is doubtful if the
first ever occurs. What *did* he call the penis? (See Introduction, p. 17; in the "Merchant's Tale" [E 2376] it is
simply "it." Also see **tool.**)

However, there are a few passages in which "penis" may
be the meaning. The first is a funny one. Palamon is described as suffering from lovesickness ("Knight's Tale,"
A 1387); he has a vision of the god Mercury, who "biforn
hym stood and bad hym to be murie." Then Chaucer
continues, "His slepy yerde in hond he bar upright," and
leaves the "his" (Mercury's? Palamon's?) ambiguous.
Robinson's note tells us that the reference is actually to
the caduceus, and the phrase in Chaucer's source was
somniferam virgam, but one wonders if there would not
be a titter in the audience when they heard this line read.
Some think that the tale needs a little comic relief;
perhaps it is here, though it would not seem particularly
appropriate in this passage.

When the merchant's wife walks in the garden to meet
(*does* she do it deliberately?) Daun John, the young
monk, she is accompanied by a "mayde child" that is still
under the "yerde"—that is, the rod (subject to discipline).
But can there be some other (rather sinister) meaning
here: she is too small for the "yerde" (penis)? I doubt it.
The little chaperone disappears conveniently from the
tale, anyway, and we hear no more about her, nor is there
any satisfactory explanation for her presence ("Shipman's
Tale," B 1287).

Chaucer uses the proverb (*Troilus and Criseyde,* I.
740) that people make a "yerde" with which they themselves are beaten, referring to the sufferings of Troilus. It
may have a vaguely obscene sense.

Most of the passages including "yerde" are manifestly

blameless, however, such as all the references to the barn-
yard in the "Nun's Priest's Tale" or the same sort of
thing in that otherwise blameworthy story, the "Summoner's Tale" (D 1798).

Let me merely list a few more occurrences where the
word means "rod, rule," so that the unwary may not be
tempted to see penises in these innocent lines: "Clerk's
Tale" (E 22) where the Clerk says he is under the Host's
"yerde"; *Parliament of Fowls* (640) in which the eagle
says to Nature that he is under *her* "yerde"; then four
passages from *Troilus and Criseyde,* all involving the idea
of "rule," and applied to Hector, Deiphebus, and (twice)
Troilus (II. 154, 1427; III. 137, 1067). [*MED,* "coilons,"
includes many fourteenth- and fifteenth-century quotations
in which "yerde" = penis. *OED,* "yard," *sb.*², 11. the
virile member, penis; citations from 1379, 1382. Cf. *Piers
Plowman* (C-Text, XI. 286): "lecherye is . . . lym-yerde
of helle," where the "lym-yerde" is: (1) stick covered with
birdlime, by which they were entrapped; or (2) the
penis.]

yeveth. See **spendeth.**

yifte. To Alison of Bath (D 39), the "yifte of God" is sex. See
also **refresshed.**

yqueynt. See **queynte.**

yswonke. See **swynke.**

index

index to chaucer's works

The Index is alphabetical, with individual Tales listed under *Canterbury Tales* and the lyrics under Short Poems. Line-number references are to *The Works of Geoffrey Chaucer,* ed. F. N. Robinson (2nd ed.; Boston: Houghton Mifflin, 1957). Page references (in italics) are to *Chaucer's Bawdy.*